Paradise Fields

Katie Fforde lives in Gloucestershire with her husband
and some of her three children. *Paradise Fields* is her ninth
novel. Her hobbies are ironing and housework but, unfortunately, she has almost no time for them as she feels it
her duty to keep a close eye on the afternoon chat shows.

KATIE FFORDE

Paradise Fields

CENTURY · LONDON

First published in the United Kingdom in 2003 by Century

1 3 5 7 9 10 8 6 4 2

Copyright © Katie Fforde 2003

Century
The Random House Group Limited
20 Vauxhall Bridge Road, London, SW1V 2SA

Random House Australia (Pty) Limited
20 Alfred Street, Milsons Point, Sydney,
New South Wales 2061, Australia

Random House New Zealand Limited
18 Poland Road, Glenfield
Auckland 10, New Zealand

Random House (Pty) Limited
Endulini, 5a Jubilee Road, Parktown 2193, South Africa

The Random House Group Limited Reg. No. 954009

www.randomhouse.co.uk

A CIP catalogue record for this book is available
from the British Library

Papers used by Random House are natural,
recyclable products made from wood grown in sustainable forests.
The manufacturing processes conform to the environmental
regulations of the country of origin

Typeset by Palimpsest Book Production Limited, Polmont, Stirlingshire
Printed and bound in the United Kingdom by
Mackays of Chatham plc, Chatham, Kent

ISBN 0 7126 5380 5

To Kate Parkin, Editor and Friend

Acknowledgements

As always, many people helped me with the research for this book. And in spite of their best efforts, there will be mistakes and errors which will inevitably have slipped through the many nets set to catch them. To them all, my deep and fondest thanks.

To Clare Gerbrands, who not only created Stroud Farmers' Market, but told me all about it. To all stallholders at the market, who not only sold me wonderful produce, but let me take up their time as well.

Ian Hamilton, Emma Gaudern, Anne Styles and Arabella McIntyre-Brown, who in many and varied ways helped me with legal matters.

To the Cotswold Care Hospice – please forgive me for getting it all wrong!

To Vanessa Kemp for making such inspiring beauty products.

To the Williams family: Tom for bees, Miranda for Forest Green Rovers and Lesley for council matters.

To my editorial team at Random House, my beloved Kate Parkin, to Kate Elton, Tiffany Stansfield, Justine Taylor, Georgina Hawtrey-Woore, all of whom worked harder and longer than they should on my behalf.

And not forgetting Richenda Todd, my first ever editor and the best, most conscientious, most sensitive copy editor in the world.

Chapter One

Nel's arm was beginning to ache. The mistletoe, heaped about her feet, was selling well. She'd already run out of the bunches she had tied together with red ribbon and was now selling the larger Stately-Home-size boughs, which had been too thick to separate into smaller sprigs. It was one of these, held above her head in an encouraging way, that was proving a strain.

She was just about to replace it for a smaller sample of her wares when a man came towards her. She'd been faintly aware of him standing at the next stall, considering mulled wine syrup and the little bunches of dried flowers and herbs known to their creator as tussie-mussies. She had time to take in that he was tall, wore a navy blue overcoat and looked Cityish, when he put his hand on the mistletoe she was holding and kissed her.

She couldn't quite believe it was happening. People don't kiss strangers on the lips in full view of half the world; or, at least, they didn't kiss Nel. It was over in a moment, and yet the feel of his cool, firm lips on hers sent a strange feeling shooting down from the underwiring of her bra to her knees. It made her catch her breath and she felt as if she had flu – all swimmy in the head.

It was amazing how many people spotted that kiss. Nel didn't usually sell things at the market – she didn't have time, she was always rushing around organising it. But this time, she was pinned down by her wares and at that moment it seemed every stallholder and every shopper had their eyes turned in her direction. She tried to pretend she wasn't blushing, took the coins he offered, handed him the bunch, and watched him walk away, relieved he didn't engage her in conversation or anything.

Her daughter skittered over, eyes sparkling. 'Oo-er,' she said in a way that Nel felt made everyone stare at her even more. 'Mum! Who was he? A bit tasty!'

Nel brushed a hand over her face, apparently getting the hair out of her eyes, but actually giving herself a moment to pull herself together. 'He was just buying mistletoe, Fleur. Now, how are you doing? Are you ready to take over for me here yet? I've been here since seven this morning and I have to speak to loads of people.' Was she still bright red, she wondered?

Fortunately Fleur had stopped looking at her mother and was searching her tight trousers and pale blue fleece for her mobile. 'I know, I know. In a min. I've just got to text Anna about something. We're supposed to be going out tonight.'

Fleur, eighteen, blonde and lovely, eventually unearthed a phone hardly bigger than a credit card and tapped away. Why someone who found writing the shortest essay such a Herculean task should prefer texting to phoning, Nel didn't understand. That was probably (her daughter had told her) because Nel thought you had to spell everything out: she didn't know the shorthand and hadn't heard of predictive text. Fleur's kindly if unintelligible explanation had been delivered to Nel when she was attempting to remonstrate with Fleur about the size of her mobile phone bill. As often happened with Nel and her children, the roles got reversed and they ended up telling her things they felt she should know, and no parental remonstrance had gone on at all.

Lavender, who appropriately sold wheat bags and lavender-filled products, 'out of self-defence, because of my name', didn't leave her stall, but she waved and winked approvingly.

Sacha, who produced beauty creams and potions in a very small way and sold them in blue glass jars, gave her a thumbs-up sign.

The trouble with knowing everybody, Nel thought, was that it made you vulnerable to people keeping an eye on you. When she had first moved here, as a young and distraught widow, she had been glad of the concern and care of the small town, but it did have its down side. She could see Reg on his fruit and veg stall giving her a saucy look, too. Living in a small community was indeed a bit like living in a goldfish bowl, and Nel occasionally felt she was the only goldfish.

She stopped trying to sell mistletoe and cast her eye over the stalls that were ranged in a horseshoe shape on the fields in front of Hunstanton Manor. It looked lovely, the stalls full of Christmas fare. There was one selling poultry and game: huge bronze turkeys in all their glossy black plumage hung next to bunches of brightly feathered pheasants, ducks and geese. Further along, strings of sausages looped up between fat bouquets of fresh herbs decorated a stall selling organic pork. Then there were what Nel thought of as the 'dippy-hippy' stalls selling brightly marbled wrapping paper, home-made candles, and nativity scenes modelled (she'd discovered after enquiry) out of wine bottles and plaster-soaked muslin, and then painted. The results were quite realistic, if somewhat sinister Biblical figures.

Everyone was there, and for once, everyone had been happy with their appointed places. They all knew that this was the last market until after Christmas and were determined to appreciate it. Some of the stallholders, the ones who produced food, went to other markets as well, but few venues allowed non-food products and so for the crafts people, the Paradise Fields market here at Hunstanton was a valued outlet. And the variety of people and products made it very popular with visitors.

3

Simon, the man Nel's children referred to as her boyfriend, had also seen Nel selling the extra-large sprig of mistletoe. Simon and Nel had been going out in a gentle way for about six months, and even Nel had to admit he was not particularly exciting, but at least he did little jobs for her, the sort that Nel found awkward and time-consuming, like cleaning out the gutters. Now, she spotted him negotiating the crowds, and could tell he was annoyed.

'Who was he then?' he demanded.

'Hello, Simon. How are you? I didn't know you were going to be here today.' Seeing that he wanted an answer, she added, 'He was just a man buying mistletoe. The kiss was only Christmas spirit. Look!' She shook her apron, the pocket of which was full of money. 'I've sold loads.'

'And you're going to give all the takings to Sam, I suppose?'

'Well, he did risk his life cutting it down off the tree. It's only fair that he should have the money.' Nel always stuck up for her eldest son, who had been addicted to tree-climbing since childhood and now climbed mountains as well.

'Mm. If stealing apples is scrumping, what's the word for stealing mistletoe?'

Ignoring the question, she twinkled up at him, 'Be a love and buy me a burger. They're organic beef and the smell of them cooking has been driving me mad. I want mayonnaise and a gherkin, and just a smear of ketchup. Please! I'm starving. I didn't have time for breakfast and it's nearly two.'

Simon returned her look gravely. 'I checked your tyres and they're all right now.'

'You're an angel. Or a Father Christmas, one of those.' She pulled down his head and kissed him, fleetingly aware that she felt nothing except his smooth cheek under her lips. 'Now, the burger?'

4

He frowned. 'I'm not sure they're hygienic. They're cooked in the open, they're probably loaded with salmonella.' His distaste was evident in the involuntary curl of his lip and the anxious glint in his eye.

Nel's feeling of warmth towards him dimmed. 'That farm sells meat at all the farmers' markets. They can't do that unless they have food-handling certificates. So, are you going to let me die of hunger?'

He shrugged and walked away.

Vivian had obviously dressed up specially. She was a physiotherapist and carried herself beautifully. As she came over, she looked magnificent with her flame-coloured hair and dramatic velvet cloak. Although a bit younger than Nel, she was her closest friend, and the reason Nel and the children had moved to the Cotswolds when her husband died.

Now, Vivian tucked a strand of hair behind an ear. 'I've sold the last of my honey, and almost all my beeswax and turpentine polish. People buy loads of it at Christmas. Does that mean it's the only time they clean their houses?'

'Personally speaking, yes,' said Nel, who had several jars of Vivian's home-made polish, mostly unopened, at home. 'It smells heavenly, though.'

'I know,' said Vivian. 'And that is not a coincidence. I've been talking to Sacha about providing her with beeswax for her lip balm, but I don't think I could ever get it pure enough. Everything has to be perfect for her stuff.'

'It's why it's so good,' said Nel, relieved that her friend appeared to have been looking the other way when she was swooped on from on high.

Her relief was shortlived. Vivian peered suspiciously at her. 'Have you been holding out on me? Who was that man who kissed you? You've been keeping him dark.'

'No, I haven't. He's a complete stranger and he bought some mistletoe. As have plenty of other people here today.'

5

'Did everyone who bought mistletoe kiss you?'

'Lots did. It's an occupational hazard. Although I suppose it's mostly been people I know, who would have kissed me anyway. It's no big deal.'

Vivian, who enjoyed an active and varied love life, disapproved of Nel's casual attitude. 'You should have maximised your opportunity. He was the most gorgeous man I've seen in weeks.'

'And I have a boyfriend, as you very well know.'

'Simon, yes.' Vivian didn't approve of Simon, and although she never said so, Nel was perfectly aware of the fact. 'Oh well,' she went on, 'he must be a commuter, down for Christmas. Or staying with his parents, possibly. He looks young enough to still have parents. Oh, sorry, Nel.'

'It's okay, mine died decades ago. But I am still young enough to have them.'

'What d'you reckon?' said Vivian. 'Has he hired a cottage to spend Christmas in the Cotswolds with friends? He was on his own, so probably not with a girlfriend.'

'I have no idea and couldn't possibly speculate!' Nel said defensively.

'Well, I certainly haven't seen him before, I would have remembered.'

Actually, Nel had seen him before, playing squash at the leisure centre. She had been going home from Weight Watchers on Monday and had looked into the squash courts to see if her son was there, possibly wanting a lift. Instead of a couple of sweaty teenagers, she had seen this stranger, hammering ten bells out of a large blond man. They were both galumphing about the court like young bulls, shoes squeaking, squash balls ricocheting bullet-like around the court. At the time Nel had wondered if this sort of squash would be better for losing weight than the low-cal kind she occasionally made herself drink instead of wine. But as her hand-eye co-ordination was atrocious, it probably wasn't a great idea – although it might be more fun than queuing for hours each week to find that, in spite of all her efforts, she had stayed the same weight as last week, and was still on the plump side of size fourteen.

She didn't say any of this to Vivian, who disapproved of dieting even more than she disapproved of Simon. 'Well, when you've found out everything about him, including his collar size, let me know, will you?'

Vivian laughed. Her ability to extract huge quantities of information about people, men in particular, in a very short space of time, was a skill she had been honing for years.

Harry, Nel's younger son, who looked so like his father it was almost uncanny, arrived, panting slightly. Like Sam, he was down from university for Christmas. 'Hey, Mum – Oh, hi, Viv – Mum, I've just overheard something that might interest you.'

'Oh?' asked Vivian. 'About your mother's bit on the side?'

Harry frowned in bemusement. 'What? No! That friend of yours who's on the council?'

'Fenella, yes?'

'She was talking to a woman while they were picking over the apples – God! People are so fussy! There I was with my paper bag open and ready and they were looking at each apple as if they might have worms in them.'

'Well, they might,' said Nel, 'but what did you over-hear?'

'Apparently there's a planning meeting. And they mentioned Paradise Fields – that was when I pricked my ears up. Something to do with planning permission. Anyway, it's tonight. I asked Fenella and she said anyone could go. I said you might be interested, and she said, yes, she thought you might be. So are you?'

Nel and Vivian both frowned, trying to cut their way through this confused report. 'You didn't pick up any

7

other bits of information, did you?' asked Nel. 'I mean, I don't understand. The hospice owns these fields. We've been using them for years. I really don't think anyone could be building on them.'

'Is Fenella still here?' asked Vivian, looking about her. 'We could ask.'

Harry shook his head, his floppy brown hair landing in his eyes. 'No. She said she had to rush. I told her I'd tell you about the meeting. She said ring her to find out the time. She couldn't remember off hand.'

'Oh God! It sounds ominous!' said Nel. She was mystified and rather concerned. 'But thank you for telling us, and for finding out. I'm sure there isn't a problem, but we'd better check. Are you busy this evening, Viv?'

Vivian nodded. 'Hot date. New man. Could be fun.'

Nel sighed. 'OK, well, I'll tell you if I discover anything exciting.'

'Oh yes. I'd hate to miss out. I wonder if Simon knows anything? Being an estate agent, he might well.'

'We could ask him,' said Nel.

'No, thank you.'

Anxious to get off the subject of Simon before Viv could imply yet again that Nel could do better for herself, Nel quickly changed the subject. 'So, what are you doing for Christmas, Viv? I don't think I've asked you.'

'Going to my aunt in the Highlands. It'll be roaring fires, whisky galore, and long walks. I might take the hot date, if he's up for it. What about you guys?'

'The same old same old, I expect.' Nel smiled to cover the dread the word held for her. She liked the Christmas carols she sang with the hospice choir, she liked fairy lights and she liked – no, loved the Christmas farmers' market where they now stood. But since her husband had died, all other pleasure in Christmas was feigned. She was so good at pretending, she doubted even her children knew how she really felt about it.

'What, at yours, with Simon and your cousin and her husband? What about the kids? Are they spending it with you?'

Nel knew perfectly well that soon the children would want to spend Christmas with their various love interests, but so far, they hadn't said so. Nel didn't know if this would make it better or worse. If they weren't around, she could go away too. Perhaps if she weren't at home, the space by the fireside, unmentioned but always there, would be less obvious.

'Simon's going to his mother's, but I think all mine will be there,' she told Viv. 'I'm a bit worried about your god-daughter, though. She's got this new boyfriend. He's from London.'

Vivian laughed. 'It doesn't mean he's a rapist, you know. London is really quite civilised these days. They have policemen and everything.'

Nel made a face. 'They met in a club. It's the first time she's gone out with anyone whose mother I don't know. Or, if I don't know her myself, I always know someone who does. It's a growing-up experience.'

'What? For Fleur?'

'No, for me. Oh good, here's my burger.'

'Hi, Simon,' said Vivian. 'I'd better go back. I left your Sam in charge of my stall,' she said, turning back to Nel. 'If I leave him to get bored, he might take the money and buy drugs with it.'

Nel laughed as she looked across at her son, persuading someone who obviously did not want them to buy a pair of beeswax candles.

Simon looked down at Nel. 'I don't understand you,' he said, pretending to take offence. 'You get huffy if I suggest the boys shouldn't put their feet on the sofa when they're wearing shoes, but Vivian accuses Sam of theft and illicit substance abuse, and you don't bat an eyelid.'

Nel smiled at him, to acknowledge he was joking. 'Have

you smelt their feet without shoes?' The truth was often disguised as a joke, and had been this time, but she didn't want this conversation now, so she bit into her burger. The mayonnaise oozed delightfully. 'This is so good! It may be the most delicious thing I've ever eaten, and you are a hero for bringing it to me. And you got yourself one. Good choice! Have a bite.' Ensuring his mouth was full and he was therefore unable to speak, she went on, 'But I'm glad Sam's around. I'll ask him to mind the shop for me while I have a last gallop round the stalls. I still haven't done all my Christmas shopping, and I've got to break it to people that there's a mountain of red tape to go through when we go official. Fleur's obviously gone off some-where, and God knows where Harry's got to. Oh bugger! That'll never come off.'

A large gloop of ketchup-tinted mayonnaise had landed on the front of her waxed jacket. Muttering and scooping it up with her finger, out of the corner of her eye she caught sight of the man who had kissed her. He was holding his mistletoe bough as if it was a major embar-rassment, watching her lick off the mayonnaise. He smiled. Nel had no choice but to smile back; to appear standoffish now would just make her look even more ridiculous than she felt. After she smiled, she blushed. Oh for a tenth of Fleur's confidence with boys, she thought. Not that he was a boy, exactly.

'Here.' Simon handed her a handkerchief. 'Why do you have to make such a mess?'

Nel wiped her finger and then started on her coat, scrubbing at the stain. 'I don't do it on purpose. But it's an old coat, it's no big deal.'

'You'll have to have it dry-cleaned,' said Simon. 'You really should be more careful.'

Nel was about to say that it was impossible to eat a burger without the contents going everywhere when she noticed that he was halfway through his, and not a drop

10

of anything had gone anywhere but in his mouth. 'Would you like me to wash your hanky for you?'

'No, thanks. I don't want it pink.'

A little offended, but trying not to show it, Nel tucked Simon's handkerchief back into his pocket. 'Thank you for feeding me, Simon.' Then she stuffed the rest of the burger into her mouth.

'I could do it again. Come for a meal with me tonight? There's a new place opened, I hear it's really good.'

Nel chewed hurriedly. 'It sounds lovely, but I'm going to be exhausted. I think I'd rather just slob out in front of the telly. When I've finished here I've got to deliver my local Christmas cards. That takes for ever.' She didn't mention the meeting. He would want to come with her, and it would make everything more complicated.

'You could just put a stamp on them, you know.'

'I know, but it's a chance to catch up with people. I'm always so busy when we're setting up, I don't get time to chat. There are bound to be things they want to ask me about the changes we need to bring things up to standard and become a properly recognised market.'

'That'll mean a lot of work. Is it really worth it?'

Nel took a deep breath, swallowing her irritation. 'There are grants we could apply for, websites to go on, advertising ourselves. As an official farmers' market, we'd get far more publicity, far more people. Fenella thinks that if I present a proper plan to the council, tell them how everyone will be following all the rules, having the right scales, stuff like that, they'd go for it. The more stalls we have, the more money the hospice gets in rent.'

'Just because Fenella works for the council, it doesn't mean she knows everything,' Simon replied huffily. He didn't really like Nel having sources of information other than him. 'And do we really want all the extra traffic?'

'It's only going to be once a month to start with!'

'That's hardly viable, financially.'

'Oh Simon, stop being so cheerful all the time. It's really wearing!'

Simon laughed, acknowledging her teasing. 'I just think upgrading this market into a properly recognised farmers' market will be a lot of work, and no proper money. Now your children have practically left home, you could get a proper job.'

Nel didn't want a proper job. Mark's insurance had left them adequately provided for and she enjoyed working at what interested her and not having a career. As they'd had this conversation many times and now wasn't the time to have it again, she just smiled.

He regarded her crossly, annoyed at his inability to interest her in earning money. 'And you could have just brought your Christmas cards with you and delivered them now.'

In fact Nel had intended to do just that, but there'd been so much on her mind when she'd rushed out into the pre-dawn that they'd got left on the hall table. 'I said, I need to talk to people. And organising the market will be a lot of work, but it's very worthwhile, and could be huge fun.' She frowned as the thought of planning per-mission on Paradise Fields floated into her consciousness. Surely the hospice owned them! Harry had probably got the wrong end of the stick. He was a lot more dreamy than the other two. 'But as I said, I want to talk to everyone.'

'You live for chat,' said Simon.

'I do, I do!' agreed Nel. 'What better motive in life is there? And here's someone who needs mistletoe. Hey, Adrian! Buy some of this for your wife. This big bit would look lovely in your hall.'

'We have home-grown mistletoe at the farm, Nel.' Adrian Stewart farmed a few miles away from the town. Nel knew him because she used to work for his wife in her catering business.

'I'm sure, but I bet you just leave it on the trees. It's no good if you don't bring it into the house. No one will kiss you in the middle of a ploughed field.'

Adrian laughed and put his hand in his pocket. 'How much will you sting me for, then?'

'You decide what it's worth. Here's a nice big bunch. Let's say a pound. It's for a good cause.'

'I thought you said Sam was getting the money,' said Simon.

'Sam is a good cause. Thank you, Adrian. Give Karen my love. I'm planning to pop over later with my Christmas card.'

Adrian kissed Nel's cheek. 'She'll be pleased to see you. She was struggling with a Christmas wreath last time I saw her.'

'Oh, I'd love to help her with that! In fact, next year, if there is a next year for the market, I might make them. They're such fun to do.'

Adrian picked up his mistletoe. 'For you perhaps. Now I've got to carry this all round Tesco's.'

Nel took it from him. 'I'll bring it round with the card.'

'If you didn't spend so much time doing favours for people, you'd have more time to go out with me,' said Simon, who never quite understood her ability to be so friendly with everybody.

'I love going out with you, Simon. You know that.' She took a breath. 'Look, why don't you come over to me this evening? I'll cook us something – or better still, buy some fish and chips – and we can rent a video. Have a bottle of wine.' This invitation took a bit of effort to make. Simon didn't really understand the concept of 'slobbing out', and Nel still felt she had to tidy the house before his visits. Still, with luck the meeting wouldn't go on too long, and she'd have time.

'Are you allowed fish and chips on your diet, Nel?'

'It's Christmas! Or nearly. Do you want to come or not?'

'Actually, I've got things of my own I should sort out. I'll take you out for Sunday lunch tomorrow, instead.'

'Lovely. Somewhere not too fattening, please.'

'I thought you said it was Christmas.'

'It is and it isn't,' said Nel, wondering if Simon would ever understand about dieting, or if, like slobbing out, it was beyond him. Extremely fit himself, and able to eat anything, he just thought people were overweight because they ate too much. Only people who suffered from it realised there was more to it than that. Seeing someone she knew turn away from the cheese stall, which sold among other products a local cheese known affectionately as Tom's Old Socks, she hailed him.

'Here, Ted! Have you got your luverly mistletoe yet? Roll up, roll up, buy your mistletoe here.'

'Hi, Nel. Give me a sprig then. Keep the missus happy. Good market, eh?'

'Excellent. But it should be even better next year, when we're official.'

'So we don't know what's going to happen to the old place then?' He indicated the house, rambling and huge, which overlooked the fields. 'I mean, Sir Gerald's heir and his wife may object to having a market on their front lawn, so to speak.'

'It's not their front lawn, and there's no reason why they should object. The market is a thing of beauty and a joy for ever. Anyway, if they were likely to be worried, they should have come back from America sooner.'

'So you haven't heard anything about what they're going to do with it, then?'

'No,' if you discounted the ugly rumour about the fields, a bit of gossip she was not going to spread. 'But there's no real reason why I should. I worked for Sir Gerald, but his son doesn't have to tell me his plans. I imagine it will cost a fortune to put back in order.'

'At least a million, I reckon. Apparently the old boy just

14

moved from room to room, as each one began to leak.'

Nel sighed, finding the conversation depressing. 'Let's hope they've got plenty of money then.'

'Well, can't stand here gossiping, I've still got to buy the wife a present. Any hints, Nel?'

'Diamonds always work for me,' she said seriously.

He laughed, as he was supposed to. 'She'll be bloody lucky!'

'I hope she is!'

Chapter Two

'Christmas is such a bloody nuisance sometimes!' said Nel. 'I mean, this is a fine time to find out that Paradise Fields has had planning permission granted on it for years. When there's no one around to do anything about it! It's unbelievable! I mean, I was sure the hospice owned those fields. God! The market has even been paying them rent for it! The thought of executive homes on them is unbearable!'

Vivian, who was just as upset as Nel but was being a little more philosophical about it, said, 'That's probably why they reapplied now, hoping everyone would be too busy to notice.'

Vivian was watching Nel decorate a Christmas cake with little figures Nel had moulded herself. Nel's mind being elsewhere, she kept making mistakes. From above them came the distant throb of music which announced there was a boy home. She didn't know which one, because although they constantly argued about the relative merits of breakbeat versus drum 'n' bass, she couldn't distinguish between them.

'So why is Christmas a nuisance? I thought you loved doing all this stuff,' said Fleur, indicating the table covered with fondant icing and biscuit cutters.

'Not the cake, sweetheart, I meant the fact that this has come up when every office in the country has closed down for a fortnight. I stormed in to see the solicitors to find out who this Gideon Freebody person was, only to be told there wouldn't be anyone in the office until after the New Year.'

'Oh.' Fleur picked up a bit of scarlet icing that a moment before had been Father Christmas's hat, and began turning it into a rose.

'It's a pain,' said Vivian, 'but I shouldn't think it's serious. No one else is going to be doing anything either. Do we know who first applied for planning permission?'

Nel shook her head. 'I talked to Fenella about it and she said anyone can apply for planning permission anywhere. You could apply for it in my garden.'

'That's awful!'

'I know. I keep telling myself not to panic, but until I know what the situation is, I can't stop thinking about it. You should have seen the plans, Viv! They want to cram untold numbers of houses in. I couldn't believe it. I still can't. Although I feel I would have known if it was Hunstanton land. I worked for Sir Gerald for years! And Michael's away too.'

'Who's Michael?' asked Fleur, trying to find a suitable place for her life-size rose on a snow scene.

'Our finance man at the hospice. He's a lawyer or an accountant – something boring like that. He should know all about it.'

'It's not just that we'd lose everything we've done to make it possible for the children to have access to the river,' said Vivian to Fleur, 'it's such an important area for wildlife, too. I simply can't believe someone has planned to build on it without any of us knowing. God knows how many creatures would lose their habitat if it went through.'

Even after knowing her such a long time, Nel was still often surprised by Vivian. She combined enormous glamour with a fondness for earthy activities like keeping bees, rambling, and birdwatching on remote islands. It was because she didn't look as if she did anything more muddy than shopping that Nel tended to forget about her trips to the Galapagos, treks across the rainforest and nature conservation holidays.

'Have you noticed that we're just assuming the hospice doesn't own the land, after all?' said Nel. 'Why is that, do you think?'

Vivian shrugged. 'It's because it's sod's law that official people are always right. The bank has never made a mistake; you always are overdrawn. Do you mind if I put the kettle on?'

'No, I'd love a cup of tea, but I do wish you two would stop picking. I don't mind you eating the rejects, but that was a perfectly good snowman you've just put in your mouth, Fleur.'

'So, how's the diet going, Mum?' asked Fleur, bored with icing and water meadows. She picked up a gadget Nel hadn't seen before and proceeded to iron her hair with it. In a little while she was going to London on the coach. Knowing her mother was worried about this, she was spending some quality time with her and Vivian before she left.

'It doesn't go, it sticks. I lose a little, gain a little, and end up the same.'

'I don't know why you bother,' said Vivian. Tall and well built, with creamy skin and flashing green eyes, she ate what she liked.

'It's all right for you, you can afford not to think about what you put into your mouth. Which is just as well,' Nel went on, 'considering how much sugar you've been eating.'

'But you're lovely, Nel. Isn't she, Fleur?'

'Mm. Cuddly and mummyish.'

Not really liking this epithet, Nel said, 'If I was six foot six, I would be the perfect weight. Sadly, or happily, even, I'm not. Besides, it's all about self-respect and keeping your standards up.'

'It's Simon, isn't it?' said Vivian. 'Because he's so skinny, he thinks you should be too.'

Nel blushed. 'No, it's for me!' She didn't want the subject of Simon to come up.

'Have you got cellulite then?' asked Fleur. She had stopped ironing her hair and was now smoothing her trousers over her hips. 'You know, orange-peel skin?'

'I know what cellulite is, Fleur, and I don't think orange peel quite covers it.'

'What do you mean?' asked Fleur and Vivian together.

Nel considered. 'Well, it's more, say – imagine if you had an ice-cream scoop, and lobbed gobbets of mashed potato at the top of my thighs. That'd give some idea of what we're talking about. Orange peel is just too small a scale.'

There was a horrified silence, and then Nel's daughter and friend both inspected her trouser-covered legs to check if this was true. Nel was slightly prone to exaggeration.

'What about your bum?' asked Fleur.

'One of life's small mercies,' said Nel, 'is that I can't see my bum. I expect that's covered with mashed potato, too.'

Vivian, having spotted nothing untoward beneath Nel's black bootleg jeans, shook her head. 'What does Simon say about it? In my experience only paedophiles and closet gays like very skinny women. Real men like flesh.'

'Simon hasn't seen my flesh. At least, not that bit.'

'What?' Vivian shrieked in shocked amazement. 'You mean you haven't slept with him? But you've been going out for over six months!'

Fleur gulped, obviously undecided as to which was weirder, her mother having sex at all, or the thought of going out with someone that long and not sleeping with them.

'I know, but Simon's been very considerate, and doesn't push me.'

'That's not considerate! That's a low sex-drive!' Vivian, who wore a column of ex-engagement rings on her right hand, was the acknowledged expert.

'No, it's not. It's me. I just find it hard to think about sleeping with another man.'

'What do you mean, "another man"?' said Fleur brutally. 'Dad's been dead for years!'

'You mean there's been no one since Mark died?'

Nel shook her head. She was older than both of her companions: why did they make her feel so naïve?

'So, Mum, what's your number?'

'What do you mean? My telephone number? If you don't know that by now, poppet, you can't possibly go to London on the coach.'

'Derr! I mean your number, the number of men you've slept with.'

'Oh,' Nel murmured.

'Well,' Vivian admitted, 'I was trying to think of mine the other night, when I couldn't sleep, and realised I could hardly count that far without a calculator. Yours can't be as bad as that.'

'Well, no.' In some ways, it was worse.

'So, what is it? More than the fingers of both hands?' Fleur persisted. Now she'd accepted her mother as being sexual, she wanted the details.

'You mean more than ten? Nope.'

'One hand then?' suggested Vivian.

'Not that either, really.'

'Then what do you mean?' They both spoke together.

She thought they might as well know the worst. 'Darlings, I can count my sexual partners on the *thumb* of one hand. I don't need my fingers at all.'

Both the other women needed a moment to work out what this meant.

'Oh, that's so sweet!' said Fleur.

'It's seriously strange,' said Vivian. 'And probably unhealthy. You should rectify the situation immediately.'

'Well, I'll tell Simon what you said.'

'Simon—' Vivian started to say, and although Fleur

didn't so much as glance at her godmother, Nel knew they were both thinking the same thing. 'It doesn't have to be Simon,' Vivian finished.

'Yes, it does! We're going out! Who else would I sleep with?'

'What about that man who kissed you in the market?' said Fleur.

Nel blushed. She'd had exactly the same thought herself. 'I couldn't. I couldn't sleep with anyone I wasn't totally committed to.'

'Or fancied the pants off,' said Vivian.

'I don't fancy people like you do! I need love, commitment, time, all those things. Anyway,' she added, wondering if she'd ever feel sufficiently passionate again, 'I'm not showing my mashed potato thighs to anyone. The moment my prospective partner saw them, he'd make his excuses and leave.'

'Nonsense! Physical appearance is only part of it,' said Vivian. 'Get yourself laid, girl!'

'Sometimes I wonder why I chose you to be godmother to my daughter.'

'Honestly, Mum, she's right. People take sex far too seriously.'

Nel's mother's heart sank. 'I hope you take it seriously, darling.'

'Don't start! I know all about sexually transmitted diseases and everything. And I have not slept with Jamie, so don't get your knickers in a twist.'

Nel, who'd had a hard job accepting that her daughter was no longer a virgin and indeed already had a higher number than she had herself, subsided. Accepting what you can't change was an important lesson in life, and Fleur seemed to have been put on earth to teach Nel *all* the important lessons in life.

'What you need is some sort of body-confidence-building course,' said Vivian.

'It sounds like the gym to me, and let's not go there!'

'Well, I never do,' agreed Vivian, 'far too boring. Although some of the men are cute. No, I meant some sort of therapy. "I am a beautiful woman and all men find me sexually attractive,"' she intoned.

'The trouble is, I'm not,' said Nel.

'Yes, you are!' Fleur and Vivian spoke as a team. 'You're lovely. Especially since you had highlights put in,' added Vivian.

'Look, I'm all right! I know I don't frighten the horses or anything, but no one is going to convince me that "all men" or even "any men" are going to find me sexually attractive at my age! Anyway, I found a grey hair the other day.'

'But that's not a problem with the highlights,' said Fleur. 'The grey doesn't show.'

'I know that, but it wasn't in my head!'

There was yet another horrified silence. Nel had never been one to shock people on purpose, but she seemed to be doing it a lot today.

'Age has nothing to do with it,' went on Vivian. 'Women can be sexy in their eighties.'

'Really?' This time it was Nel and Fleur sounding amazed.

'Of course, I don't know that from personal experience,' went on the thirtysomething Vivian, 'but I'm sure it's true. It comes from within.'

'There's no point in my going on a course, then,' said Nel.

'That is the point I am trying to make, sweetheart. If you *felt* you were the sexiest woman on earth, you would become her.'

'Would I?' The man who had kissed her batted back into her mind like a persistent moth on a lightbulb. She realised she had taken in the fact that he had very curly eyelashes as well as the ability to affect parts of her she'd forgotten she had.

'Well, it would make a difference,' said Vivian.

22

'I'll have a look in the bookshop and see what they have in the self-help line.' Vivian and Fleur were still regarding her in the way that made Nel feel nervous. They did tend to gang up on her rather. Any minute now they'd insist on her having her colours done and she'd never be allowed to wear black again. To distract them, she said, 'What I really need, of course, is a book called *Fit for an Affaire*. You know, that would tell you what to do to your body if you're thinking about having sex again after years without it. I bet it doesn't exist.'

'Mm, I could write it, though,' said Vivian thoughtfully. 'I could think of all sorts of good tips. And not just the ones everyone else would think of.'

'What like?' asked Nel.

'You know, like putting leave-in conditioner on your pubic hair. Or in your case, a little hair dye.'

Nel ignored this dig. 'You don't do that, do you? Put conditioner on it?'

'Yes! And why not? We all spend a fortune on our other hair. Why not pay some attention—'

'Honestly!' Fleur, who by now had finished putting on her make-up, forced the zip of her bag closed and got up. 'Sometimes being with you two is like living in an episode of *Sex and the City*.'

'Yes, you may take my eye-shadow to London,' said Nel, who had spotted it in Fleur's stash, 'if you promise to ring me the moment you get there.'

'To London, or to Jamie's house?'

'Both. And—'

'I will. I'll phone, I'll be the perfect houseguest, and I will be careful in London, and I'm only going for two days. Sam's taking me to the bus.' Fleur laid her cool cheek against her mother's. 'Love you. See you later. Well, Christmas Eve.'

'I think it's time to move on to wine, now,' said Vivian when the sudden quiet told them the house was now empty except for themselves. 'Have you got any, or shall I pop out for some? There's none in the rack.'

'There's an emergency "bogoff" behind the cornflakes in that cupboard. I have to hide it, or the children keep taking it to parties. People say life is too short to drink cheap wine. I think it's too long not to. I'll just finish this, then I'll try to find a corkscrew.'

'The day I can't find a corkscrew, I'll become teetotal. It's in this drawer, isn't it?'

'It might be. It should be, but it doesn't necessarily follow,' Nel said doubtfully.

'It is!' Vivian was triumphant. 'So, are you and the kids going to eat all that cake?'

'Good Lord no! It's for the hospice Christmas raffle. Viv, you don't think there's anything different about Fleur, do you? Not extra jumpy, or anything?'

'No. She's lovely as ever, and getting more like you every day.'

As Nel and Fleur were constantly told how alike they were, and as neither of them could see it, she ignored this. 'It's just that Simon thought she was the other day, and asked me if she was on drugs.'

'I think it's highly unlikely.' Vivian paused for a minute. 'Are you just worrying because her boyfriend lives in London? They have drugs in Bristol, you know. Here, too, actually.'

'I know! It's just that round here, if anything happened, I could be with her in minutes.'

'Do the boys smoke dope or anything?'

'Probably, but they don't do it here, and don't let me know anything about it.'

'They're very protective.'

'Yes. But what about Fleur? You really don't think there's anything different about her?'

'No, I don't. I think Simon worries too much. And he makes you worry, too, which is worse.'

'He means well.'

'I always think that's the worst thing anyone can say about anyone.'

Nel ate a misshapen holly leaf she didn't want. 'I didn't mean it in a bad way. Simon is a good man. He's concerned for my family.'

Vivian patted her friend's arm. 'I know. But I'm sure he's got lots of good points as well.'

Later, alone, Nel, waiting to wash the floor after the dogs had licked up all the spilt icing, thought about the water meadows.

She had taken the children there the first summer they arrived. It was the school holidays, and she was struggling to do something nice with them. Something normal.

There were children already playing, ranging from toddlers to school-age ones. Some of the older ones were organising the younger ones into a game of rounders. A group of mothers established round a bench smiled at Nel, encouraging her to place her rug next to theirs. They asked her if she was new to the area and clearly felt a little awkward when she told them she was a widow.

'Oh God,' said one. 'We've just spent the last half an hour complaining about our husbands and their irritating ways.'

'It's all right,' said Nel. 'My husband used to think it was helpful if he rinsed out his coffee mug, completely unaware that he hadn't washed the rim at all and there were drips all down the side.'

'And now you'd do anything to have him leave drips down the sides of the mugs?' said another woman.

'And hear him snoring, and farting in bed, and all the other disgusting things that men do.' Nel paused to regain her composure. 'But it was still very irritating at the time.'

'What did he do?'

'Something in the City.' Nel shrugged. 'To be honest, I

25

always wondered if the pressure of work had something to do with him getting ill.'

'Oh? Was it a heart attack?'

Nel shook her head. 'Cancer. It was very quick.' Then she smiled, to keep back the tears which were threatening. 'Very good insurance pay-off though!'

A woman, who perhaps saw how close to weeping Nel was, said, 'So you can afford the chocolate therapy then?'

Nel nodded, biting her lip. 'Unfortunately, my hips can't.'

It had been a golden afternoon, a turning point for Nel and her family. From then on they felt embraced by the community, and while their grief was still omnipresent, it became more livable with.

At last the dogs, a trio of Cavalier King Charles spaniels, having made their ears disgustingly sticky, decided that there wasn't anything left on the floor, and Nel started with her mop. Once she had washed one bit of floor, she decided she might as well do the rest. Simon had said he might pop round and 'might' often meant 'would', so Nel really had to make the necessary adjustments to the house. She would have preferred a quiet evening on her own.

She had told Simon early on that she couldn't bear the thought of a stepfather for her children, not while they were living at home. Her two sons were away most of the time, at university, or travelling, or just out, but she knew they would resent a man in their house, telling them what to do. Nel wasn't sure she liked the idea either. She might have to make changes, and she didn't want to. But Simon was kind, took her out for meals, and did the sort of jobs that were easier for taller, stronger people. Being on her own had made her very independent, and able to tackle most jobs around the house, but sometimes it was nice not to have to drag out the ladders, but simply hand over the appropriate tools instead.

Her cosy kitchen had been partly built by her (in that

26

she had put the flat-packs together herself). She had also created a wine rack out of a crate, and a useful cubby-hole for cleaning materials out of a painted wooden box which the Girl Guides had thrown out. It was cluttered, but that was how she liked it. A twelve-year-old Fleur had stencilled flowers round the ceiling, but fortunately they had now faded to an acceptable dimness. When it was tidy, which was hardly ever, it was extremely attractive. In fact, people would never get out of it, which was trying if Nel was cooking for a dinner party, and didn't want to be watched. It was sunny in the mornings; and big enough for the family if everyone was in a good mood, and to entertain in (just about), provided people weren't too formal. Fortunately, Nel didn't know any formal people.

Through the door was the sitting room. It had two sofas, an armchair, a fireplace and a television: too much furniture really, but the lavish number of table lamps, pictures and books made it snug in winter. And in summer, the window, which ran the width of the room and had a deep window-seat in front of it, filled the house with light. Of course, it too looked better when it wasn't littered with newspapers, drinks cans, games machines and pet hairs, but when she lit the candles on the mantelpiece (in spite of Simon pointing out her habit was turning the ceiling black), it gave Nel a lot of pleasure.

Upstairs there were four small bedrooms. Hers was almost full of the double bed she had shared with Mark, her husband. After his death, when the family had moved into the house, they had all shared it, clinging together in their grief, until, worn out with weeping, they decided it was time to get on with their lives.

The kitchen floor clean (at least where it showed), Nel moved on to the sitting room and hoovered up the worst of the dog hairs. She didn't really have the energy for entertaining, having spent all day icing Christmas cakes, but her last telephone conversation with Simon had ended badly. She had been annoyed with him for not reacting suitably when she rang him to tell him about planning permission being reapplied for on what she had always thought was land belonging to the hospice. He had said – rather sarcastically – that she could always lie down in front of the bulldozers. He had also made her worry, possibly unnecessarily, about her daughter. As Vivian had pointed out, Nel's worrying gene was quite well developed enough without him agitating it. But to assuage her guilt, if he did come round, she would offer to cook him a meal.

She dialled his number, hoping something had cropped up, and that he couldn't come. It hadn't.

'It's not going to be anything exotic,' Nel warned him, trying to put him off. 'But the children are all out of the way, so we can have a bit of peace.'

'You should be able to have peace when they're home, Nel. It's a lovely house, or it would be if it wasn't so full of their clutter. They've all got bedrooms. And they're not really children any more.'

There was a silence. Even if Nel had wanted Simon to move in, her non-interventionist child-rearing methods would have put him off. Fleur was due to go to university next autumn, like her brothers, and Nel was aware she'd have to make a decision about him soon. But now didn't seem the right time. 'Children are always children to their parents, Simon. Think of your mother.'

He chuckled. 'I do, frequently. Now, what time do you want me to come round?'

'About eight. I'll make us a cheese soufflé.'

'A man could marry a girl for her cheese soufflé, you know.'

Nel laughed awkwardly and said goodbye. After her chat with Vivian and Fleur, while she'd been sweeping and plumping cushions, she'd thought about her moribund sex life, and whether, or how, she should revive it. But having a sex life was one thing, getting married quite another. Besides, Simon's mother would be the sort of mother-in-law bad comedians made jokes about.

Now she fetched kindling to light the fire, wishing there was a child around to do it for her. Nel was perfectly capable of lighting a fire, but long ago her children had decided they were better at it, and as she was hopeless at getting them to do chores, she was grateful for any they undertook for themselves.

When they first began to get to know each other, Simon let it be known that he thought Nel indulged her children, but told her kindly it was probably because she was a single parent and they had no father figure. Nel had been furious, stating she'd indulged them just as much when Mark had been alive. After that, Simon had kept his opinions about her children to himself for quite a long time.

By the time Simon arrived, there was a superficial order. The dogs were nestled on freshly shaken throws on plumped-up sofa cushions; there were new candles alight; and the fire was going well enough not to make Simon's hand itch for the poker. Nel had even remembered to place the logs from front to back, so he wouldn't feel obliged to tell her this was the best way.

After she had sat him down in front of the fire with the paper and a glass of wine, she retreated to the kitchen. While she was grating cheese and measuring flour, Nel thought yet again about what Fleur and Vivian had said that day. 'Use it or lose it,' Vivian had told her, after Fleur had gone. Now could be the time. Perhaps she should put a bottle of white wine in the fridge, to add to the one that Simon had brought. Perhaps she should redo her already redone make-up, and make eyes at him.

Nel sighed. Actually they quite often did sit together on the sofa, and enjoy a companionable sort of cuddle, but it never went further than that. Simon wasn't very good at kissing, so she didn't encourage that, and he never put his hand on her breast. If he did put it on her knee, over her skirt and her tights, it never went further up her leg. Was there something wrong with him? Or was it her, giving out all the wrong signals? Perhaps she had 'touch me not' invisibly tattooed on her forehead, so that only men could read it. If so, the man buying mistletoe hadn't spotted it.

While Nel had dismissed the incident as Christmas spirit, she couldn't quite stop thinking about the perpetrator. It had been such a brief contact, just the gentle pressure of his lips against hers for a second. She was a romantic fool even to think about it, let alone mentally replace Simon on the sofa by the fireside with that unknown squash player. And yet, when she did that, she didn't feel there'd be any difficulty about turning a cuddle into something more passionate. It would be quite – very, even – easy to let her fingers explore between the buttons of his shirt, and eventually undo them.

Briskly, she returned her mind to her cooking, and it was only after she had made an extremely garlicky vinaigrette for the salad when she remembered her plans for the sofa. Then she had to explain to Simon why she had suddenly giggled.

Chapter Three

꒰ঌ✦ଡ଼꒱

The fact that after what seemed to be about a million phone calls Nel had actually managed to get an appointment with the solicitors didn't make her one jot less irritated; in fact, rather the reverse. As usual, she had arrived ten minutes early. It was now fifteen minutes after the appointed time, and her anxiety and boredom levels had risen to dangerous heights.

She looked around her, plucking at the frayed arm of her chair, wondering how, when everyone knew solicitors earned a fortune, they could let their waiting room get into this condition.

The walls had probably been magnolia to begin with, but had darkened to a shade which, Nel decided, the National Trust would probably have called Under-housemaid's Garret Grey. The curtains could have been any colour, but when Nel got up to look between the folds, she discovered they had originally been pink. Definitely Antique Potpourri, she thought, liking this new game.

However, when she'd failed to find anything clever to describe the carpet, which was too faded actually to have a colour, she turned to the magazines for entertainment.

'Well, at least they're seasonal,' she muttered. 'After all, Christmas is pretty much the same, year after year, even if it was over a week ago. The fact that they keep going on about how to celebrate the Millennium needn't really matter.' She reflected that Christmas had gone quite well, considering, in as much as no one had fallen out and the turkey was properly cooked, and then she picked up

31

another magazine, grateful it was nearly a year before she needed to think about it again. When she'd read what films she'd missed during 1999 and had gone on to another magazine only to come across instructions on how to build a small gazebo in her back garden, she realised they weren't seasonal at all, they were simply old.

She had just got out a tissue and was dusting the artificial flowers ('Graveyard Taupe') when a woman, who was faintly familiar, came in.

'Mr Demerand will see you now,' she said.

Stuffing her dusty tissue back into her pocket, Nel got up, feeling caught out and more irritated than ever. 'Mr Demerand' might at least have had the courtesy to be punctual.

The woman opened a door. 'Mrs Innes,' she announced.

Nel walked in. There were three people there, two men and a woman, but the only one she saw to begin with was the man who had kissed her under the mistletoe.

This was a shock. In her imagination, the solicitor responsible for everyone's anxiety was ancient, and wore half-moon spectacles and rusty black clothes, like the wicked bankers in *Mary Poppins* or something out of Dickens. This solicitor, if not particularly young, was definitely what her daughter would call 'fit'. And as she'd seen him playing squash, Nel knew that he was fit in the ordinary sense as well.

'I must apologise for the office,' he said now. 'We've only just moved in. It's partly so I can borrow some space when I'm not in London. It could do with a bit of refurbishment.'

He made no sign of recognising Nel, and although she was not surprised – was greatly relieved in fact – she also managed to feel insulted. She gave her surroundings a quick glance. The office was a great deal larger than the waiting room, and had roughly the same colour scheme. The furniture was large and chipped and would be much sought after in thirty years' time, but now it belonged in a recycling scheme.

'So it's your office in the provinces, and it'll be empty most of the time?' Nel hadn't intended to speak until spoken to, but her mouth obviously hadn't consulted her brain, and the words came out unbidden.

One eyebrow raised in surprise. 'It's not quite like that . . .' he began.

Nel turned her attention to the other people in the room. They were a little younger than Nel, the woman a lot younger, and extremely well dressed and assertive-looking. They also looked as if they could afford as much legal help as they needed to allow them to do whatever they wanted. They seemed to be a team, with the solicitor. She hated them on sight.

'I'd be happy to help you out with the refurbishment,' said the young woman.

Hearing her speak, Nel realised that she not only looked like a star of a prime-time American television series, she sounded like one, too. She had a soft, caressing voice, with a hint of huskiness in it, the sort of woman that men would listen to simply for the pleasure of hearing her voice.

'Kerry Anne's an interior designer,' explained the man, who was slightly familiar. 'She's really good.'

Jake Demerand took control. 'Mrs Innes, I'm so sorry for keeping you waiting.' He took her hand and crushed it briefly, but there was still no sign of recognition in his eyes. Mm, obviously a monster, she decided. The fact that he didn't look like a twenty-first-century Scrooge didn't mean he was less of a villain.

'Allow me to introduce you to Mr and Mrs Hunstanton,' he went on. 'Pierce and Kerry Anne. Mrs Innes?' He raised a dark eyebrow, demanding her first name.

She regarded him for a moment before saying, 'Nel.'

'We've met, I think,' said Pierce Hunstanton. 'Years ago,

when I was last in England? You worked for my father, didn't you?'

'That's right,' said Nel. 'I remember meeting you.' Pierce had been born when Sir Gerald was forty, long after he'd give up hope of having a son. She smiled at the memory of how happy Sir Gerald had been when Pierce had got married. The man she had met back then had seemed pleasant enough, if not as much of a character as his father. He had got older, of course, but he still seemed pleasant enough. If he hadn't been planning to cheat a children's hospice out of what it rightfully owned, Nel might have liked him.

His wife, on the other hand, was what Vivian would call a piece of work. Wearing an enchanting little suit, which looked dauntingly like Chanel, she was so immaculately made-up you could hardly see she was wearing make-up, she just looked fizzing with health and beauty. Her hair was a glossy cap that showed off her perfect cheekbones, and her perfect teeth were a row of evenly sized pearls. Her whole persona declared that here was a woman who could move mountains without chipping her nail varnish. Nel's spirits, already subterranean, descended even further.

As they all sat down, having shaken hands, Nel wished she'd taken up Vivian's offer to come with her, but at the time it had seemed totally unnecessary. At the quick meeting the hospice committee had called before her visit, the members had unanimously elected her their spokesman, mostly because she was the most passionate, and she hadn't anticipated feeling lonely. Their finance person was still in the Maldives, and was out of contact. The chairman was skiing. Still, Nel reassured herself, anger and passion could be very brave-making.

'Now, Mrs Innes,' said Jake Demerand. 'What is it you would like to say?'

Nel instantly felt patronised, although for no logical

34

reason that she could see. 'Nothing of any importance, only to point out that you – someone – seems to have applied for planning permission on land that is not yours.' She gave a smile she hoped was as patronising as Jake Demerand's had been.

'What makes you think it isn't ours?' asked Pierce, genuinely surprised.

'The fact that Sir Gerald gave it to the hospice years ago, long before I became involved in it. It's vital to us. We use it for recreation, for fundraising, for access to the river. There's a boat specially adapted for the children with disabilities.'

'Surely the children could find somewhere else to play?' asked Kerry Anne, inspecting her surroundings, her mind apparently on colour schemes, false walls and glass bricks.

Her lack of interest added to Nel's increasing fury. 'I dare say they could! But we couldn't have a steam yacht rally anywhere else! We raise thousands every year from that, and the year before last, we used the money to build a jetty and a road down to it. Apart from anything else, we have assets in that bit of property, and it's ours!' She was about to mention the rent paid by the market but thought better of it.

'I'm sure the hospice finds the land very useful,' said Jake Demerand, 'but that doesn't alter the fact that it doesn't own it.'

'We need to build on the land to generate enough money to renovate the house. I'm afraid my father neglected it terribly,' said Pierce.

'And I am so looking forward to getting started on it. We're going to keep the principal rooms in period, but the rest of it is going to be such fun.' Kerry Anne laughed and then glanced at Jake, as if checking his reaction.

Nel clenched her teeth very hard. The hospice's major source of fundraising, possibly its whole existence, were to be sacrificed, so Kerry Anne could have 'fun' and Pierce could have a few repairs done. It was outrageous, but she mustn't cry or scream, or do anything to make her appear more hysterical than she appeared already.

'But the hospice must own it!' she insisted as calmly as possible. 'I know Sir Gerald thought they did. He told me he'd made arrangements for them, years before. What else would he have meant?'

'I can't possibly speculate on what he meant,' said Jake, 'I can only reiterate that they do not own those fields. Let me show you the deeds of Hunstanton Manor.' He produced a huge, folded sheet of paper.

'I dare say it doesn't have it on some absolutely ancient deeds,' said Nel. 'Have you looked at anything more recent than thirty years ago?'

'I have, and they clearly show that the land belongs to the Hunstanton Estate, and always has done.' Jake Demerand said all this without any show of emotion, of regret, remorse or anything except cool disinterest.

'I have such confidence in you, Jake,' said Kerry Anne, patting his hand. 'I know you wouldn't have made a mistake.' She peeped up at him through her lashes. That was something Nel had once tried to do to her first boyfriend, and had given herself a violent headache in the process.

'Well, someone must have!' insisted Nel, trying to ignore Kerry Anne's behaviour. 'Some bloody solicitor or other! I know it was Sir Gerald's intention that the hospice should have that land.'

'They had the use of it for a long time, out of the kindness of Sir Gerald's heart. Now they must find somewhere else for their fête,' said Jake Demerand.

Nel wanted to kick him. 'It's not a fête! It's a – a – an extravaganza! People come to it from all over the country!'

He shrugged, as if she were quibbling over mere semantics.

'Look,' Nel went on. 'It's all right for you. You've got the Big House, you don't need to build on that land! Even

36

if we don't own it, you could at least have the decency to let the hospice go on using it!'

'The Big House is going to cost nearly a million pounds to restore,' said Pierce Hunstanton. 'If we don't build on that land we can't afford to do it. It would be very sad if such a wonderful slice of history were to disappear, just because it was allowed to fall down.'

'Yeah, and I really want to spend time in an old mansion,' added Kerry Anne, spoiling the effect of her husband's little speech.

'I don't want to see the house fall down, either,' said Nel. 'But which is more important? Saving a stately home or a hospice?' She tried to set aside her personal gratitude for the London hospice which was so helpful in Mark's last weeks. 'What about the hopes and dreams of children who have life-threatening illnesses? That means they are going to die,' she said unkindly, in the direction of Kerry Anne.

'I think we all know what a hospice is,' said Jake Demerand. 'And I'm sure we're all very sorry that they can no longer use the land. But the fact is, the land belongs to the Hunstanton Estate and they need to build on it.'

'Doing up an old house can't cost that much,' persisted Nel, reluctant to leave until she'd tried everything. 'Couldn't you raise a mortgage on it or something? What are you planning to do with it? Line it all in marble and gold leaf?'

'Time-share,' said Kerry Anne, after a quick glance at her husband. 'Very superior apartments for people who like a few days in the country every so often, perhaps to entertain friends, but who don't want to live there.' Her slight shudder revealed how she felt about actually living in the country herself. 'We're going to turn the attics into a penthouse for ourselves. Although I doubt if we'll spend much time there.'

'You're not even going to live there, and yet you're going

to stop the market in the fields?' said Nel, forgetting she hadn't been going to mention the market.

Pierce nodded.

'It's outrageous!' went on Nel. 'Do you know – no, I suppose you don't – but all the stallholders pay—' Just in time she stopped herself saying 'rent'. Knowing her luck, if they found out about that, they would demand to have the money back.

'What do they pay?' asked the solicitor.

'A donation – it's a donation – a small proportion of what they earn at the market to the hospice.'

'What market?' asked Kerry Anne, ignoring the references to the hospice.

'At present there's an occasional, informal farmers' market held in the fields, just in front of the house,' said Jake. 'There was one just before Christmas.' He looked at Nel, and while there was nothing in the look, she knew he hadn't forgotten that he'd kissed her, after all.

Kerry Anne shuddered. 'I don't want a lot of cheap clothes and thrift-shop furniture making the place look like a garage sale.'

'It's not that sort of market,' Nel explained. 'As Mr Demerand said, it's a farmers' market. Sort of.'

'What do you mean?'

'I mean the produce for sale is very high quality, produced locally, mostly organic – vegetables, meat, cheese, yoghurt and cream. No one sells clothes.'

'I don't eat meat,' said Kerry Anne.

Nel took a patient breath. 'Maybe not, but if other people do, wouldn't you prefer them to eat meat that's been reared in a kind, humane way? And there's the cheese.' She bit her lip at the thought of Kerry Anne eating cheese called Tom's Old Socks.

'We don't eat dairy either.'

'Well, there's the vegetables! You've got to eat something, after all.' Although, looking at you, you probably

38

just lightly spritz yourself with mountain dew and survive on that, she added silently.

'I am very careful about what I put into my body.' She smiled at Jake in a way that warned him she was about to make either a joke or a risqué statement. It turned out to be a cliché. 'The body is, after all, a temple.'

Nel winced. Her body wasn't a temple. It was perfectly functional, got her from A to B with no problems, but no one, not even Nel, worshipped at it. And no one, she was perfectly sure, would ever look at her temple in the way Jake Demerand was looking at Kerry Anne's. She may have only been able to judge this from the back of his head, but it was still a safe bet that he was practically drooling. How could she have spared him the briefest thought? He was obviously a womaniser. Simon might not make her heart race because of a simple kiss, but at least he couldn't be accused of that.

Nel cleared her throat. 'Sometimes we have a different sort of market, with antique furnishings, linens, a lot of it from France – *brocante*.' (Sounded much better than bric-a-brac, Nel thought.) 'As an interior designer, you might be interested in that.' Please God.

'I may well like *visiting* a market like that – I'm always on the lookout for interesting pieces, but I don't want one on my doorstep.' She smiled, and Nel wondered if her teeth were naturally that white, or if she'd had her teeth bleached.

'So you're planning to settle in England permanently?' Nel addressed Pierce again.

'Obviously,' answered Kerry Anne. 'Otherwise why would we be restoring the property? But we'll spend most of our time in London, naturally.'

There was a faint knock on the door, and the nice woman who Nel now definitely remembered asked, 'Would anyone like tea or coffee?'

'That would be nice,' said Jake. 'Kerry Anne, I know

39

you like herb tea, and we have some camomile. What would you like, Mrs Innes? Pierce?'

Nel and Pierce both said, 'Coffee, please.'

'So that's one herb tea for Mrs Hunstanton, and for the rest of us, coffee,' said Jake Demerand.

Nel smiled at the woman, just in case she ever needed a spy in the enemy camp. The Hunstantons might legally own the land, but they weren't going to build on it if Nel had anything to do with it. If she needed someone to photocopy incriminating documents, steal the deeds or reveal evidence of an unethical affair, she'd better get the office staff on side as soon as possible. Although, knowing her luck, her potential ally would probably say that Jake Demerand was 'a lovely man' and wouldn't have a disloyal thought, let alone use office equipment without authorisation.

'It's not just the hospice,' said Nel. 'Hundreds of local people would be disadvantaged by this building plan.'

'Several dozen local people would be advantaged by it,' said Pierce Hunstanton.

'Not local people,' said Nel. 'Incomers. People round here who need homes wouldn't be able to afford executive housing.'

Kerry Anne yawned. 'Oh God! Don't tell us we're moving into Nimby land, and the people resent anyone who wasn't born and raised in the village for three generations.'

'Three generations hardly gives you the right to vote round here.' Nel smiled to disguise the fact she was being bitchy. 'Although actually, they were all very welcoming to me when I came here with my children ten years ago. But I lived in the area, my children went to the local schools and I was active in the community. I still am. What villages and small towns resent is people who just come at weekends, don't contribute to the local economy and make the place a desert during the week.'

'On the other hand,' said Jake, who Nel was beginning to think of as the devil, 'if people earn their money outside the community, but spend it inside it, the local economy benefits hugely. Think how many jobs a building project like this would provide.'

Luckily for Nel, she'd had this argument hundreds of times. She was usually on the other side of it, fighting in the corner Jake now occupied, but she still knew all the words. 'It's only short-term employment. When the building is completed, the builders and labourers are all laid off. The community has lost their facility and the houses are empty for most of the time.'

'We are not planning to build small houses,' said Pierce Hunstanton. 'Our houses are unlikely to be bought by weekenders.'

'They're not likely to be bought by local people either. What will happen is that people who work in London' – she shot a hate-laden glance at Jake – 'will leave their wives and families down here during the week. The children will be sent to boarding school and the mothers . . .' She paused, her argument and her spirit flagging at the same time.

'Well, what will the mothers do?' Jake, who hadn't shown any signs of having a sense of humour up to now, seemed to be laughing at her.

'Nothing very constructive. Shopping in Cheltenham, probably.'

'I find retail therapy very constructive,' said Kerry Anne and then laughed. She made Nel feel unbearably frumpy and gauche. She was young and sophisticated and in a position of power. Nel felt past her best, untidy and trying to push mud uphill. Both men laughed with Kerry Anne, amused at her womanly wiles and her fondness for spending money.

Nel got to her feet. She only had right on her side, and at that moment she'd willingly have swapped it for one tiny atom of Kerry Anne's confidence. But what the meeting had given her was a whole lot more determination to see the Hunstantons off, to prove to Jake Demerand that she wasn't just a woman you could kiss under the mistletoe and then dismiss. She had lots of friends and between them they would become forceful and effective. There would be a protest, people would camp in trees, inter themselves in drainpipes, and chain themselves to earth-moving equipment. Eventually, the Hunstantons would admit defeat.

'I'd love to stay here chatting,' she cooed, 'but I've got a campaign to organise. Thank you so much for meeting with me.' She smiled at Kerry Anne and her husband. 'It's been very informative.'

She didn't smile at Jake as she stepped over his shiny shoes to get to the door, but she was very friendly to the woman whose name she at last remembered was Margaret.

She'd arranged to meet Vivian in the local wine bar after the meeting.

'It was awful,' Nel told Vivian as she sat down and took a sip of the white wine Vivian had ordered for her. 'Absolutely awful. The hospice doesn't own the land at all. It's the Hunstantons', to build on if they want.'

'Are you sure?'

'The solicitor, Jake Demerand' – she clenched her teeth on the words – 'offered to show me the deeds. I realised then there was no hope.'

'Not no hope, just that we don't own the land.'

'That's what I thought!' agreed Nel. 'We just stop them building on it, then we can go on having the use of it. We'll start a campaign.'

'Will you have time, what with organising the farmers' market stuff?'

'Oh yes, I'll have you to help me!'

Vivian sighed. There would never be any question of her not helping. Not only was she as committed to the hospice as Nel was, she would have helped just for Nel's sake.

'So, tell me about the young interlopers.' Vivian liked to know about people.

'Well, Pierce Hunstanton is a bit younger than me, I suppose, OK-looking, but not very exciting. But his wife was so gorgeous she'd make anyone look dowdy. Jake Demerand could hardly keep from licking her feet, he was so besotted.'

'Doesn't sound very promising.'

'It wasn't. They've obviously got pots of money but according to them, the house is going to take about a million to restore, which is why they need to build.' Nel made a disgusted face.

'So what's Jake Demerand like? Ancient and black-clad with half-moon spectacles?'

'That's just what I was expecting! How funny! But no.'

'I suppose Jake is quite a young name. So?'

For some reason, although until this moment Nel was convinced she always told Vivian everything, she didn't tell her that he was the man who had kissed her under the mistletoe. 'He's – well, tall, dark and handsome. Bit of a stereotype.'

'Mm. It's funny, but no one ever says small, fat and handsome, do they? Yet lots of the most attractive men are nothing to write home about in the looks department. So he likes animated Barbie dolls, does he?'

'He appears to. But you might be able to convince him otherwise.' As she said this, Nel realised she didn't want Vivian sweeping Jake Demerand off to bed, even if it would help their cause, but nor did she want to admit she felt anything except dislike for him.

'Actually, I've got my sights on someone else at the moment. Besides, I think you should take a crack at him.'

43

'You've got to be joking! He'd never look at me in a million years!' Nel paused. He had looked at her, for a brief moment. 'Anyway, he's probably married.'

'Doesn't necessarily make any difference. Go on, it would be good practice for you.'

'Vivian, I was married for a long time; I believe in fidelity. I would never do anything with anyone who was in any kind of relationship. I think it's immoral.'

Vivian yawned. 'All right, keep your stays on. It was only a suggestion. You've got to do something about your sex life and Simon's not going to do it for you.'

'Viv!'

Vivian picked up the menu. 'What are you going to eat?'

'Salad. That woman was so thin she'd make the presenter of that programme Fleur likes so much look porky.'

'Sounds bony to me.'

'To be honest, she wasn't. She glowed. But all that you were saying the other day about men liking flesh is clearly nonsense.'

'Not all men, obviously, but I also told you my theory about men who only want to sleep with women who look like their skin has been airbrushed onto their bones—'

'They're paedophiles or latent homosexuals,' Nel chanted patiently. 'Much as that theory would suit my case, I don't think it applies here.'

'So, what was she wearing?'

'A dear little suit. It looked like Chanel, but what do I know? The nearest I get to designer clothes is TK Maxx. Her shoes were heaven too. Lovely little boots with extremely high heels. I suppose she might have really ugly feet. Model beauties so often do.'

'But she didn't look like trailer trash?'

'Not exactly. So depressing.'

'Do we need a little trip somewhere?' suggested Vivian.

'I'd love to, but I've got no money and no time.' In spite

of her disparaging remarks in the solicitor's office, Nel enjoyed retail therapy as much as anyone, even if she did stick to sale rails, charity shops and the energy-sapping TK Maxx. 'I was hoping to get the Hunstantons to let us go on using the fields for the market until we become official, although I may wait a day or two before storming that barricade again. But I've loads to do, and we've got to get this campaign going.' A young man came up to their table with a pad. 'What are you eating?' Nel asked Vivian.

'Rosti with mushrooms. It's to die for.'

'I think I'll have that too.'

'I thought you were going to have salad.'

'Changed my mind. It's too cold. And I couldn't compete with Kerry Anne even if I were a size ten. Make that two mushroom rostis and we'll share a salad. Thanks.'

When the young man had gone, Vivian leaned forward. 'So, you're thinking of giving Kerry Anne a run for her money, are you?'

'No! Of course not! I told you.'

'It's just in all the years I've known you, I've never known you admit to fancying anybody.'

'I never said I fancied him. I hate him.'

'Practically the same thing, darling.'

Chapter Four

❧

'All right, love? You're looking a bit down.' Reg, the green-grocer, flung the bag over to twist the corners.

The effect of a cheering lunch with Vivian obviously hadn't worked for long if Reg noticed she was feeling depressed. 'It's this building application. Have you seen it? They're going to put houses on the water meadows – Paradise Fields. We all thought the hospice owned the land. It doesn't.'

Reg shook his head. 'It's bad. How will the hospice manage without the money it raises from the do's? Not to mention the rent the stallholders pay.'

'Don't mention that! If the Hunstantons find out they may demand back payment! I was hoping, with the market going official, and getting much bigger, that we'd get loads more!'

'You may be able to move the market to another site,' Reg suggested.

'Yes, I'm going to look into that. As long as we don't have to pay the council – or at least, not much – the market should survive. But I – somehow – have to arrange for the hospice still to benefit from it! We need the money so badly. And our jamborees! How are we going to have them without a site with river frontage for the steam boats? I'm thinking of organising a campaign to stop the building, until someone finds a rare newt or something.'

'Are there any rare newts or anything?'

'I have no idea, but there'd better be. I can't think what else will work.'

'And even that might not do the trick nowadays.' Reg rearranged a pyramid of beetroot. 'Tell you what, why don't you go along to the chairman of the football team? He might help you.'

'Why would he?'

'Because they use the other bit of land, across the road. Their junior teams practise there, to save the pitch getting all muddied up.'

'I don't know if I knew that.' Nel thought for a moment. 'I suppose it's because football is a winter thing, and we use the meadows more in the summer.'

'Your lads not play football then?'

'No. They had no ball control, according to their PE teacher. You don't know who the chairman of the team is, do you?'

''Fraid not. Not since old Bill Chapman died. They've got a new one now. But the best place to find him would be at a match.'

'I've never been to a proper football match, with grown-ups in it.'

'Time to start. There's one on Wednesday. You go along to that, and then ask to have the chairman pointed out to you. He'll be delighted to see you.'

Reg, Nel knew, had a soft spot for her, and a very kind heart, in spite of a somewhat brusque exterior. She doubted if the chairman of Meadow Green Rovers would be that thrilled to see her, but he might be glad of support if he knew and cared about his junior teams' practice ground being built on. On the other hand, perhaps they'd already got somewhere else to practise, so he wouldn't give a damn.

'Who can I go with? I don't want to go to a football match on my own. That would be just too sad.'

'What about those strapping sons or yours?'

'As I said, not into football. They would come with me if I asked them, but I'd have to get them to come down

47

from university, and I'd rather find someone who actually wanted to go.'

'No use looking at me, love. I'm not into football either.'

Nel continued her shopping, eyeing up all the friends that she met for potential footy-loving characteristics. Eventually, in despair, she told of her dilemma to a friend she didn't see that often. Sheila was an extremely positive person and Nel made a note to get her involved in the campaign. She was surprisingly helpful about the football match too.

'Oh, Suzy'll go with you. She's a big fan of Meadow Green.'

'Would she mind? I haven't seen Suzy since she was little, and she probably wouldn't want me with her at a football match.'

'She wouldn't mind at all. She'd be delighted. I'll ask her when I get home.'

'So how are her A levels going, then?'

'She's working extremely hard, but you can never tell, can you?'

Nel shook her head. She wasn't sure that Fleur was working at all, let alone extremely hard. All her enquiries were answered by soothing noises and, 'Don't worry, Mum.'

'I'll get Suzy to give you a ring later.'

'That would be so kind, as long as you're sure she wouldn't mind.'

Suzy, on the phone later, assured Nel that she'd be delighted to take her along. 'Wrap up really warm, and wear comfortable shoes, or boots: your feet get freezing. I'll get a lift to yours.'

On Wednesday, although Nel had not gone there to enjoy herself, she couldn't help picking up on the buzz of excitement of being in a crowd of people all on the same mission: going to 'the match'. It was an evening match and the darkness added to the feeling of expectation that Nel found developing. Suzy's infectious enthusiasm helped. Although they were the same age, Suzy, Nel discovered, was a very different child to Fleur. Suzy was interested in politics, world poverty and the ozone layer. Fleur was interested in her friends, her social skills and clothes. Having lots in common with them both, Nel found them equally delightful.

Once at the ground, Nel parked the car where Suzy suggested. 'Dad always parks here because you can always get out easily. We need a car park, really, but then we need a lot of other things, too.'

Nel was surprised at how many people were thronging to the match. 'Is it always this busy?'

'It's an important match. If we win this, we're up for promotion, which is why we need a revamp. But don't worry, it's a very friendly crowd, if we stay away from the opposition.'

'Thanks. I'm not that keen on crowds.'

Suzy wrapped a scarf of the appropriate colours round Nel's neck. 'Don't worry, I'll look after you.'

Role reversal again.

'I'm a season-ticket holder, so I go in here,' explained Suzy, who was proving the perfect companion. 'You go through that turnstile. We can buy chocolate now, or wait until half-time and buy pies,' she went on. 'Only please don't have a pasty as we always lose if any of us buys a pasty.'

'It's all right, I've already eaten. There are about a thousand calories in a pie.'

'I know. That's what makes them so delicious, but I've eaten too. I'm afraid the best place to stand is all the way over there.'

'You don't happen to know who the chairman is, do you? You seem to know everything else.'

Suzy laughed. "Fraid not. He's new and doesn't get to every match. But I'll ask around. Hey, Rob? You don't know if the chairman's here tonight, do you? And if he is, which one is he?'

'Yeah, I think he's here. And I think that's him. Do you see? He's got his back to us, talking to that man in the anorak?'

Neither Suzy nor Nel could see, but knowing he was present was a start. Although Nel was starting to enjoy herself in a way she hadn't thought she would, she didn't want to have wasted an evening waiting for someone who wasn't there.

Football banter went back and forth between the group of regulars as they waited for the kick-off. Nel couldn't understand much of it, except the bits when they talked about the dreadful condition of the buildings.

'The showers are so bad, the players warm up running up and down trying to catch the drips,' said one.

'Yeah, and the water that does come out is full of rust. Our Kevin played up here as a junior once. Don't think anything's changed since.'

'Hey, they're off!'

With Suzy at her side explaining things, Nel found herself getting caught up in the match. She got excited when a goal was scored, and although she didn't join in with the chants (everyone seemed to know what they were, even before anyone started), she found the whole experience extremely enjoyable.

It wasn't, she explained at half-time as she ate a thousand-calorie meat pie with Suzy, that she wanted to become a regular, 'but I can see how people get bound up in it. I'm just sorry my boys didn't get interested. I wonder if I didn't encourage them enough.'

'My brother's not into football and Dad is, so I don't suppose it's your fault,' said Suzy. 'Have a chip?'

'You realise I've just blown an entire week's dieting just with the pie. The chip will turn me into Colonel Blimp by next Monday.'

'Why Monday?'

'When I get weighed.'

'I really don't think dieting's good for you, you know.'

'It's funny, but it's only people who don't need to who say that.'

Nel's feet were very cold by the time Meadow Green Rovers had won their match. 'It means they're up for promotion,' reiterated Suzy, still enthusiastic, but losing hope that one day Nel would understand the offside rule.

'That's good. It'll give me something to talk about when I go and speak to the chairman. Now, can I just march up to him and say hello, or is there an etiquette I should know about?'

'No idea. I expect you can just go up to him. He's not royalty, after all.'

'Are you going to come with me? Or do you want to meet up with your friends?'

'I'll meet you later. Have you got your phone on you?' Nel nodded. 'Send me a text when you're ready.'

'I don't do texting. I'm over thirty.'

'Mum does! And she's well over thirty!'

'So am I actually. I'm going now. See you soon.'

Nel was considered by all who knew her to be friendly and outgoing. Only she knew that inside she was extremely shy. Now, for instance, although she was holding her head up and had a smile at the ready, inside she was convinced that the chairman wouldn't want to talk to her, and she'd have to fight her way back through the crowd rejected.

She got herself near the middle of the throng before asking someone if they'd mind pointing out the chairman to her. The someone obliged, and Nel plotted a course in the direction of the navy blue overcoat indicated.

She cleared her throat. 'Excuse me! Oh! It's you.'

Jake Demerand was the last person she wanted to see.

'I was looking for the new chairman. I was told it was you. Can you point him out to me, please?'

'I'm afraid it is me.'

'What?'

'I am the new chairman of the football team.'

Nel's feet hurt. She was cold, and her pie was beginning to give her indigestion. 'Oh God! This is so awful!'

'Why? You weren't hoping for the position yourself, were you?'

'Of course not! It's just I was going to ask the chairman of the team for some support for my campaign.'

'What campaign?'

'Derr!' Nel heard herself sound just like Fleur but didn't care. 'The campaign I'm going to organise to stop your millionaire clients from building on the water meadows!'

'If my clients were millionaires they wouldn't need to build on them.'

'They don't need to build on them anyway, it's just that that woman wants to turn the whole place into something likely to get her in the house magazines. All Hunstanton Manor needs is a few new tiles on the roof, and it would be fine! People's standards are just too high!'

He laughed, and she realised she was being ridiculous. It was the shock of meeting Jake Demerand when she was expecting a friendly, grizzled man in a sheepskin coat who would pat her on the shoulder and say, 'You leave it with me, love. We'll stop them toffs puttin' 'arses on them water meadows.' Perhaps her *EastEnders* addiction was dangerous, after all.

'Listen, Mrs Innes – Nel – why don't we carry on this conversation over a drink?'

In any other circumstances in the world, Nel would have said yes, Simon or no, Simon. She took a breath. 'Because not only do you talk in clichés, Mr Lawyer Demerand, but there isn't a spoon long enough in the world.'

'What are you talking about?'

'You've heard the expression, I'm sure. "If you sup with the devil, use a long spoon."'

There was a short silence. 'I'm sorry you think of me as the devil, Mrs Innes. Because I assure you I don't think of you in those terms at all.'

'Oh, don't you? Well, you will. When I get my campaign up and running, you're going to be sticking pins in wax models of me.'

'Really?' Irritatingly, a smile flickered across his face.

'Oh yes. You'll find I'm a force to be reckoned with. You'd better warn your clients to scale down their plans, because that land is not going to be built on while I live and breathe.'

'Well, I do hope you continue to live and breathe but I'm afraid you're wrong about the building. It's going to happen. There are some starter homes planned and the council are going to be delighted.'

'God! I believe you want the water meadows lost for ever! Did you know that the junior football teams practise on them?'

'No, as it happened, I didn't. But I do now.'

'And doesn't that affect how you think about things? Poor little boys, freezing cold, in shorts, with nowhere to practise.' Too late she realised she probably shouldn't have said those negative-sounding things.

'Well, of course it's a shame we don't have a nice warm indoor stadium for them.'

'You weren't planning to build one, were you?'

'No. But it explains why you can't get me excited about that extremely damp bit of ground you've just described.'

'How do you know it's damp?' Nel replied after a moment's thought.

'Because I help train the junior team.'

'Oh.' Deflated, Nel paused. But she soon rallied. 'Well, you can't have done it for long. You're new to the area.'

'Not that new. It's just that I've only recently come to your attention.'

'You haven't "come to my attention"! I would pay you no attention whatever if I hadn't thought you – or rather the chairman of the team – would support my campaign!'

'No? I saw you watching me play squash, you know.'

'What?'

'I saw you watching me and my friend play squash. What is it that takes you to the leisure centre on Monday nights?'

'I don't know what you're talking about,' she lied, knowing only too well.

'Oh yes, you do. You didn't have a sports bag with you, so what were you doing?'

'I'm not going to tell you! It's none of your business.'

'It must be Weight Watchers. I don't know why you bother. You've got a lovely figure.'

'Oh f—' Nel bit hard down on her lower lip as she realised what she had been about to say.

'Don't apologise. I expect I deserved it.'

'I wasn't going to apologise. And you certainly deserved it.'

'It's just you're not in the usual run of women, you know.'

'No woman is "just in the usual run of women", that's a terrible thing to say,' Nel retorted indignantly.

'You do seem to make me say terrible things. And I obviously have the same effect on you.'

'What do you mean?'

'You were going to tell me to – er – how shall I put it?'

'Don't tempt me to help you out! See you in court!

As Nel made her way back through the now thinning crowds to Suzy she didn't know if she wanted to laugh or cry. However hard she tried, she couldn't ignore the fact that Jake Demerand was not only the most attractive man she had met in years, he was one of the most attractive

54

men she had met *ever*. And the fact that there was obviously some sort of spark between them was not helping. He was the enemy. She held him responsible for the building plans even more than she did his clients. He probably gave them the idea.

'I'd better go,' said Nel when Vivian had been given a quip by quip account of her meeting with the chairman of the football team, aka Jake Demerand, over a hurried drink. 'It's the dreaded WW tonight, and I haven't been since before Christmas. I've probably put on a stone.'

Vivian yawned. 'You'd have noticed your clothes getting tight if you had.'

'I think they've just stretched. I'll give you a ring if anything of interest crops up.'

'*Anything* of interest,' said Vivian. 'Not just anything to do with the hospice or the farmers' market.'

'They are closely linked, you know. The farmers' market is a nice little earner for the hospice.'

'Oh, go away and torture yourself!'

Thus, late, aware that the white wine she'd drunk might smell on her breath, and not wearing suitable light clothes, Nel fell into Weight Watchers just before the talk was due to start.

Getting out her wallet, she searched for her card, finally finding it buried beneath all the other stuff in her handbag. She handed over a note, then, carrying everything in one hand, she pulled off her boots with the other and went to the scales, where the leader was waiting. Then, throwing it all onto the floor, she said, 'I'm terribly sorry, I just got all behind. Well, I've always been that, really . . .' As usual at this nail-biting moment, Nel made pathetic jokes, as if low humour could somehow stave off the ghastly truth. 'I haven't been since before Christmas, but, then, you know that.'

'Never mind, you're here now,' said the young and

lovely girl, who, rumour had it, had produced three children without adding a single pound to her svelte hips. 'How did you cope with the festivities?'

'Well, to be honest, I didn't think about dieting. I just ate whatever I wanted.'

She stood on the scales, holding her stomach in and not breathing, in an attempt to make herself lighter.

'Well! That must be a first! You've lost two pounds! Do you know what you did?'

Nel shrugged, delighted but mystified. 'Just rushed around a lot, I expect.'

'Exercise.' The group leader handed Nel back her card. 'I'm always telling my ladies to get out there and exercise!'

Nel smiled, taking the booklet which followed her card and picking up her boots. Would watching a football match count as exercise, she wondered? Or did you actually have to play it?

Not wanting to hold up proceedings, Nel bought several boxes of Weight Watchers chocolate bars and piled them up under her chin, anxious to escape before the group leader made her feel obliged to stay for the talk. It wasn't that she didn't know it helped to stay, she did, but she just didn't have time. So she staggered out of the door under the boxes of chewy bars, holding her boots, aware she was red in the face.

What *had* she done that was different? she wondered. She'd eaten out so much over the holidays. Perhaps it was because if she ate out she always had salad, and if she stayed in she often had pasta. Maybe she should write a diet book called *Eat Out Every Night* – it could be a companion volume to Viv's *Fit for an Affaire*.

Nel stopped dead. She couldn't believe her eyes. As if by some sinister alchemy she had summoned up the very man who had made her think she wanted an affaire. She was so shocked, she dropped all her boxes and her boots.

56

Jake didn't look shocked, he was frankly laughing, his face alive with merriment. Devil or not, his laugh was too infectious not to respond to. She'd been found out, and Nel was always ready to laugh at herself. 'I am so busted!' she said. She picked up a boot and pulled it on.

He was in his squash kit: black shorts, white shirt, and a fetching gleam of moisture. As he knelt to pick up her boxes, she noticed how enormous his feet were in his squash shoes. What was it they said about men with big feet? She suppressed the thought.

'You are indeed busted!' He straightened up, handed her the chocolate bars and looked down into her eyes. 'I'm sure you don't need to come to Weight Watchers, but I'm quite pleased you did. Would you like to come for a drink? Or am I still the enemy?'

In some ways, he was even more of the enemy than ever, because he was flirting irresistibly, and making her do it back. 'I can't.'

'Why not?'

If only he wouldn't look at her like that! He was doing it on purpose, to torment her! She knew he wasn't interested in her, so why was he being like this? Well, she wasn't going to give in. He could practise his charm on Kerry Anne, she'd be much more receptive.

'I've got to get back.'

'Why?'

She took a deep breath. 'There's a television programme I promised to record for Fleur, and I can only do it if I'm there when the programme's on.'

He nodded. 'That's a real shame. Next week, perhaps?'

She definitely couldn't handle this. He was the opposition. She couldn't go out with him: she mustn't even see him if he was going to have this effect on her. Nel decided that she was never going to that Weight Watchers again. She'd find another class somehow – or give up.

'I don't think so.' She wedged her boxes more firmly

57

under her chin. 'Now I really must go, or I'll miss the beginning of the programme.'

It was Saturday morning, Nel was in the chemist, studying the buy-two-get-one-free offers, trying to decide whether it was really good value to buy six months' supply of toothpaste in one hit, when she saw the only person in the world she loathed.

Vivian always told Nel that she was very dull when it came to disliking people. People Nel declared she couldn't stand would, after Nel had got to know them a little better, become, 'She's all right when you get to know her. She's just not a very good communicator.'

This time, Nel determined, observing Kerry Anne Hunstanton inspecting body scrubs, she was going to keep right on hating her, and not find out about her difficult childhood, her alcoholic father, and end up either feeling sorry for her, or worse, liking her. She glanced at her; why did she marry Pierce? For his money? For his crumbling stately home?

Suppressing her sudden curiosity Nel scooped three giant tubes into her basket and moved on to the section euphemistically referred to as 'feminine hygiene'. Here the special offers were very bulky and it was while she was trying to apply logic to the packing of them that she looked up and saw Kerry Anne right in front of her.

'Oh, hello.' Maybe, she suddenly realised, if I took the trouble to get to know this girl, I wouldn't come to like her, but I might be able to find out what's going on. It was too much to hope that Kerry Anne'd be able to stop the building, but Nel smiled anyway.

'Hi! Nel, isn't it? I wonder if you can help me. I can't seem to find any decent beauty products in this place. What I really want is . . .' She named a brand Nel had barely heard of, and would certainly not be available in a small branch of a chemist in a small town.

58

'I'm afraid you'd have to go to Cheltenham for something like that.'

Kerry Anne shook her head impatiently. 'I was there yesterday. Nothing. I tried every shop, and none of them had anything I would care to put on my face.'

'Well, as you see, this is a small branch—'

'So where do you go for moisturisers and stuff like that? London? You have lovely skin.'

This last was clearly not meant as a compliment, more a statement of fact, but Nel was still flattered. She also just might have the key to getting on Kerry Anne's good side. It would be a shame to waste it.

'I buy all that type of thing from someone who makes their own products. She sells them at the market,' she added. She was tempted to say that unless Kerry Anne got her husband to withdraw all plans to build on the water meadows, and go on allowing the market to be in their backyard, she wouldn't tell her where she could buy these products anywhere else.

'Makes all their own products?' repeated Kerry Anne. 'How bizarre! I'm really interested in cosmetics. I mean, it's so important not to put crap on your skin.'

'Absolutely,' murmured Nel.

'But it seems weird to make your own.'

'Not really. After all, all these companies' – she gestured to the counter – 'make all their own products. My friend just does it in her home instead of in a vast factory. She uses natural, pure ingredients, combines them, and then sells what she makes in blue glass jars.'

'And are they any good?'

'Oh yes. Her anti-wrinkle serum is really excellent. Not that you need to worry about wrinkles – yet.'

Kerry Anne shuddered, even at the word. 'Well, where can I buy these things? If they really are so good?'

Nel thought fast. Kerry Anne was rich, and obviously a woman prepared to spend a lot of her money on keeping herself beautiful. If Nel took her to where Sacha made her products, Kerry Anne would spend a fortune. Sacha would be thrilled to have such a big-spending customer and visiting her might soften up Kerry Anne beautifully – and not just on the outside. Perhaps it would change her mind about building on the fields.

'Well,' Nel began. 'You could just wait for the next market. Or go to Bath. I think Sacha sells her stuff there . . .' She paused enticingly.

'Or what?' To Nel's satisfaction, Kerry Anne immediately picked up the implication of an alternative.

'Or you can go to her outlet and buy them direct.' Nel was not surprised to see Kerry Anne's eyes widen in interest. Almost all women liked bargains, and the word 'outlet' did sort of imply cheapness. Nel would of course warn Sacha in advance, and make sure she charged Kerry Anne double what everyone else paid.

'Could you tell me where to go?'

'I could, but I'm too well brought up,' Nel mumbled and then went on, louder, 'It would be better if I went with you. It's rather difficult to find. Or you could wait for the next market. It's due in three weeks.' The words 'deferred gratification' came into Nel's head, and she realised this concept would be totally foreign to a woman like Kerry Anne.

'I don't think Pierce wants it to happen,' said Kerry Anne. 'We think it would be better if people got used to the idea that the fields are no longer available to them.'

'In which case,' said Nel, sweetly, 'I can't really take you to my friend. You couldn't expect her to welcome you when you're planning to cut off her main customer base.'

Kerry Anne's gaze narrowed. She seemed torn between disappointment and wanting to make it clear she did not respond to blackmail.

'It's only fair to let there be one last market, don't you think?' Nel went on. 'It would give stallholders a chance to tell people where else their products can be bought. After all, you're not going to be living there by next month, are you? Probably not even a year next month. It wouldn't make any difference to you.'

Kerry Anne sighed. 'I guess not. I could talk to Pierce about it.'

Nel smiled sweetly. 'Talk to' and 'tell' were obviously interchangeable for Kerry Anne. 'Do. And then, if he agrees with you, you can get in touch if you want me to take you to where my friend makes her products. You can't call it a factory, exactly. I really think it would interest you.'

Kerry Anne fumbled in her Prada bag and produced a card. 'Here. It has my cell phone number on it.'

Nel found a broken pencil and a crumpled receipt in her pocket and wrote on it. 'And here's my telephone number. Try and persuade Pierce, won't you?'

'Great, thanks.' Kerry Anne looked into Nel's basket, where the toothpaste and the shampoo were buried under packets of sanitary protection. 'Do you still need all that stuff?'

Nel bridled. 'Oh yes. I'm using it to insulate a chill-out room in my house, so I can practise my primal screaming.' She smiled in a sickly way and moved on, not sure if the sarcasm was obvious, and aware that Kerry Anne might now think she was not only ancient, but a witch as well. The wretched woman probably thinks I'm about sixty. No wonder she said I had good skin. I wish I was a witch. I'd send her cellulite.

Exiting onto the street at roughly the same time as Kerry Anne, it was somewhat embarrassing for Nel to see Jake Demerand. Why on earth did he turn up everywhere she was? She couldn't get away from the man. More annoying still was the fact that he saw both women. Supposing Kerry Anne told him what she'd said? He'd think she was a mad old crone, too.

61

'Oh, are you two getting to know each other?' he asked, sounding surprised but pleased.

'Oh yeah, Nel's going to take me to where someone makes beauty products in their own home. I love that idea. By the way, thank you for the other night, Jake. It was so fun.'

Jake acknowledged this gracefully, and Nel suddenly felt slightly sick.

'Well, must get on,' said Nel, not looking at Jake, 'Lots to do.'

'You will take me to your friend's place?' said Kerry Anne.

'If you really want to. Give me a ring. Now I must go!'

At the bottom of the high street, she nearly bumped into Simon.

'Nel! Hi! You look very—'

'What?' Nel snapped, feeling extra sensitive. 'How do I look?'

'Pretty, actually. You look pretty.'

Nel smiled warmly, patted his coat and moved on. 'Sorry, must dash,' she called as she went on down the High Street. 'I must see Fleur. I'll see you tonight.'

She reached her car, only ten minutes after its ticket expired, and realised Simon had never said she was pretty before. What on earth had come over him? Why was he saying it now?

Chapter Five

Fleur was sitting at the kitchen table, a mug of tea in front of her, propping herself up on her hands.

'Hi, darling,' said Nel as she came in from the back door. 'Have you had breakfast? I bought some croissants.'

When she first had children, Nel had resolved always to make the first thing she said to them each day positive. While she had found it quite hard, particularly when her boys refused to get out of bed in time for school, it did mean the rows didn't start until a good ten minutes into the day. Fleur had definitely been a bit jumpy at Christmas, but with the house full of the children's friends, there had been no opportunity to talk to her about it. Thus it was very nice to have this time alone together.

'Mm, thanks, Mum.'

This didn't look like a good moment. Fleur was not a morning person, but she seemed less so than ever today.

'Tired?'

Fleur nodded.

Nel bit her lip. She often wondered if, being a single parent, she worried for two, but she couldn't help herself. 'But you will get that essay done?'

'Mum! I told you! Don't worry. I'm going to see Jamie, but I will do it, although I don't think it's fair them giving us one so near the beginning of term.'

'Your exams are coming up, and Jamie lives in London.'

'I know that. I do have his address, you know,' she added irritably. 'In case you've forgotten, I stay there practically every weekend.'

Nel turned away from her daughter's sarcasm and put the kettle on. She had not forgotten that Fleur spent all her weekends in London, and she hoped that Fleur had not forgotten that she had promised Nel faithfully that she wouldn't leave the house until the essay was done. Nel had never been the sort of parent who could now have said, 'You're not leaving this house until that essay is written, young lady! And don't you smart-mouth me!' She had relied on good sense and explanation from a very early age, telling her more critical friends that you can only be the sort of parent you are. You can't pretend to be strict and decisive if you're not. Simon found this particularly hard to grasp.

'Sweetheart,' she began. 'You did agree—'

'Yes! And I'll do it! Now stop nagging . . . !'

'If you think that's nagging . . . !'

'No, I know it's not nagging, but it is early in the morning and I'm not a morning person.'

'It's not that early. I've seen the printer about getting leaflets and petition forms printed, shopped and walked the dogs.'

'But you're a lark. I'm an owl. No, Villette, you can't get up. I'm too tired to cuddle you. And you, Shirley.' The dogs retreated to their bed, where they arranged themselves in layers.

Nel kissed her daughter's cheek before releasing the croissants from their wrapper and putting them in the oven. 'Shall I clear the table for you to work on? Or will you do it in your room?'

'It's all right, Mum, I'll do it in the sitting room.'

'While watching television, I presume.'

Fleur smiled. 'That's right. Have we got any cherry jam?'

Nel searched the fridge for the appropriate jar, aware that it was not Fleur's homework she was worrying about. She always did get it in on time, somehow. Nor was Nel

64

concerned about Jamie. Although she had yet to meet him ('Like he'd want to come down here, Mum!'), she felt moderately happy with the relationship, having spoken to his mother on the phone once when Fleur had left her mobile at home. It was what Simon had said about young women taking drugs that was forming a knot of anxiety in her subconscious.

When he had first brought the subject up, she had dismissed it as one of Simon's things. But although at the time she'd sworn she'd know if her daughter took drugs, in her heart she wasn't so certain. How would she know? How would she recognise the signs if she didn't know what the signs were? If only there was some sort of sensor you could tape to their foreheads which would flash if they took anything untoward. Failing that, she wished her eldest son was at home. He and Fleur were very close and she might tell him things she wouldn't tell her mother. Although she and Fleur had an intimate and loving relationship, her children did protect Nel from things they thought would worry her.

'No cherry. What about raspberry?' Nel said eventually, having collected a little clutch of jars, the contents of which would have looked very interesting under a microscope.

'As long as it's red.' Fleur got up. 'Can you bring them in when they're ready? I'll get my school bag.'

'I spoil you, you know that?'

'I know. But you like it, really.'

Later, once Fleur had written, but not typed the essay, Nel drove her to the bus station.

'You won't miss the bus back on Sunday, will you? You can't miss school now.'

'Mum, have I ever missed the bus?'

'Not yet, I'm just making sure you don't. I'm a bit worried about you seeing so much of Jamie when I haven't met him.'

'You'd like him, Mum, really you would. It's just there's nothing to do down here.'

Nel refrained from mentioning beautiful countryside to ramble in, ancient buildings to admire, and the general calming effect of nature. After all, it was still winter.

'Well, ask him if he'll come and stay with you. It's not right that it's always you schlepping up to London all the time. He should spend a few hours on a bus and spend all his allowance!'

'I'll suggest it, but I don't expect he'll want to come. There are no good clubs here.'

'There are clubs in Bristol!' Nel remembered only too well her anxiety when her sons had started going to them.

'Not like London clubs. Now don't worry, Mum, I'll be fine. I do know how to look after myself.'

'I rather hoped that Jamie was looking after you.'

'Mum! You're so old-fashioned! How's your love life, by the way?'

'You mean Simon?' Nel deliberately misunderstood her daughter.

'No. I mean the man who kissed you under the mistletoe.'

'He's not my love life, he was suffering from a momentary aberration, and I've since discovered that he's the spawn of the devil. Now, what time is your bus?'

It was only on her way home that Nel realised yet again that Fleur had changed the subject to get her mother off her case. She decided to ring Sam at university, something she didn't often do.

'Hi, Mum, what's up?' he said, after he had been fetched, leaving Nel listening to several sorts of music for a good five minutes.

'It's Fleur, have you seen her lately? In London, I mean?'

'Well, she and I don't like the same music, so no, basically.'

'But do you know which clubs she and Jamie go to?'

66

'Not really. Why?'

'I'm just a bit worried about her. There's something not quite right. I'm worried she might be taking drugs or something.'

'Oh Mum!'

'It's a perfectly legitimate concern. She spends all that time in London, and I've never met Jamie.'

'He's a perfectly nice guy,' Sam said soothingly.

'I'm sure. I just don't know anything about him, and you know me, I worry.'

'At Olympic standard, Mum.'

'No one's offering me a medal. But that's not the point. What I'm asking is, can you find out where she and Jamie go, and then if they're the sorts of places where you can get drugs.'

'You can get drugs everywhere.'

'Don't tell me that! But some places must be worse than others, don't you think?'

'I suppose so. Actually, Mum, while you're on, you couldn't send me a cheque, could you? The electricity bill's come in, and it's mega.'

Nel sighed. 'All right.'

'I'll pay you back in the holidays, when I'm working.'

'That's OK. Just find out where Fleur goes, will you?'

Although she usually avoided telling Simon about any problems she had with her children, when he took her to a local pub for a meal that night, she found herself discussing Fleur.

'I know I said I'd know if she was taking drugs, but then I realised that I probably wouldn't. The parents never do, in these cases you read about in the paper.'

Simon picked a mussel out of its shell. 'It would be easier if you didn't let her spend so much time in London.'

'I know it would, but Jamie's there, and although I keep suggesting he comes to stay with us, she says there's

67

nothing to do down here. And I suppose there isn't much, for young people.'

'You could ground her.'

'No, I couldn't. I've never been that kind of parent, I can't start now. Besides, I've never known how you do grounding – I mean, you tell children they can't go out, but if they decide to disobey you, how do you prevent them?'

'You stop their allowance or something. Other parents seem to manage it.'

'Yes, but it's different for us.' By now she was thoroughly regretting bringing up the subject of Fleur and her love life. 'Good mussels?'

'Excellent. How's your salad?'

'That's very nice, too. Have you got any news about the development, how the plans are going? You realise I want you to tell me that it's all going pear-shaped, and no council on earth would allow people to build on those meadows.'

'Can't oblige, I'm afraid,' said Simon, his mouth full of French bread. 'Although, to be fair, I haven't heard information to the contrary, either. These things take time, even after outline permission has been granted.'

'That's a relief.' Nel folded a leaf of lollo rosso and pushed it into her mouth. 'It'll give me plenty of time to galvanise people.'

'You may not get as much support as you think, and it's unlikely to do any good anyway. Councils have targets for new housing they have to meet. They're not going to turn down anything they can possibly accept.'

'I'm not against houses, just houses there! Apart from the hospice, it's such a wonderful local resource. And there's the wildlife.'

'That may be so, but people need houses, and ultimately people are more important than newts and frogs.'

'We don't know that,' said Nel, who had had a couple of

glasses of wine. 'We don't know that newts and frogs might not be all that stands between us and total decimation.'

Simon raised an eyebrow. 'I think we do, Nel.'

'Even so, I can't just stand by and let it happen. Even if I fail, I've got to give it my best shot, otherwise every time I saw them, I'd feel guilty.'

'You feel guilty about too many things, you know.'

'Women do. It's to do with having oestrogen.'

'You're a funny little thing sometimes, Nelly.'

There were times when Nel quite liked being a funny little thing, but now, probably because she was worried, she'd have preferred Simon to tell her she was strong and independent, and could move mountains if she put her mind to it.

'Are you going to have pudding?' she asked.

'What, after my steak? I shouldn't think so. Why?'

'I just wanted to have a bit of it, that's all.'

'Why not have one of your own?'

'Because I don't want a whole one.' Nel suddenly wished she hadn't chosen her meal with her diet in mind. She yearned for a spoonful of sticky toffee pudding, or banoffie pie. In some ways Simon was an unsatisfactory eating companion. He just didn't like food enough.

It was a week later and Nel had just come in from taking her dogs for their pre-bedtime walk, when Sam phoned. 'I've done that bit of espionage you wanted, Mum.'

'Espionage? I thought you were doing media studies?'

'Twit. No, I've found out where Fleur and Jamie hang out. It's a club called Chill. Not my sort of music at all.'

'I don't care about the music, what about the drugs?'

'I told you, the drugs are the same all over, pretty much.'

'Wretched child! I mean, is it particularly bad for them? Does everyone who goes there take them?'

'Mum, if you think Fleur's taking drugs, why don't you just ask her?'

'She'd be so insulted if she isn't, and I'd be so devastated if she is. Besides, she might not tell me. I'd rather find out first, and then decide how to deal with it.'

'It's up to you. Let me know if you want me to come with you, or anything,' Sam said patiently.

'Come with me where?'

'To the club. If you need to go there, you don't want to go by yourself.'

'Oh, God! I'd never thought of that!'

'I really think you're worrying unnecessarily, Mum.'

'But you always do think that.'

'And ninety-nine times out of a hundred, I'm right. But I'll tell you what, I'll ask around and if I hear anything I think you need to know, I'll tell you. OK?'

'Just as long as you think I need to know the same as what I think I need to know.'

'Mum, you're talking rubbish.'

'Oh, OK. I'll try not to worry too much.'

Nel didn't know if the amount she was worrying was too much, or the right amount, but she did quite a lot of it as she pottered round the kitchen. Although she really enjoyed the company of her children as young adults, she did slightly yearn for the days when she knew where they were at all times. Fleur was in London with Jamie; she wouldn't see her until Sunday night, which would not be a good time to ask her if she was taking drugs. Monday morning would be no better, in fact far worse. Vivian would speak to Fleur if asked, but Fleur would be furious. However much she loved Vivian, she wouldn't take it kindly if Viv came round to supper and then told Fleur her mother was worried about her – a special form of trust would be broken. Nor could she involve Jamie's mother. Fleur would never forgive her if she rang Jamie's parents and demanded to know if their son was leading her daughter astray. No, she'd have to sort it out by herself.

She had just switched on the dishwasher when the phone rang again.

'Sorry to ring again so soon, Mum,' said Sam. 'Are you in bed?'

'Just going. What's up?'

'I've just heard some goss about Chill. I think there might be a bit more going on down there than at most clubs.'

Although sweat had formed at Nel's hairline, she tried to sound calm. 'But that doesn't mean Fleur and Jamie are doing it too.'

'No, it doesn't. But if you want me to come with you to check it out, I will. Anytime except next weekend. Angela's invited me to stay with her parents.'

'Who's Angela?'

'New girlfriend. The weekend after would be fine, though.'

There was no way Nel could wait a whole fortnight before finding out if Fleur was ingesting dangerous substances. 'No, it's OK. I'll deal with it.'

'You sure, Mum?'

'Course. She's my daughter, after all. There's a farmers' market I want to see in London, and it's on this week. I'll go and visit that, and then stay on.'

'If you're positive that'll be OK . . .'

'Honestly!'

All week, in between handing out application forms for the official farmers' market, asking every shop and office in town, not to mention every primary school, nursery and playgroup, if they would have a petition form to protest against the building plans, Nel interrogated Fleur. It had to be very subtle interrogating, and Nel felt it was. Fleur thought otherwise.

'Mum, if you want to know if I'm doing drugs, why don't you just ask me?'

'Well?'

'It's none of your business. I'm nearly eighteen!'

'And you're definitely going to see Jamie this weekend?'

'Yes! And I'm going to stay with Hannah the weekend after, remember. It's her eighteenth.'

At least that would be one Saturday night Nel needn't worry about her. Hannah's mother was notoriously strict and had always made Nel feel like a bad parent. But if Hannah's mother could get away with demanding her children were home by eleven on a Saturday night, Nel could only be grateful.

'So,' said Fleur, 'if you've finished with the third degree, I'll go to bed! I've got to go to school in the morning!'

All this pouting and flouncing was so uncharacteristic that Nel knew what she'd be doing the following Saturday night; she'd be going clubbing.

On Thursday night she phoned Simon to ask him to go with her. She'd tried to avoid it, but all her other potential fellow victims had genuine reasons for not going.

Vivian had been willing but had to get up early on Sunday morning, so Nel told her not to come. 'Besides, who's going to look after my animals if we're both away?' she added.

Nel and Vivian had a reciprocal arrangement with regard to this. 'I'd *love* to go another time, though; we could get Simon to dog-sit. In fact, are you sure you couldn't go on Saturday week instead? We could stay with my friend from college. We'd have a ball!'

'Sounds lovely, but Fleur's staying with Hannah that weekend. It's her eighteenth.'

'Hannah with the scary mother? Oh, shame.'

'Besides, I'm not sure how much fun I'd be, spying on Fleur, while you two go on the pull.'

'True. What about Sam, or would he be too embarrassed?'

'Nothing embarrasses Sam, but he's been invited to his girlfriend's parents for the weekend.'

'I didn't know he had a girlfriend.'

'Nor did I,' Nel said with feeling.

'So will you ask Simon to go with you?'

'Yes.'

Vivian left a tactful pause before saying, 'Are you sure Simon's into clubbing?'

'It doesn't matter! I'm worried about Fleur, not looking for a good time.'

'Then Simon's the perfect companion. Where are you going to stay?' Vivian glided over this little dig.

'Simon's got friends in London who I'm sure will put us up. They did when he took me on that theatre break.'

'Oh yes, when I thought he should take you to a fabulous hotel.'

'It's not like that between us! Anyway, I must go. I haven't actually asked Simon yet.'

'Try not to worry about Fleur – she's a sensible girl.'

'I know that really, but I can't stop fretting. Still, it's not all bad! I forgot to tell you I lost two pounds the last time I went to Weight Watchers!'

'Two pounds! That's nothing! There's no point in you starving yourself to lose two pounds.'

'It's a bag of sugar, which is not nothing, and now I *have* to ask Simon. I know he's not ideal but he's all I've got.'

But a few moments later, Nel realised that in fact she had not got Simon. He refused to go.

'I think it's ridiculous, you chasing up to London to see if Fleur is taking drugs. You should just stop her going to London if you're worried.'

'I'm going to visit a farmers' market!'

'Honestly, how do they have farmers' markets in London? They don't have farms!'

'The products have to come from within a hundred

73

miles of the M25. They're extremely popular. People like buying direct from the producer.'

'You don't have to go to London to research all that, but I don't blame you for being worried about Fleur. There was another case in the paper the other day, some foolish girl taking an E on her birthday and dying.'

Nel hissed. She didn't read papers except for the lifestyle bits and the crossword, and she'd managed to filter out too many details about the girl in question from what news she heard on the radio. She did not need Simon to remind her of it.

'Please, Simon. I'm asking you, as a favour, to come with me.'

'And I'm saying no as a favour. I don't think you should go. You spend far too much of your time running round after your children when they're not even children any more.'

'So, even though I'm asking you, *begging* you, even, you won't come with me?'

'No.'

'Fine.'

'Nel, don't take this personally—'

As there wasn't another way to take it, Nel put the phone down.

Nel didn't like leaving the dogs alone in the house at night, but Vivian had said she'd come over and tuck them up, so Nel felt they would be all right. On Saturday morning she fed them, walked them and gave them pigs' ears to chew, then caught the early train to London. The farmers' market would be over by the time she got there if she waited until a more reasonable time.

It was always tricky, getting dressed in the country for two very different appointments in town, Nel decided. She wished Vivian had been going with her. It might even have been fun. As it was she finally decided on black trousers,

74

little black top, V-necked jumper, also black, and a sort of informal jacket which was long enough to cover her bottom. Over this she put a winter coat which had been Mark's. It was extremely heavy but extremely warm. She wore it partly in case she missed the last train home and needed to sleep on a bench: it would act as a sort of tent; and partly because she liked to wear something of Mark's – socks, a jumper, a T-shirt – if she was doing something frightening that involved the children. It allowed her to imagine she wasn't a completely single parent. A fuchsia-coloured pashmina over the top made the outfit slightly more suitable for daytime wear than unremitting black.

Twelve hours later, it was an anticlimax to have got herself from Notting Hill Gate on the tube to Oxford Circus and followed Sam's directions to the club to find it closed. Her feet were killing her; she had been on them all day, and while visiting the market had been fascinating and extremely useful, it had been exhausting.

She had spent most of the afternoon, after the market was over, going round the art galleries. She'd then taken herself to a small arthouse cinema and slept through something very highbrow in black and white. Still, she'd been more in need of a nap than she had been of an improving retrospective view of the Spanish Civil War, seen through the eyes of a blind child and his grandmother.

Now, after a cup of strong coffee, she had got herself to the right place, and it was all locked up. A notice on the door said it didn't open until ten o'clock! She knew things started much later in London, but ten o'clock! No wonder Fleur was always so tired.

The thought that Fleur might see her lurking outside sent Nel walking down the side street she was in, looking for shop windows. There were none. There was nothing she could possibly be doing except waiting for the club to open, and as there was no queue forming, and she assumed there wouldn't be for a while.

75

She set off for Oxford Street; at least there were shops there. She'd gone off down yet another side street, which at least had some lovely shoes on display, when a taxi pulled up behind her. One glance told her it was full of men, and she looked hastily back at something in pink with a strange-shaped heel. One of the men got out and said her name.

It was Jake. 'Nel? What are you doing here?'

Nel gulped with shock and confusion. What was he doing here, appearing out of the blue again? It was weirder than the film. Not knowing what else to do, she shrugged. If she'd been on more familiar territory she'd have made some sharp riposte. 'Just hanging around.'

'Why?'

'Nothing to do with you. Get back in your taxi, your friends are waiting.' She didn't want him feeling sorry for her.

'Not till I've found out why you're hanging round Oxford Street at this time of night.'

'I'm waiting for the clubs to open.' She smiled. In spite of her anxiety, it still sounded funny to her.

'Why?'

'So I can go clubbing, of course.'

Jake frowned, and looked back at the waiting taxi. 'Look, we can't talk here. Come with me.'

'No! Don't be silly! You're with your friends, and why should I come with you?'

'Because I can't leave you here on the street.'

'Yes, you can. I'm a free woman, over twenty-one. What can happen to me?'

'I wouldn't put anything past you. Move over, lads, we've got an extra passenger.'

'But—'

'Don't make me drag you into the taxi with me. I don't usually have to work that hard, and my reputation would never recover.'

Nel hesitated.

'Please?'

Then Nel laughed – fatal if you're trying to resist doing something you quite want to do, like get into a taxi with a familiar, if not friendly face, rather than hang about on a London street planning a one-woman drugs bust. 'Oh, all right, then.'

One of Jake's companions moved to share the flip-up seat, making almost enough room for Nel and her coat on the bench seat. There were already four men in the cab before Jake followed her. It was a squash.

'We'll take you with us to the restaurant,' said Jake. 'Then we'll go clubbing. Everybody, this is Nel Innes. She's going clubbing and it's too early, so she's going to have dinner with us. OK?'

'Jake, I can't butt in like this!'

'Yes, you can,' said one of the other men, who, now Nel looked at them, all seemed terribly young. 'We don't often get to see Jake's totty.'

Nel giggled nervously. 'I'm not Jake's totty! I'm just someone he knows from the country.'

'Let me make some introductions,' Jake said.

Nel immediately realised that as they all had the same haircuts and very similar clothes she had no chance of remembering their names until she got to know them a bit.

'This is a sort of works do,' Jake explained. 'We don't usually have them on a Saturday night, but no one here has got a girlfriend at the moment, so we agreed on tonight. We have a meal first, and then we go on somewhere.'

'So you can go on the pull?' asked Nel, seriously.

The young man opposite her nodded. 'That's right.'

'Well, I won't get in your way. I've got stuff of my own I need to do.'

'Here's Luigi's,' said someone as the cab drew up. 'The firm's paying for the cab, right?'

Chapter Six

❧

The men with Jake were extremely nice to Nel, she thought.

'Let me take your coat,' said one. 'God! It weighs a ton!'

'It was my husband's, and it was his father's, so it's ancient. But very warm.'

'I should think so,' said Jake briskly as he went and hung it up for her.

The group was obviously well known at the restaurant. '*Ciao, ragazzi!*' said the head waiter. 'Oh, you have a lady with you. How nice!'

Nel tried to match her smile to the mood of those around her. 'Hello.'

'She's with Jake, Luigi,' said one of the men, who, Nel had to keep reminding herself, could not be thought of as boys.

'Really?' Luigi looked Nel over critically yet appreciatively. Nel could have felt offended, but somehow didn't.

Luigi pulled the table out from the banquette and Nel squeezed round so she could sit down.

'Now, let's get some drinks in, for goodness' sake,' said Jake. 'Nel, have a Brandy Alexander, it will do you good.'

'What is it?'

'Just have it,' said Jake crossly. 'And we'll have the usual quantity of beers, some sparkling water and a bottle of red wine. That do for everyone?'

Judging by their expressions, 'everyone' was rather surprised by Jake's brusqueness.

'You're the boss,' said one.

78

'That'll do, Dan. Now let's all sit down.'

'Let's introduce ourselves again,' said Dan, 'or Nel won't have a hope of remembering all our names.'

'She doesn't need to remember your names,' snapped Jake.

'Yes, she does,' said Nel. 'I'm hopeless at it, but it's good practice. Besides, I can't call you all "you".'

'Right,' said Dan, taking the lead. 'We all work together. I'm Dan, this is Nathan, Paul, and Jezz. And we're all dateless on a Saturday night, so we decided to go out together.'

'On the pull, as you said,' said one, possibly Paul.

Nel decided to ignore this. 'And I'm Nel.'

'We know,' said Dan. 'There's only one of you, so it's easy for us to remember.'

'I'm going to the loo,' said Jake, and got up.

'Well, this is a turn-up for the books,' said Dan, when Jake had gone. 'We didn't know Jake had a girlfriend in the country.'

'Oh, I'm not his girlfriend! Perish the thought! I mean, I'm sure he's awfully nice and all that, but . . .'

'But what?'

'It was just coincidence that we met this evening.'

'We know that,' said the one next to her – Jezz? 'But he wouldn't have got so worked up when he saw you if you were just acquaintances, would he?'

'I don't know how worked up he got, but actually we're adversaries. He's acting for the Hunstantons—'

'And you're the one objecting? All is now made clear.'

'So,' went on Nel, probing in spite of herself, 'you don't have to worry about him two-timing his girlfriend in London.'

'Has he got a girlfriend in London?' asked Paul. 'He's kept that dark!'

'Of course he hasn't,' said Dan. 'If he had we'd know about it.' Dan turned to Nel. 'Jake got divorced about

79

three years ago. He hasn't shown any sign of being interested in a woman since.'

'Once bitten, twice shy, I expect,' said Nel.

'How about you? Married? Divorced?'

'Widowed, actually, but not looking for a new relationship.' It hadn't taken Nel long to realise that Jake's London colleagues took far too much interest in his personal life.

'Why not?' asked the one with very short hair and a shiny face, who Nel assumed must be Nathan.

'None of your business, Paul,' said Jake, rejoining the party. 'I must apologise for my colleagues, Nel. They're worse than a bunch of girls for wanting to get everyone paired off. Has everyone ordered?'

There was a chorus of 'No!'

Nel had begun to enjoy herself. In the company of these friendly, entertaining men, she almost forgot why she was there in the first place.

'You're all very frivolous for lawyers,' she said.

'Is that a complaint?' asked Dan.

'Certainly not, I just didn't expect you to be jolly. I would have thought you would spend your spare time discussing the finer points of law.'

The guffaws and hoots which greeted this remark could have felt unkind, except that Nel was used to being laughed at by her children, and could tell when the humour was affectionate.

'I'm afraid lawyers are just as bad as everyone else,' said Jake.

Nel regarded him. 'And worse in some cases.'

The moment of stillness was quickly buried by another joke, but Nel wished she hadn't made that remark. It was inappropriate. However badly she felt Jake was behaving over the building and her rather abortive attempts to protest against it, he was being nice to her now: the brusqueness had disappeared and he was proving as entertaining as his colleagues.

She couldn't let it stand. She put her hand on his to claim his attention. 'I didn't quite mean that like it sounded.'

He gave her fingers the smallest squeeze, to acknowledge her apology, and the awkwardness was past.

Jake didn't laugh quite so much as his colleagues. They were younger than him, but she got the impression that he was usually a bit more lively than he was being now. It was her presence, she realised. She had spoilt his evening. She resolved not to allow herself to be talked into dawdling, and leave the minute she'd had a cup of coffee. She could get a taxi back to the club.

'Who's for pudding?' said Dan. 'Nel, have the zabaglione, it's to die for.'

'I think I should be getting off—'

'Sit down,' said Jake, firmly. 'Have a pudding. And Dan's right about the zabaglione. It's not even fattening.'

Nel glared at him with a mixture of horror and outrage. 'How do you know?'

'It can't be, it's full of air. Besides,' Jake put his hand on hers. 'It's still far too early to go to Chill.'

'Are you going to Chill?' Paul asked. Come with us instead. We're going down to the Pool Hall. The drinks are a rip-off, but the music's great.'

Nel found herself laughing. A Brandy Alexander and two glasses of red wine had certainly taken the edge off her anxiety. 'I'm not going clubbing,' she said firmly. 'I'm going to check up on my daughter.'

'Is she pretty?'

'Very,' said Nel. 'Or at least, I think so.'

'She's very pretty,' said Jake.

'I didn't know you'd met her.'

'I haven't met her, but I saw her that time at the market. I recognised her easily, she looks just like her mother.'

81

Nel realised there was a compliment hidden in there somewhere, but couldn't accept it. 'She doesn't, you know. She's blonde and blue-eyed, and I'm – not.'

'You're still alike. Something about the eyes.'

Nel sighed. She simply couldn't see the resemblance.

'So, "zeebag" all round?'

'No, not for me, really,' said Nel. She had a card and a certain amount of cash, but she didn't want to use it all on her share of the meal.

'So it's just the lads, then, thanks, Luigi,' said Dan.

'If now is still too early, what time can I go to the club, then?' asked Nel.

'Not till midnight at the earliest,' said Paul.

'Good God!'

'Is she still at school?'

'Yes. A levels soon.'

'I've never worked so hard for anything before or since as I did for my A levels,' said one.

'Nor me. GCSEs were a happy breeze. A levels stank.'

'Your parents must be very proud of you.' Nel suddenly felt parental, something she hadn't felt all evening.

'Yeah, I suppose. They were thrilled when I got good grades. Have you got other children, apart from your daughter?'

'Yes, two boys at university. One's in London, and he would have come with me to the club, only he couldn't.'

'You don't look old enough to have children at university,' said Paul.

Nel smiled in a way that made it quite clear she knew she was being flattered, and didn't believe it. 'Thank you. I'm also Queen of the May.'

'No, really,' Dan persisted. 'Don't you agree, Jake?'

Jake didn't answer immediately. 'I think Nel's a very attractive woman. Age has nothing to do with it.'

Fortunately for Nel, who was completely dumbfounded, the puddings arrived at that moment. Tall glasses full of golden foam were set in front of all the men.

'Are you sure you don't want to change your mind?' asked Dan.

'Quite sure. It does look heavenly, though.'

'Here.' Jake passed his spoon across the table. 'Try it.' He put the spoon into her mouth, and although they were in a crowded room, at a table full of laughing people, Nel suddenly felt the gesture was curiously intimate, as if it was something he shouldn't have done in public.

'It is delicious,' she said. And it was: warm, fluffy and alcoholic.

'Have another mouthful,' said Jake.

She opened her mouth to refuse, and another spoonful was delivered. 'Really, that's enough,' she said when it was gone.

Jake was serious when he looked into her eyes. 'Coffee now, then.'

Nel didn't drink coffee often, but she nodded when the others ordered it. If her clubbing experience wasn't to begin until after midnight, she'd need some nervous energy.

'Grappa?'

'Whatta?' Nel couldn't help flirting with Dan. He was so safe and friendly.

He laughed back. 'It tastes of lighter fuel, but it's somehow delicious. Have some.'

Nel decided that there was probably a cashpoint machine somewhere between here and the club, and that she should just stop worrying about the money and enjoy herself. It was still only half past eleven.

Three cups of coffee, two grappas and several amaretti biscuits (all of whose papers had been lit and wishes sent) later, Nel got up to go to the Ladies.

Once there, she pulled her fingers through her hair a

few times and put on some lipstick before actually con-
fronting her reflection. Long ago she had realised there
was no point in knowing how awful one had looked all
evening. Once these preliminary preparations were over,
she took a good look.

Her long black V-neck jumper was satisfyingly slimming. It covered her tummy and hips, and with her black
trousers and long jacket, it was a flattering look, if somewhat sombre. She had never worn black to mourn her
husband, but now society felt mourning was no longer
appropriate, she wore it a lot. She had a good colour, and
it didn't drain her like it did so many people.

But she was going to be too hot; already her cheeks
were a little flushed. She decided that Mark's overcoat
would keep her warm enough on the way to the club,
went back into the cubicle and removed the jumper. Under
it she was wearing a little black top, which might have
been underwear, or might have been a proper garment.
With the jacket on top this would have looked moderately respectable if it hadn't shown quite so much
cleavage.

Nel inspected the cleavage. It was, she decided, quite
nice. But was it appropriate to show so much of it, even if
it was one of her best features? When you're young, she
reflected, there are bits of your body you don't like, and
you feel if it weren't for your thighs, or your nose, you
would be perfect. Now she was over forty a bit of critical
scrutiny brought her to the conclusion that her teeth, her
skin and her cleavage, were all . . . OK, but the rest of her
was best ignored. Mark had always liked her bosom. Simon
had probably never seen as much of it as was on display
now, and Jake . . . ? She tugged her top up a bit. What Jake
thought about her top half was neither here nor there.

She put her jacket back on. Her arms were one of the
bits she no longer liked to display, except in summer when
they were tanned.

She stuffed the jumper into her capacious handbag, clawed at her hair a few more times, partly out of nervousness, and went back to the others. It was lucky her hair was in a style which could take a fair bit of clawing, she thought. She'd have wreaked havoc with an elegant chignon long since.

'I'm going to take you to the club,' said Jake. 'The others are going to the Pool Hall.'

The trouble with leaving a group of men to go to the loo was that it gave them the opportunity to make decisions without consulting you. But the thought of actually going into the club by herself (that's if she was even let in), was incredibly daunting. It was one thing to know that it was the right thing to do, that you were doing it for Fleur, to tell yourself that that was what you were going to do. To actually do it, especially alone, was another thing entirely. Knowing she didn't have to was a great relief.

Nel's mother had always described her husband Mark as a 'man to ride the water with'. She'd probably describe Jake the same way – only of course she'd be quite wrong, thought Nel, which proved that not even dead people know everything. What would her mother have thought of Simon? Wondering why she should choose this moment to ask herself that question, Nel decided her mother would say he was a nice man, but would never set the world on fire.

Now she said, 'Oh, OK. What about my share of the bill? If I put in twenty pounds, will that be about right?'

'The firm is paying,' said Dan. 'It owes us. And we have an entertainment budget that is seriously underspent. So put your money away.'

Nel put her head on one side. 'You seem to have thought out that little speech in advance.'

'Yes, well, Jake said you were bound to be difficult about letting us pay.'

She regarded him, unsure if she should be indignant or

not. 'I have no idea why you would have thought that!'

'Experience,' said Jake. 'You're always difficult.'

Silenced, Nel allowed Dan to hold her overcoat and got into it.

Once outside the restaurant, a taxi drew up quite soon and Jake opened the door for Nel. 'We'll take this one. Get in, Nel.'

'But I haven't said goodbye!'

Each of the four men kissed her warmly and she kissed them back. They were very smoothly shaved and smelt of cologne. Nel decided it was nice being kissed, and wondered, as she settled herself into the taxi, if fancying men younger than yourself was a sign of getting old. Before they'd travelled more than a few yards she'd decided that yes, it was.

'This is very kind of you,' she said, a moment or two later. 'I would have been all right on my own, and I've spoiled your evening.'

'Have you ever been to a club before?'

Nel thought back to her very well-spent youth. That was the trouble with getting married young; you don't get much time to misbehave. 'Well, the odd discothèque, you know.'

'Exactly. And you haven't spoilt my evening. I spend a lot of time with those lads.'

'So you live and work in London, mostly? Not in the country?'

'At the moment I'm between both places. We've taken over a local firm—'

'Oh yes, with those lovely offices.'

'Which have now been painted, at least.'

'And did Kerry Anne choose the colours?'

'Look, I thought you asked me if I worked in London or the country. I'm trying to tell you. Stop interrupting.'

Nel stopped, mostly because she wanted to listen to his explanation.

'The local firm was struggling. There's a historic link between us and them, so I'm going down to re-establish the business, and while I'm about it, decide if I want to move out of London.'

'And have you decided?'

'No. It depends on several things.'

Nel managed not to ask if Kerry Anne was one of the things. He would hardly admit it if she was. Kerry Anne was married to one of his clients, after all. Although he had given her that 'so fun' time. She sighed, and chided herself for being old-fashioned and jealous at the same time.

'I spent my school holidays in that part of the world, and the friend I spent them with still lives there,' went on Jake. 'He was the one I was playing squash with, when you first saw me.'

'Oh?'

'Yes. Here we are.'

Nel pulled up the collar of her coat and tried to look suitably cool – not easy when encased in several kilos of wool. She let Jake pay the taxi-driver, but had her money ready to pay for him to go into Chill.

The bouncer looked them over, but didn't comment, although Nel felt he must have wondered why they were there. It would have been a million times worse without Jake, she knew. In fact it might not even have been possible. Knowing she wouldn't be able to talk much once they were actually in the heart of the club, Nel put her hand on his arm. 'I'm really grateful to you for coming. They might not even have let me in.'

'That's OK. Let's get your coat checked, and go and find some action.'

Nel had been worried that Fleur would spot her and be furious. Now she was actually inside the club she realised it was going to be very difficult to spot Fleur, even when looking intently. And if she did manage to make her out among the other blonde girls in black trousers and strappy tops, would she know if she was taking drugs? Her whole plan suddenly seemed incredibly flaky. What had she been thinking?

'Drink?' Jake bellowed at her over the top of the music.

Nel nodded. 'Fizzy water, please!'

While she was alone she inspected the crowd and listened to the music. No one was taking any notice of her, she realised, and began to relax a little. She quite liked the music, too, but then she had always liked Fleur's music better than what issued forth from the boys' bedrooms. Theirs had no lyrics, no tune, and far too many electronics for her, and Fleur's was far too 'middle of the road' for them.

Jake came up and put a glass in her hand. Nel smiled her thanks and took a sip, thinking how odd it was to be in a club with Jake, the man who until recently had been fixed in her mind as the one who had kissed her under the mistletoe. And after that he had turned into the devil incarnate who, almost single-handed, was depriving the hospice of Paradise Fields.

'This isn't water!'

'No, it's vodka and tonic. I thought you needed a bit of Dutch courage.'

'But I asked for water!'

'You can have water next time.'

'Next time, I'm getting the drinks!'

Jake smiled. 'Drink up, then we can dance.'

Nel couldn't help smiling back. She wanted to dance, she liked dancing. One of Mark's few faults had been that he didn't like dancing, and only did it extremely reluctantly – and very badly.

Nel soon lost her inhibitions and was getting into the music when Jake put his hand on her shoulder and pointed. It was Fleur. She was with a tall young man who looked both handsome and prosperous, but not, Nel decided, significantly older than Fleur.

Jake pulled Nel close and said in her ear, 'What do you want to do?'

Nel turned, and Jake bent down so she could speak into his ear. 'Just observe her, and see if anyone tries to give her anything, or if money changes hands.'

'I doubt if it would go on out here,' said Jake.

'I'll know if she does anything odd. At least, I hope I will!'

Jake took Nel into his arms. 'It'll be easier for you to spy on Fleur if you're not jumping up and down. And it's less likely she'll spot you.'

'You're not telling me I draw attention to myself when I dance, are you?' She tried to pull away, but he wouldn't let her. It was certainly easier to talk when they were close.

'You dance in a very original manner,' he said.

Nel groaned, and let herself melt into Jake's arms.

Dancing with Jake was really very pleasant, she decided. If she didn't have to keep her eyes on Fleur, she could have closed them and swayed about to the music quite happily. He smelt lovely. His aftershave was not too pungent, but it was obviously something very expensive. And his suit jacket felt very soft. Probably cashmere, she decided. He had taken off his tie, and his shirt was blue-white in the ultraviolet strobes which zigzagged across the floor.

She couldn't tell if he was equally happy to be holding her, of course, but he did seem to nuzzle into her a little, although that could have been her imagination. But when he pushed his fingers up into her hair, she knew her mind wasn't playing tricks on her. And she liked the feeling rather more than she would have admitted. Trying to distract herself from the feel of his touch on her neck, she wondered if the reason she pulled at her own hair so much was because she missed Mark's caresses. Simon never

89

touched her hair – possibly because he liked it tidy, something it never was.

From her slowly rotating viewpoint, Fleur seemed to be behaving in a perfectly normal way. She was drinking something from a bottle, and seemed to dance with a lot of people at once, but that was fine.

Nel's feet began to hurt, in a way they hadn't since the last time she had been to a club. Jake was probably bored out of his mind. She reached up to pull his head down so she could speak to him. Just for a split second, it looked as if he was going to kiss her. But then he presented his ear to within a few inches of her mouth.

'I think I've seen enough. Shall we go?'

'If you want to. It is a bit noisy.'

'And I don't think Fleur is going to do anything revealing.'

'Then let's get out of here.'

He forged a path through the crowd, in the nick of time, as it turned out. Just as she left, Nel turned for a last look at Fleur and saw her daughter frown, as if she'd recognised her mother. I'll have to lie, she thought. I'll say I was in town, having dinner with friends – a friend – and we thought we'd go dancing. I'll say I never saw her, or of course I'd have come over and said hello.

'Come on!' Nel muttered under her breath, as the girl took ages finding her coat. 'I'm sure Fleur spotted me,' she said to Jake. 'She might not have recognised me for sure, but I really don't want her to follow me. This is no place for a confrontation.'

'Well, I'm glad you worked that out, finally,' said Jake, putting a two-pound coin into the saucer as Nel's coat was produced.

'What do you mean?' Nel's voice seemed to be an octave higher than usual, and sounded very squeaky.

'Come on. Let's go home.'

Chapter Seven

❧

'Right, I'm going to Paddington,' said Nel as the taxi drew up. 'Can I give you a lift?'

Jake grunted and opened the door; Nel got in. Then he gave the driver an address.

'But I want to go to Paddington! To catch a train!'

'I know the timetable by heart, and I can promise you there is no train at half past one in the morning.'

'Well, I can wait there until there is one!'

'No, you can't! I couldn't possibly let you spend the night on the station platform until God knows what hour in the morning! Who do you think I am?'

Nel took a breath and tried hard to stop feeling outraged. 'Listen, Jake, I've been really grateful for your support this evening. *Really* grateful,' she repeated, thinking how unsupportive Simon had been. 'But I can't intrude on your time a moment longer. I've already ruined your evening. Now I just want to go home. And if I have to wait for a train, so be it. I'll be fine.'

'Have you ever spent all night on a station, in winter?'

'That is not the point—'

'Yes, it is. You'll be picked up by drunks, harassed by beggars and mugged for your overcoat.' The corner of his mouth twitched, and, maddeningly, so did Nel's.

'My overcoat will be like a tent.' She retorted, trying very hard not to respond to his half-smile, which suddenly seemed incredibly sexy.

'It will be, but you're not sleeping in it. Not tonight.'

'Well, I'm not staying with you!'

'Listen, Nel, I do understand about you not wanting to inconvenience me in any way, and I appreciate your concern. But quite frankly I'm tired, I don't want to spend the whole night arguing with you, and if you refuse to come home with me, I'll feel obliged to drive you back to the country myself. And I think I'm over the limit.'

'Oh.'

'Or I could arrange a minicab, but that will cost a fortune. I'm not mean, but I do resent paying over fifty pounds to someone who may not even get you home safely.'

'I could go to a hotel,' Nel persisted stubbornly.

'Oh, stop being bloody ridiculous. Sit back and enjoy the ride. I've got a perfectly good sofabed you can sleep on.'

'I haven't got a toothbrush or anything.'

Jake sighed deeply, and leant forward to speak to the driver. 'Could you stop if you see an all-night shop, please? Madam needs a toothbrush.'

'Honestly! Now he'll think we're sleeping together!'

'Rubbish. I didn't say you needed condoms.'

Nel huddled in her coat, shaking with indignation. When a One Stop appeared at the corner of a street, she got out and went into it, wondering if she should refuse to re-enter the taxi. As she stalked the aisles, looking for what she needed, she concluded there was something incredibly slutty about buying a toothbrush in the middle of the night, however pure one's intentions. She added a pot of moisturiser to her basket, and then her hand hovered over the condoms. She didn't want them, she doubted if she remembered how to use them; it was so long ago – before they were married – that she and Mark had struggled with the hard-to-open sachets. But some defiant streak in her wanted just to plop them in on top of her more legitimate purchases. It was something to do with living up to the reputation she was sure she had by now.

She didn't do it. If Jake saw them, and she couldn't trust him not to go through her bag, he'd think she was coming on to him, and she would die, literally die, rather than let him think that.

'You took your time,' he said as she sat back down beside him.

'Well, I was just deciding which magazine to buy.'

He looked in her bag, as she knew he would. 'But you didn't buy one!'

'No, and I didn't spend time looking for one, either! It just took a while to find the toothpaste. They don't have a special section devoted to loose women's requirements, you know!'

'Are you a loose woman?'

'No, but I felt like one in that shop. I'm sure the man thought I was planning to sleep with my gentleman friend, and was wondering who would possibly want to sleep with me.'

Jake stared at her. 'Oh, I'm sure he wasn't wondering that.'

Nel turned away to look out of the window, aware that she'd said far too much. Being with Jake shifted her identity somehow, from mother to woman, and it didn't feel safe.

When they reached their destination, Nel insisted on paying for the taxi, pushing Jake away from the window with such vehemence that he almost fell over.

His flat was tiny and reassuringly cluttered. He switched on a table lamp which he dimmed to glow-worm brightness and turned off the main light, but the mess was still clearly visible. Piles of papers were on every chair, and the table was hidden under a heap of files.

Jake swept several Sundays' worth of newspapers off the sofa and onto the floor. 'Sorry about the mess. I'm not here often enough to do anything about it.' He didn't seem unduly apologetic, and she wondered if she'd ever be able to be like him about mess and other people.

'Only one bedroom, I'm afraid,' he went on. 'I'd offer you the bed and sleep on the sofa myself, but I know you'd kick up.'

'I do not kick up! I'm a very reasonable person.'

'You're mad as a box of frogs. Now, let me take your coat.'

Without it, Nel felt underdressed. She tugged at her top to hide the large amount of cleavage that was now on show.

'Don't keep doing that,' said Jake, having laid her coat tenderly on the back of a chair. 'It draws attention to it, and it's very distracting. You've been doing it all night.'

'Have I? I'm sorry.'

'No need to apologise. It's the sort of distraction I like.'

'Is it?'

A moment later he had his arms round her and was kissing her.

Nel was tired and had had a fair bit to drink. Also, all her tension about Fleur seemed to have been dissipated. Her fears that she may have been taking drugs were probably all just neurosis, encouraged by Simon. Now, her defences were down and it was only too easy to nestle into him, close her eyes and kiss him back.

Without lifting his mouth from hers, he manoeuvred her to the sofa and drew her onto it. Then they were both horizontal, he slightly on top of her. When at last he stopped for breath, she said, 'What on earth am I doing?'

'Kissing me,' said Jake decisively. 'And doing it very well, thank you.'

'But I—' Opening her mouth was a fatal mistake; Jake had it covered in an instant.

This is so nice, thought Nel. So, so nice. I'd forgotten how lovely it is to lie next to someone and kiss. But I really, really shouldn't be doing it. She fought free. 'Jake, I . . .'

Jake, prevented from kissing her mouth, laid his lips on the cleavage he'd complained had been so distracting. It felt like heaven. All Nel's suppressed sexuality surfaced. Suddenly it wasn't enough to have his lips on the place where her breasts met, she wanted her breasts bare, so he could caress them, take her nipples in his mouth.

He pulled down the little black top (which *was* really underwear) and revealed her bra. Oh God, thought Nel, my bra. It was one of those designed by architects for a television programme, and though extremely comfortable, supportive and practical, it was about as sexy as armour-plating. But – Nel thanked God more fervently than she'd thanked him for a long time – it was black. Her white bras stayed white for about two washes.

She sat up, trying to summon the will to stop doing what was giving her so much pleasure. He took advantage of her position to remove her jacket. Then her arms, which no one saw except in summer, were exposed, and being held, gripped in his fingers. She wasn't sure arms were on the list of erogenous zones, but his hold on hers was making her melt just as much as everything else he was doing.

Nel decided she was being too passive; her clothes were being flung off at a rate of knots. Jake's tie was in his pocket, but otherwise he was fully dressed. Her fingers fumbled with his shirt buttons. She struggled to get the first one undone.

'How did people manage when men wore shirt studs,' she breathed, abandoning the button while he got his hands behind her to undo her bra.

'I expect it was a technique people learned,' he said, revealing his own expertise as he removed her bra.

Nel swallowed, her breathing uneven. No man had seen her breasts for a very long time and at first she felt extremely self-conscious, but when she saw Jake's reaction to them, she just felt sexy and powerful.

She made another attempt at his collar but he pushed her hands away and just pulled the two halves apart until the button flew off. She found herself wondering briefly who would sew it back on, until his shirt and jacket came off together and she saw his chest. If she'd thought about it, she'd have known he was fit, with all the sport he did. But seeing his bare chest, with its well-defined pectorals, shadowed with hair, made her gasp. She had an overpowering desire to feel it against her own torso, to trail her nipples over his muscles.

'Shall we go to bed?' breathed Jake. 'It would be more comfortable.'

Nel shook her head. She was in the throes of passion, but she knew if they changed venues, sense would come rushing back, and she'd stop. She didn't want to stop. She didn't want to be sensible. She wanted, more than anything else in the whole wide world, to go on doing what she was doing, to have sex with Jake. It was the first time for ten years, and she didn't want her brain, or her conscience, or anything coming between her and this blissful experience.

'Hang on a minute then.' Jake leaned over and burrowed at the side of the sofa. There was a grinding noise and a jolt, and the back of it tipped back and the seat slid forward. 'That's better.' He laid her down so she was flat on her back and, propping himself on one elbow, did all the things her breasts wanted him to do.

A little later, he struggled with the zip on her trousers.

'You have to hold the top bit together, otherwise it catches,' she breathed. A moment later she regretted giving him the hint as she recalled her knickers. Big knickers had better be in, she thought, knowing they weren't, knowing that to be a sex kitten these days you had to wear a thong.

Jake didn't comment, didn't even look, as he slid down trousers, pants and tights together. They got stuck on her boots.

'This is ridiculous,' breathed Nel, struggling upright.

'Don't move.' He pushed her back and kept her there by stroking her stomach as he struggled, one-handed, with the zips. Could he feel the stretch marks, she wondered? Would he find them off-putting?

She sighed when she was completely naked, and so did he. 'God, you're so sexy,' he breathed.

Nel stopped worrying about her knickers or her stretch marks and laughed. She felt sexy. She felt desirable, wanton, and totally feminine. She fumbled at the hook at the top of his trousers. Impatient, he brushed her hands away and did it himself.

'You're not going to just rip them apart, then?'

'I've haven't got that many suits, and this is easy.'

The sensation of skin against skin was ectasy. It had been so long since Nel had felt that electricity. She lay back and he lay on top of her, crushing her slightly before rolling over and pulling her on top of him. She paused a moment before moving off him and paying his body the sort of attention she felt it deserved. She wanted to read his body with her fingers, examine every curve and hollow. Her mind may have forgotten the joy and beauty of a man's body, but her senses hadn't. When she'd studied every silken inch of his torso, she echoed the movements of her fingers with her mouth. She took his nipples gently between her teeth and felt them respond immediately. He groaned softly and she moved onto his chest hair, tugging at it with her mouth. He sighed deeply, sat up, and took over.

Nel had only ever made love to one person in her life, but somehow, between them, she and Jake swiftly worked out how to make each other happy. Possibly, she reflected, because everything he did to her sent her skywards, and similarly, everything she did to him seemed to please him. It was only afterwards, when he moved off her, and they were both panting and hot from their exertions, that Nel allowed her brain to take back control of her thoughts.

'That was so bloody fantastic,' said Jake, still breathing heavily. 'You are the sexiest, most brilliant woman.'

Nel's body was sated, happy from sex which had no right to be so utterly satisfying. But now emotion rushed in: doubt, guilt, the horrible realisation that she'd just had sex, for the first time in ten years, with a man she hardly knew.

'Can I get you anything?' he asked, concerned at her silence.

Nel sat up, reaching for what clothes she could find and holding them to her, even though some of them were Jake's. The elation of a few moments ago was suddenly offset with a despondency as deep as the elation had been high. She'd changed her life irrevocably, and she'd done it without thinking. It was as insane as flinging yourself off a cliffs on impulse. Somehow, she must scrabble herself back to sanity, to what she knew and valued and trusted. If she could have expunged the whole experience from her memory, she'd have done it.

'Listen, Jake.' God what to say? She tried again. 'That was very nice. Very, very, nice actually, but it shouldn't have happened. And I don't want you to feel obliged to ring me or get in touch with me in any way.' She paused, alarm building inside her. 'In fact, you mustn't. We'll just draw a line, and move on. And could I use the bathroom please.'

'Nel – darling, what's wrong?'

'I think you know what's wrong, what we just did is wrong.' At his look of utter bewilderment, Nel's alarm boiled over into panic. She had to think. 'Could you just tell me where the bathroom is please?'

Jake got up, and Nel tried to avoid looking at his

splendid, squash-playing body as he opened a door. 'Here,' he said, taking something out of a cupboard. 'Have a clean towel. Do you want your toothbrush and stuff?'

Nel nodded, gripping the clothes with all her strength, even though no one was trying to take them away from her.

When her plastic bag was in her hand, and the bathroom door safely closed, she burst into tears. She couldn't think straight: there were too many emotions battling within her. She switched on the shower, as much to hide the noise as anything, and cold water shot round the room as she lost control of the shower head.

Eventually she pulled herself together sufficiently to reattach it, adjust the temperature, and then get under it.

The hot water pouring over her was very soothing. It must be a power shower, she realised, picking up bottles at random. She would have to wash her hair, of course; she opened a bottle of Vosene. Trust Jake to use Vosene, she thought, such a horrid smell. Then she started to cry again. Mark had used it too.

Fifteen minutes later, she emerged, her hair wrapped in a towel, wearing a robe which smelt of Jake. She was clutching a bundle of clothes, although she knew that some of them, Jake's, might not recover from their experience.

Jake was now wearing a pair of jeans and a sweatshirt, somehow managing still to look disturbingly sexy. Nel knew her face was red, she had no make-up on, and a combination of tears and shampoo had probably made her eyes puffy and pink-rimmed.

'Here,' said Jake. 'I've found you some pyjamas to sleep in. And I've made Horlicks. Do you like Horlicks?'

Nel nodded, still not trusting herself to speak. Jake tenderly took the clothes as she sat down on the edge of what was now a sofa again.

She cleared her throat. 'I'm afraid they got a bit wet. I had to wrestle with the shower and at first it won.'

'It is a bit unruly. Why did you take my clothes?'

'It was a mistake.' Nel sipped her Horlicks, relishing the soothing, sickly-sweetness of it. 'It has all been a terrible mistake. Which is why I want you to promise never, ever to refer to it. We must just pretend it didn't happen.'

Jake looked astonished. 'But it did. And it was fantastic. How can you pretend it didn't happen? Or not want it to happen again? I wouldn't have put you down as someone who went in for one-night stands.'

She wriggled uncomfortably on the sofabed. 'I'm not. I don't have sex at all. This was just an aberration.'

'You don't have sex at all? Why ever not?'

Nel shrugged. 'I'm a widow.'

'Yes, but you're also a woman! A very sexy and attractive one. How long is it since your husband died?'

'Ten years.'

'Ten years! Are you telling me that this is the first sex you've had for ten years?'

Nel nodded. In spite of her remorse, which threatened to overcome her, she couldn't help feeling just a little bit smug that he hadn't been able to tell.

'Well, you certainly haven't forgotten what to do.'

She shrugged. 'Well, I suppose it's like riding a bicycle—'

'Sweetheart, if you think that was like riding a bicycle, you haven't ridden one for even longer than ten years!'

She let herself smile. 'I have actually, but I don't think I'll be riding one again anytime soon.'

He came and sat beside her, and put his arm round her shoulders. 'Come on, let's go to bed, and we'll see if you can still remember what to do in the morning.'

Nel moved away from him. 'No! I meant what I said. We must pretend this hasn't happened, never refer to it, draw a veil. I'll sleep here.'

'But why? We could have something absolutely fantastic between us!'

100

'We could have fantastic sex between us, I'll grant you that, but nothing else. But I'm not someone who just has sex. This was a momentary lapse. I didn't mean anything by it.'

Jake got up, frowning. 'I think you're mad.'

'I know that. But I still want you to promise me you won't ring or try to see me or anything. I'm sorry to be so . . . so . . .'

'Neurotic? Cavalier?' She couldn't tell whether the expression on his face was hurt or anger.

She nodded. 'Cavalier is about it, when you've been so kind. But that's how it's got to be, I'm afraid.'

'But why? Why can't we go out? See if we have anything else in common apart from fabulous sex?' Now she saw his expression was disbelief. Probably couldn't believe his luck.

'Because, apart from the fact that we're on opposing sides on an issue that is very, very important to me, I have three grown-up children. I can't just have relationships with people.'

'Yes, you can! Anyway, you've got that Simon.'

She was horrified. Now, not only would he think her a very easy lay, he would think she was a two-timing slut. 'How do you know about Simon?'

'I saw you with him at the farmers' market and I asked around.'

'About me?' Nel squeaked.

'Yes, about you.'

'You wanted to know what kind of madwoman you were up against, I suppose.'

'You could say that,' he muttered, with a touch of exasperation.

'Well, I think I should go to bed now.'

'Fine. I'll find you some bedding.'

'I don't need much. A sleeping bag would be fine.'

'Oh shut up!' He was definitely angry now.

He produced a pile of pillows, a duvet and some sheets. 'Would you like me to make up the bed for you?'

'Don't be ridiculous! Go to bed!' Her attempt at authority was marred by the quiver in her voice.

'I'll just use the bathroom first, if that's all right by you.'

'Fine! Oh, and Jake . . .'

'What?'

'Thank you for having me to stay.'

He gave her a look which indicated she might have gone too far, that any moment he might arrange a repeat performance of what had gone on before. To her relief and disappointment, he didn't. He just said tightly, 'Don't mention it. It was a pleasure.'

As she lay in the dark Nel pondered on the strangeness of men. He should have been delighted that she didn't want a relationship. He wouldn't want one with a woman who might well be a couple of years older than he was. She was letting him off lightly. Fantastic sex – she sighed – but none of the complications.

She got up when she calculated it must be dawn. She put on a side light and found her clothes. Some of them were still wet, but she found the sweater she had removed at the restaurant in her bag. That was dry, thank God. Then she put on the coat.

She had hoped to leave silently; she hadn't noticed him setting a burglar alarm the night before. But at least she was safely in the lift before its strident shrieking alerted the whole building to her departure.

It was still dark outside, and, looking at her watch under a streetlamp, Nel saw it was only five a.m. Too early to have woken Jake. It was a shame about the alarm, but it couldn't be helped, people in London were so security conscious. And she'd had to leave. She couldn't face him again, not until she'd had time to recover. Which might take a long time.

As she walked towards the nearest traffic lights, where the chances of a taxi were a bit higher, she wondered if she looked different. Would people be able to tell she'd had sex? Orgasms? Would her children, Vivian, Simon? God, she hoped not! She'd never live it down. Her reputation would be shot to pieces. Instead of the good, virtuous person everyone thought she was, she'd be recognised as the whore she obviously was deep down. She sighed. Well, not whore exactly, that was a bit unkind, even when she was metaphorically beating her breast, but definitely wanton. Or wanting, even.

Right now she felt as terrible as it was possible to feel without having done something really dreadful, like mugging an old lady or committing a murder. But she had wanted to make love to him. Very, very much.

She found a newsagent just opening up, and bought a street map. Then, on her high-heeled boots, which Jake had removed so summarily the night before, she walked to Paddington Station. She still had to wait hours for a train.

Chapter Eight

❦

It didn't dawn on Nel that she'd had not only sex, but unprotected sex, until the train reached Didcot. Then she started to feel sick and shake with anxiety. Mark's coat around her was a reproach. How could she have been so thoughtless? Fleur would never have let that happen. She was not only a sex-starved slut, she was stupid as well.

She closed her eyes and burrowed into the navy wool, but she couldn't rest. Just supposing she got pregnant?

It was highly unlikely. She was over forty: fertility went right down then, everyone knew that. All she had to do was to wait for her next period, then relax.

Nel knew that her chances of relaxing, ever, let alone after however long it was until her next period was due, were nil. When was her period due, for goodness' sake? She didn't keep a record; she didn't need to. If she was going away, she might calculate vaguely for packing purposes, but that was all.

She racked her brains, but couldn't distinguish one period from another, probably because she was so worried.

What would her children say? How would they cope with having an elderly single parent for a mother? Of course, they were used to her being a single parent, but not the mother of a baby.

People would think it was Fleur's, and that she was bringing it up for her. How unfair! To be castigated by society for her mother's folly! It was possible that society didn't go in for castigating these days, but it would still be horribly embarrassing for Fleur, for the boys, for them all.

Well, it mustn't happen. She would take the morning-after pill, then she wouldn't have to worry long, only until the train arrived and the chemist opened.

She remembered the first time her children had nits. She had discovered them in Fleur's hair one Saturday morning, and had the whole family on the doorstep of Boots at nine o'clock. She was beside herself with horror and shame and the conviction that she was an unfit mother because she hadn't spotted them before. The woman who sold her the toxic chemical fashionable at the time had been completely calm. She had even given her a little lecture (all lies probably) about nits only liking clean hair, and posh people getting them just as often as anyone else.

It was this memory which made Nel realise she couldn't possibly buy her own emergency contraception. She knew the people in Boots, if not personally, at least by sight, and one of Fleur's friends worked there. However discreet everyone was, Nel didn't want even two people knowing she'd had unprotected sex.

She winced again. It was Sunday! How could she have forgotten that? Now she'd have to find out which the emergency chemist was. She could go to another town, of course, somewhere where no one knew her, that would reduce the embarrassment factor. But supposing it made you terribly ill? What would she say to Fleur, if she came back from school and found her mother groaning on the sofa, or worse, actually in bed?

No, she'd have to confide in someone, which meant Vivian.

Now, Vivian would have been the perfect person to turn to if Nel had just picked up a stranger at the club, lost her marbles completely, and slept with him. But the moment Vivian knew it was Jake whom Nel had lost her marbles with (God, that sounded so vulgar!), she would go on and on about seeing him again, and having an affaire, and getting rid of Simon.

Well, too bad. Nel would have to stand her ground and convince her that there was no future in the relationship, not even a wonderful, fleeting affaire. Nel sighed so deeply it was almost a sob. She didn't want commitment, or for ever, she just wanted her life to go on undisturbed. And she wanted sex. This thought was oddly settling. Nel pulled up her collar and dozed.

Nel rang Vivian as soon as she got off the train. 'Sorry to ring you at this ungodly hour, but I knew you were getting up early this morning. You couldn't be a love and pick me up from the station?'

'Where's your car?'

'I walked down.'

'And you're too hungover to walk back? Nel, I'm surprised at you.'

'It's not that, but I do need to talk to you.'

'Well, you can, but I've just let your dogs out, and I'm off to my bees just now. You'd have to come with me.'

'How are they?'

'The bees? Dunno. They've been asleep all winter.'

'Not the bees, the dogs!'

'Fine. The health of my bees is far less reliable.'

'Yes, sorry.' Nel loved the romance of the bees, loved honey, loved beeswax, and thought them utterly fascinating – as long as she could be fascinated from a safe distance. And Vivian didn't really understand people with phobias about flying insects, which, though apparently they didn't want to sting you, frequently did.

'I'll put some spare kit in the car.'

'I could walk, I suppose. You could call in on your way back.'

'No, these lot are miles away, and it sounds as if you've got good goss. I'll be down in about five minutes.'

'So,' asked Vivian, when Nel had got herself and her coat into the car. 'Did you stay with Simon's friends?'

'No.'

'So did you come straight back after the club closed?'

'No! I'm not an android! I do need sleep.'

'Some of them stay open all night.'

'I know that now! I had no idea! We didn't go until after midnight, and we were early.'

'We? Did one of the boys go with you?'

'Viv, if I tell you the whole story, do you promise not to scream?'

'Course. I'm a woman of the world, but it sounds good.'

'Well . . .' And Nel began.

Vivian screamed. 'You slept with Jake Demerand? Solicitor to the Hunstantons, the man who kissed you under the mistletoe?'

'Did I tell you that?'

'Oh for God's sake! I'm not stupid!'

Nel was forced to accept this as true. 'Anyway, I didn't sleep with him, we had sex.'

'I can't believe it! I didn't even know you knew him that well!'

'I don't. It was all by accident, chance.'

'Darling, you don't have sex with men as gorgeous as Jake Demerand by accident. It takes months of planning, expert strategy, and you, who are practically a virgin—'

'I'm the mother of three grown-up children and I was married for years,' Nel reminded her irritably.

'. . . practically a virgin, certainly no femme fatale—'

'Thank you!'

'I don't mean that you're not very attractive, just that you're not exactly in the habit of pulling on a Saturday night, and you seem to have achieved this with no effort at all.'

Nel groaned.

Vivian drew up in the gateway to an orchard. 'Right, come and tell me all about it while I work. No holding out on me.' She turned round and rummaged in the back seat. 'Get that tent off and prepare to take the veil.'

'I'm not that much of a loose woman . . .'

'Here, take this,' said Vivian, handing Nel a white tunic, hat and veil attached.

Nel paused uncertainly. 'Viv, why did you get a new anti-bee outfit?'

'Because my old one had holes in and didn't work.'

Nel had thought as much. 'Can't I just wait in the car?'

'Certainly not! I want to hear every last detail, and it's high time you stopped being so neurotic about a few bees.'

As Nel needed quite a large favour from Viv, who might not want to ask for emergency contraception in her home town either, she did as she was told. She took off Mark's coat and exchanged it for the holey anti-bee armour.

'Here, carry this lot, will you?'

Nel received a wooden box full of bee paraphernalia with good grace, and followed as Vivian strode ahead, glamorous as ever in her wellingtons. The hives were on a slight incline and when they were a little way away from them, Vivian dumped her own load on the ground.

'It's the first time I've looked at the bees since I tucked them up last winter. They may well have all died.'

A small, cowardly, part of Nel hoped they had died, then they wouldn't buzz so much. 'They don't usually all die in the winter, do they?'

'No, but there's always a first time. They quite often do die for no particular reason. Can you manage that kit?'

'Really, Viv, I think it would be better if I just stayed here.'

'You don't have to go right up to the hives, but come nearer, then you can take notes for me.'

As this seemed to indicate that Vivian had forgotten Nel had a story to relate, Nel didn't argue, she just resolved to keep upwind and as far away from the bees as possible.

Vivian stuffed a bit of hessian into her smoker and set light to it. 'So, how did you meet Jake? Come on! Did you arrange it? Number five hive.' Vivian puffed at the squat, wooden structure.

'No! I met him quite by chance. I was window-shopping when a taxi full of men, including Jake, drew up behind me. He must have spotted me.'

Vivian took out a hooked tool, burrowed into a seam on the top of a hive with it, and gently pulled.

'Oh my God, bees,' said Nel, as several of them flew out and landed on her.

'Don't panic. They don't want to hurt you. I've got a goose's feather if you want to brush them off.'

'I don't know how you can keep so calm!'

'Practice. This hive all seem fine. Bit of mouse damage at the bottom, but otherwise all present and correct.'

'And very noisy!'

'So then what happened? Pass me that bit of food, will you? I'd better give them something to eat.'

'Is this it?' She handed Vivian a square of brown something which Nel might have been tempted to eat herself, had she been in that sort of mood, it looked so like fudge.

'So? You're holding out on me, Nel!'

'Not on purpose. It's these bees. They're very distracting.'

'So what happened?'

'With Jake? Well, the others were his workmates; it was some sort of staff do. They made me go with them. We went to an Italian restaurant. It was fun.'

'What were you wearing?'

'What I'm wearing now, only without the veil.'

'Sorry, wasn't thinking for a moment. Number seven. No obvious activity. Let's have a look at a super.' She prised out a narrow rectangle full of wax. 'Oh. What a shame. You're safe to come and look, they're all dead.'

Nel didn't want to look, but also didn't want to tell Vivian her most intimate secrets at full volume.

'Now, I wonder why that happened?'

'And after that, Jake and I went to this club.'

'There's no clue at all. Perhaps it's a virus. I hope they don't all get it.'

Nel was torn between relief at being free from the third degree she had been enduring, and irritation that Vivian seemed to have lost interest in her story.

'Go on,' said Vivian, examining another rectangle full of wax and dotted with holes. 'They've had plenty to eat. They've just died!'

'Go on with what? What number did you say this hive was?'

'Seven. And you know perfectly well. What happened when you went to the club?' Viv clearly hadn't lost interest.

'Oh my God! It was amazing. Unisex toilets, a vibrating floor—'

'Enough with the floor, already. What happened between you and Jake? Did you kiss while you were dancing?'

'Certainly not!' Did she have the right to sound indignant, Nel wondered?

'And did you see Fleur, by the way?'

'Yes, but of course I couldn't see if she was up to anything.'

'I could have told you that you wouldn't be able to.'

'So why didn't you?'

'Because you wouldn't have listened. You are rather prone to panic, Nel. Sometimes.'

That *was* unfair. 'I think I'm coping with these bees quite well!'

'These bees are only half-awake! Now, could you please move the story along from you being in the club, failing to spot Fleur snorting cocaine, to you sleeping with Jake

– sorry, having sex with him. It's just a figure of speech. We're on number ten hive now, by the way.'

'Why don't they go consecutively?'

'Because if I get rid of one, or it collapses, or something, I don't want to renumber them all. So?'

'Well, Jake insisted I stayed the night. He bullied me into it,' Nel said defensively.

'I'm not blaming you for that. God, you wouldn't want to spend all night on the platform at Paddington!'

'Paddington has been done up. It's very salubrious, and it would have been a great deal better if I had spent the night there!'

'Nonsense! You could have been kidnapped and taken to cardboard city.' Vivian had clearly forgotten her bees for the moment. 'So did he just say, "How about it?" and you said, "Why not?" and there you were?'

'Of course not! We were arguing, and he kissed me, and one thing led to another.'

'There's a whole lot in between you've missed out, Nel.'

'You know the facts of life. You can fill in the details for yourself.'

'I suppose so. But why did you leave so early in the morning? The mornings can be really good, you know.'

'I do know, but I didn't share his bed.'

Vivian looked as astonished as Jake had.

'Why on earth not?'

'I was so embarrassed! I made him promise never to mention it again, and, in a minute, I'm going to make you promise the same thing.'

'Why in a minute? Not that I would promise. I have every intention of mentioning it as often as it takes to get the details—'

Nel interrupted. 'We didn't use a condom.'

'Oh.' Silenced, Vivian looked down at the super she had been examining, then replaced it. 'That is quite bad. Where are you in your cycle?'

'I have no idea!'

'Really? I always know, but then I'm in perfect sync with the moon.'

'You would be.'

'Being an older woman, you are less likely to get pregnant.'

'Plenty of women get caught on the change.'

'You're nowhere near your menopause!'

'Well, thank you for that, but it means I could get pregnant.' Fighting panic, Nel took a deep breath. 'Viv, I need the morning-after pill. And you have to get it for me.'

'Why!'

'Because I can't go into the chemist and ask for it!'

'Why is it any better for me?'

'Because you're younger, and lovely, and are always having affaires.'

'I don't have unprotected sex, though.'

'You'd have to if a condom split.'

Vivian sighed. 'OK. I'll come with you. We'll go to Gloucester where no one knows us.'

'How do we find out which chemist is open?'

'They have it on the doors of all the other chemists.' She paused. 'Why do I have to come with you?'

'I could say so you accept responsibility for what you've done,' she said sternly, 'but actually, because there are bound to be instructions. You'll need to listen.'

'Oh, I see,' Nel said meekly.

'So why don't you want to see him again?'

'I would have thought that was obvious!' She could feel herself getting worried up again. 'Now, if you don't mind, I'd like to stop talking about it!'

'Nel—'

'No, really. I'm fine, or at least I will be, but I would appreciate a change of subject.' She paused, hunting for one. 'What about the petition? Have you had much support for our petition?'

Vivian examined Nel for signs that the subject of her sex life was really over. Resigning herself to the fact that it was, she answered, 'No, actually. I mean the people I've told about it have signed the form, but we've had no publicity.'

'I think we need to launch a campaign, get the press involved, all that stuff,' said Nel.

'Yes. The trouble is, how to get the press interested? The local press wouldn't be a problem, but we want national coverage. I know!' Vivian put down her smoker. 'Our four-year anniversary on Thursday! Let's turn the celebration into a big party! Get some entertainment, invite the local TV and radio bods! Mind you, there'd be no guarantee they'd come. But you could make a cake! You're good at that!'

'Make a cake?'

'You know, in the shape of a steam launch or something. Like you used to do for the kids' parties.'

'Right, yes, good idea. I'll do that.'

'There's that extraordinary committee meeting this week, but we can't wait till then to raise it: I'll ring round everyone and get their OK. I can't see why anyone would object.'

'Well done, Viv. That's a really good idea. Give this campaign a bit of oomph. Sometimes I think we're the only committee members really committed to saving the meadows. The ones I've talked to have all just assumed the building is inevitable.'

'Chocolate cake would be nice. In the shape of a steam boat, possibly? To remind people of the jamborees, what they'd be losing if the fields are built on.'

Nel smiled. It was comforting to turn back into a person who made cakes in the shape of things. The role of woman who had wild unprotected sex with strangers didn't really suit her. If only she could stop thinking about Jake.

'Right,' said Vivian. 'When I've finished here, we'll drive to Gloucester.'

Nel's dogs were very pleased to see her. She was pleased to see them. Although it was only a day since she'd last seen them, so much had happened, it seemed like a lifetime – or a good week, at least. After each one had had a chance to lick a good layer of skin off her and gone back to their chosen spot on the sofa, Nel pottered about her kitchen, doing the clearing up she hadn't had time for the morning before.

'I'll just put last night out of my mind, like I told Jake to do. I won't think about it,' she said to Villette, the eldest, most matronly dog, mother of the other two, who'd heard the fridge door open.

Villette wagged her tail.

'Not that you forgot, did you? After the first time you were mated, you became a complete hussy. Oh my God, I do hope that doesn't happen to me.'

The thought of herself behaving like her little spaniel, who, in a beguiling but totally wanton way, made up to every male dog she met, was horrifying. 'What would Simon think?'

She must have conjured him up, she thought a moment later, after she had answered the telephone.

'Nel? Where have you been, I've been ringing for ages.'

'I went to help Viv with her bees.'

'Oh. What about last night?'

'I went clubbing last night, I told you.'

'You didn't go, did you? I thought if you had no one to go with, you'd give it up as a bad idea.'

'Simon, you were the one who told me you thought Fleur might be on drugs. You can't expect me just to do nothing.'

'Yes, but going to a club, on your own—'

'I wasn't on my own. Jake Demerand went with me.'

114

'And who is Jake Demerand?'

'Apart from being chairman of the local football team and the solicitor in charge of putting buildings on the hospice's meadow.' To punish him for being so unsupportive, she added, 'He's the man who kissed me under the mistletoe. I thought you knew all that.'

There was a short silence. 'Well, I didn't. Why did you ask him to go clubbing with you? You hardly know him!'

'I did ask you first. But actually, I didn't ask him. He happened to see me, and offered to come too.'

'Oh. That was quite kind of him, I suppose.'

'Very kind, actually.'

'Nothing happened, did it? He didn't grope you on the dance floor, or anything?'

'No, we just went back to his place and had mad, passionate sex on the sofa!' The truth presented as a lie was still a lie, but Nel knew Simon would never believe this particular truth.

There was another pause, a sigh and a sort of grunting sound which could have been an apology. 'I am very fond of you, you know, Nel. And while you must have thought it mean of me not to come with you, I thought it was a wild-goose chase.'

'And I shouldn't be encouraged in it?'

'Exactly. Did you see Fleur, by the way?'

'Yes.'

'And was she taking anything?'

'I couldn't see. But I did see her boyfriend, which was quite reassuring. It wasn't a wasted journey.'

'I'm glad. I must take you out for a nice meal.'

'Why?'

'Because I want to talk about our future. Fleur's going travelling when she's done her exams, isn't she? Having a gap year before uni?'

'I think so. I don't know for sure. It depends if she can save up enough money.'

'That's what I thought. It would be a good time for us to join forces.'

'Would it?'

'Don't let's talk about it now, you're obviously in a bad mood with me. But we'll go somewhere nice, and talk about it then.'

'That would be lovely,' said Nel as unenthusiastically as she could without being rude. 'But now I must go. I've got loads to do.'

'Of course. I'll be in touch.'

Although she did have loads to do, Nel didn't do any of it. She lay on the sofa and waited for her dogs to lie on top of her and provide warmth and comfort. Hard as she tried, she kept having flashbacks from the night before. She kept hearing Jake's voice (he had a lovely voice) breathing something in her ear, and seeing bits of his anatomy: a wrist, a foot, his hand on her waist. With a huge effort of will she managed not to think about any other bits of him for the time being, but keeping her mind off him completely was going to be extremely difficult. Would she be able to function at all normally now?

Firmly, she directed her thoughts to Simon. She knew what he was angling for, and the thought of living with him was not pleasant; he wouldn't ever have left the mess in the kitchen in order to lie down and think. On the other hand, if she had a proper boyfriend, she prob-ably wouldn't go about having sex with strangers. Perhaps she needed Simon to put order in her life. If her children were out of the way, they wouldn't mind who was living with her, would they?

Simon and Vivian would say it wasn't any of their busi-ness, it was her life, her house, she could share it with whomever she liked. But Nel didn't quite agree with them. She felt her young adult children needed a base as much as younger children did. Whether it was her wanting them to need it, or a real need, she couldn't decide. As her eyes closed she realised she was thinking about Jake again. She fell asleep still thinking about him.

'Hi, Mum.'

It was Fleur, standing over her, somehow making Nel feel reproached.

'Hello, darling! Why didn't you ring? I'd have picked you up from the station.' Nel swung her legs off the sofa and sat up.

'My battery's dead, and I felt like a walk.'

'Why, darling, what's wrong?' Fleur only liked walking if it involved shopping or the dogs.

'Mum, did I see you at the club last night?'

Nel grimaced, guilt piling on guilt, unable to tell the lie she had concocted in her mind at Chill. 'Yes, I'm afraid you did.'

'Were you spying on me?'

Nel felt she could hardly deny it. 'I was worried about you. Simon said . . .'

'Yes? What did Simon say?'

'Well, nothing really. He just thought I should keep an eye out for you, in case you'd got into bad company in London.'

'He should have known that you always keep an eye out for me, and that my choice of company seems to be a lot better than my mother's!'

'Sweetheart, I know you're angry, and you're perfectly justified, but let me tell you about it from my point of view. Come on, we'll have a cup of tea first.'

'But spying, Mum! It's the sort of thing Hannah's mum would do!'

'Would she go clubbing?'

This did make Fleur smile a little, which was a good start. Nel and Fleur usually had such a good relationship, Nel found rows not only exhausting, but very upsetting. She hoped she could avoid one now.

'I do realise how it must look from your point of view. But you know I worry, I always have, even before Daddy died, and when Simon said—'

'"Simon said see if she's on drugs", so you went to spy on me!'

'Actually, Simon said don't go, and he didn't say he thought you were on drugs, he just pointed out the item about that girl who took one tab of Ecstasy – one tab – and died. It's very scary for me, you having a life in London I know nothing about.'

Fleur shrugged. 'London's just the same as here, only it's good. You'd really like Jamie's mum.'

'I'm sure I would if I had the chance to meet her. Or even Jamie. That would be a start.'

Fleur sighed the deep gusty sigh of the truly put-upon. 'Oh, OK. I'll ask him to come down one weekend. But you're not to discuss me with Simon. He's not my dad, and never will be.'

Nel had to acknowledge the truth of this, but she also had – for once – to be firm with her daughter. 'I won't ever do it again, but you're to promise me you'll never take anything stronger than pot. I don't approve of it, but I do accept people take it without turning into dribbling idiots.'

'Christ, Mum! They're thinking about making it legal! But if it sets your mind at rest, I'll tell you I have tried it, and I didn't like it. And I don't fancy taking anything else, either.'

'That's such a relief!' Nel felt a bubble of happiness form in her throat. Her turmoil about Jake had overshadowed the nagging doubts about Fleur, but only temporarily: this was wonderful news.

'Of course, what you really should be worrying about is how much I drink. Hasn't Simon pointed out that article about the boy who died on his eighteenth birthday through drinking the cocktail his mates made for him?'

'All right, Fleur, you've made your point! How about some hot buttered toast?'

'Yeah! Now, Mum, tell me, was that the man who kissed you under the mistletoe before Christmas?'

'I don't know what you're talking about, darling.'

'The man you were at the club with.'

Nel sighed. 'OK, yes, it was. But we didn't arrange it . . .'

'Huh! And you think you need to spy on my private life! I think you should be thinking more about your own!'

Nel wanted to bury her head under the biggest cushion she could find. Instead, she put the kettle on.

Chapter Nine

❧

It was Monday morning and Nel was studying a picture of a Mississippi paddle-steamer, mentally converting it to cake, when the phone rang. It made her jump. Only part of her mind had been on cake tins, piping nozzles and icing, the greater part had still been on Jake Demerand and what had happened between them – not the terrible aftermath, but the blissful moments when thought had been suspended, and only instinct mattered. The phone's jarring reminder of the real world was not pleasant.

'Is that Nel Innes?' cooed Kerry Anne.

'It is.' Nel recognised her voice. Kerry Anne was a bucket of cold water in human, telephonic form on all her wickedly enjoyable reminiscences. She represented everything Nel was fighting against.

'It's Kerry Anne Hunstanton here. I want you to take me to where that woman makes her own cosmetics.'

'Oh?' You do, do you? she thought. Well, I'm not going to do it for nothing, young lady. I'll get my pound of flesh in return, thank you very much.

'Yes. I can't get to London and I'm right out of cleanser.'

'Well, of course I can help you out, but there was that little something you were going to do for me?'

'I talked to Pierce about the markets, and he says they can carry on until the building work begins.'

'When is that likely to be?'

'God knows! We're still having difficulty with the plans. Something to do with which sort of bricks to use.'

Good, thought Nel. Perhaps they would be rejected for

ever, and she and Vivian needn't half kill themselves saving the fields. Only that morning, when she had been up in the attic looking for one of the children's old books, which she dimly remembered as having a picture of a paddle-steamer in it, she had spotted some polythene that a mattress had once been wrapped in. She had been about to throw it away, but then thought that it might come in very useful if she and Viv were obliged to take up Simon's suggestion and lie in front of the bulldozers. Water meadows were, by their very nature, watery.

'So, when can you take me? Will you take me?'

Still Nel didn't reply. She was awfully busy – how to make exotically shaped cakes was really the least of her problems – and she wanted time to make use of Kerry Anne's eagerness. On the other hand, time spent in Kerry Anne and Sacha's company would distract her mind from saturnine lawyers who could perform magic just by breathing, which would be a good thing. Reliving the highlights of Saturday night was bad. She should be concentrating on the dreadful consequences of her folly. The trouble was, discovering sex again after all those years was like the first piece of chocolate after a long, strict diet; absolutely delicious and leaving you wanting more. Thank goodness in this case there was no chance of Nel repeating the wonderful, terrible experience.

'Please?' Kerry Anne's dulcet, confident tones took on a pleading quality which the mother in Nel immediately responded to, against her better judgement. She sighed.

'I'll arrange it with my friend and get back to you. Are you free any time?'

'Right now, pretty much, although I'm off to visit my family in California at the end of the week.'

'Fine, give me your number, and I'll get back to you.'

'I've already given you my number!'

'I've lost it.'

Kerry Anne related it.

'Right, I'll try and organise something in the next few days.'

'Thank you. This could be just what I need.'

Nel put the phone down thoughtfully, determined that Kerry Anne would get nothing that didn't benefit others in some way. She had quite enough already. Then Nel sighed again, thinking she'd almost let Kerry Anne and Pierce do what they liked with the fields, if she could only keep Jake to herself.

She rang Sacha before she forgot or allowed herself to get distracted; sex seemed to have addled her brain.

'Hi, Nel! Haven't heard from you for ages! How are things?'

'So, so. What about you?'

All the enthusiasm died from Sacha's tone. 'Don't ask. I'm still searching for somewhere to live. The house part isn't a problem, but finding something with space is quite another.'

'But I thought you'd found somewhere.'

'It fell through.'

'What about renting somewhere to make the cosmetics? You don't have to do it from home, do you?'

'I'd have to do it on a much grander scale to make it financially viable to rent anywhere separate. I may have to give up Sacha's Natural Beauty.'

'Oh, Sacha, that would be awful. Just when things are beginning to take off and I really need anti-wrinkle serum in my life! But seriously, you have to fight for things you care about. You can't just lie down and accept things.' She wondered briefly if all her analogies would refer to lying down in future. Not that she'd done much of that. 'The perfect place does exist, you just haven't found it yet.'

'Yeah, well. You get tired, eventually.'

'Of course. If I wasn't so tied up with this Paradise Fields thing, I'd help you scour the country. In fact, I'll ask around when I visit farms applying to come to the market. Someone may have a spare building they'd let you have for nothing, or nearly nothing.'

'That would be kind. Now, how can I help you?'

'Well, I was wondering if I could bring a potentially very good customer to see what you do, but you may not want me to.'

'Oh yes, bring her along. While I'm still in business and I might as well sell what I can. Who is she?'

'Kerry Anne Hunstanton. You know? They inherited Sir Gerald's place?'

'Oh yes. I wrote to them to see if I could use their barn. It's in quite good condition and would be perfect for me.'

'What happened?'

'Nothing. Except I got a letter from the solicitor saying no.'

Nel's breath caught, even though she couldn't be sure it was even Jake who sent the letter. It might have been an underling. 'What a shame.'

'So how do you know Kerry Anne Hunstanton?'

'I met her when I was in the solicitors', finding out if the hospice owned Paradise Fields, which they don't, by the way. Then I met her again in Boots. She was frantically looking for something or other and I mentioned your products. She was very interested, and now she wants to visit you. So it's all right if I bring her? You must charge her absolutely top whack for everything, mind.'

Sacha laughed. 'As long as you don't mind doing a bit of work. What about Tuesday?'

'Tomorrow?' It wasn't super convenient for Nel, she had a paddle-steamer to make.

'Yes, I'm going to Oxford the day after. There's a house with a building in the garden which might do.'

'But that's miles away!'

'And the house is pretty small, but I'm examining all the options.'

On the other hand, Nel could design and get the basic

cake made this afternoon, and decorate it tomorrow afternoon. 'I'll bring Kerry Anne about eleven, OK?'

Nel decided that keeping busy was the best way to get over Jake Demerand and felt she should be grateful he should appear in her life when she had so much to be busy with. Unfortunately, both the water meadows and the farmers' market were connected with him in some way, and so weren't really a distraction. Of course, Kerry Anne was connected to the fields too, but visiting Sacha was always a treat.

Kerry Anne and Pierce had rented a cottage on the other side of the town. Kerry Anne was looking lovely when Nel picked her up. Not long ago, Nel would just have envied her her beauty, and put it out of her mind. Since her experience with Jake, she had been thinking a lot more about herself and her beauty routine. There was no doubt about it, it may have been a one-night stand (in fact, Nel forced herself to admit, that was exactly what it had been), but it had awakened a part of Nel which had been dormant for a long time. *He* may have been a one-night stand, but perhaps she should think about finding someone who wouldn't be. Somehow, this didn't include Simon.

'So where are we headed?' Kerry Anne asked when she had disposed her elegant limbs in Nel's far from elegant car.

'It's not far. Just a short way out into the country.'

'But it's just a cottage!' exclaimed Kerry Anne as Nel drew up in front of a little redbrick house surrounded by fields.

'But a lot goes on inside it.' Nel rang the bell.

Sacha was the best advertisement for her own products it was possible to find. Younger than Nel, older than Kerry Anne, her glowing complexion could give even Kerry Anne's youthful dewiness a run for its money.

'Come in both of you,' she said, holding the door wide.

'Sacha, this is Kerry Anne Hunstanton. Kerry Anne, Sacha Winstone, creator of Sacha's Natural Beauty.'

Kerry Anne nodded, but wasn't quite as effusive as Nel thought she should be.

'Hi.' Sacha put her hand in Kerry Anne's. 'Do you guys want a drink or something, or would you like to see where it all goes on straightaway?'

'Let's go and see what you do,' said Nel, who needed the therapy she knew Sacha's workplace provided.

'Follow me then, and mind the stairs.'

'But it's tiny!' said Kerry Anne, as the three of them climbed the stairs into Sacha's attic. 'I was expecting a factory!'

A white melamine workbench stretched across the narrow end of the room. Behind it were rows of shelves on which stood bottles of different sizes, but all of them small. At right angles to the bench was a sink, a gas burner, and crates packed with larger containers and tubs. On the opposite wall, labelled plastic boxes were stacked to the ceiling. Every inch of the attic was filled with what was allotted to it, nothing out of order, everything tidy and ready to hand. Whenever Nel saw Sacha's attic, she realised what she could do with her own, if it wasn't so full of junk.

'It is small, but it works. And everything is made on a very small scale. That way I can make sure the quality is always perfect. I would like a lot more space, of course, but this is all I have. Now, what particular product are you most interested in?'

'Cleanser, definitely,' said Kerry Anne. 'My pores are so clogged, if I don't cleanse properly soon, I'll break out.'

'Well, I'm out of cleanser, but we can make some. It's quite time-consuming, and my recipe only makes four pots, but as I've got help, we could probably double up.'

'Did you say four pots? You only make four pots at a time?' said Kerry Anne, not sure if she should be impressed or appalled.

Sacha nodded. 'As I said, I like to be certain that every item that leaves here is of the same high quality. Right, girls, put on a hat and gloves, please.'

Nel put a paper hat on over her hair and pulled on some gloves. 'Do you really go through all this every time, even when you're alone?'

'Of course. How would it look for me if someone found a hair in something? I treat the cosmetics as if they're food, that way I know everything is pure. Right, now, what are we making? Cleanser.'

Kerry Anne was transfixed as she watched Sacha get out a plastic mixing jug, and then a small, slightly battered notebook.

'I keep all my recipes in here. It took me a while to develop this cleanser. It's a copy of that one all the stars buy—'

Kerry Anne interrupted with a name in an awed voice.

'That's it. But I've refined it a bit, so I think it's better. Now, what do we need? Shea butter. Mm! Smell that! If you read out what we need, Kerry Anne, I'll find it.'

Kerry Anne read out ingredients and Sacha assembled them. Nel had seen Sacha work before as she was one of the people Sacha would ring if she got behind with orders and needed a hand. Nel knew how magical the processes were, the tiny quantities, carefully measured out, eventually turning into products which were as soothing and softening as they were exclusive.

Kerry Anne was getting more excited by the minute as she flicked through the book. 'Lip balm! Can we make lip balm? My lips get so dry and there's only one . . .'

This time it was Sacha who supplied the name. 'Only mine has one or two essential oils in it that that one doesn't have. And the pink version uses natural colour. We can do that after we've done the cleanser. Nel, would you be a love and get me some jars? They're under the bench behind you, behind the box of labels. Great, and the lids are just behind them.'

'I can't believe this,' Kerry Anne was trembling with excitement. 'This is so fun!'

'It is fun. I shall really miss it if I have to give it up. Hard work though.'

'Well, if you usually do it all by yourself . . . Now what do I do?'

'Just give it a good stir while I measure out the powdered walnut shells.'

'Why don't you employ some help?' asked Kerry Anne, giving the contents of the jug a good sniff. 'That smells so good!'

'As you can see, I have no space, and if I rented somewhere larger, I'd have to sell in far greater quantities to make it viable.'

'But you could keep on like this, though?' Kerry Anne watched with the tip of her tongue poking out as Sacha levelled off her tiny measuring spoon.

'Unfortunately not. My lease has run out, and my landlord wants this house for his mother to live in, so he can keep an eye on her.'

'So you'll have to leave here?'

'Yup. By the end of next month. But I'm going to look at a place in Oxford tomorrow. Now, we put this in a *bain marie* – you know, like in cooking? And heat it very, very gently . . .

'. . . it sets pretty quickly in winter,' Sacha said a few moments later. 'In summer I have to put it in the fridge.'

'Wow.' Awed, Kerry Anne looked into the blue glass pot at the cleanser she had helped make.

'When it's completely cold we'll label it.'

'I don't know about you two,' said Nel, after a couple of hours had passed and several dozen little blue jars, plastic bottles and tiny pink potion bottles had been filled, 'but I need a cup of something. Shall I go down and put the kettle on?'

'That's a good idea,' said Sacha. 'Kerry Anne, you must be gasping. I get very carried away and forget about things like meals and hot drinks. I even forget to go to the loo until I'm desperate.'

'I can perfectly understand that,' said Kerry Anne. 'It's so fascinating. What can we make now?'

'Well, I'm going to make a hot drink,' said Nel, aware that the other two were operating on a different plane. 'What would you like?'

'Do you have 'erb tea?' asked Kerry Anne. She looked up from the bottle she was filling with a syringe. She was more precise even than Sacha with her quantities.

Sacha named several varieties of her tea. 'I know Nel will have peppermint.'

'It's the only one I like, apart from proper tea, and I know you don't have that.'

'You don't use caffeine either?' Kerry Anne was ecstatic. 'I know it wrecks the skin.'

'I'm not sure about that, Nel gets through a fair bit of caffeine and her skin is fine.'

'That must be because she uses your products. Which proves how wonderful they are if they work so well on an older skin.'

Nel, not sure if she should laugh, cry or throw something, looked at her watch instead. 'Oh my God! I've got to go! I've got a cake to finish!'

'But you're good at making cakes,' said Sacha. 'You're always making them!'

'Not in the shape of a paddle-steamer, I'm not. I only used to do that sort of thing for the kids when they were little. It's terrific fun, but it takes hours. I must dash! Kerry Anne, do you want to come with me, or what?'

Kerry Anne looked like a child about to be dragged away from the biggest ride at Alton Towers, just before she'd reached the top of the queue.

'I'll run you home later, if you like,' said Sacha, who

128

was pleased with how much work she'd got through. 'Kerry Anne is really good at this. I'd like it if you could stay a bit longer. I'll make you something to eat as well as the cup of tea Nel isn't going to make.'

'That would be great! I haven't had so much fun in years. Thank you so much for bringing me here, Nel.'

Nel regarded Kerry Anne, who looked touchingly young and vulnerable in her white paper hat. She must warn Sacha later that she wasn't as innocent as she looked. 'That's fine. I'm glad you're enjoying yourself.'

As she negotiated her car out into the road, Nel realised she was in danger of softening her attitude to Kerry Anne. She'd been rather sweet in her enthusiasm, much softer than the glacial beauty of the meeting in Jake's office. Yet she was clearly determined to push the building through: Nel mustn't forget that. The trouble was, she inevitably became fond of people when she got to know them better. To know all was to forgive all. But as her sons often pointed out, not many people shared this philosophy and it did tend to make you vulnerable. And look what had happened the moment she stopped hating Jake Demerand! Or had she stopped hating him? Love and hate were so closely aligned.

Oh my God! She almost swerved as she realised she had allowed the 'l' word into her thoughts. You may have felt in a bad way before, girl, but let that little word encroach into your consciousness, and you'll really be in trouble.

Nel had to call in at the supermarket before going home. Cake sculpture required a lot of supplementary equipment. She didn't have time to be discriminating; anything that might come in useful was hurled into her trolley. She gathered large circular biscuits; every kind of small sweet; chocolate buttons, chocolate fingers and animals; food colouring; cocktail sticks; silver balls, hundreds and thousands; sugar roses; in fact, almost everything the Home

Baking department sold plus catering packs of icing sugar. She always used to have much of this stuff in her larder, but it had been years since she had last made such a complicated cake. It had been a helicopter. The dogs had eaten it while Nel was giving out party bags. Fleur had been extremely upset, but Nel had been secretly relieved; there was only so much hyperactivity she could cope with. But any dog that even sniffed at this one would be banished from the sofa for life.

Her back was aching, her teeth felt ready to fall out she'd tasted the icing so often, and the kitchen floor was encrusted with sugar, but it was a masterpiece, even if she shouldn't think so herself. She even went so far as to photograph it.

Because it had to feed a lot of people, and be a centrepiece for the party, it had to be on quite a large scale. Nel had used her largest square tin to make the base, and cut it into a boat shape. With another square of cake, she had built a cabin. The paddle wheels were huge chocolate biscuits with dismantled liquorice all-sorts for the flaps. It was surrounded by a sea of blue icing, each wavelet topped with a wiggle of foam. The river didn't often get rough enough for white horses, but what the hell, she was an artist!

She was only sorry that none of her children were home to admire her creation. The boys were of course at university and Fleur was with her girlfriends in town. Of course she should have been at home, working, but since the clubbing fiasco, Nel had decided not to nag. Fleur might decide to ask her mother a few pertinent questions, and Nel was not only hopeless at lying, but blushed far too easily for a grown woman.

With the utmost care, she put the cake on a high shelf in the larder, having scrutinised the ceiling above for cobwebs. Then she laid a sheet of tissue paper delicately on top of it. She decided to put off washing the kitchen floor until tomorrow, and retreated upstairs to the bath. The dogs would give the floor a good lick, after all.

The following morning, Nel decided that making the cake had been the easy part; getting it to the meeting at the hospice would be the tricky bit. But at least her car had nothing much else in it. As the party itself was on the following day, when she would be loaded to the gunnels with bran tubs, prizes to go in the bran tubs (which she had not yet wrapped), cloths to cover trestle tables, a tombola machine, oversized dice and a million other things not yet on her list, she decided to take the cake early.

She laid it on the back seat as if it were a newborn baby. She had great difficulty in preventing herself putting a seatbelt round it, and had to content herself with packing it round with cardboard boxes, so if she had to brake sharply, it wouldn't budge.

It was a pity it was a formal meeting. Most of what went on at the hospice was casual and fun, in spite of the very serious reason for its existence. But occasionally, and this was one of the occasions, all the patrons and bigwigs were invited, and Nel and Vivian always put on their best clothes accordingly. It was possible there would be news about getting a new director. Nel and Viv had wanted a woman, but they were not sure any had applied.

The building did look dreadfully tatty, thought Nel, as she opened the back door of her car to retrieve her high-heeled shoes. And the drive was as muddy and pot-holed as any farm track. Perhaps instead of raising money so the children in wheelchairs could get to the jetty, and therefore the boat, they should have had the drive retarmacked. But they always put the needs of the children before things like that. Even now a group of them were kicking a football around near the basketball hoop.

131

Very carefully, she drew the cake out of the back of the car and put it on the bonnet. If the big cheeses didn't appreciate that work of art, they didn't deserve her. Except that she didn't do it for the big cheeses, she did it for the children.

She was debating whether to carry the cake in before she changed her shoes, and then come back out, or put on her heels and risk falling over in the mud when she became aware that the group of children was coming nearer. For the first time she wondered what they were doing there. It was term-time, none of the committee members would be likely to bring their children to kick a ball around, not in winter. She became aware that they were wearing a sort of football strip, so their presence must be official in some way. There was a man with them, saying goodbye, but he was being followed.

'OK, take this on your head,' he called.

The ball missed its target, landed badly, ricocheted off a stone and landed in the cake.

'Oh shit!' said someone.

Chapter Ten

Nel was too shocked to react instantly. It was too much, looking at a muddy football resting in the middle of her paddle-steamer. And the fact that she was covered in mud herself didn't register until she automatically put up a hand to wipe her eye and realised why she couldn't see properly.

'I'm most terribly sorry.'

Of course it was Jake. Of course it would be him who caused this catastrophe. And of course he would be looking immaculate while she was covered in mud. Sod's law (and whoever Sod was, he seemed to have too many laws and they were all very unfair) stated that the person who least deserved to be covered in mud and have her cake ruined would suffer those disasters, and that the man who had caused them would end up mud-free and proud.

Or would he? Nel didn't swear, shout, or even speak. She just removed the football, covered now not only with mud, but with chocolate, butter cream (made with real butter) and brightly coloured sweets, then she aimed it very carefully at Jake Demerand's silk tie.

'Ooh, sir! We're so sorry, miss!' said a voice, anxious, yet keen to see what would happen.

'Gorr! Look at that cake! It's ruined!' said another.

'It were a boat, wunnit? Look at them sweets!'

Looking down, Nel saw that all the children who had been playing football now surrounded her. They were looking back and forth between Jake and her with pleasurable anticipation: there was going to be a fight.

Which meant there couldn't be. Nel would have to think of a revenge which could be performed without witnesses, but soon. She didn't hold the popular opinion that revenge was a dish best served cold; if she wanted her own back, she wanted it back immediately, with heat.

He was laughing. He was obviously trying to hide it, but he was definitely laughing, possibly because he realised what Nel had intended and knew she couldn't go through with it.

A tiny part of Nel was laughing, too, only it was swamped by the part that had spent so long making the damn cake.

'It's OK, you guys,' she said breezily. 'I can knock up another cake in a brace of shakes. You go off and finish your game. Find your teacher,' she added somewhat acidly. Carefully, she put the cake down on a low wall which supported the balustrade, then she threw the football as far as she could. She watched the boys chase after it, and spotted a young man in a tracksuit with a whistle round his neck run up and meet them.

'I'm so sorry, Nel, that must have taken you hours. Is there anything we can do to save it?'

Nel didn't answer; she just looked him steadily in the eye and picked up a handful of cake. Then she smeared it all down the front of his tie. 'I should make you eat it all, with your hands,' she said, wiping her own on the bit of tissue paper which had been covering the cake.

To his credit, he went on laughing. A beautiful silk tie deliberately ruined, and he laughed. Some part of Nel gave him massive brownie points for this. After all, the cake thing, although far more serious, had been an accident. It was a shame he spoilt it by putting his hands on her shoulders.

'Nel, I'm so sorry!'

'Don't you "sorry" me!' She dragged herself free, felt behind her for another handful of cake, and let him have it, down his face, his collar and shirt, so it wasn't only his tie he needed to worry about. Then she stalked into the building, leaving the cake and Jake behind. Just as she opened the front door she heard a car drive up, and Vivian calling out of the window.

'What on earth has happened? Who are you, and why are you covered in cake? Oh my God! It's you!'

Nel was wearing her old and muddy shoes, and a fair amount of mud had splattered over her face. There was no way she could go straight into the meeting without doing something about it.

'Don't ask me why I look like this,' she said to Karen on reception as she signed in. 'Ask the next man to come in what happened. I'm off to the Ladies. I hope there's no one in there?'

'Don't think so. Most of the kids seem to be in the art room, and the volunteers are with them.'

'I don't know,' said Nel seriously. 'Some people think they're just here to have fun.'

Karen laughed, and Nel went down the corridor.

Her reflection in the mirror was not encouraging. Her white silk shirt, the one she always wore for committee meetings, would take an awful lot of washing to get clean. When the boys first played rugby, she had learned there was something about mud which made it cling like no other stain. Her navy jacket, part of a suit she had bought at a charity shop for just these occasions, responded rather better to being scraped at with a paper towel, as did the skirt. It was a shame that half her eye make-up came off with the mud on her face. After rummaging in her bag for a bit of kohl pencil for a few moments, she gave up and hoped mud would have the same effect as eyeliner and mascara. Then she blotted her hands on more paper towels, pulled her hair about for a bit and went to take her place in the boardroom, murmuring apologies for her lateness.

'You're not late, Nel,' said a woman in her seventies, a stalwart of the hospice and a good friend of Nel's. 'We're waiting for Vivian, and of course our consultant.'

Consultant? That must be what Jake was doing here. But why?

'What do we want Ja— a consultant for? I thought we were discussing losing our income from the farmers' markets? Mind you, I'm cautiously optimistic about finding a new venue, provided we can comply with the regulations.' As if Nel weren't busy enough, she had been researching possible new sites and now had a shortlist: none was as appealing as Paradise Fields though. 'So why do you think they've got – a – consultant in?'

'Perhaps he's going to tell us how to maximise our assets.'

'I don't think so! He's the Hunstantons' solicitor! I just met him outside,' she added. Nel felt deeply depressed. Why was he here, appearing in every aspect of her life, like a dark, desperately attractive nemesis, preventing her from functioning normally? She suppressed a sigh. She would find out soon enough.

Vivian and Jake came in together. They were both laughing. For a split second, Nel knew what jealousy was as she saw her best friend, younger and infinitely more gorgeous than she had ever been, sharing a joke with a man, who, even while she had been grinding cake into his shirt, she wanted with every part of her.

Nel fiddled with the papers in front of her. If Jake and Vivian wanted each other, there was nothing she could do about it. Viv might hold back if Nel asked her to, but what would be the point? Jake would never look at Nel, now he had seen Vivian, who was, she thought sadly, looking particularly lovely today.

Much to Nel's huge relief, they couldn't sit next to each other, because the chairman, Chris Mowbray, a middle-aged man who had once been Big in the City, but had taken early retirement so he could be Big in Good Works, got up to greet Jake in what seemed to Nel to be a rather obsequious way.

Nel and Vivian had never liked Chris Mowbray much. As soon as he had arrived in the town he had got himself onto every committee and had become chair of this one extremely quickly. The trouble was, they had said at the time, it wasn't easy to find people to take on such positions, so that anyone who was willing was instantly voted for.

Now, he ushered Jake into the chair next to his. Nel could see him murmuring but couldn't hear what. Jake caught Nel's eye and gave her a sort of half-grin. It could have meant 'sorry' again.

Nel looked down at her papers to hide her own grin of response. It was too soon to forgive him, but however smug Jake might be, however much he was fawned upon by the other committee members (who obviously were a bit surprised to see him without a tie, but with a lot of greasy spots on his shirt and suit), there was no getting away from the fact that he looked like he'd been in a food fight. Which of course he had.

'Are we all here?' said the chairman. 'I think we'll make a start. Can you sign the book as it goes round?'

Nel's neighbour passed the little hard-backed notebook to her and she signed it, noting as she did so that there was still cake under her nails.

'Now, this is an extraordinary meeting, have we all got our financial reports with us?'

Nel realised she had forgotten hers. She had been too preoccupied with getting the cake into the car to pick them up off the kitchen table. Her neighbour put her own report where Nel could see it.

'Apologies for absence? Only Michael and Cynthia? No one's heard from anyone else?'

Nel found a pen in her bag and began to doodle on her agenda. Could they not just cut to the chase and tell everyone what Jake the Cake was doing here? Thinking of this sobriquet cheered her up somewhat.

'Before we begin, I should tell you why we have Mr Jake Demerand here.'

'Yes,' said Nel. It came out rather loudly.

'There was an unfortunate incident with Mrs Innes's cake,' said Jake, as if to explain Nel's rudeness. 'A football accidentally landed on it.'

'It wasn't my cake,' she said, still more loudly and more belligerently than she really intended. 'It was the birthday cake for the hospice, for the party. Tomorrow.'

'Oh dear. That is a shame.' Chris Mowbray looked down his nose at her. 'Nel does make quite good cakes for the hospice and the amounts they raise, though small, shouldn't be discounted. However, I'm sure you can knock another one up in no time.'

Nel's hackles rose instantly. He had somehow managed to imply that making cakes was all she did for the hospice. As for 'knocking another one up in no time', she'd like to see him try!

'Well, I didn't have an opportunity to see it before it was squashed by the football,' said Jake. 'But I can vouch for its deliciousness.' He looked at Nel. 'I inadvertently ate some.'

Nel added some thorns to the stem of the rose she was drawing, biting her lip. She was steaming with rage but also unable not to respond to Jake. Revenge was definitely better hard and hot and not cold and premeditated. Like sex, really.

Instantly the thought was formed, she blushed. Do not think about sex, she ordered herself severely. Do not! You are here for the hospice! He is the enemy! Anything that happened between you is over! Anyway, now he's met Vivian, he's not going to look at you. Except that he was looking at her, and she blushed even more hotly, in case he was reading her mind.

'So,' she demanded, 'why is he here? I mean, is it ethical to have Mr Demerand on the committee when he's acting for the Hunstanton Estate? He's hardly disinterested.'

'Could I just explain—?'

Nel, who was usually very well behaved in committee meetings, found herself getting more outraged and more outrageous with every word the chairman spoke. 'It's just not democratic, roping people onto the committee without consulting the rest of us, just because – because they want to ingratiate themselves into the community! Surely we should be allowed to vote on who we are to work with?'

'Nel! Could you please address your remarks through the chair!'

'She has a point,' said Vivian. 'Mr Chairman.'

Jake put up a hand. 'Could I just explain? I'm here to represent my clients, to make sure their interests aren't jeopardised in any way. That OK with you, Mrs Innes?'

Nel blushed. He shouldn't have looked at her like that. It wasn't fair.

Chris Mowbray made the sort of gesture that told the committee that he never had been able to deal with women on a professional level. Nel noted it with a shudder. Chris had squeezed her rather too hard on more than one occasion while they were shuffling round the dance floor.

'I don't know how your clients' interests could be jeopardised. They own Paradise Fields, land which enables us to raise huge funds for the hospice, and there's planning permission on it. What more do your clients want, Mr Demerand?'

Jake looked at Chris Mowbray, as if prompting him to speak.

The chairman cleared his throat and got to his feet. 'I think all the members of the committee are familiar with the situation. Of course, it is a shame for the hospice that we can no longer use the fields . . .' He paused and sent a ghastly smile in Nel's direction. 'But I'm sure your delicious cakes will go some way to making up the shortfall.'

Nel wanted to stalk out. She had never felt so patronised in her entire life. But she couldn't stalk out. She needed to be here, to find out what was going to happen.

'But we will be able to have our spring jamboree as usual?' said Vivian. 'Nothing will have happened to the fields by then.'

'That will, of course, be at the discretion of Mr and Mrs Hunstanton,' said Chris Mowbray, deferring to Jake with a bow.

'Can you tell me what it is you mean, exactly?' asked Jake.

'It's our twice-yearly fundraiser,' explained Nel's neighbour, Muriel. 'We have two big dos a year, to do most of our consciousness-raising and fundraising. We have one in the spring and one in the autumn. It would be a great shame if we weren't allowed to use the fields this year.'

'We can't presume to use the fields. They don't belong to us,' Chris reminded them.

'We know that. Now,' muttered Nel, drawing furiously.

'I'm not in a position to comment on whether Mr and Mrs Hunstanton will allow the fields to be used again—'

Nel put up her hand. 'But Kerry Anne said we could use them! She told me.'

Jake regarded her sternly. 'But I will assure them that it will be for the last time, and that the hospice needs to raise money,' said Jake.

'We don't want any special favours,' said Chris.

'Yes, we do!' said Viv. 'We're a charity!'

Muriel put her hand up. 'Mr Chairman? Can we just confirm: is it absolutely inevitable that the fields are to be built on? There's nothing we can do to stop it?'

'I'm afraid so.' Chris Mowbray smiled in a way that

made Nel suspect that, in fact, he was pleased. He wanted the fields to be built on. Why on earth was that?

'Have you got any plans for us to look at?' asked Vivian. 'So we know what's what?'

Chris shook his head sadly. 'I'm afraid not—'

'It's all right,' said Jake, 'I have a set here.'

'Oh,' blustered Chris. 'I didn't realise they were ready. Well by all means have a look at them, if you think they'll mean anything to you.' He picked them up, keeping them folded. 'But I beg you, you ladies in particular, not to try any stunts, like lying down in front of the bulldozers.'

Nel at once winced and wondered – why was he using exactly the same expression Simon had used? But she felt too angry to cry, and too miserable to spend much time wondering. It was just an expression, after all. Was this the end of her campaign? Was there no way to save the fields?

'Can we see the plans?' demanded Vivian. She twitched them out of Chris Mowbray's fingers and opened them. After a moment she said, 'Hang on. By the looks of things there are more houses than would fit on Paradise Fields.'

Chris Mowbray twitched the plans back again. 'I think you're mistaken, Vivian.'

'Who are the builders?' asked Muriel. 'Are they local?'

'Gideon Freebody,' said Chris Mowbray. 'Very reputable builder.'

'Ha!' said an elderly man, who hadn't spoken before, and who never did say much. 'Reputable! My eye!'

'He's like a character out of *The Archers*,' whispered Chris to Jake. His comment was audible to Nel, but she hoped not to the speaker.

She wrote a quick note on her agenda. *What's his name? Abraham something*, wrote back Muriel. *Nice old chap.*

'Did you want to address the committee?' asked Chris Mowbray loudly. 'If so, could you kindly do it through the chair?'

141

Abraham got to his feet. 'I just said, Gideon Freebody is not a reputable builder. His houses fall down and he rips people off!'

'That's tantamount to slander!' said the chairman, affronted.

'Not if it's true, it's not,' said Abraham.

'Well, we're not here to discuss the merits or otherwise of the builders,' went on Chris Mowbray.

'Could you let me see the plans, please?' persisted Abraham.

'Oh very well, if it will make you happy. Now I really think we should press on. The first and most important item on the agenda is the roof,' said the chairman.

'What about a new director?' asked Vivian. 'I would have thought that was pretty important, too.'

'Important, certainly, and we are doing all we can, but so far no suitable candidates have presented themselves. Now, if I can go back to what I was saying about the roof, I've had quotes from three builders, but they are all for much the same amount.' He named three astronomical figures.

'Bloody hell!' said Vivian.

'Here, here,' said Nel.

'How are we going to get our hands on that sort of money?' said someone else.

'There are a few grants we can apply for,' said Chris. 'But, basically, it's a fundraising job. Which rather puts the matter of the water meadows being built on into the shade.' Chris regarded Vivian and Nel in turn. 'We'll use tomorrow's party to spearhead a new campaign, but I have to say, I'm not hopeful. People worked very hard raising money for the jetty and the road, which as it turns out was a complete waste of time, I don't know if we're going to be able to raise that sort of money again so soon. There's only so many bring-and-buy sales and raffles people can support.' He looked at Nel in an almost accusing way, as if she organised tombolas and car-boot sales just to annoy people. 'There are Nel's cakes, of course.'

'And fundraising isn't going to be any easier if we lose the farmers' market money,' said Nel. 'You seem to forget that it isn't only the jamborees we arrange that make us money. The farmers' market gives us quite a large lump, every time it's on. And if it gets on a more official footing, and happens every fortnight or so, it would be a lot more money. But there's no guarantee yet that it *will* get off the ground, or that I can arrange for it still to support the hospice. I don't think you're taking the loss of the fields anything like seriously enough.'

'Look, I can see you're upset, seeing that two years' fundraising has been entirely wasted—' Chris started impatiently.

'I don't think it's been a waste of time having the jetty,' said Vivian. 'I think the two summers the children have been able to use the boat have been well worthwhile. They've loved it. And I can't help feeling that someone on the finance committee should have realised we didn't own the land. Nel and I are fundraisers, we don't have access to the deeds of the house or anything, so it's not our fault it has turned out to be a wasted effort. What's the alternative to replacing the roof? Plastic sheeting and buckets underneath?'

'The alternative is closing the hospice, selling the building and trying to find somewhere else,' said Chris.

There was a stunned silence. 'That's out of the question!' said Nel, aghast. 'The hospice is part of the community! Apart from all the upheaval, having to close, possibly for a long time, while we find new premises, it would take ages to make a new hospice local people's number one charity! Moving would be fatal.'

'I have to agree with Nel,' said Nel's friend, Muriel. 'The changeover would be a year at the very least. And what would our children do in the meantime?'

'Unless we close down all together,' said a man who didn't usually say anything. No one was quite sure what he did, as he only ever turned up at committee meetings and was never seen at any other time. 'I mean, there are other children's hospices.'

'Over my dead body!' said Muriel, leaping to her feet.

'And mine!' agreed Nel.

'Mine too,' said Vivian.

'There's no need to get so excited, ladies,' said Chris, making Nel even more excited with his patronising tone. 'No one is seriously suggesting we close the hospice down.'

'Aren't they?' asked Nel. 'I thought that was exactly what Mr – Mr – he suggested!'

'It's only a thought,' said the Mr in question.

'Not helpful,' said Vivian.

'So what are we going to do?' asked a retired vicar with a bad heart.

'We're going to raise the money for a new roof,' said Nel, and then realised that she shouldn't have. 'I mean, I think I can say that, on behalf of the fundraising committee.' She glanced anxiously round at her fellow members of the team, and was relieved to see that while they didn't seem totally enthusiastic at the prospect, they did at least acknowledge money would have to be raised.

'And how do you propose to do that? Cake sales?' The chairman wasn't even pretending to be polite any more.

'Excuse me,' said Abraham, getting to his feet. 'I've a suggestion.'

The chairman tutted and sighed. 'What is it, Mr – er – I was hoping to close the meeting soon.'

'I could build houses on that land – not so many, but better quality – and still leave a bit of river frontage for the children to play on. And what's more, while I'm at it, I could reroof the hospice.'

'I'm sure it would be very nice for the children to be

able to go paddling, but you seem to be forgetting, Mr . . .' He cleared his throat to hide the fact he didn't know the speaker's name. '. . . that Mr and Mrs Hunstanton have already agreed that Gideon Freebody should have the contract. They stand to make a lot of money out of this deal. They're not likely to be interested by a couple of two-bed semis.'

'I'm not talking about two-bed semis – at least, not just a couple of them.'

'How on earth would someone like you be able to raise the money necessary for a project this size?' said the chairman.

'That's for me to know and you to ponder on,' said Abraham. 'Now, if you'll excuse me, I've got work to do.'

Taking the plans with him (much to Nel's satisfaction), he walked out of the meeting.

'Well! Of all the bloody cheek!' said Chris Mowbray. 'He's walked off with the plans! Go after him, someone!'

'No need,' said Jake quietly. 'We can get another set easily enough.'

'I'd have liked another squint at them myself,' muttered Viv. 'I didn't have time for a proper look, but I'm sure all those houses couldn't have fitted onto just Paradise Fields.'

'I don't expect they've got gardens, or anything. It's all so depressing,' said Nel.

'Bloody ridiculous! But I suppose we'd better get on.'

After that, Nel deliberately tuned out of the meeting. It seemed it was a *fait accompli*. The fields were lost. The only consolation was to hope that Abraham did have an alternative solution. If the fields had to be built on, it would be nicer to think of some dear old man who cared about the hospice doing it, and not some faceless builder with a strange name, who, according to Abraham, built bad houses.

At last the chairman declared the meeting closed and

there was a hurried scraping of chairs as people raced for the door. Nel and Vivian waited for the rush to die down before speaking to each other.

'I don't suppose you fancy coming back to mine and talking about this?' asked Nel. 'I've got to make another bloody cake, and I would do it with better grace if I had someone to share a bottle of wine with while I was at it. Fleur won't be home; we can thrash some ideas about while I cook. Send out for a balti, later, perhaps?' She tried to make it sound tempting, but she could see that Vivian didn't look as if she could come.

'Oh God, I'm sorry!' said Vivian, putting her hand on Nel's sleeve. 'I promised Mum I'd take her shopping the moment the meeting was over, and I can't let her down, as I've had to change the arrangement about three times already. I'll come over first thing tomorrow, if that's any good.'

Nel shook her head. 'Don't worry. I'll have to do the cake now, or the icing won't be set properly before tomorrow afternoon.'

'I'm so sorry to let you down. This is awful, Nel, we will have to do some serious thinking about how to raise a proper amount, not just dribs and drabs added together.'

'We will, and we will think of something. We always do. Give my love to your mum and tell her I've got some books she might like to read, and that I'll bring them over some time.'

Vivian kissed Nel. 'That's really kind. You know what she really enjoys, not like her kindly neighbour who doesn't think she should read anything with sex in it.'

Nel returned the kiss with a hug. 'We'll get together soon, huh?'

Chapter Eleven

Nel was unlocking her car when Jake came up behind her. 'I'll come home with you and help make the cake.'

Nel turned. 'No, it's all right. I can manage.'

'But I want to come. It's my fault the cake was ruined. The least I can do is help.'

'I don't need your help! I did the last one on my own. Besides, if you came, your car would be stranded here.'

'I could follow you home.'

'I'd rather you didn't.'

'Then I'll come with you now, then.'

'No!' Nel squeaked as he walked round the car, at the same moment wondering if she'd locked the passenger door.

She hadn't. Jake was sitting in the car before she could get in herself. 'Could you please get out of my car?'

'Well, I could, but I'm not going to. I ruined your cake: I want to help you make another one.'

Nel got in next to him. She had often wondered how women, when they referred to 'throwing men out', did it. After all, he was much bigger than she was, and no amount of pushing and shoving would shift him if he didn't want to be shifted. She could have called for help, but she didn't want to draw attention to the situation.

'Well, that's very kind of you, but I forgive you for ruining the first one, and want you to get out of my car.'

'Well, that's very kind of *you*, but I'm not going to get out, so you might as well just drive home.'

As Chris and the man who suggested closing the hospice

down were now approaching, obviously intending to talk to Jake, Nel started the car. She didn't want to give either them, or Jake, the opportunity to hatch up more skulduggery. 'Very well, if you insist on coming home with me, there's nothing I can do to stop you.'

'No.'

'But you won't like it. It's a very untidy house, full of dogs and cats who all leave hairs all over you.'

'That's my favourite sort of house.'

'Hah!'

She swept round into the supermarket car park. 'I'll have to buy some ingredients. You wait here.'

'I'll push the trolley.'

'No! We might meet someone I know! Think how embarrassing! People will think we're a couple! Only they won't, because all my friends know I'm with Simon.'

'Oh, him.'

'There's nothing wrong with Simon!' Nel was so used to defending him to Vivian and Fleur, she did it out of habit.

'I'm sure. You'll just have to think of some other way of describing me if we meet anyone you know. I quite like "bit on the side".'

Nel bit her lip. Her sense of humour was threatening to ruin her bad temper with Jake again. 'Oh yes. I can see me saying that.'

Jake smiled slightly, seemingly totally unconcerned about her reputation. He pulled out a trolley. 'This big enough?'

Nel snatched it from him, irritated once more. 'I'm making a paddle-steamer, not the QE2.'

'Same difference, when it's cake. Now, what do you need?'

'It's like going shopping with the boys!' she said a little later, when the trolley was full of things she was not at all sure she needed. 'They just pick things up and say, "Can we have this?" Only the things they choose are at least mostly quite cheap.' She looked resentfully at some delicious-looking olives that had no place on any cake. 'Oh hi!' she greeted an acquaintance.

Jake, who was a little way behind her, and should have stayed there, pretending they weren't together, came up.

'This is Jake,' said Nel.

'I'm from the hospice,' said Jake. 'I'm going to help Nel make a cake.'

The acquaintance, whose name Nel had momentarily forgotten, regarded Jake with amazement, and Nel realised she shouldn't have worried about people thinking they were a couple. No one would ever believe they were together in that way, Jake was too gorgeous. Nel had a sudden urge to tell this woman that although at the moment she was looking a complete wreck, with not only half her eye make-up missing, but with a lot of mud in strange places, she and Jake had slept together. She clamped her lips together so she couldn't.

'You didn't introduce me,' said Jake when they had moved on.

'I forgot her name. Sorry. And you could have just stayed looking at something else.'

'Not ashamed of me, are you, Nel?'

'Well, you weren't too pleased having to take me to dinner with all your workmates!'

'That's perfectly reasonable. They take the rip out of me terribly.'

'Oh, so you can dish it out, but you can't take it!'

'You know something? You're attractive, even when you're being ratty.'

She narrowed her eyes at him. 'You do know they sell sharp knives and big pairs of scissors at this supermarket, don't you?'

'You just get more and more exciting. Now let's buy

149

some chocolate buttons. I haven't had chocolate buttons for years. Oh, and squirty cream. I love that!'

There had been a short, sharp row at the checkout when Jake insisted on paying. When forced to admit defeat, Nel said, 'Well, if I'd known you were paying I'd have put a bottle of Baileys in the trolley.'

'Oh, do you like Baileys? I can pop back and get some.'

Nel found herself blushing. It was a sweet gesture, one Simon would never have made. Simon, if she found she'd forgotten something really vital, and had to go back, would sigh and tut and ask her what was the point of making a shopping list if she didn't look at it.

She put her hand on his sleeve. 'Oh no, I was joking!'

'Are you sure?'

'Yes! It's a bit sweet for me, although Fleur likes it.'

'OK. Here, let me push the trolley. It doesn't steer very well.'

As they made their way through the car park to the car Nel wondered why, when Simon said that sort of thing, she felt irritated and patronised, but when Jake said it she felt cherished.

At home, as she put the key in the door, Nel realised that the house was in a state. She had rushed out that morning, before the meeting, to visit someone who was thinking of becoming a stallholder at the farmers' market. It would be their first official market, and Nel knew they would take a bit of persuading that it was worth going through all the necessary hoops. But she needed a certain amount of regular stalls, or the council wouldn't consider them. The market was going to be even more important to the hospice now, if she could arrange for it still to be a source of regular income.

She opened her mouth to tell Jake all this, and then shut it again. He probably wouldn't be interested, and why should she apologise for the state of her house? If she was too busy to do housework, what business was it of his? Her home was her castle, he could like it or lump it.

'I'm sorry about the mess,' she said, aware too late that the words had come out like an inward breath, automatically.

But Jake had put down his bags of shopping and was talking to the dogs, who were all jumping up at him, whimpering, as if no one ever usually spoke to them at all. He didn't hear her apology, and obviously didn't care about the mess as he wasn't looking round her kitchen in shocked silence, like Simon had the first time he had arrived unannounced.

While Jake was allowing the dogs to lick icing off his trousers, Nel put the bags on the table, and noticed that one of the animals had been sick in the sitting room. She fetched a dustpan and her rubber gloves. It happened quite often, so she had a routine.

'Put the kettle on, would you?' she called from her knees as she scooped and scrubbed, to keep him in the kitchen where it was messy, but vaguely hygienic. 'I won't be a minute.'

'If I move to the country, I'll have dogs. It's one of the things I don't like about working in London.'

She could hear him filling the kettle. She just wanted to shove a few things under cushions while she had the chance. 'What are the other things?'

'Oh, the general pace of life. Property prices. I'm renting at the moment, but it seems such a waste of money.'

She came back into the kitchen. 'But would you like living in the country? What about the culture? Theatre, cinema, art exhibitions?'

'It's only an hour and a half on the train. I could still do all those things.'

'I suppose so. Right, let's get the oven on.'

'But you've got a range! Aren't you going to cook the cake in that?'

Nel shook her head. 'If you're going to question every-thing I do, you can go home. Now, wash your hands, please.'

He gave her a look which told her that bossing him about probably wasn't a good idea. It provoked a smoul-dering sort of glower which promised retribution of a kind Nel had forsworn. 'How do you like your tea?' she added quickly.

Fleur came home while they were waiting for the cakes to cook. She breezed in, chattering the moment she got through the door, unaware that her mother was not alone.

'Oh,' she said, silenced halfway through a diatribe against the amount of research they were expected to do, 'when it's Art, for Godsakes!' She came to a sudden halt when she saw first that her mother was not alone, and second who her companion was. 'Umm – making another cake, Mum? I thought you did that yesterday.'

'I did—'

'There was an accident. All my fault,' said Jake, who was sitting at the table carving letters from rolled out liquorice all-sorts. 'That's why I'm helping your mother make another.'

Nel was grateful for the interruption of Fleur's arrival; she thought Jake had been about to bring up the subject of that Saturday night. There were lots of reasons why she didn't want to talk about it, mostly because she didn't want him to thank her for understanding it was a one-night stand, and that was all. She knew the truth but she didn't want to discuss it with Jake.

'Fleur, this is Jake Demerand. Jake, my daughter, Fleur.'

Jake got up and took hold of Fleur's hand. 'Hi.'

'Hi.' Fleur wasn't easily silenced, but the sight of a man she herself had described as gorgeous in her kitchen, with her mother, did the job – for a few seconds at least.

'Cup of tea, darling?' said Nel. 'Jake, another one?'

'I'm awash. Why don't I open the wine now?'

A glass of wine sounded wonderful. Nel glanced at the kitchen clock. It was after six. 'Better not. I'll have to drive you back to your car soon. In fact, I could do it now. Fleur will help me with the cake.'

'If you think I'm going to let you do the fun part on your own after I've carved out the name, you're in for a surprise. I'll take a taxi home later.'

'Mm, wine, good idea,' said Fleur. 'I'll just get the corkscrew from my bedroom.'

Simon would have given Nel an 'I know you're doing your best, but it must be very difficult for you, bringing up teenagers without a father' look. Jake just burrowed about for wine glasses. It was really odd, Nel reflected, hunting in another cupboard for Bombay mix and crisps, how easy it was to be with Jake. He was a hot-shot London lawyer and she had slept with him. Not only that, he represented the enemy, literally, with regard to the water meadows. And yet having him in her kitchen, chatting to her dogs, rummaging in her cupboards, was somehow fine.

'Why were you late home?' enquired Nel when Fleur reappeared.

'Oh, I was in town. I bought some black trousers.'

'So how many pairs is that now?'

'Eleven,' said Fleur promptly. 'I couldn't get to sleep the other night and I counted. Lots I just keep for messing around in.'

'When will the cakes be cool enough to ice?' asked Jake.

'Not for ages,' said Fleur. 'But we can take them outside if you like. They'll cool quicker there. It's freezing.'

'OK. I'll take the big one, and you tell me where we can put them.'

'Don't put them where the foxes can get them!' called Nel as Jake and Fleur disappeared through the back door.

While she was alone she looked frantically in the freezer. She'd have to cook something for them all to eat, but what?

Fortunately, the farm she had visited had given her a whole tray of cracked eggs, and in spite of the cake, there were still plenty left.

'Spanish omelettes all right for supper?' Nel asked, when Jake and Fleur came back in having found a place for the cakes which they could observe from the kitchen.

'Oh great, my favourite! Thanks, Mum!' said Fleur, giving her mother a squeeze which was not only affection, but contained quite a lot of 'doing all right there, girl!' about it, too, as she went through to the sitting room and turned on the television. Nel had never been in this position with her daughter before, and she wasn't sure if it was funny or embarrassing.

'I really like them too,' said Jake. 'Does that mean I can hug you as well?'

Nel found herself blushing and hoped he wouldn't notice. 'No. You can peel potatoes. Do you want a knife or a peeler?'

'A peeler. Do you really think you can just pretend Saturday night didn't happen?'

'The world is divided into people who do potatoes with knives, and those who like peelers. I like peelers myself.'

'Stop rambling and answer the question.'

Nel stopped gathering crumbs with her cloth. 'No. And I'm not pretending it didn't happen. I'm just never referring to it again.'

'But why not? It was fabulous. At least, it was for me, and I kind of got the impression you liked it too.'

'I did! But can we please not talk about it?' She gestured towards the sitting room.

'I'm sure she knows the facts of life.'

'Yes! But not the facts of *my* life!'

He laughed. She wished he wouldn't do that. It made his eyes crinkle and his eyelashes appear particularly curly.

'Seriously,' she went on. 'We can't talk about it now. Or ever!'

'That's ridiculous. We need to talk about it. We had unprotected sex.'

Nel kicked the door to. 'Please! Don't say things like that in front of my daughter! It's hard enough trying to make sure she has morals and things without her finding out that her mother is a slut!'

'You are not a slut!'

'And you are not to discuss what happened between us with my daughter in the house!'

'Fair enough. Come out for a drink with me then.'

'No!'

'You're being ridiculous! Either we talk about it now, or you come out with me and we talk about it elsewhere.' Up to this point he had sounded remarkably good-natured in the face of her stubbornness, but there was definitely an edge to his voice now.

'We can't have' – aware that she was getting agitated, she lowered her voice – 'a relationship. There's no point in discussing Saturday night.'

Jake crossed the room and opened the door to the sitting room. 'Agree to come out with me, or I tell Fleur everything.'

'That's blackmail! You can't expect me to give in to that!' She was nervous, but she didn't really think Jake would tell Fleur.

'Fleur!' said Jake. Nel went cold suddenly. 'Tell your mother you wouldn't mind at all if she went out for dinner with me.'

Fleur turned round, trying to suppress a smirk. 'Of course I don't mind, Mum. You're old enough to make up your own mind about these things. Just don't come back too late and make sure you've got your homework done first.'

Nel made a sound like a tennis player who's just hit a really hard ball. It didn't quite sum up her feelings of exasperation, but it helped. It also made it clear to Jake and Fleur what she felt about them.

'So, get out your calendar and we'll make a date,' said Jake.

'And what am I supposed to tell Simon I'm doing?' she asked, not expecting an answer.

'That you're meeting with the solicitor representing the Hunstantons,' said Jake.

Fleur got up from in front of the television and came into the kitchen. 'Tell him you're discussing tactics.'

'What? I'm asking the solicitor for help in saving the fields? I don't think so.'

'Why do you have to tell him anything?' said Fleur, picking a cube of fried potato out of the pan. 'You're not engaged or anything, are you? Just go out with who you want!'

Jake raised an eyebrow and sort of smiled. The combination was too much. She opened her mouth to say she didn't want to go out with Jake, but she didn't, she just stood with it open.

'I really think it's important that you keep abreast of all developments, as they happen,' said Jake.

'So do I,' said Fleur.

'Very well,' she snapped, trying not to respond to the two sets of twinkling eyes which regarded her. 'But there had better be some developments – good ones!'

'Oh, I think I can guarantee that.'

Nel blushed furiously and tried to frown at Jake without Fleur noticing.

He raised his eyebrows briefly, confirming he really had meant what she'd thought he'd meant. 'Right, where's this calendar then.' Jake then took the calendar, which was designed for families, and mostly full of dentist and vet appointments for the children and dogs (the animals had their own column) and meetings for Nel, and found a slot. 'You don't seem to be doing anything Friday next week? I'm working in London, but I could be down for seven. We could meet up at eight? That suit you?'

Nel shrugged. 'Fine. My feelings on the matter obviously aren't important.'

'Mum!' Fleur was shocked. 'That's a bit rude.'

'Sorry. I'm just a bit worried. Do you know that the hospice roof needs replacing and it's going to cost thousands?' she said to Fleur.

'How awful. Shall I make a salad?'

'That would be lovely. The potatoes and onion are done, I'll just have a look for something meaty to put in.'

By the time they sat down to eat, they had opened another bottle of wine Fleur had produced from somewhere. Nel put her hand over her glass. 'I've still got to ice the cake. I've got to keep my wits about me.'

'But you've got us to help you, Mum. It'll be fun. Do you think I can take a picture of it and add it to my portfolio? Cake is art, isn't it?'

'Oh, I'm sure it is. Fine art, even,' said Nel, who didn't really care about art at that precise moment. She was tired and worried.

'Have another glass of wine,' said Jake. 'Iron is good for women.'

Nel scowled at him. It may have been true, but she didn't like him knowing too much about women. It would give him too much insight in her own character, and would indicate a lively past. A lively past didn't make him any less attractive, but it made her feel even more out of her depth with him. 'Have some salad. It's good for men.'

Jake laughed again. If only he wouldn't do that, thought Nel.

After the meal Jake said to Nel, 'You go and sit down. We'll make coffee and clear up, won't we, Fleur? Then we can get going on the cake.'

'Yes, off you go, Mum,' agreed Fleur. 'Do you want ordinary tea or mint?'

'Mint,' she said. 'I sense I'm going to get indigestion.'

'I hate to say this,' said Nel, a couple of hours later, 'but I'm not sure this cake isn't better than the first one.'

'I'm definitely taking a picture of it,' said Fleur. 'I need to bulk up my portfolio. I could even make a cake as my final piece.'

'Well, I'm very proud to have had a hand in it,' said Jake. 'I've never seen such a fantastic paddle-steamer in my life. It's beautiful.'

'You've both been wonderful,' said Nel. 'I couldn't have done half so well without you.'

Jake caught her eye and held it. 'I'm almost pleased the first one got ruined.'

As she'd been in danger of thinking something similar herself, Nel contradicted him hurriedly. 'Well, it's nice to have the chance to do things better.' She yawned, suddenly overcome with fatigue.

'You're tired. Would you like me to go?'

Nel had been enjoying herself. It had been fun, doing the cake with Jake and Fleur, who seemed to get on terrifyingly well, but it wasn't real. Playing with icing and eating chocolate buttons would entertain him for an evening, but he would soon tire of the everyday, cornflakes-but-no-milk sort of life which was hers. He was London restaurants, bachelor flats and beautiful suits, not hairy sofas and dogs being sick on the carpet. Eventually, the warp and weft of her life would irritate him, and eventually, he would break her heart. It was harsh, but it was the truth and reality was sometimes a bitter pill, which had to be chewed thoroughly, not swallowed and then forgotten.

'Well, it has been fun and you have been extremely helpful with the cake. But the birthday party is tomorrow and I've got loads of things to organise for it.'

'I did make a lot of hard work for you, didn't I?'

Fleur had disappeared, probably to the bath, and they were alone. 'You didn't mean to.'

He reached for her but she held him off so he only got hold of her wrists. It was enough to send her heart racing and make her short of breath. He looked as if he was considering kissing her. Terrified of what would happen if he did, she pulled free. 'Are you coming to the party tomorrow?'

'I can't,' he said. 'I've got to be in London all day. I'm getting the early train.'

'Then you should go. Let's phone you a taxi.'

'It's all right, I can walk into town from here. Burn off the chocolate buttons. Nel—'

'I really don't want to talk about it.'

'I was only going to make arrangements about Friday.'

'I don't think we should do Friday.'

'I think we should definitely do Friday.'

She was too tired to argue with Jake as well as with herself. She sighed and gave in to both her opponents. 'Oh, OK.'

'I'll pick you up here, at eight. Say goodbye to Fleur for me.'

Then he kissed her cheek and let himself out of the door.

Nel closed her eyes, staying quite still, as if that way she could hold on to the moment. Then she ran up the stairs and shouted to Fleur through the bathroom door, 'Will you leave it in for me? I'm still covered with mud and sugar.'

'OK. Oh, and Mum?'

'What?'

'Have you been holding out on me?'

'What do you mean?'

'With Jake? He's the one you took to Chill, isn't he? You never told me you'd got to know him.'

'I'm not going to stand here talking to you through the bathroom door.'

Nel stomped off to her study and switched on her computer. A few games of Freecell while she waited for the bath might calm her down. While it was booting up she concentrated very hard on not thinking about Jake. Away from his office he was so nice, such fun, so incredibly sexy. In fact, if she cast her mind back, he'd been pretty sexy when she'd met him in his offices, too. He exuded sexiness from every pore. Not thinking about him seemed almost an impossible feat.

Her computer, operating at last, needed subtle adjustments before it would bring up her game. She knew she could have changed the default settings and got it to bring it up immediately, but somehow she'd never got round to it. Now, as she clicked and pressed keys, she realised that she was doing it on automatic and was really thinking about Jake. She dragged her mind away from his crinkly eyes, the way his wrists protruded from his shirt cuffs, the feel of his hands on her arms. She realised that since Saturday, if she wasn't thinking really hard about something else, she was thinking about him.

Fleur appeared, draped in white towelling. 'You can have the bath now. It's nice and hot.'

'Thanks. I'll just get this game out . . .'

'And you've definitely been holding out on me. How come you know Jake?'

'I met him at the solicitors when I went to tell them that the hospice owned the fields. It's such a pity they don't. Now they're going to be built on.'

'We were talking about Jake.'

'Well, you were, I was trying not to.'

'First you go clubbing with him—'

'That was pure chance! I was all set to go on my own.'

'Then I come home and find you all cosy cosy in the kitchen.'

'Not that cosy. He insisted on coming home with me from the meeting, which I didn't know he was going to be at—'

'Grammar, Mum . . .'

'In fact, he got in my car and refused to get out. There wasn't much I could do about it.'

'It sounds like a load of excuses to me.'

'The truth often does.'

'Which is what I've always told you.'

'Remind me, which one of us is the adult here?'

'Me,' said Fleur. 'You're refusing to answer perfectly reasonable questions about your boyfriend.'

'He is not my boyfriend, Simon is!'

'I'd dump that horrible Simon and go for Jake, if I were you.'

'Simon is not horrible!' Nel protested. 'He's very nice! He cleans out my gutters.'

'Jake helped you with the cake.'

'You helped me with the cake. You wouldn't clean out the gutters.'

'You don't know Jake wouldn't. Anyway, you can't only go out with people who do DIY.'

'That is the principle reason for me going out with anyone,' Nel explained. 'After years of doing it myself, I'm on the lookout for someone who can put up shelves.'

'I'm sure Jake could if he tried.'

'Anyway, none of this is relevant. Jake isn't interested in me at all, he just felt bad about ruining my cake.'

'So why did he ask you out, then?'

'Out of politeness. He's very polite.' Nel didn't actually believe this, she just hoped Fleur would.

'And getting in your car and refusing to get out doesn't sound remotely interested, either. Or polite.'

Fleur did sarcasm very well, thought Nel, considering she'd always tried to avoid it herself when talking to her children. She sighed.

'And he did kiss you under the mistletoe,' persisted Fleur, sensing Nel's weakness.

'I wish you wouldn't keep going on about that. It was weeks ago, and it was only Christmas spirit.'

'So, what happened after he took you clubbing? Did you go back to his place?'

The role reversal was getting beyond a joke about role reversal. This was becoming a serious interrogation. 'I did spend the night with him, yes. But I got an early train home in the morning.'

'I know you must have got a train home, what I want to know is what happened when you got back to his place.'

Nel decided to give Fleur the same line as she had Simon. 'Oh, Fleur, we had mad passionate sex on his sofabed – what do you think happened?'

'All right, I was only asking. Now you know what it feels like, getting the third degree.'

'OK, I'll never ask you anything again, now go and get dry before you freeze to death. I'm going to get in your bath.'

Fleur's bath, even if it was full of toxic chemicals and bits of stick disguised as sandalwood, was a sensible place to end a long day. She really should turn her mind to the party tomorrow. And Simon, who *was* her boyfriend.

She pulled off her clothes and climbed into the water. As she sank her shoulders beneath it, she realised she wasn't thinking about either of those, she was still thinking about Jake. He had become the default setting of her mind.

Chapter Twelve

❧

The next day began badly. There was a letter from the council saying that unless Nel could guarantee at least twenty stalls for every market they would not allow her to open. Thus she had to have letters from at least twenty potential stallholders, and ideally several dozen extra spare, undertaking to support the market and come every time.

She offered a brief prayer of thanks that at least she had made good progress in her search for a new home for the market, and then said to Fleur, 'It's so unreasonable. These people lead busy lives, they can't be writing letters all the time! On the other hand, if we had that many stalls every time, it could turn into a nice little earner for the hospice.'

'Jamie's coming down weekend after next,' said Fleur, who wasn't listening.

'That's nice,' replied her mother, wondering when 'Please can me and (some nice little girl) have a sleep-over?' became an announcement of a visit. 'I'm looking forward to meeting him,' she added, deciding not to ask.

'Mm. Would you smell this milk? I think it's off.'

'Then I don't want to smell it. Give it to the dogs and see if this morning's has arrived yet.'

'Mum! You know milk gives them diarrhoea! Mum – are you listening?'

'No,' said Nel, who was fretting about the council's letter again. 'It's the party today, and if I've got to visit every farm and smallholding I'm going to have my work cut out. If I don't get enough people, I won't get my grant, which I need for advertising, and publicity – stuff like that.' She switched on the kettle, and tried to refocus on her daughter. 'Shall I do a special meal for Jamie on Friday night?'

'You're going out on that Friday night. With Jake, remember?'

Nel sighed. 'I was trying to forget.' It was a lie. She was trying to decide if she should cancel. It wasn't that she didn't want to go, it was that she couldn't square it with her conscience.

'You're not engaged to Simon,' said Fleur, who knew her mother worryingly well.

'You're not engaged to Jamie, but you wouldn't go out with anyone else.'

'That's different. Simon's the only person you've been out with since Dad died. You should play the field a bit more before settling down again.'

'Have you been talking to Viv?'

'No, but I expect she'd say the same.'

'I'm sure she would, that's why I thought you'd got together.' Nel felt a little calmer after her first sip of peppermint tea. 'What about Saturday night? Or Sunday lunch?'

'Thanks, Mum, that's a really nice idea, but we'll be going out on the Saturday, and he's got to leave by twelve on Sunday. He's got a lot of work to do.'

'I won't have much opportunity to get to know him, then. Saturday lunch?'

'Don't worry. You'll see him. What are you going to wear on Friday?'

'Fleur! Some of us have more important things to do than to think about what to wear on a date that's over a week away!' But in spite of that, they still did think about it, she thought remorsefully.

'Of course,' went on Fleur, 'what you need for the market is a chef, someone to cook the products that are for sale. I saw something about it in a magazine at school. They have one at a farmers' market in Scotland.'

Nel considered this. 'It is a good idea. But who could we get? I don't know any chefs.'

'I bet Jake does. He's just the sort of bloke who would know all the young talent from London who are desperate to come down and turn some failing pub into a restaurant.'

'I wish you wouldn't say bloke. It's so vulgar. How do you know so much about it, anyway?'

'I told you. It was in a magazine. Anyway, can't stay here chatting. I've got to get to school. No chance of a lift, I don't suppose?'

Nel glanced at the clock. 'Honey, at this time of day, you'd be quicker to walk. The traffic will be horrendous.'

'That's all right, I don't mind being late. I'll just say we were caught up in the rush hour.'

Nel sighed. 'OK, then, get the dogs in the car and I'll give them a quick walk in the woods afterwards. Then I can get on with the party. I wonder if I've still got that tea chest we used for a bran tub last time? Or did it get turned into a prop for *Jane Eyre?*'

'Prop for *Jane Eyre*,' said Fleur. 'Someone put their foot through it.'

'That's all I need! Having to find a bran tub at this stage.'

'Oh, just use a dustbin, Mum!'

'Oh! Good idea. Now where's Villette? On my bed, I expect. You round up the other two, and I'll go and get her.'

'Well, I think that went OK, don't you?' said Vivian. 'The press all turned up and took photos.' She dried another glass.

Nel, who was washing up, ran a glass under the tap. 'Yes, and we just about managed to convince them that it was always intended as a campaign to raise money for the roof, and not to save the fields.' She shook her head as she remembered how many lies she had told, in such quick succession.

'Oh don't worry about things like that!' Viv was putting the glasses into boxes, 'they wouldn't have remembered why they were there, anyway.' She carried a box of glasses over to a table. 'It was a pity Jake couldn't come. Did he go back with you and help with the new cake?'

'Yes. And Fleur did, too. She took a picture of it for her portfolio. I think she's thinking of doing a cake for her final piece. Edible art. Should go down well.'

'Changing the subject?'

'No, but I'm going to change this water. Viv, you don't know any chefs, do you? Fleur suggested we got one to come to the market to do a cookery demonstration and encourage the punters to buy stuff.'

'Not off hand, but I'll have a think. You should ask Jake. He's bound to know of someone.'

'Jake and I are not on those terms, and would you care to take a turn at washing now? My hands have gone all wrinkly.'

'You should wear gloves.'

'I would, but these have been here for ages and have gone all slimy.'

Vivian turned on the hot tap. 'You know he'd be far better for you than Simon—'

'Viv! Jake is not interested in me, and Simon is just fine. I'm of a certain age, I'm only going to attract a certain type of man now.'

'Bollocks. Will you tell him that Jake helped you make a cake?'

'If it comes up! But I'm not going to make a point of it. He'd think I was trying to make him jealous, and I'm too old to play games.'

'No woman is ever too old to play that sort of game,' said Vivian firmly. 'Anyway, what makes you think Jake isn't interested in you? He slept with you, didn't he?'

Nel shrieked, and looked over her shoulder to make sure no one had heard. 'That doesn't mean a thing! At least, not in the long term! It was a spur of the moment, spontaneous—'

'Lovely?'

'—Action. It does not have long-term potential. Women like me do not go out with men like Jake. Understand?'

'No.'

Nel sighed. 'I'm a mother, I'm over forty, I'm over-weight! Jake is younger, gorgeous and single. He could go out with anyone he likes. He's not going to pick frumpy old me. Now, can we please just drop the subject? It's making me depressed.'

'OK. Your choice. But I think you're barking. So what are you up to now?'

'I'm visiting all my potential stallholders tomorrow. I've got to make them write to the council and convince them they'll support the market regularly. If I don't have at least twenty, they won't let me do it. They are so damn cautious! If they let us start slowly, we'd get more people in time.'

'And twenty is loads. We never had more than about ten before.'

'I know! I could probably do it if I was allowed crafts, but they're being a bit iffy. I don't know why. Gwen Salisbury – you know, the potter who produces all that lovely blue stuff – is a farmer's wife. And she's really local. I think I'll go in person and twist their arm on this one.' Nel dried her hands on a very wet tea towel. 'I would have gone to see the planning officer, but that seems a bit pointless now. The fields are going to be built on. It's just a matter of who by.'

'Shouldn't that be by whom?'

Nel shrugged. 'I'm just the chief cake-maker – I don't do "whom".'

Nel put Fleur firmly into the car the following morning, having decided to face the council as soon after nine o'clock as possible, before she could find a list of excuses not to go. She had spoken to Simon the night before and he had suggested he go with her, but Nel had declined his kind offer. If he went, he would do all the talking and her points and anxieties would not be expressed. It was slightly galling, she thought, that he wanted to be with her when she wanted to be alone, and yet when she was begging him to come clubbing with her, he refused.

It gave her a pang to pass a door marked 'Planning Department' while she negotiated the miles of corridor to the department she needed to see about the farmers' market. But while building on the fields now seemed inevitable – a thought that was deeply depressing – at least if she got permission to have the market in the town itself, it would still give the hospice a little regular income.

Rather to her surprise, she walked out of the council offices an hour after she had entered them in slightly better spirits. Not only had the woman now in charge (Nel's original contact having gone to another department) confirmed that the council were behind the scheme and would give her a small 'start-up' grant. She gave Nel a lot of statistics about increased footfall, opportunities for tourism, and the spin-off benefits for current businesses and she agreed that high-quality crafts would be a good addition. She was also very enthusiastic about having a chef cooking meals with food from the stalls.

'What we want,' she had said, 'is Jamie Oliver, off speed. And I know just the person!' the woman went on. 'He's a nephew of mine. He's been working for a restaurant in London, but has moved down here so he and his girlfriend

168

can get married. He's renting at the moment, but if we get those starter homes . . . Anyway, he might be just the person you want. He's gorgeous. The women will love him. Leave it with me, I'll get in touch.'

'Thank you,' said Nel, wondering if the woman would be so helpful if she'd known Nel's original mission had been to prevent those particular starter homes being built. Still, she'd had a major reality check since then. 'That would be really useful. He would have to have passed all the relevant exams regarding hygiene, of course.'

'Of course,' said the woman. 'We take those things very seriously in this department.'

So, as Nel negotiated her car out of the car park, she had to admit that her spirits were better. One part of her plans was going well. She also had her date with Jake to look forward to, and however much she was trying to protect herself against inevitable heartbreak, she couldn't help feeling excited.

Nel decided to go first to a farm where she was sure of a friendly welcome, a cup of coffee, and possibly a piece of home-made cake. They not only produced several sorts of organic meat, including Nel's favourite burgers, but they could be relied on to write a letter declaring their support.

'Have you thought about asking for deposits?' asked Catherine, a pretty dark-haired woman.

'I thought about it, but rejected it as too complicated. I'd have to keep the money separately, and it would be dreadfully fiddly.'

'You'll have to set it up as a business sometime, Nel.'

'I've got my grant, which should come through some time, and that will tide us over for advertising and what have you, and although I know I should be happy we might have a new home for the market, I can't help feeling sad about Paradise Fields.' She paused. 'You do know about the plan to build on them, don't you?'

169

'Given that I know you, yes I do. What sort of houses are there going to be? Do you know?'

'Well, it really depends on who gets the contract to build them. There's one builder who wants to put up executive housing and rabbit hutches, and another, a really sweet man, who wants to put up fewer houses, with much better materials.'

'Oh!' Catherine suddenly became very animated. 'I've got some gossip! It might even be useful gossip!' She lowered her voice confidingly, although only her husband and Nel were present. 'Apparently, the solicitor acting for the Hunstantons . . . what's his name?'

'Jake Demerand,' said Nel – too quickly, she realised too late.

'That's him. Apparently a builder that a friend of mine knows – not well, I don't think, but they're members of the same golf club – can't remember which one. Which one was it, Robin?' she referred to her husband while Nel mentally bit her nails, urging her friend to get on with the story.

'Anyway,' Catherine went on, after her husband had looked at her blankly, 'apparently this builder said that the solicitor Jake . . .'

'Demerand,' snapped Nel.

'. . . was involved in some dodgy deal or other. Something to do with having an old peoples' home, and using the site for building. Made shedloads of money out of it.' Catherine seemed triumphant. 'That's good, isn't it? I mean, if the Hunstantons' have got a crooked solicitor, it will weaken their application, won't it?'

Nel felt peculiar. Instinctively she felt the gossip was lies; no way was Jake Demerand anything but honest. She didn't technically know him well enough to know this for a fact, but every cell of her body told her so. On the other hand, if, by some bizarre chance, he had made lots of old people homeless, it might be worth restarting the protest campaign she'd abandoned in depression at the meeting on Wednesday. For a sickening moment which literally made her feel faint, she debated which was more important to her, saving the fields, or trusting Jake's integrity.

'Are you OK, Nel?'

Nel smiled and sipped her coffee. 'I'm fine, I just felt a bit funny for some reason. Hungry, I expect.'

'Have some more cake. Are you still going to Weight Watchers?'

'Haven't been for ages. I feel so guilty.'

'Load of nonsense,' said Robin.

'So what do you think?' To Nel's regret, Catherine hadn't finished with Jake. 'If the solicitor is dodgy, will it help?'

Robin, who didn't talk as much as his wife, said, 'I doubt it. If they found out anything bad about the solicitor, the Hunstantons would just hire another one.'

'But perhaps we should tell them,' said Catherine. 'After all, they have a right to know.'

'But it's only gossip,' said Nel. 'If we told the Hunstantons, and it turned out not to be true, he could sue us for slander or something.'

'True,' said Catherine. 'But I just thought I should pass on any little snippet. Shame you can't use it. More coffee?'

'No, thanks. I'm full of cake.'

'Apparently this builder is tendering for the work,' said Catherine. 'He thinks it's in the bag. Which is one of the reasons I told you about the solicitor.'

'Did you sign my petition? I had more or less given up hope of saving the fields, but now, it might be worth a punt.'

Catherine sighed. 'I doubt it. Not one of our letters protesting against the plans did any good, did they?'

Nel had to acknowledge this was true.

'Hey!' Catherine said suddenly. 'Have you thought of

having home-made fudge? There's a woman over in the Forest who makes fudge to die for, and I'm not kidding.'

Robin finished his coffee and plonked his mug down on the table with a thump. 'But she makes it in very unhygienic conditions. You quite often find dog hairs in it, the saucepans are ancient, and the kitchen floor is so sticky you can hardly walk across it.'

'Mm, sounds like home,' said Nel. 'I might go and investigate her, if only for a free sample.'

'Talking of which, you must take this joint with you. Someone ordered it, then cancelled.'

'Well, you must let me pay you for it—'

'Don't be silly!'

Nel didn't have any time that day to investigate anyone she didn't know, but realised even if all the people she did know wrote letters supporting the market, she still didn't have nearly enough. She would have to seek out other products. The trouble was, while it was perfectly acceptable to have more than one cheesemaker, say, she would feel a bit disloyal to her friend who produced it if she positively looked for competition. On the other hand, if the market couldn't function because she didn't have enough people, it was a greater disloyalty. I wish I was an animal, thought Nel, developing a headache, then I wouldn't have to have morals. I could just follow my instincts. Then, remembering what had happened when she 'just followed her instincts', she decided to end the day – and the week – with Sacha, and demand some soothing potion to cheer her.

Sacha was very pleased to see her. 'Nel! Darling! You are the best! Thank you so much!'

'It's nice to be appreciated,' said Nel, helping herself to a seat. 'But what for?'

'For introducing Kerry Anne to me! She's amazing! She came and helped me again the day after you brought her – I decided not to go to Oxford – she took loads of stuff with her to America yesterday, and she's absolutely positive that pretty soon she'll have orders coming out of her ears! It's fantastic!'

'But will you be able to produce it all?'

'It'll be a struggle, but when Kerry Anne gets back, she's going to help me.'

'So I can't hate her any more, then? Viv will be furious.'
'Why?'

'She says it's boring the way I never hate anyone. She says that people who are always nice about other people are boring. I have to practise being waspish for her. If I know that Kerry Anne has helped you—'

'She has! But I'll *really* have to have bigger premises soon if I'm going to make the products for her health spa. That Oxford place wouldn't have been right—'

But Nel had fixed on a different issue. 'Health spa!' she interrupted.

'Yes. In the old house. Should be fantastic.'

'But I thought it was going to be turned into time-share apartments!'

'Well, the health spa is her latest plan. I think' – Sacha coughed modestly – 'she was a little bit inspired by my stuff. And it's much more her, really.'

Nel suddenly frowned. She suddenly remembered Kerry Anne with Sacha's recipes in her hand. 'You don't think she's up to anything bad, do you? I mean, she could steal your secrets, sell them to someone else, and clean up!'

Sacha laughed. 'Well, she could, if she knew the recipes. But she only knows them up to a point.'

'And Kerry Anne isn't going to become your partner, is she? You know partnerships are almost as bad as marriages to dissolve?'

'I won't go into anything without taking advice. I'd get a good solicitor.'

'That would be sensible. Kerry Anne's got one, after all.' At least, she assumed Jake Demerand was a good solicitor. Was it her brain that told her that? Or her heart? She bit her lips to bring herself back to the matter in hand. 'Now, Sacha, did I ask if you'd write a letter to the council? Before they give me the go-ahead for a bigger market, I've got to prove I've enough stallholders committed to supporting me. Oh, and do you know anyone else who makes or produces anything vaguely edible?'

Chapter Thirteen

Nel was surprised, but pleased to be rung by the nice woman from the council the following Monday.

'I've got the number of that young chef, my nephew, from my sister. Shall I give it to you?'

'Well, that would be very useful, but won't he be a bit surprised if some strange woman rings him up out of the blue?'

'Oh no, I've warned him that you might phone. He's very keen.'

Striking while the phone was hot, she dialled the number and was lucky. The young chef could see her, and could be fitted in on her way to or from a potential ice-cream maker, a willow-hurdle maker, and a farmer who didn't want to be involved himself, but whose wife made wedding hats. Nel didn't really feel wedding hats were what people went to farmers' markets to buy, but, on the other hand, a visit might be fun. She decided to go and see the chef first, because she knew that he was a definite must. The others were just maybes.

The minute he opened the door to his cottage, Nel knew he would be perfect. He was huge, young, fair and handsome, with boyish charm in spades. All women would respond to him on one level or other and he might make even the likes of Fleur interested in cooking.

'Ben Winters.' He shook her hand. 'Come in. Sorry the place is such a mess.'

'I'm Nel Innes.' As she followed Ben into the hall she glanced through the open door of the sitting room.

Hideously familiar, she felt tired just looking at it. Nel had visited her sons at their universities; she was accustomed to student accommodation. In fact, she felt she lived in it herself a lot of the time, but the living room of this little cottage was bad, even by her generous standards. The floor was so covered in crumpled beer cans you could hardly see the layer of crisps which covered the swirly red carpet. Games machines were heaped around a pile of videos and cartridges and tomato-smeared plates stacked with pizza crusts occupied the fireplace. Every surface was covered by the detritus of food, alcohol, cigarettes or electronic entertainment equipment.

It was such a shame. He looked perfect, his manner was endearing, and he may very well cook like Gordon Ramsay, but if he wasn't up to standard hygienically, it was no good. How would she explain it to the woman from the council who had suggested him? It would be so embarrassing. 'I'm so sorry, but your favourite nephew' – or whatever he was – 'lives in something out of a documentary about garbage or a piece of art up for the Turner Prize.'

'Come through to the kitchen, and I'll make you a cup of coffee. You might like to try a cinnamon whirl as well. They're pastry based, but not too cloying, I hope. I've just taken them out of the oven.'

Nel's volatile spirits recovered when she saw the immaculate state of the kitchen. It was as clean and tidy as the sitting room was filthy and chaotic. 'What a relief!' She laughed. 'I thought I was going to have to turn you down.'

'What? Turn down my cinnamon whirls?' His disappointment was enchanting. 'That would be a first!'

'No! Turn you down as the chef for the farmers' market. Everyone and everywhere has to comply with very high standards of hygiene. Even though you wouldn't be cooking here, I expect your kitchen would be inspected.'

'I am a qualified chef! I have passed all my exams in that sort of thing!'

'That's all right then. Can I sit down?'

Nel sat at the kitchen table and watched this large, handsome boy move about making coffee, producing plates, sifting icing sugar through a tea strainer onto the plate of pastries. He was built like a rugby player, and yet he moved about with grace and economy of movement, everything appearing under his hand the moment he wanted it. Nel was not a professional in these matters, but she felt that he would be able to cook anywhere and make it look easy.

The cinnamon whirls melted almost before they got to her mouth, and didn't linger there long, either. 'These are fantastic!' she said. 'Oh, I'm so glad I've given up going to Weight Watchers.'

'Weight Watchers? Why?'

'The normal reasons. Now, tell me what else you can cook. You won't have an oven at the market. It'll all have to be done on gas burners.'

'Well, I've been practising pastries because they've always been my weak spot, but really, I like to use fresh ingredients, cook them quickly, and eat them without too much in the way of sauces and fancy bits. I love doing pan-fried stuff. I plan to have my own restaurant in ten years.'

'Wow! And would you be happy to do demonstrations for us in the farmers' market?'

'Oh yes, Helen – whom you met? – she told me all about it. She said you probably wouldn't be able to pay me, but that I wouldn't have to pay for the ingredients either, and that it would be a good way of getting my name and face known in the area.'

'Well, I would hope to be able to pay you. If I get enough stallholders, and they all pay their twenty quid or whatever, I should be able to take a bit of it for you. I'm not actually going to be paying myself, just to begin with. I've just had an idea!' she added suddenly. 'Why don't we have a farmers' market at the spring fundraising jamboree for the hospice?'

'Sorry?'

'I must sound mad, but I've just thought we could have an inaugural farmers' market at a fundraising event I organise. It would be good for the event, and would advertise that the farmers' market should be continuing on a different site! It could be great!'

'And you'd like me to do some cookery demonstrations? Cool!' He smiled, a wide, white smile which could sell beer to breweries, coals to Newcastle, and, if necessary, ice to Eskimos. 'Would you like to try some pâté I've made? I could sell that at the farmers' market.'

Having sons did not make Nel susceptible to young men, or so she believed. She concentrated on sounding professional. 'Only if you use a local source. If you want to make pâté, you should get together with someone who produces the main ingredient—'

'Duck.'

'—and make it with them.' Then she forgot about being downbeat and businesslike. 'I know a duck person! I'll give you the address. I think they also keep rare breeds of some sort. Can't remember what. I must contact them about the market. I'd forgotten I knew about them until you reminded me. You should definitely get in touch.'

Nel was reluctant to leave the haven of Ben's kitchen and his boyish exuberance, but as staying would require more eating and she already felt slightly sick, this didn't seem a good idea. She found her way down narrow, winding lanes to the hurdle maker.

'Most farmers' markets only do food,' she told him, after she'd seen what he could create with willow. 'But I'm working on the council to let me have good quality crafts – pottery, blacksmithing, that sort of stuff. I think

they'd go well alongside food products, and if they're produced locally, why not?'

'Well, thank you.' The man was in his thirties, bearded
and wearing a boiler suit. Several young children clus-
tered round him and, in the kitchen, his wife was making
tea. 'It'd be good to have a regular outlet. I spend most
of my time laying hedges, but you've got to have something to do when the weather's bad. Come in and get
warm.'

They were a nice family. The kitchen was snug and not
too tidy, and Nel felt at home there. 'I expect you know
the market is having to move from Paradise Fields,' she
said eventually. 'I know you're a bit far away for it to
affect you directly, but it's a terrible shame. It's very rare
and precious meadowland. It's also where the children's
hospice does its major fundraising.'

Ewan looked at her thoughtfully. 'I'm sorry about that,
but people do need houses. Who's the builder?'

'Well, at the moment it's someone called Gideon
Something.' She sighed. 'A dear old chap on our committee
– Isaac or Abraham, something biblical – said he might be
able to build something better, but quite honestly—'

'Abraham? I know him! I used to work for him. He's
a good bloke. Good builder, too.'

'But he must be getting on a bit.'

'He took early retirement. Made a pile before he did,
mind. Is he interested in this bit of land? That's good. He
builds nice houses.'

This was a bit unexpected. Ewan was green from his
boots to his woolly hat with ear-flaps; Nel would have
sworn he'd have been against building even a bus shelter
if it was on a bit of grass, let alone an executive housing
estate on rare meadowland.

'We do take the children there sometimes in the
summer,' said his wife. 'They play on the rope swing. It
would be a shame to see the meadows built on.'

179

Ewan shook his head. 'No. People have got to live somewhere. Are there any starter homes planned? You can't object to that. But Gideon Freebody's a thoroughly bad bloke.'

'You seem to know a lot about it. How come?'

'I was a brickie by trade until I settled down here. We saved up and bought this bit of land with trees on it, and now I work on the land, mostly. But Gideon Freebody should be locked up. His houses fall down before the paint's dry.'

'Oh.'

'He made a lot of money from buying up old peoples' homes, letting them fall into disrepair and then knocking them down and building expensive houses on the sites. He had a dodgy solicitor who helped him get away with it.'

Nel felt as if someone had punched her directly on her heart. She didn't dare ask the name of the dodgy solicitor in case she recognised it. She might be able to dismiss Catherine's gossip as gossip, just, but to hear it from two different sources made it harder.

Ewan drained his tea mug. 'You should go and see Abraham, see what his plans are.'

'Do you know where he lives?'

'Not far from here. I'll give him a ring if you like. See if he's home. He works from there, so he might be.'

Nel was not at all sure that she wanted to visit Abraham the builder. She knew nothing about builders, and wouldn't know what to say. She put out a hand to stop Ewan, but he had already picked up the telephone. Ewan, for all his gentleness and love of nature, was clearly very determined that people should do what he felt to be the right thing, even if they had other ideas.

Nel listened to him making arrangements, telling his mate that this woman would be on her way. She couldn't get out of it now. Once he was off the phone, he turned to her in great excitement. 'This is an amazing coincidence. He's been trying to get hold of you. He needs to talk to you asap – can you go round now?'

Nel sighed. 'OK. Can I use your loo?'

Abraham lived in a large, new house that had more charm and elegance than she was expecting. There were no inappropriate diamond panes, knicker blinds or sentimental children supporting birdbaths in the garden, nor did the doorbell play the first few bars of the William Tell overture when she rang it. Waiting on the doorstep, Nel chastised herself for prejudice; even builders who've made a packet building houses she wouldn't personally care to live in could have good taste in their personal lives.

Abraham seemed pleased to see her, and even given her bad record for hating people, Nel found herself succumbing to his old-fashioned manners worryingly easily.

'Come in, my dear. My wife's at the hairdresser's, but she'll be back shortly and will make us a cup of coffee. I realise you don't want those meadows built on at all, but I think if you see what I've got in mind, it'll soften the blow a little.'

It was hard not to be soothed by his fatherly kindness. Nel followed him into the dining room, on the table of which were spread the plans.

Nel had seen them before, when she'd inspected them in the council offices at the planning meeting before Christmas, but she was glad of an opportunity to see them in more peaceful surroundings. They were also on a larger scale. She peered at them. They didn't seem to be the same plans.

'You see it's all very ambitious,' said Abraham.

'Very expensive, of course.' Nel was confused, still trying to fit what she was looking at now, with what she had seen before. The larger scale would make a difference, of course. But still . . .

181

'Hang on, Abraham, I'm sorry to be stupid, but how are all those houses going to fit onto Paradise Fields?'

'By pulling down the hospice and building on that land as well.'

She felt all the blood drain away, for a moment she thought she was going to faint.

'That's why I tried to contact you. I realised you didn't have a clue the extent Gideon Freebody was planning to build.'

She sat down on a chair which was pulled out a little way. 'But why didn't anyone know about this?'

Abraham shrugged. 'Because they didn't want you to know.'

'Who? Gideon Freebody?'

Abraham shook his head. He seemed to have information she needed, but was clearly reluctant to give it to her for some reason.

'You mean someone at the hospice?' She felt hot all over. 'Chris Mowbray?'

The old man nodded. 'Reckon so. You look a bit pale, love. Do you want a drink of water?'

Nel nodded, wanting not so much the water, as the time on her own to gather her thoughts.

They were still un-gathered when he came back with the glass.

'You think he's planning to sell the hospice for building land?' she asked, when she had taken a sip.

Abraham nodded.

'That would explain how they could get all those houses onto the space, but where's the access?'

'Here,' Abraham pointed.

'So why's that in a different colour? Sorry to ask such stupid questions.'

'It's not a stupid question. It's a very sensible question. It's in a different colour because the Hunstantons don't own it. At least not any more.'

'Then who does?'

'It's not exactly clear. You see it's not outlined in the same colour as whoever owns this land here.'

Nel peered more closely, and pulled the plan at a different angle. 'That's the hospice!'

'Reckon it is. Was it the dower house for Hunstanton Manor?'

'Mm. Sir Gerald gave it to them years and years ago. It's why we thought the hospice owned the meadowland.'

'I dare say he didn't feel he could give too much of his son's inheritance away. But that little strip of land, a ransom strip, you might call it, could be very useful to the hospice.'

'How? It's not very big.'

'Well, without that, Gideon Freebody's revised, bigger plans would never get planning permission. There isn't sufficient access without that land.'

'And you think it might belong to the hospice.'

'Aye.'

'But why?'

'Something a little bird told me. I'll not say who, I'll just say I think you should check it out. Before someone else does. Whoever owns that land has a lot of power in all these shenanigans. Without that strip, there'd be no point in pulling down the hospice building.'

Hope flickered briefly. 'We couldn't stop the building all together?'

Abraham laughed. 'Nay lass, you'll not do that. The Hunstantons are set on building, and they've already got planning permission for Paradise Fields. But you'll stop Gideon Freebody in his tracks, though.'

Nel's head was whirling. She couldn't believe that people, Chris Mowbray in particular, could be so devious. Could she trust anyone? 'What about you? What about your plans? You don't have to do anything dreadful for your scheme, do you?'

Abraham chuckled. He was remarkably calm, useful when Nel felt on the verge of hysteria. 'No! My scheme's much smaller, and the feeder road on the other side will be more than adequate.

'I've always liked to produce quality. It pays in the end. Ah, that's my wife home. Fancy a cup of tea or coffee and a piece of home-made shortbread?'

Nel didn't, really, she wanted to go away and think about the implications of everything she had learned. Supposing the hospice wasn't listed and so could be pulled down quite easily? Supposing it did become too expensive for them to maintain? Could they depend on Abraham doing the maintenance for ever? Could they sell a dilapidated building for enough money to have something new and purpose built? Or, if they just sold the ransom strip, might that raise enough money to keep the hospice going for a little while – but for how long? Every way she looked at it the situation was hideously complicated.

But Mrs Abraham, whose name was Doris, produced tea and shortbread, and Nel couldn't refuse it. Doris was as motherly as her husband was fatherly, and it was soothing to be in their gentle company.

'Tell me about this hospice,' said Doris, as if sensing Nel was in a state, and needed to be calmed. And her sensible, kindly voice did indeed steady Nel. 'Abraham's hopeless about telling me what's going on. I hear you do wonderful work.'

It was good to be made to answer, equally sensibly, when she really wanted to throw herself onto the carpet and howl. 'Oh, we do. I just hope we can go on doing wonderful work.'

'What might stop you?'

Passionately Nel described the work that went on, the difficulties with the fields (suitably censored, for the sake of good manners) and the problems with the building itself. She had to be given another cup of tea halfway through to sustain her.

'You see,' she finished, 'we really needed the meadows, to raise funds year after year. We need the river frontage too, so we can get the children onto the boat.'

Abraham didn't quite tap the side of his nose and nod, but nearly. 'You leave it to me,' he said. 'Don't forget in my proposal the kids can still get down to the river.' He finished his tea with a practised slurp. 'But you check the deeds of the hospice and find out exactly who controls what. And, if I may suggest, see who stands to gain from what.'

Nel set off in the direction of the ice-cream maker, thinking hard about what Abraham had said about the deeds. She'd spent long enough in his company to be confident that he was an honest man, and his offer to reroof the hospice told her that his heart was definitely in the right place. Of course he stood to make money out of it, but making money wasn't actually a sin. Making money out of disadvantaged people definitely was: old people, or children with life-threatening illnesses.

She changed her mind about the ice cream. She turned her car in a field gateway and went back towards town. She wanted to do what she had done so much of when she first came to live here: she headed for the hospice.

She was lucky, a small boy wanted to be read to, and so Nel had an excuse to make herself and him comfy on the flop cushions, a pile of books beside them. Being with children always put life in perspective, because you couldn't pretend with children, you just had to be yourself. Nor did you have to wonder about their motivation. If they wanted a story, they wanted a story and Nel was only too happy to oblige. When her own children were little, she would quite often find that they had fallen asleep while they were being read to, but she'd carry on and finish the story anyway. There was very little scope for doing different voices in adult fiction.

When the little boy got bored with having *The Cat in the Hat* acted out for him, and went off to do something else, Nel heaved herself to her feet and went into the office.

'Karen,' she said, trying to sound like her usual, casual self, and actually feeling like a spy, 'I don't suppose I could have a look at the deeds, could I? There's something I want to check up on about this building plan.' It was all perfectly true, but it felt like a tarradiddle.

'I don't think they're here actually, Nel,' said Karen, opening the filing cabinet and rummaging through folders. 'I think Christopher's got them. He took them home to check up on them himself.'

'Oh well, I expect he's had the same thoughts as I had. This alternative building idea could be really good for us.'

'Why don't you go and see him at home? He'll probably have the deeds handy, as he only took them a couple of days ago.' Karen laughed. 'He might be playing golf, of course. He's been really keen on it lately. Would you like me to ring him now, and see if he's there?'

'No, don't bother. I'll just call on the off chance. I can ring him later to make an appointment if he's not there.'

Christopher Mowbray was there, but the deeds weren't. Nel was not surprised, not now, when she was almost certain he was up to something. He probably had had a copy for ages, and had just taken the ones in the hospice so no one could examine them. 'Oh no', explained Chris, unusually affable. 'I lent them to a friend. He's into local history and wanted to see them.' Nel could hardly object. The deeds weren't her responsibility, and they would probably be of interest to local historians. 'Why don't you come into the sitting room and have a sherry?'

'That would be lovely,' she said.

Christopher Mowbray's sitting room was, Nel couldn't help noticing, the epitome of a new house: what she'd been expecting from Abraham, the builder, and not found. It had the diamond-pane secondary glazing, the fireplace made out of reconstituted Cotswold stone, the nooks filled with Capodimonte figurines. It also had a sound system which took up an entire wall, but no books. It smelt of some toxic chemical that made it feel very clean but somehow institutional. Nel remembered he was divorced and wondered if she was wise to have sat on the sofa where he could sit next to her.

Rather than reveal her own concerns, the moment she had the Tío Pepe in her hand Nel said, 'So, tell me, what are your thoughts about the building on the meadowland? You do agree that getting Abraham to do it would be much the best thing for the hospice?'

He sat down beside her, making the leather seat sag, so she inevitably slid towards him. 'Actually, Nel, I have to disagree. I don't think Abraham – is that his surname or his Christian name, by the way?'

'I don't know. Everyone just calls him Abraham.'

'Whatever. But I don't think Abraham's going to be able to come up with a plan that is remotely attractive to the Hunstantons. He's an old man. He's not into all the new technology. No, I think Gideon Freebody's plans are the ones the hospice should back.'

'But why, when Abraham thinks he might be able to keep river access for us? I know we'll still be losing the fields, but being able to get to the boat would be better than nothing. Would that mean that the hospice would be safe?'

Chris Mowbray shook his head and Nel took a sip of sherry, which she didn't like very much, and shifted away from him a little. She hated the space between her and another person being wrong, either to far or too near. Christopher Mowbray was definitely too near. 'Small beer,

I'm afraid. It would be much better for the hospice to support the bigger plan.'

'But why?'

Nel edged away some more. She wasn't in the habit of thinking of herself as the sort of woman men made passes at, but even she couldn't misinterpret the signals she was getting now.

'I'm afraid, Nel' – he put his hand on her knee. She could imagine it leaving a greasy stain on her trousers – 'there are some things I'm not at liberty to tell you. But take it from me, Gideon Freebody's are the ones.'

'This sounds very suspicious, Christopher!' Nel laughed, not remotely amused.

'I know it must sound like that, but really, it's for the hospice.' He leant forward confidentially and she realised he had bad breath. 'We might get a brand-new hospice building out of it. What would you say about that?'

On the face of it, it was very hard not to be thrilled with the notion, but Nel mistrusted it with every cell in her body. She knew now that Viv had been right, twice. 'Well, of course, it could be brilliant. You'd have to take it to the committee. My concern would be what would happen to the hospice while the new one is being built. And should we be making decisions like this while we're without a director? Surely the new person should have a say in such a major change.'

'Oh, don't worry about that, Nel. I'm sure we could sort something out. And I think it would be easier to get a new director if we had a new building.'

Internally, Nel groaned. She took another sip of sherry. 'Do you think so? Well—'

With perfect timing, the telephone rang, giving Nel precious moments to think of what to say, and how to get herself out of there without causing offence. While he might be extremely offensive to her, Nel couldn't afford to offend him back.

Christopher had turned his back to her and was speaking softly into the receiver. 'How nice to hear from you. Dinner? When? That would be lovely. Tell me, is – your husband there? I'd like to set up a date for some golf.'

Christopher might have been talking quietly, but his interlocutor certainly wasn't. The tones were muffled, certainly, but obviously female – and American. Kerry Anne?

By the time Christopher Mowbray was off the phone, Nel had escaped from the slippery clutches of the sofa and was on her feet, on target for the door.

Chapter Fourteen

'It's no good. I'll have to cancel. I've got a spot.' Nel had been thinking all day of excuses why she couldn't go out with Jake. She had been driving all over the county researching potential stallholders, almost praying to break down in the Forest of Dean.

'Put some toothpaste on it and cover it up with make-up,' said Fleur, quite brutally, Nel thought.

'Really? Does that work?'

'It's supposed to. I read—'

'No, don't tell me, you read it in a magazine.' Nel peered into the mirror. 'Do you ever read anything except magazines?'

'Only on aeroplanes and the beach. Oh, and school stuff. It's not like you to get spots, Mum.'

'It's my hormones. I must be due for my period, which is a pain but I suppose at least it means I'm not pregnant.' The word was out of her mouth before she knew she was thinking it. Oh God, I'm no good at this! You obviously have to practise to be a scarlet woman on the sly.

'Mum!' Fleur was horrified and amused. 'How could you possibly be pregnant? Unless you've slept with Simon and not told us.'

'It's just an expression,' Nel said, blushing so hard her spot disappeared. 'A habit, sort of. I mean, aren't you always relieved when your period comes?'

'Not really.' Fleur investigated an old mascara stick. 'I'm on the pill. I know I'm not pregnant.'

Fleur's calmness should have been a relief to Nel, but

instead, it seemed to point up her own panic. For although she had taken the morning-after pill, she wouldn't be sure it had worked until nature confirmed it. 'And I'm a celibate old bat, so I know I'm not too!' said Nel. 'But I've still got a bloody great spot on my chin,' she added, to deflect the subject a little.

'It's a tiny spot and I'll lend you my concealer. Put it on after the toothpaste. Now I must go and get ready myself. I'm meeting Jamie at the station.'

'You're sure you don't want me to pick him up? I don't mind being late, or even cancelling.'

'If you cancel, Mother, I will never speak to you again! And no, we'll walk up, or take a taxi. It's a shame he's getting down here so late.'

'Well, at least it means you can check that I look all right. And you really look. The boys just say I look lovely without their eyes ever leaving the television screen. Mind you, your father used to do that, too. Except when he'd ask me if I was wearing whatever it was I had on when it was too late to change.'

'Sometimes you make Dad sound less than perfect.' Fleur sounded a little indignant.

Nel laughed. 'Sweetheart! You don't fall in love with people because they're perfect! One of the signs is that you can see all their faults, perfectly well, and yet you still think they're the best thing ever.'

'Are you in love with Simon?'

Nel sighed. 'Probably not. But I am very fond of him.'

'You never get in such a state getting ready to go out with him.'

'That's because we were just friends for ages. He'd seen me looking terrible before we were an item.'

'Did you tell him you were going out with Jake tonight?'

'Sort of.' She had told Simon she had arranged a meeting with the solicitor to discuss the plans. She hadn't told him the exact circumstances. In his turn, he had told

191

her he'd seen said solicitor in a restaurant with Kerry Anne. While it could have been perfectly innocent, the thought was like having a stone in one's shoe. No matter how often you tried to shake your foot, the stone was always painfully digging in.

'What do you mean you sort of told him you were going out with Jake?'

'I thought you had to go and get ready. You still have to decide exactly which pair of black trousers you are going to wear with which little strappy top.'

'Huh! You're as bad! Your bedroom looks like a jumble sale! Clothes all over the bed! Although I do think you look nice. Those trousers are very flattering and the jacket is heaven.'

Nel hugged her daughter, wishing for a moment Fleur was still a little girl, and she was still a mother who thought only of her children. She was still a mother of course, nothing could alter that, but her thoughts had strayed somewhat.

'It took me ages to get the dog hairs off it. But thank you for liking it.'

'Any time. Can I borrow your eye-shadow?'

Jake arrived to collect her fifteen minutes late. Nel was just beginning to think she could relax in front of the television, and then pounce on Fleur and Jamie when they arrived, when the doorbell rang.

'I'm so sorry I'm late. I got held up in traffic. It's hell on the M4 on a Friday night.' He kissed her cheek. 'You look stunning.'

'You mean you drove down from London to go out with me?' Nel was blushing, both from his compliment and the fact that his kiss, chaste as it was, had made her heart pound. 'You should have cancelled and stayed in town. The traffic wouldn't be so bad tomorrow.'

'But I didn't want to cancel. If we took a rain check,

God knows when I would have got you to agree to go out with me. It was hard enough this time. Shall we go?' Jake was, by this time, stroking all three dogs simultaneously.

'I'll just get my coat.' Nel felt like a girl on her first date. She wished she'd had a glass of wine or something first, to settle her nerves. When Fleur had suggested it, Nel had felt she needed a clear head. Also, when she was nervous, wine tended to turn her face rather red.

'Goodbye, girls,' said Jake solemnly. 'I'll look after your mistress for you.'

The word mistress made Nel flinch, but she trusted Jake wouldn't have noticed. He took her arm and ushered her to his car and opened the door. While she was sitting waiting for him to go round and get in his side, she reminded herself of what Catherine had said. He'd been responsible for turning old people onto the street; she mustn't trust him.

The car smelt of leather and his aftershave. It had a dashboard with enough instruments for an aeroplane. It was heavy, and shiny, with a walnut fascia, and was quite unlike the cars Nel was used to. It could have been bought with money made out of turning those old people onto the street, she thought, and then reminded herself that that was only gossip. But he's still a smooth operator, her lecture went on, you may not be a girl any more, but you're still from the country, and terribly naïve. You're not equipped to go out with slick men from the city, who can seduce a woman just by touching her arm. Guilt flooded over her. What was she doing, going out with Jake, when she was more or less committed to Simon?

Last night, when he'd rung her, she had hinted to Simon that she'd been told something about Jake which needed investigating. But, she was forced to admit, it was so that if he ever wanted to go out with her again, she had an excuse for Simon ready. She sighed. Really, she had fewer morals than Villette.

'Why the sigh?' asked Jake as he sat down next to her. 'Are you tired?'

'A bit. I've been rushing round all day, trying to find people who'll commit to supporting the farmers' market. What have you been doing? Turning green fields into building sites?' She hadn't meant to mention the fields, but nerves had nearly had her saying 'turning old people onto the street'. At least she hadn't said that.

'Mm, well, shall we agree not to talk about work?'

'But what else shall we talk about? We've got nothing else in common.'

He laughed. 'We've got plenty of other things in common, only you don't want to talk about them.'

Blushing in the darkness, Nel said, 'No, I don't.'

'Then I'll look for neutral topics that won't make you blush.'

She looked at him, horrified. How did he know she was blushing? But his eyes were on the road ahead. The reference to blushing must have just been by chance.

'How are you on opera?' he suggested.

'I know nothing whatever about opera. You can't just pick something out of the air. Conversation has to come from somewhere.' She paused. 'Where are you taking me?' If she chose the topic, it would be safer.

'Somewhere new that's just opened, near Frampton. It sounds really good. I was lucky to get a table on a Friday night.'

'How lovely.' She took a long, calming breath, being careful to let it out slowly, so he wouldn't hear.

'The Hunstantons told me about it.'

'Oh.'

'Or does that qualify as talking about work?'

'You don't have to be silly about it.'

'How are your children? Fleur? She's a very smart girl.'

194

'I know. Too smart, maybe. But I'll miss her terribly when she goes travelling, on her gap year. I won't know what to wear without her to ask.'

'Do you ask her advice a lot, then?'

'Oh yes. She knows far more than me about most things. And having a daughter is a very useful fashion accessory. They stop you making dreadful mistakes.'

'Well, she's done a very good job on you tonight. As I said before, you look stunning.'

'Thank you.' Blushing again, Nel wondered if Fleur would consider giving her a quick course on how to accept compliments gracefully. Or, better, how to prevent oneself blushing. 'Do you like opera?' she said, having failed to think of any other neutral topic.

'I thought you said you knew nothing about it?'

'But if you do, you can tell me, and save me the trouble of making conversation.'

'I would hate to put you to any trouble. Let's just sit in silence until we get there. You could shut your eyes and have a little nap.'

'I expect you need a little nap, after driving all the way down from London. I should have cooked supper for you.'

'Nel! I wanted to take you out! Now just shut up and enjoy the ride. It's not far.'

To her horror, Nel found she quite liked being bossed about. It was restful.

'Right, I think it's just off this turning here. Yes, there we are, The Black Hart.'

Nel hadn't actually been asleep, but her thoughts had been wandering a bit. Now she was back to panic mode with a start. It's an omen she thought. Harts are always white! I'm not even sure they come in black! He is a crook! Black Hart must mean black heart. What have I done!

'I'll just see where we can park without you having to

step out into a puddle,' said the crook, sounding suspiciously like a gentleman.

While Jake was looking for a place which pleased him, Nel thought she spotted Simon's car. She was notoriously bad at recognising cars but she was slightly better at number plates. It was definitely Simon's car.

What should she do? Say now? Demand to be taken somewhere else? No, Jake wanted to be here, he'd had difficulty getting a table, he had already driven hundreds of miles. It wouldn't be fair to make him move, especially when she couldn't think of anywhere else they could go. If she saw him, she would just explain to Simon that they'd had to bring their meeting forward, and tonight was the only available window. Jake was a man who'd have windows; he was busy and came from London. And it may not happen. It looked quite a big pub, upgraded to a restaurant. It may not be necessary to lie at all.

'It is a bit muddy there,' said Jake, having parked and come round to Nel's side. 'But it's the best I can do. Would you like me to carry you over the patch?'

'No! I've spent most of my day on farms. I've coped with far worse than mud!'

'Not in those shoes, I bet.' He took her arm. 'But I thought we weren't supposed to be talking about work?'

With him holding her arm, it was going to be hard for Nel to talk about anything. Just as well he let it go the moment they got inside.

Nel spotted Simon while Jake was helping her off with her coat. He was sitting with his back to her at a table for two. His companion was a woman who appeared to Nel to be a little younger than she was.

'This isn't the coat you were wearing the other night,' Jake commented. 'It weighs less than half as much.'

As a pretty waitress in jeans, a strappy black top (just like the ones Fleur lived in) and a little white apron was hovering around, Nel couldn't reprove Jake for mentioning 'the other night'. 'That was my late husband's,' she said repressively. 'I got this one from the Oxfam shop last year.'

'Very nice too,' said Jake, amused. He wasn't appalled, as Nel had half hoped he would be.

'Would you like to go straight to your table?' asked the girl, who was about Fleur's age, too. 'Or to the bar first?'

Jake looked enquiringly at Nel. The bar was beyond where Simon was sitting. If they went to it, they would cross his sight line. 'I think I should tell you,' she said, 'that Simon is here. I'd rather go straight to the table.'

'Fine.' Jake seemed extremely calm and, as they walked to their table, he asked, 'Did you tell him we were going out tonight?'

'Sort of.'

'What do you mean "sort of"?'

'You're as bad as Fleur! I said there were things to do with the hospice that needed discussing. I didn't say we'd arranged a time or anything.'

'So if he comes up and threatens to thump me, I'll say we're working.'

'He won't do that. He's a nice man. He doesn't thump people.'

'Is he alone?'

'No. He's with a woman.'

'Well, do you want to go and thump him?'

Nel laughed. 'No! I'm no better than he is, for a start, and besides, I don't do jealousy.'

Just as she said it, she remembered her reaction on seeing Jake look at Kerry Anne that time in his office. When Jake and Vivian came into that meeting together. And when Simon told her Jake had taken Kerry Anne out. Perhaps she did do jealousy, after all. But, interestingly, not for Simon.

He held out her chair for her and she sat down. 'You are a very unusual woman, Nel.'

That was a bit too serious for Nel. She enjoyed Jake's

197

company when he was being silly and a bit confrontational. She didn't think she could handle deep looks, not in public. She picked up her menu. 'Let's just forget about Simon and enjoy our meal. Wow, this looks fantastic.'

'Good, I'm starving. I didn't have lunch,' said Jake. 'Are you hungry?'

Nel wasn't, particularly, she was too nervous, but she said, 'Come to think of it, I didn't have lunch either. Just a rather large bit of cake at Amanda's. Oh, you won't know her: she's a beef farmer. Sorry, that's work.'

'Just concentrate on what you want to eat,' said Jake. 'We can argue about the rules later.'

Nel forgot about Simon being there until he appeared at their table while she was eating her steak, a filet mignon which lived up to its description on the menu as tender, delicious and small enough to eat. She was wondering if she had the nerve to ask who had supplied it.

'Hello, Nel!' Simon sounded half cross and half guilty. His companion hovered at his shoulder. Definitely younger than me, Nel thought, but no teenage daughter. Her clothes were terrible.

Nel got to her feet, relaxed by two glasses of red wine. 'Fancy seeing you here! Have you met Jake Demerand? He's the solicitor for the Hunstantons.'

Jake put out a hand, and Simon took it. 'Yes. Nel wanted a meeting about the fields, and this was the only time available. Running two offices, very time-consuming.'

'Oh,' said Simon. 'This is Penny. We're working too. She's looked at several houses and can't decide which one is best for her.'

'Hello, Penny,' said Nel, wondering why Simon had brought her over when he so obviously felt guilty about it. He could have just slipped out of the restaurant with Penny and, for all he knew, she would have been none the wiser. 'Buying a house is such a hard decision. Harder than choosing a husband, in some ways.'

'I wouldn't say that exactly. If you buy the wrong house you can always move,' said Simon. 'Marriage is for life.'

'Or until it irretrievably breaks down,' said Nel.

'I'm surprised to hear you say that, Nel,' said Simon. 'Nel is a widow,' he said to Penny in a slightly lowered voice.

Nel felt mildly annoyed. She was a widow, but was that the defining thing about her, like being an artist or a teacher? 'That's not what I do as a profession,' she said. 'What do you do, Penny, or are you a divorcee, or a young mother, or a grandmother even, although you look far too young for that?'

'Stained glass,' said Penny, looking as uncomfortable as Simon.

'Look, why don't you two take a seat?' said Jake. 'You can have coffee while we finish our meal.'

It was only polite. He more or less had to say it, but Nel fervently hoped Simon would refuse. He didn't.

'Oh, well, that's very kind,' said Simon. 'Are you all right to hang on a bit longer, Penny?'

Penny shrugged, and sat in the chair Jake held out for her.

'So, what sort of house are you looking for?' said Nel, feeling sorry for her.

'Small, with a garden, south-facing, and a big attic I can work in. Not too far from town.'

Nel laughed. 'A perfect gem, in other words. Have you seen anything you like?'

'Yes, but they've all got something wrong with them.'

'To go back to my husband analogy,' said Nel, who had realised too late that she might have had too much to drink, 'I think you have to fall in love with a house. Think: this is home! Even if one of the bedrooms is poky, or the kitchen is falling apart.'

'Is that how you bought your house?' Simon asked, and then went on, 'Nel's house is a perfect gem. It has four double bedrooms, a sitting room, a dining room and a good-sized kitchen. Oh, and a utility room. And the garden is a very decent size indeed. Big enough for a building plot at the end.'

Nel laughed to hide her annoyance. Even allowing for the fact that Simon was an estate agent, he shouldn't tell complete strangers the intimate secrets of her property. 'But unfortunately I'm not planning to move. I did fall in love with it, and we're still living together happily.'

'Sorry, Nel,' said Simon. 'I forgot what I was doing there for a minute.'

The waitress appeared, looking questioningly at Simon and Penny. 'We're just having coffee,' Nel said. 'Does that go for you two?' She had abandoned her steak, and thought she was probably full. But Jake had other ideas.

'No, we want the pudding menu. Nel needs fattening up.'

'No, I don't! Quite the opposite! I should just have black coffee.'

'But you know coffee late at night stops you sleeping,' said Simon.

Oh God, thought Nel, now everyone thinks he knows this first hand. 'Well, I'll have peppermint tea, then.'

The waitress scribbled.

'Hang on,' said Jake, 'I insist on you having a pudding. My mother taught me that only a cad takes a woman out to dinner and doesn't give her pudding.'

'Really?' Nel was intrigued.

'No, not really, but it's the kind of thing she would have taught me, if she'd thought of it. I fancy the tiramisu. I know it's terribly retro, but I still like it. What about you, Nel?'

'Oh well, if you insist, I'll have the pot au chocolat.' And if Simon says if I'm having chocolate I must be due for my period, which is why I've got a spot, I'll deck him.

Then she remembered with relief that Simon didn't notice things like that. 'Are you two going to eat something, or have you had pudding already?'

'Oh no, thank you. I've had more than enough to eat,' said Penny.

'And I expect you're worried about which house to buy,' said Nel kindly.

'I'm sure Nel would go and look at some with you, if you wanted her to,' said Simon.

'Simon! I am a bit pressed for time at the moment!'

'But you know you love looking at houses, and would hate Penny to make the wrong decision.'

'I think Nel probably feels that only Penny can know if she's fallen in love or not,' said Jake. 'So Nel going with her wouldn't make a difference. It's not as if they are old friends or anything.'

'That's quite right. Have you got a girlfriend who could go with you?' Now she was off the hook, Nel felt guilty for not wanting to help.

'No,' said Simon. 'That's why I'm asking you.'

'But Nel really is very busy,' said Jake. 'That's why we had to meet tonight. All her days are filled. Which reminds me, have we finished our work, Nel?'

Nel didn't know whether to laugh, cry or retreat to the Ladies. 'I think so. Excuse me, I'll just go and powder my nose.'

When she had reapplied Fleur's concealer and refreshed her lipstick, she went back, to find that Simon and Penny had gone.

'What a relief,' she said, without thinking.

'I know. I am sorry I had to invite them to sit down.'

'There was nothing else you could do, in the circumstances. But I am glad you got rid of them. And thank you for getting me out of house-hunting with Penny. Simon's quite right, I love going round houses, but I am so busy at the moment.'

'I know,' said Jake. 'Besides, he had no right to commandeer your time like that without consulting you.'

'Well, I suppose we are old friends . . .'

'I agree with Fleur about Simon.'

'What?'

'You definitely shouldn't marry him.'

'You haven't discussed Simon with Fleur!' Nel was outraged.

'No, but I bet she says you shouldn't marry him.'

Nel bit her lip to hide the fact that she was smiling. 'It hasn't come up.'

'It will.'

'Not necessarily! Really, I don't like you making assumptions about my private life when you hardly know me!'

'This isn't about you. It's about Simon. He has his eye on your house.'

Nel laughed. 'No, he hasn't! What rubbish! What on earth makes you say that?'

'He's an estate agent. It's a very desirable property.'

'But he knows I'd never sell it. I love that house. The children love that house. It's mine.'

'Good. But Simon loves it too.'

Nel thought about this. 'He's never said anything about loving it. He mostly just thinks it's a mess.'

'But I bet he helps you with the DIY.'

'Yes! That's because he's a kind person, and he's fond of me – us. There's nothing sinister in it.'

Jake made a 'have it your own way' gesture with his hands. 'Ah, here's pudding.'

'This is so wicked,' said Nel a few moments later.

'Nonsense. It's been scientifically proved that chocolate is good for you.'

'You don't need to tell me, or any woman that. They know it instinctively.'

'So in a little while you're going to feel all relaxed and happy?'

'Quite likely.'

'And so then you'll be willing to talk about that Saturday?'

Nel dropped her spoon. 'No. I'll never be that relaxed and happy.'

'You can't deny what happened between us. It was explosive and spontaneous and wonderful.'

'I'm not denying it happened! I know it happened, but I don't want to talk about it!'

'But don't you want to repeat the experience?'

'No! Yes! But we can't! I'm committed to Simon. I don't have affaires.'

'Why not?'

Nel regarded him, stunned. 'Well – because! I'm a respectable woman, a mother. Besides, I think you might be younger than me.'

'Who cares? I've always liked older women. They're more experienced.'

This really made Nel laugh. 'Not this older woman. I think Fleur is probably more experienced than I am, although I hate to say it.'

'Well, I think it's time you changed your mind about affaires. I think you might like one.'

Nel picked up her spoon again and took another mouthful of the perfect marriage of cream and chocolate. It was the nearest thing to heaven this side of the pearly gates. Far, far, nearer than making love to Jake would ever get her. Another spoonful failed to convince her and she sighed.

'I think you need a brandy. Several brandies,' said Jake.

'No, I don't. I think we should talk about work.'

Chapter Fifteen

He sighed. 'OK, what do you want to nag me about?'

Nel chuckled. 'I don't want to nag you. I just want to talk about safe things.'

'I see. You don't want to talk about how attractive you are, and how foolish Simon is not to have got you down the aisle long since?'

'No!' she squeaked. 'Honestly! Anyway, what makes you think Simon wants to get me down the aisle?'

'The fact that he knows the internal measurements of your house, for one thing.'

'That's nothing! Estate agents like that sort of detail. Anyway, he knows I'm not interested in anything full time and permanent until the children have well and truly left home.' She frowned a little, hoping Simon did know this, and was not confusing Fleur's gap year travelling with her actually leaving home.

'Oh, why is that?'

He seemed genuinely interested, so Nel answered. 'I can't bear the thought of another man telling them off. I didn't even like it when Mark did it, and they were his children.'

'That's easy, you'll just have to find a man who won't tell them off. Anyway, they're practically grown up now.'

'Not easy, actually. In my experience all men are bossy, which means it's just as well I don't need one, and manage very well without.'

'You may be able to manage without but you're not doing it. You've got two men interested in you and one of them does DIY.'

She laughed, until the thought crossed her mind that Jake might very well make money out of making old people homeless and it cast a shadow on her enjoyment. But it was still only gossip. Could she challenge him about it? She ought to, but somehow, as he looked at her with his eyes alight with mischief, she found the words stuck in her throat. She did the best she could. 'And the other works for dubious projects, which involves desecrating places where children play. Sick children, some of them.'

'And who makes love to you without any prior warning, although, to be fair, I think that was pretty mutual.'

Nel was already fairly pink, but this made her blush more deeply. 'Jake!'

'I know, you don't want to talk about it. But you can't forbid me to think about it. Or to want to repeat the experience.'

He regarded her with a combination of desire and amusement, and, in spite of her best intentions, Nel's body responded. 'We can't! It's out of the question. I've explained!'

'Not to my satisfaction, actually. And I won't be gagged for ever. I'll give you a bit of time to think it over, but then I'll insist on talking about it.'

The waitress brought a glass of brandy and another of water. She put the brandy down in front of Nel, who had no recollection of drinks being ordered.

'You're not trying to get me drunk so you can have your evil way with me, are you?'

'No.' He held her eyes with his. He was smiling, mocking, almost, but he still made Nel swallow and look away. 'I promise you, when we next make love, which is how I prefer to describe it, you will be in full command' – he paused, with lethal emphasis – 'of all your senses.'

Nel looked hastily into her brandy, doubting if she would ever be in full command of her senses ever again.

'So, what have you been doing with yourself this last week?' he asked.

'I've been checking out potential stallholders for the farmers' market. And I saw Abraham.'

'Abraham? Oh, the builder.'

'Yes.'

'Has he got the Gideon Freebody plans still? For the proposed building?'

'Yes.'

'And did you get a good look at them?'

'Pretty much. Why do you ask?'

He looked straight at her; the smile had utterly vanished. 'I just think you should look at them. Thoroughly.'

She frowned. 'Why? Is there something about them I should know?' Did Jake know about the little strip of land outlined in a different colour? What was he trying to tell her?

Jake made a gesture with his hands. 'I can't actually say. It's confidential. But I do think you and Abraham should make sure you read those plans thoroughly. All research is interesting. And remember, where there's a will there's a way.'

'What?'

'Where there's a will, there's a way.' Jake was folding the gold foil from his mint into a ring and wouldn't meet her eyes.

Nel wondered if he'd been slipping extra alcohol into her wine. He might as well have been talking in code, the sense he seemed to be making.

'And remember, there *will* be an answer to your problems.'

'Jake! Are you talking nonsense, or are you trying to tell me something? If you are, could you make yourself a little clearer?'

'I've already said far too much. Would you like anything else? More brandy?'

'No, thank you. It's been lovely, really it has. Thank you so much. But I should go home now.'

'I really enjoyed it too, but I'm going to give you a little time to do your homework.'

'Homework? What are you talking about?'

'I want you to think very carefully about your policy on affaires and why you're so against having them. After all, if you can't have an affaire when you're single, when can you have one?'

'You do definitely have a point there. So you do have affaires?' She kept her tone light, but some part of her wanted to ask him about Kerry Anne, and this was the nearest she dared get.

'Only in the down time between wives.'

She smiled, although it wasn't the answer she wanted. 'How many wives have you had, Bluebeard?'

'Only one. But there were a couple of LTRs. I don't think I shall marry again.'

'Oh.' Her spirits descended by a further mile or two, unaccountably, as she certainly didn't want to marry him herself. She managed a smile. 'It's just as well I didn't have my eye on you, isn't it?'

'Absolutely,' he smiled. 'It's lucky I'm the wicked solicitor, with dubious morals, working for the bad guys.'

Nel nodded. 'That does pretty much sum it up.'

They didn't talk much on the way home. Anti-climax was already hitting Nel. She'd had a lovely time, but it wasn't real life. It was just a single, shining jewel among the pebbles. Life was mainly pebbles.

After an exhausting day – and a rather disconcerting evening – Nel expected to collapse straight into a deep sleep when she got home. But as soon as she fell into bed, she found herself annoyingly awake. Everything she and Jake had discussed went round and round in her head.

Could she trust him? Could he ever have anything to do with her real life? He was so terribly tempting, but there was so much she didn't know about him. And what was going on with that whole talking-in-code thing? Had she just been imagining it?

The answer came to her at about four o'clock in the morning. Jake had indeed been talking in code. He had been talking about wills. All that 'where there's a will' stuff had been to give her the hint. She needed to look at Sir Gerald's will. She'd ring Abraham in the morning and tell him. Finally she slept.

Because of her late night, she was still asleep when the phone rang irritatingly early the next morning. For once the dogs hadn't thundered on the kitchen door to be let upstairs and into Nel's bed, and she was in her deepest slumber. She picked up the phone. It was Simon. 'I just rang to see if you got home all right last night.'

She bit back an infuriated 'what on earth are you phoning me at this time in the morning for?' because she knew the reason. He was checking up on her. 'That's very kind of you. And I did. Did you?'

'Of course. I just wanted to make sure that man had got you home safely.'

'He's not still here, if that's what you're asking, Simon.'

'No, no! I wasn't suggesting—'

'Good, because it really is none of your business.'

'Isn't it? I thought we were going out together, Nel.'

Nel sighed, feeling his reproach. 'Yes, we are. I'm sorry, I'm really tired, and was just drifting back to sleep.'

'And I've disturbed you. I'm so sorry. But while I'm on, you must let me know if there's anything I can do to help with the farmers' market. I mean, have you thought about going through the *Yellow Pages*, and ringing up all the farmers in it?'

Nel's fuzzy brain couldn't think further than a cup of tea at that moment. 'No, I hadn't, and it sounds incredibly tedious, although it is a good idea.' She yawned.

'I'll do that for you,' said Simon. 'I'll go through them all, and ring them.'

That made her wake up. 'Simon! That would be amazing! Would you really do that?'

'Absolutely. I'm not sure I've been supportive enough over this whole thing. Last night, when I took Penny out to help her decide about her house' – these words seemed to be underlined – 'I thought perhaps I'm more supportive to clients than I am to you. Because that's all she was. Penny, I mean. She was a client.'

'It's all right. You told me at the time.'

'And you were just going out with Demerand because you wanted to ask him stuff about Paradise Fields?'

Nel hated Simon's habit of referring to people by their surname. It had a fake public school ring to it. 'Yes.'

'And did he tell you anything?'

'Not really.' Somehow she didn't want to tell Simon about his hints with regard to the plans now. 'But it was a useful meeting. I don't think I'm going to be writing minutes on it, though.'

Simon laughed. 'You funny old thing! I'll let you get your beauty sleep now, and ring you later.'

'Much later, please, Simon. After ten o'clock, anyway.'

She glanced at her watch and got out of bed. It wouldn't be too early to ring Abraham and tell him what Jake had told her. With luck, he would know how to find out what was in someone's will. He did.

'It's quite simple, you just ring up the Probate Office and they copy it for you. I had to do it for a friend a little while ago. They're very efficient.'

'And you think we'll be able to find out who owns that bit of land?'

'A nod is as good as a wink to a blind horse,' he said

mysteriously. 'It'll tell us what Sir Gerald left to who. You leave it to me. I'll get onto it.'

Cheered by Abraham's positive response she went back upstairs to dress, thinking that the previous evening had turned out to be really useful, even if that hadn't been her motive for going. Simon was going to make several hundred phone calls on her behalf, and she knew that Abraham was on the right track when it came to the plans. She glanced at her watch. While she decided what would be the most constructive next step, she might as well make lunch for Jamie and Fleur. She knew if presented with roast potatoes and gravy, Fleur, at least, would stay and eat, which seemed a priority at the moment.

When a completely blasé Fleur and a slightly shame-faced Jamie appeared, the kitchen was full of the smells of roasting meat, trays of roast potatoes and Yorkshire pudding hissed and crackled in the oven, and the windows were slightly steamed up. The place had a homely, lived-in look.

'Hi, you two. Hi, Jamie.' Nel smiled with relief at the nice, respectable-looking boy whom she might have hand-picked for her daughter. All that anxiety. 'I'm afraid you've missed breakfast, but lunch is just about ready. I'm making gravy.'

'Mum! Roast lunch! Beef or lamb?'

'Lamb. Catherine gave it to me; I had to freeze it but I'm sure it'll still be good. And don't worry, I've done Yorkshire puddings.'

'I think it's so unfair that you can't have Yorkshire pudding unless it's beef,' said Fleur to Jamie. 'So Mum always does them, whatever meat we're having.'

'I love Yorkshire pudding, but my mum's not very good at it,' said Jamie, looking at the tray of golden puffs of batter Nel was taking out of the oven.

'Oh, nor's mine,' said Fleur. 'She gets them out of a packet.'

'That's right, give away all my secrets. Now, be a love and set the table? What would you like to drink, Jamie? Orange juice, as it's your breakfast? Or wine, because it's lunchtime?'

Jamie looked at Fleur anxiously.

'Or would you like to start with orange juice, and then have a glass of wine?' Nel went on.

'That would be really nice, Mrs Innes,' said Jamie. 'If it's no trouble.'

'Oh, call her Nel,' said Fleur. 'Everybody else does.'

'Then let's sit down. It's a shame the boys aren't here. It would have been a family meal.'

'My mum thinks all this sitting down together as a family is too much like hard work and overrated, so we only do it for special occasions. Mind you,' she said a little reproachfully, 'Mum didn't warn me about this.'

'Darling, you can't really expect to invite Jamie for the weekend and not have at least one decent meal. What would his mother think?'

'Oh, she works full time,' said Jamie, 'so we have a lot of ready meals. I can cook quite well, and my dad.'

'Have another potato. I've done loads. And pints of gravy. And have you got brothers and sisters?'

'Don't give Jamie the third degree!'

'I'm not! I'm giving him roast potatoes!'

A couple of hours later when Jamie had insisted that he and Fleur do all the washing up, including (and thus earning himself a gold star) all the greasy tins, Nel shooed them out of the house to take the dogs for a quick walk.

Unable to settle to anything relaxing, she decided to clean the house and embarked on it with a thoroughness which irritated her. Cleaning was such a waste of time, she felt normally, it only had to be done again the next day. Now she did it for therapy, to help her think. But her thoughts were gluey and unconstructive, clogged with emotion. Her feelings, whatever they were, for Jake did not help. Even if he wasn't a crook she was pretty sure he wasn't interested in more than just an affaire, and Nel didn't have affaires. She was fairly certain about that. She wouldn't have considered having one while Mark was alive, and hadn't wanted once since.

The trouble was, she realised, she felt lust so rarely. There'd only been one, brief, holiday romance before Mark. Then there was Mark, and now there was Jake. Simon she liked, had liked for a while, possibly even loved, but she didn't react to him in the way she reacted to Jake. Sitting next to Simon on the sofa was cosy; sitting next to Jake on the sofa would be explosive. She wrung out her cloth and wished she'd put on rubber gloves. Her hands would need pints of Sacha's cream to recover.

She plunged them back into her bucket. But did you need that kind of inflammatory desire for a relationship? Or could gentler, more considered emotions develop into love and companionship of a lasting kind?

A huge spider fled from her scrubbing brush. 'Before Christmas I'd have said yes, definitely,' she said aloud. 'But now I know I can feel such passion, would I be happy without it?'

Early evening, exhausted, and the furniture only half put back, she rang Vivian. Talking to her about the new crisis with the fields would stop her thinking about her emotions for a little while. Emotion, like cleaning, was very wearing.

'Hi Nel! How are you?'

'I've been better, frankly. I haven't had a chance to get you up to speed, but the things I've found out about the building plans would make your hair curl.'

'My hair already does curl.'

'This is serious! Listen!'

'Oh shit!' said Vivian, a few minutes and several questions later. 'What can we do?'

'Nothing until Abraham finds out who owns that bit of land, then we can make a plan. In the meantime, I thought we could try convincing the Hunstantons that the new, bigger plan – the one involving the hospice land – is a really bad idea. We could start on Kerry Anne.' Nel did not sound enthusiastic. Her feelings for Kerry Anne vacillated between chilliness and downright hatred. 'Although personally, I'd rather not.'

'But what's the point of talking to Kerry Anne? She's not the organ grinder. We should be talking to Pierce.'

'Viv! I've just had the most fantastic idea!'

'What, you're going to seduce Pierce and make him give up his dreams of avarice?'

'No, you are!'

'Nel—'

'Oh come on, Viv. He's not that disgusting, and it would be in a good cause. Seducing him would be child's play for you.'

'Now listen, Mrs Innes, my number may be a bit higher than yours, but I'm not a slut. Mind you, your number's increased by fifty per cent recently, hasn't it?'

'Shut up.'

'Anyway, it would be completely unethical. I like sex but I'm not a home-wrecker.'

'No,' Nel said enthusiastically. 'Not "a" home wrecker! You'd wreck hundreds of them! Stop them ever being built!'

Vivian sighed. 'Very funny. I also think you're being defeatist. We were hoping to stop any building at all. So what is the point of getting the Hunstantons on side?'

'I may be wrong, but I think it would be easier to fight Pierce and Kerry Anne, individuals, than it would someone like Freebody who has probably done hundreds of similar schemes.'

'Nothing to do with a certain solicitor, is it?'

'No!'

'And have you heard from a certain solicitor recently?'

'Hardly! We only went out last night. I'll email his office to thank him. Simon brought me flowers this afternoon though!'

'Really? What's he feeling guilty about, then?'

'Nothing! He'd just made dozens of phone calls for me and brought the details round.'

Viv's response was a deep sigh. She was clearly un-impressed.

Chapter Sixteen

The following week, Nel was driving back from visiting a woman who made particularly unpleasant homespun bags, which Nel had resolved not to have anywhere near her market, however well the producer complied with the regulations, when she found herself near the pub where Jake had taken her to dinner.

Although she spent her whole time warning herself off him, she decided to indulge herself with a little sentimental detour. After all, in the years to come, it might be the little memories of their brief times together which would keep her going through the dark days and nights.

There were roadworks just by the pub, and while she waited at the temporary traffic lights she had a good opportunity to inspect the car park. She remembered him finding somewhere to park so she wouldn't have to step in a puddle. So thoughtful.

Then she saw his car. He was there! Her heart jumped and she half considered turning into the pub and finding him. She could make some excuse; if he was busy with clients she needn't speak to him, she could simply ask directions or use the loo and leave. Suddenly her need to see him again was overpowering. She was just looking in her rear-view mirror and regretting that the awkward entrance and the roadworks meant it would be better to go on to the next roundabout than to try and negotiate her way into the car park from here, when he came out. He was with Kerry Anne.

'Don't panic,' she told herself, perspiration already

forming at her hairline and down her back. 'Pierce will appear at any moment. It's just a business lunch, but maybe it'd be better not to go in.'

The traffic lights were still red. Now she urged them to change so she wouldn't be tormented by the sight of Kerry Anne and Jake together. She couldn't stop watching them. She saw him walk with Kerry Anne to another car – her car, apparently. So they hadn't come together. Was that significant? And where was Pierce?

Of course it must be just business. But three things arrived simultaneously in her mind and collided with bitter precision: the image of Kerry Anne flirting with Jake the first time Nel met her in his office; Simon's voice coolly telling her he had seen Jake and Kerry Anne having lunch; and the memory of the American voice on the telephone at Chris Mowbray's house.

Kerry Anne. Jake. Chris. Chris who was so keen on Gideon Freebody's plans. Jake who seemed so keen on Kerry Anne, who wanted to make as much money as possible out of her husband's inheritance. As the Hunstantons' solicitor, Jake was in a very good position to persuade Pierce and Kerry Anne that selling the land to Gideon Freebody was the best thing to do. If they sold to Abraham, or let Abraham develop the site, Gideon Freebody would get nothing. And if Jake was in league with Gideon Freebody, that would be the last thing he'd want.

Nel suddenly began to really sweat. She felt sick, and her head swam as if she was physically ill. Oh God, I am so stupid! She wanted to cry, not the sentimental tears which slipped out of the corners of her eyes several times a day, but the kind of racking, heart-tearing sobbing she hadn't done for a long time. Jake was making up to her, had seduced her, even, because she was the most engaged person on the board of the hospice. The other committee members, except of course Vivian, tended to follow Chris

Mowbray's lead. Chris must have been confident he could steer them towards Freebody, but not her. Jake had been primed to keep her quiet, so she wouldn't make waves.

Maybe she did always see the good in people, but she was not entirely stupid, she knew a rat when she saw one, knew when she'd been stitched up. She wiped her forehead in an agony of remorse and despair. For a moment, she felt she'd despoiled Mark's memory and their happy years together, allowing her senses to cloud her brain like that. She rubbed the space between her eyes with her finger fiercely, as if trying to erase what she had done.

Kerry Anne was now searching in her bag for keys. Jake took them from her and opened her car door. She turned to him, stood on her tiptoes and put her arms round his neck, pulling his head down so she could reach.

The car behind her alerted her to the fact that the light had gone green. He hooted, loudly, and stuck his head out of the window and shouted. She put the car in first gear and moved off, unable to see Jake's reaction. It was terrible, not knowing if he had responded to that tender, affectionate gesture.

But whether he did or not, this confirmed it. There was definitely something going on between Jake and Kerry Anne. She'd been mad to pretend to herself that there wasn't. Now she'd seen it, with her own eyes.

In some strange way it was a relief to know the worst. Her thoughts and dreams were all despoiled by the sight of that tall man leaning down to kiss a tiny, pretty, greedy woman, but at least she knew. She was out of her misery. She bit her lip to stop herself crying. If she cried she'd have to pull over and do it properly and she wanted to get home. *Out of one's misery*. Such a strange expression. What it really meant, in this case, is that she was tipped so deeply into her misery that she may never claw her way out of it.

*

217

Fleur was at home when Nel got there. 'Hi Mum, cup of tea?'

'Actually, darling, I think I need something stronger. Have we got any whisky? Burrow about behind the cornflakes and see what you come up with.'

Nel went into the sitting room and hauled the nearest spaniel onto her knee. There was nothing like a spaniel on your tummy for instant comfort. But at that moment it would take a whole Crufts' worth of spaniels to make a dent in her despair. Still, it was good to have Fleur to talk to, to be normal in front of.

'Simon rang,' called Fleur from the kitchen. 'I've found some. How do you like it?'

'In a glass. Very simple. What did Simon say?'

'Nothing much. He just wants you to ring him back.'

Nel groaned, more loudly than she'd intended. Recently even the thought of Simon made her feel as if she was pre-menstrual, edgy and irritated. Now she doubted if she could even be polite to him. Fleur came into the sitting room and handed Nel a glass. 'Don't you want to ring him back, then?'

'Golly, this is huge. No, don't take it away! I'll manage. I will call him back, but not now. I've had such a strange day. I think I'll ring Viv in a minute.' Nel didn't know if it was so she could tell Viv 'I told you so' or for a good bitch about life, men and Kerry Anne. Probably both.

'Well, Simon's got a newspaper cutting or something which he says might be useful for the anti-building campaign.'

Nel relaxed as the first sip of whisky reached her stomach. 'That's odd. I thought he knew the building was inevitable.'

'Mum! Surely not! Those are our fields!'

'I didn't know you cared! And no, they're not our fields, they belong to the Hunstantons, and they're putting houses on them.' Without the glimmer of hope that she had Jake in her life, this fact was even more unpalatable than ever. 'Now our project is to convince the Hunstantons to use our nice friendly builder, and not someone who apparently gives the ugly face of capitalism a bad name.'

'What on earth are you talking about?' Fleur perched on the arm of the sofa, holding a glass of water.

'There are two builders. One will re-roof the hospice for the cost of the materials and the other will put dozens of rabbit hutches up and leave us no river frontage.'

'Rabbit hutches would be quite sweet. I like rabbits.'

'Fleur!'

'It's all right. I know what you mean really.'

Nel sighed and closed her eyes. 'And if that wasn't bad enough, what I also suspect might happen is that we might lose the hospice building too. I've a horrid feeling that our chairman is planning to sell it to the builder – the bloated plutocrat one, not the nice one.'

Fleur nodded wisely. 'Tricky.'

Nel managed a weak smile. 'Which explains why I've turned to strong drink, and why I want to see Viv.' It wasn't the real reason, but she didn't want Fleur to know that.

Fleur had lost interest. 'I'm starving. Why don't you ask Viv round for a Balti? You could order it and she could pick it up. Save you cooking.'

Nel laughed, in spite of feeling so depressed. 'I thought you might like to knock us up a light, low-fat meal, full of free radicals and anti-oxidants?'

Fleur shook her head. 'I do pasta or pasta, nothing complicated.'

'Ooh! What with one thing or another, I don't think I told you! I met the most heavenly chef last week!' It was good to talk to Fleur about normal things. 'He's going to cook for the farmers' market. So sweet! He might even inspire you to lift a wooden spoon from time to time.'

'Mum! You're not thinking of having a toy boy, are you?'

'Of course not! As if!' said Nel, wondering how much younger a man had to be to qualify as such, and deciding Jake was far too dangerous to be thought of as a toy. She sighed again. Oh for the feel of his arms round her, just once more. This was all so painful. She gulped her whisky, so Fleur wouldn't hear her groan again.

Despairing of ever getting anything to eat, Fleur got up. 'Shall I get the phone and you can ring Viv? A girl could die of hunger round here.'

'You're very expensive to keep, you know, Fleur.'

Fleur grinned. 'Yes, but I'm worth it.'

Viv agreed to come, told Fleur what she wanted and Nel left the comfort of the sofa to attack the kitchen. The prospect of a girly evening with Viv and Fleur penetrated her misery a little. She had, after all, been perfectly happy before she met Jake. There was no earthly reason to think she couldn't go back to being happy. The phone rang while Nel was making preparations for the Balti, spreading sheets of newspaper over the plasticised table cloth, so it wouldn't get stained with turmeric-coloured ghee. She took the plates out of the oven before she answered it. It would be Simon, ringing back, and her heart clenched with guilt for not having invited him to join them. It was Jake.

Her mouth became instantly dry. 'Oh, it's you.' How could she even pretend to talk normally to him?

'Who where you expecting?'

'Simon.'

'Oh, I see.'

With an effort, she sucked some saliva into her mouth so she could speak. Supposing he'd seen her looking at him in the car park? It would be so humiliating. 'I really should have phoned you to thank you for dinner . . .'

'So why didn't you?'

'I haven't got your phone number.'

220

He laughed. 'That would explain it. Shall I give it to you?'

'Well, no, don't bother. I can thank you now, while you're on. Thank you so much for dinner the other evening. I really enjoyed myself. I hope you got my email about it.' Her voice sounded flat and artificial and she hoped he wouldn't hear. The last thing she wanted was for him to know how much pain he had caused her.

'Well, I'm glad about that. What are you doing now?'

'Viv's coming round with a Balti. We're going to discuss the hospice.'

'Oh, can I come?'

How many women did he need at one time? Kerry Anne at lunchtime – and it must have been a long lunch – her and Viv and Fleur this evening. 'No. It's girls only. And people who care about the hospice only.'

'I care about the hospice.'

But not quite as much as he cared about Kerry Anne. 'Not enough, otherwise you wouldn't encourage people to build on the land.'

'I'm not encouraging anyone, I'm just facilitating something which is bound to happen.'

'Call it what you like, you're still the enemy as far as the hospice is concerned.' She squeezed her eyes shut, hoping that it was only the Hunstantons he was facilitating, and not Gideon Freebody. Now that she was calmer, she had remembered his curious hints at dinner about the plans, and was very confused.

'So I won't come round, then?'

'Please don't.' Why didn't she – couldn't she – say 'no' firmly, and mean it? Why did she still want to see him, in spite of everything? 'Viv and I really have got work to do. The Balti is just to please Fleur.'

'Are you having onion bahjis?'

'I expect so, Fleur ordered it.' Although the conversation was really over and he might be the most devious, pernicious slug on the planet, she wanted to go on hearing his voice.

'I love bahjis.'

'Do you?'

'Nel, are you all right? You sound a bit odd?'

'Do I? I expect I'm just tired.'

'You were tired the other night, but you didn't sound like you do now.'

'Different sort of tiredness perhaps. Anyway, I've got to go now. Goodbye.'

'Mum! Was that Jake on the phone? Why were you so funny with him?'

'Like I said, I'm tired.' She turned away so Fleur wouldn't see that she was also close to tears.

She'd always known in her heart that Jake wouldn't give her a second glance if someone young and lovely came along. Now she'd had proof of it with her own eyes. And she'd lost her senses so completely, she'd gone to bed with him. Despair closed over her. She could imagine Chris Mowbray, the Hunstantons, Gideon Freebody, discussing the matter.

'She's the troublemaker,' Chris would have said. 'Take her to bed, Jake, get her eating out of your hand. She's over forty, she's a widow, she'll be grateful. You'll only have to do it once. It'll be worth it to keep her out of our hair . . .' The pain was like acid on her soul, that she, a fine, upstanding pillar of the community, mother to all the world, should have let herself be made love to (there was a shorter, harsher expression she couldn't bring herself even to think) by someone who was using her for his own purposes.

She would have poured herself more whisky, only Fleur was looking at her strangely and she didn't have time to drown her sorrows just then.

Viv arrived at that moment, laden with leaking plastic carrier bags, so she couldn't get even more depressed.

She'd have to wait until Fleur had gone to bed before she could confide in Viv, to tell her what she'd seen. And even the relentlessly positive Viv would find it hard to say something positive about that.

While Viv was getting past the dogs, who loved her a lot and so made it a time-consuming exercise, Nel had time to consider that even if he hadn't seduced her to keep her sweet and biddable, he was a very bright, attractive man, and his attention span was probably not very long when it came to women. He had probably suffered from Attention Deficit Disorder as a child. She couldn't expect to hold his interest for more than a few weeks. And she knew that feeling like that was nothing to do with her being over forty and a widow.

Over several thousand calories and several poppadoms, Nel and Viv discussed the hospice, Nel leaving out any reference to Jake. 'I can't say I'm very hopeful about things at the moment,' said Nel, aware that Viv was looking at her intently and feeling obliged to give her a reason for her despondency that Fleur would accept. 'I mean Christopher and the Hunstantons and Gideon Hardy and Willis, whatever his name is, are all in cahoots. I bet they know who owns that strip of land and have got it all sewn up. Do you want tea, or would you like another lager?'

'Tea, please—' Viv stopped as the doorbell rang. 'Expecting anyone, Nel?'

'If that's Jake,' said Nel crossly, tripping over the dogs in an attempt to get to the door, heart pounding in a pathetically girlish way, 'I'll kill him.'

'Why should it be?' called Viv. 'Have you been holding out on me?'

'Oh, hello, Simon,' said Nel. 'Was I expecting you? Did Fleur forget to give me a message?' She knew this was unfair. Fleur never forgot to give messages. (The boys frequently did.)

Simon shook his head. 'No, I just came round to give you another list of farmers out of the *Yellow Pages* who might be interested in becoming stallholders. People I couldn't get through to before. And also . . .' he paused. 'I thought you might be interested in this.' He waved a sheet of paper at her. 'I got it off the Internet.'

'Well, thank you very much for all the contacts, Simon. That's really kind. It must have taken you hours. You'd better come in.' She tacked on a smile of welcome, several seconds too late, and felt mean. He'd done all that work for her on Saturday and now, and she didn't even feel grateful, let alone behave gratefully. And Simon only wanted her for herself, not for anything else. 'Viv's here. We're just having a Balti and talking over hospice stuff.'

Simon came into the kitchen. Although he tried, he couldn't disguise his expression of disgust as he regarded the confusion of foil dishes, dirty plates, plastic bags exuding finely chopped lettuce and onion, broken poppadoms and bottles of lager.

'Hi, Simon,' said Vivian. 'Come in and get a plate, there's loads here.'

'No, thank you, I've eaten. I just came round to show Nel this. And you, I suppose.'

Nel took it between finger and thumb, but still managed to get ghee on it. 'Sit down, Simon, do,' she said.

It was a copy of an article from a local paper. She read it quickly. It was a report of a court case in which a builder and a solicitor were cleared of illegally demolishing a large old peoples' home so a housing estate could be built on the site. Nel couldn't bear to read every word; the gist was bad enough. Jake Demerand wasn't named, but there was a picture of him leaving court. It was blurry, but unmistakable.

'Let's have a look.' Vivian took it from her. 'It looks like Jake. Still. He got off.'

'I just thought Nel should see it,' said Simon. 'It could help her anti-building campaign.'

'It's not just Nel's campaign, Simon. All the hospice committee are against the building,' said Vivian. 'Our entire major fundraising goes on on that site. And we need waterfront access.'

'I think I'll make tea,' said Nel, wanting to get the subject off Jake and the hospice. 'Did I tell you? I met the most divine chef for the farmers' market the other day. He'll be perfect. And a wonderful chef, too.'

'You should watch out, Simon,' said Fleur. 'I think Mum may be planning to get a toy boy.'

'Think of it!' said Vivian. 'A man who's good in bed and cooks! There can't be a better combination.'

Simon shifted uneasily in his chair. Nel sighed. Vivian was too raunchy for Simon, and she was sure Viv did it on purpose. She could behave perfectly well, but when Simon was there, she always went out of her way to be shocking. Could she possibly ally herself to a man who didn't get on with her best friend? She couldn't do without her friend, that was for sure; no man on earth would be worth that.

'You don't know he's good in bed,' said Fleur, causing Simon even more embarrassment.

'Well, you might have to train him up a bit,' said Vivian. 'Give him a few pointers. But all that youthful energy, wow! And then some delicious little snack. Sounds perfect.'

'I'll give you his address,' said Nel, wishing she was in the mood for this sort of conversation. 'Now let's get back to the hospice.' She drained a bottle of lager, aware that Simon hated women who drank out of bottles. She wasn't that keen on it herself, in fact, but she had run out of glasses. 'What we're aiming for now, Simon, is to convince the Hunstantons to go with Abraham's plan, which will get the hospice reroofed, and not Gideon Whatsits', which by all accounts will be dreadful.'

225

Simon shook his head knowingly, making Nel feel more irritable than ever. 'I've been playing golf with Chris Mowbray lately, and he thinks the Hunstantons will be better off with the bigger builder.'

'Well, let's hope they're not taking their advice from him!' said Vivian briskly.

'They could do worse. He knows a lot about business investment.'

'So if you're all pally-pally with Chris Mowbray,' persisted Viv, 'why are you telling us stuff you think might stop the building?'

'Tea, anyone?' said Nel. She hated conflict at the best of times and now, when her heart was disintegrating, her threshold for it was lower than ever. She knew Viv didn't trust Simon.

Simon glanced at Nel. 'I just thought you ought to know, that's all.'

It was to do with Jake, realised Nel. It's his way of telling me he's a swine. Well, thank you, Simon, but I'd worked that out for myself.

'Did anyone else want tea, or is it just me?'

'I'll have a Women's Tea,' said Vivian, 'if you've got any. I need something powerful. I'd be on the whisky if I wasn't driving.'

'Simon?'

'I'm not drinking that witches' brew you and Viv seem so fond of, but I'll have a cup of coffee. Instant is fine.'

'Oh, good,' murmured Nel to herself, 'because that's all there is. Fleur?' she said louder. 'Want anything made out of hot water?'

'No, thanks, Mum, I'll stick to lager.'

'Isn't it a school night?' asked Simon. No one took any notice. 'You mustn't mind too much about the building. People need homes, Nel.'

'I know that. And people are going to get homes. It's just the right ones we want,' said Nel, dunking tea bags,

226

badly wanting to go upstairs and have a good cry. 'So why, if we all accept that Paradise Fields are going to be built on, are you dishing the dirt on Jake Demerand?' She hadn't meant to say that. It was probably the whisky making her say things she would regret.

'He's just a bit too much of a smooth operator for my liking. I was telling Kerry Anne . . .'

'What?' demanded Vivian. 'What were you telling Kerry Anne?'

'That Demerand might not be the best solicitor for them.'

'I'm a bit confused,' said Fleur.

'Serves you right for drinking lager on a school night,' said Viv.

Fleur ignored her godmother. 'You come round here with something off the web for Mum, to help her with the campaign, and then tell her you think the Hunstantons have got the wrong solicitor. Surely that's a good thing, if she doesn't want a housing estate on Paradise Fields.'

Simon laughed. 'That wasn't quite what I meant, Fleur. The fields have had planning permission for years. There's no way you can stop that now.'

Fleur was enjoying arguing with Simon when no one could legitimately stop her. 'I'm sure we could if we tried hard enough. Dug ourselves in, like Boggy, or whatever his name is.' She retrieved Simon's bit of paper from the aloo gobi. 'Now, how can this help us?'

'I don't think it can,' said Nel, passing out mugs. 'If we prove to the Hunstantons that their solicitor was involved in a dodgy deal, they'll just get another solicitor—'

'And the next one might not be quite so attractive,' put in Vivian, unhelpfully.

'—so it won't make any difference,' Nel finished.

'The problem is, we none of us know what the Hunstantons are likely to do,' said Vivian, sipping her tea. 'We none of us know them, really.'

227

'Chris does,' said Simon. 'He's getting to know them. I reckon he'll talk them into making the right decision.'

'Right as far as you're concerned,' said Fleur. 'I suppose being an estate agent, you're bound to want more houses to sell.'

Nel frowned at her. Being a free spirit was one thing, being rude another.

'Well, I don't think we should be discussing what is basically hospice business outside the committee,' said Vivian, who would usually have been willing to discuss anything, anywhere, if the gossip was juicy.

'Quite right,' said Nel, beginning to gather up the detritus of the meal. She wanted everyone out of her house so she could think.

They all seemed to start talking at once. Nel tuned out of the argument, too downcast to know what she felt about anything just now.

'Tired, Nel?' asked Simon a little later.

Viv and Fleur were stacking the dishwasher and Nel had gone into the sitting room, ostensibly to gather up any mugs and glasses, but in fact to get a bit of peace. Nel wasn't really pleased to have been followed, but she didn't have the energy to stop Simon taking her into his arms.

'A bit,' she mumbled into his jacket. 'I've had a really busy day.' She tried to pull away, but he wouldn't let her.

'Let me make it better,' he breathed and made as if to kiss her.

She convulsed in his arms and moved her mouth out of reach. Not today; she couldn't cope with his lovemaking today. 'I'm sorry, Simon. I'm not in the mood.'

'I just thought we ought to be thinking about our future, with Fleur nearly off your hands . . .'

She disengaged herself. She didn't like him talking about Fleur as if she was some sticky substance to be removed with a special cleaning product.

'I'm sorry,' he went on, putting his hands on her shoulders. 'I've rushed you. You need more time to think. But I want you to know my feelings for you. When all this hospice business is over, I'll take you away somewhere, for the weekend, and remind you of . . .'

'Of what? What will you remind me of?'

He laughed, to show her he knew he was being teased and didn't mind. 'I'll remind you that you're a woman, with womanly needs.'

Nel retreated a few steps and sat down on the sofa. 'Womanly needs' sounded like sanitary protection or vaginal deodorant. 'I'm sorry. I'm being awfully unresponsive. I suppose I'm too taken up with the hospice and the farmers' market to think about anything else.'

Viv came in. 'It's all a bit better in there now, so I'll push off and leave you two lovebirds to watch the news together.'

Nel got up quickly. 'But I haven't paid you for the Balti!'

'My treat. Don't bother, honestly.'

'No, really.' Nel pushed Viv towards the door. 'I'll get my bag. I've got things I must talk to you about,' she added when they were out of Simon's earshot.

'What is it?' asked Vivian in a stage whisper.

'Oh, just something I saw. It's probably not important . . .'

'It's obviously important to you. Come over tomorrow and talk about it.'

'You're not doing anything to the bees, are you? I don't need any extra stress.'

'No! I'll just be at home. I haven't got any appointments until the afternoon. Now you go and get cosy with Simon on the sofa.'

'You never used to encourage me to do that.'

'I now know that you're out of danger. Anyone who's slept with Jake is not likely to lower her standards to Simon.'

'Viv! I'll be around at about nine. I've got a whole list of calls to make later, but I'll have to take the dogs out first.'

When Nel went back into the sitting room, Simon was ensconced on the sofa, doing as Viv had implied he would be, watching the news. He patted the seat next to him. 'Come and sit down. It's cosy sitting here, watching television.'

Nel didn't much like the news. She found it distressing and she couldn't do anything about it. It was why her television viewing tended to be what other people considered rubbish, and her life full of helping others.

She sat by Simon and closed her eyes, allowing his arm to go round her shoulders, even though it meant she couldn't sit comfortably.

'This is nice,' said Simon. 'I could get used to this. You and me, together, in front of the television in a companionable way. After all, we're too old for passion, don't you think?'

Nel closed her eyes. Perhaps she was too old for passion. Perhaps passion was unhealthy for the over-forties. Perhaps she'd better just let Simon move in and forget about Jake. Irritatingly, a tear forced its way past her tightly closed lids. She sniffed.

Chapter Seventeen

꧁※꧂

'So, what is it you couldn't tell me last night?' said Viv, opening the door. 'In front of Simon.'

Nel took time to greet Hazel, Viv's little whippet, who came and stayed with Nel and her dogs so often she was practically one of the family. 'You like to cut to the chase, I must say!' she complained. 'No, "Hello, Nel, have a cup of tea," or anything.'

'Hello, Nel, have a cup of tea or anything, and then for God's sake tell me what was making you so odd last night.'

'Was I odd? I was probably drunk. I drank half a tumbler of whisky when I got home.'

'You weren't drunk, honey, but you were on edge. Come and tell Aunty Viv everything.'

They went into the kitchen, which was everything Nel wished her kitchen to be, only smaller. The cupboards were natural wood below, and glass fronted above. In the cupboards the glasses and bowls were arranged either in rows or piles. The matching china mugs hung on hooks beneath. The work surface itself, also natural wood, shone with beeswax polish and was uncluttered by anything except an Alessi kettle and a Dualit toaster. Even Viv's washing-up accoutrements were stylish and elegant. A beautiful wooden bowl full of fresh fruit sat on the circular kitchen table, but that was all. Where Viv opened her post, paid her bills, read the paper and did the crossword puzzle, Nel didn't know, but it obviously wasn't where she herself performed all those activities.

231

'Sit down. Let me make you some juice,' said Viv. 'You need a pick me up, not caffeine. What would you like? Apple and mango is nice. Perhaps with some carrot?' Viv extracted a juicer from a cupboard and set it on the side.

'Do you want me to peel the carrot?' asked Nel from the table, wondering, not for the first time, how Vivian managed to be so tolerant of Nel's chaotic lifestyle when her own was so ordered.

'Nope. It's all ready in the fridge. So what gives?'

'Lots of things really. I know for a fact that there's something going on between Kerry Anne and Jake.'

'You can't know that! Unless you've seen them with your own eyes—'

'I have! She was kissing him. She had her arms round his neck and he was bending down to her.'

'What did he say when he saw you? How did he behave? Was he guilty? Embarrassed?'

'He didn't see me. I was in the car coming back from a dreary woman who weaves – possibly her own hair – and I saw them in the car park of the pub where he took me to dinner.'

'Oh.'

Nel sighed. 'Bloody men! You think that place would be sacrosanct, wouldn't you?'

Vivian shook her head. 'I'm afraid they would just think it was a good place to eat and read nothing more into it than that.'

'Well, now I know he slept with me for underhand reasons.'

'Now why do you say that? Even if you're right about him and Kerry Anne—'

'I did see them together, Viv.'

'But what could his ulterior motive be? I don't understand what you're getting at.'

'To keep me quiet! I mean, who, of all the committee,

apart from you, is most likely to make waves, to protest, to argue with Christopher about selling the hospice land?'

Viv looked unconvinced. 'Muriel can be quite feisty,' she joked.

'Well, he's not going to sleep with Muriel, is he! She's well over seventy and has two plastic hips!'

'There's me.'

'Of course, and I'm sure you would have been his first choice.'

'So, if he didn't fancy you like mad, why didn't he sleep with me? I feel quite insulted!'

'Because, airhead, you obviously have a full and satisfying sex life! You're not a widow, overweight, over forty, desperate, and therefore grateful.'

Viv shook her head. 'I'm quite sure you're wrong.' She pressed a button and reduced a carrot to liquid.

'I'm not making it up. I did see him with Kerry Anne, and – did I tell you? – when I was at Chris's, trying to see the deeds, Kerry Anne rang up. So unless she's having an affaire with Chris too, that more or less proves there's something going on between Chris and the Hunstantons.'

'I admit that if you had Jake you wouldn't want Chris.' A couple of apples shared the fate of the carrot.

'Personally, I'd rather die childless than have anything to do with Chris.'

'So you're not that desperate then.'

'No one could be that desperate. The thought of him – touching me – it's positively revolting.'

Viv wiped a knife round a mango, separated the halves, and then scored one half and turned it inside out so it looked like a hedgehog with squared-off prickles. 'It's a strange thing. The thought of someone you fancy doing stuff can be so lovely, and the thought of someone you don't doing exactly the same stuff can make you want to heave.' Another swoop with her knife, a burst of hideous noise, and the cubes were history.

Nel sighed, watching as Vivian poured most of the contents of the jug into a glass.

'Here, drink that.'

Nel sipped gratefully. 'This is delicious. I'd make things like that, only I can't face having to wash the juicer.'

'It's no trouble if you do it straightaway.'

'I'm sure. But I wouldn't do it straightaway. Something would stop me. And the children would eat the mangoes.'

'The joy of living alone. So, we think we know there's something unsavoury going on between Jake and Kerry Anne: most unethical. So do we think he is unethical in other ways?'

'We don't think, we practically know! There was that thing Simon got off the Internet. If he is working secretly for Gideon Freebody, the Hunstantons are hardly getting impartial advice!'

'Have you brought the cutting with you?'

'No, it got covered in ghee, I had to throw it away.'

Vivian carried her own glass of juice to the table and sat down. 'And we think Chris Mowbray has something to do with them too, which means that the hospice only has us, and Muriel, to protect it.'

'Otherwise, if Chris and that other man on the committee have their way, the hospice building will be pulled down, and houses built on the site.'

'And however much money we got for it, it would never be enough to build from new, it never is. It's why ancient buildings can never get insurance. That juice really is delicious,' added Nel. 'It would help if we knew how Abraham was getting on researching the will. If we knew for certain who owned it we'd be in a much stronger position. I suppose we just have to wait until he gets the copy of the will.'

'So what are we going to do?'

'Well, if I'm right, and Christopher is dishonest and devious, we'll have to think what he will do, and have a plan ready.'

'The legal side of it could be very tricky. I don't suppose we could get Jake to help us?'

'Not exactly! Not when we more or less know he's dishonest.' Nel put her elbows on the table and rested her head in her hands.

Viv patted her shoulder. 'Oh, love!'

'No, no, I'll be fine. I'm just thinking.' What she was thinking was how terribly hard it was to concentrate when one's heart, if not actually breaking, was seriously damaged.

'I still think you might be wrong about Jake, you know.'

'Viv, I saw him—'

'You saw Kerry Anne kiss him. It could have just been an innocent peck on the cheek. Everyone kisses everyone these days.'

'You don't need to tell me that,' said Nel, head and arms still propped on the table. 'Bloody mistletoe!'

Vivian shrugged. 'It was Christmas. He fancied you.'

'I don't think so, Viv. Think about it. Why should he pick me? Why not just buy the mistletoe and leave? Because someone had told him that I'm on the fundraising committee of the hospice. They may even have said I have a certain amount of influence.' She paused. 'Don't laugh. I do know a lot of people, and while we don't have a director, the hospice is in a vulnerable position. Perfect for someone to make a killing with.'

Vivian ran her finger up the side of her empty glass. 'I still don't see that you would be worth seducing for your contacts, however many people you know. Besides, why should Jake do that? He's working for the Hunstantons.'

'Yes, but if he and Gideon Freebody, and Chris Mowbray and whoever, are planning something dreadful, who better to set it up than Jake? He's perfectly placed to convince the Hunstantons to go with Gideon Freebody. And, if they need the committee to sell him the hospice's land, to get me eating out of his hand, sleep with me, make me fall in love with him' – a pain so sharp it could almost have been caused by an actual weapon stabbed her in her solar plexus – 'so I won't make waves.'

'Have you fallen in love with him, Nel?' Vivian whispered her question.

Nel bit her lip and nodded. 'Guess so. I don't know what other condition makes you feel like I do.'

'Falling in love should make you happy.'

'But not in this case. Oh, it did make me happy to begin with, when all I had to worry about was making Simon unhappy, not that I did worry about it much. But now! It sucks, Viv! I don't know what to do with myself, although keeping busy does help. I do nothing but think about him. I hate him, but I can't put him out of my mind. It's like being in a nineteen-fifties science fiction movie.'

'What?'

'You know, when your brain is taken over by aliens, you look the same on the outside, but inside you're just a mess of snakes.'

'Oh, love!'

'But back to practicalities. What are we going to do?'

'Well, worst-case scenario, Jake slept with you because he wanted something, he might find he has to sleep with quite a lot of people, including Muriel.'

'Hang on, I've just remembered something. When Jake took me out to dinner he hinted I should try and get a good look at the will. What was that all about?'

'Nel, love, make up your mind. Either he's an arch criminal or a gorgeous solicitor but he can't swing both ways.'

'Why not? Heaps of people are double agents.'

'Not exactly heaps.' Viv glanced at her friend and, realising Nel was suffering from logic failure, got back to the matter in hand. 'We have to come up with a plan. You know, in some ways it's good this has all happened now, when you're so busy. You haven't time to be broken-hearted.'

'Yes, except it's like when I got married to Mark.'

'I'm not slow, but I do find you hard to follow sometimes, Nel.'

Nel sighed. 'I kept thinking, I wouldn't be going through all this wedding thing if it wasn't for Mark. And then I thought, I wouldn't have to go through all this wedding business if it wasn't for Mark.'

'And your point is?'

'Oh, I don't know. My mind is a mess of snakes.' She frowned. 'I've just had a thought.'

'Is that a good thing?'

'In judo you make your opponent's weight work against them.'

'And that's relevant how?'

'If Chris Mowbray and Jake hatched up this plan ages ago, Chris must think I have influence with the hospice.'

'I have my doubts about that, to be honest,' said Vivian, but not unkindly.

'But I don't think it's my influence in particular. I expect Chris believes you're influential too, but they probably decided I was the softer target. You obviously have a full and varied love life. Unlike me.'

Vivian sighed, clearly debating whether to bring out her usual lecture on how Nel was a very attractive woman, or to say that actually, her sex life was very discreet. 'I wish you wouldn't think of yourself like that. And I may be getting plenty elsewhere, but I wouldn't have turned Jake down if he'd tried it on.'

'Wouldn't you?'

'No. He is very attractive. Very attractive indeed.'

'So you don't think I'm a complete idiot for succumbing?'

'No! But we do need to focus. What do we think Christopher's next step would be?'

'Well, he knows I wanted to look at the deeds, so he may suspect I know more than I should. He fobbed me off, but I expect he'll call a meeting. He'll want to nail this before I think of a way to stop him.'

'We could call a meeting ourselves. Pre-empt him, tell the committee what we know,' suggested Vivian.

'We could, but it would be easier if he called it. For a start, he's used to calling them, and no one will think it odd if he does. And for a second, if we call one, he'll know for certain we're on to him.'

'True. But supposing he comes out into the open, puts the plans for the building scheme and everything that entails – selling the hospice land to Gideon Freebody – on the table, and the committee vote to go along with it? It would look very appealing. No more worry about keeping up the building, no more wretched fundraising, cash for brand-new premises at some point. It will save everyone so much work.'

'What he will have to do is convince people it won't matter about the hospice not existing for a couple of years,' said Nel. 'Have you got a pad and a pencil? I need to scribble.'

Vivian produced them from the first drawer she looked in.

'Everything in its place, eh?' Nel said wistfully. 'My worry is, among other things, that there is no intention to rebuild the hospice, that the money would quietly filter away into Chris Mowbray etc.'s pockets.'

Vivian sighed. 'We do need professional legal advice. I know, not from Jake, obviously, although I'm sure you're wrong about him.'

'Viv! I saw him with Kerry Anne. And he was in that picture! I know cameras lie all the time, but they don't if they don't set out to.'

'OK, so we need to lobby. We need to think who on the committee would be on our side, and produce our own plan.' Vivian gathered up the glasses and then started washing her juicer.

Nel picked up the pencil and began to doodle.

Viv looked over her shoulder at her. 'When you said scribble, I didn't know you meant it literally.'

Nel ignored her. 'Wait a minute. I've had a thought!'

'Another one,' Viv said sarcastically.

'Hang on, let me spell it out. I need to get it clear in my mind. If what Abraham says is right, and Gideon Freebody wants to build as many houses as possible, then he'll need to pull down the hospice building.'

'Yes. There did seem to be an awful lot of houses when I saw the plans for that tiny minute.'

'But he needs that strip, because without it he can't get to hospice land. There's no point in pulling down the building without it.' Nel thought for a moment. 'No one seems to know who owns that strip—'

'That's why Abraham's digging up the will,' Vivian interrupted. 'The will must say who the land's been left to.'

'Yes, that's what I mean,' Nel carried on excitedly. 'Sir Gerald told me before he died that he'd made provision for us, that the hospice would be safe. So what if *we* own the strip? What if that's what he was talking about? He's bequeathed the hospice a ransom strip to protect it.'

'But surely the hospice committee would know if it had been left some land,' Vivian objected.

'Not necessarily. As we don't have a proper director at the moment, the solicitors would just have to tell Chris Mowbray. And if we're right about his interest in the building plans, it's not the sort of information he'd be likely to pass on.'

Vivien paused. 'But the hospice owns the house. What's the difference?'

'The difference is, we could sell the strip! To other people! We divide it into tiny pieces and sell them off, one by one! That way, Chris Mowbray has no control over it, and can't persuade the committee to sell it to Gideon Freebody!'

'How do we stop Chris Mowbray – or Gideon – buying them all himself?'

Nel frowned. 'We make them quite expensive – we'll need to find out how much we could reasonably charge. We could ask Simon.'

Vivian dried her hands, came over and put her hand on Nel's wrist. 'I know this is going to sound really horrible, but could we *not* ask Simon? I know you trust him with your life, but I just feel . . .'

'You've never liked him.'

'I have tried. And I will go on trying. And if you marry him I'll try really, really hard! But could we not tell him our plans at this stage?'

Nel sighed. 'He is the obvious person to ask about property values, but if you feel that strongly, we'll find someone else.'

'There must be loads of people we could ask. I wonder if we could make it that you were only allowed to buy one bit each?'

'Good idea! Only, of course, it would mean having to find lots more people to buy bits. I wonder how many we'd need. Or how we should work it out.'

'You mean, should we divide the land into a certain number of sections and sell them, or should we calculate how many we're likely to sell and then divide it.'

Nel nodded. 'I wish I was better at maths.'

'Are your boys any good at it?'

Nel brightened up. 'Actually, yes! Sam's very good at that sort of thing. Takes after Mark. I'll get him to come down next weekend. It'll cost me the train fare, but that would be a good investment.'

'If we go into the meeting really well prepared, knowing who's on our side, we'll be fine. God, this is all assuming we own the strip. I hope Abraham finds something concrete soon. What else have you got on today?'

'Well, I've got to see the ice-cream maker I had to take a rain check on the other day. What about you?'

'I've got a—' She stopped as the phone started ringing. 'I'll just get that. With any luck it's my afternoon client cancelling, which means we could make a proper plan and perhaps start lobbying. Hello! Oh, Chris.'

Nel watched in horror as her friend confirmed with her expression that it was Chris Mowbray she was talking to.

'A meeting? Why?'

It was far too soon. They were no way ready to go into a meeting and take on the committee.

'The twenty-seventh?' said Vivian. 'But that's only a week away. Yes. I can make it. It just seems rather short notice. What's it about? The building on the fields?' She made desperate faces at Nel, to make sure she was listening. 'But what's it to do with the hospice? Oh, all right. See you then, then.'

'What did he say when you asked him what the building has got to do with the hospice? What's the official line?'

'He said he'd tell us at the meeting.'

'Oh my God!' said Nel. 'He must have something he thinks we'll swallow. And what can we do in a week? I can't even remember the names of all the committee, let alone work out if they'd be on our side or not.'

'If we just think carefully, we can work out quite a few.'

'We can rely on Muriel,' said Nel. 'What about Father Ted?'

'He's not called Father Ted, it's Ed.'

'I've got an appalling memory for names.'

'You should take some of the supplements I take. It would really help.'

Nel put her elbows on the table and rested her head in her hands again. 'Are we just bailing out the boat with a teaspoon when the waves are coming in over the bow?'

At Vivian's frown she went on, 'I mean, are we just thinking of who we can get to raise their hands at a committee meeting, when in fact we should be doing something much more major?'

'Like what?' Viv produced a snow-white dishcloth and wiped away a tiny spot of juice off the table.

'Like convincing Pierce he'd do better out of Abraham than he would out of Gideon Hardy and Willis.'

'But he won't, will he!'

'Well, maybe not. But if Abraham builds very lovely, expensive houses, it might be a lot nicer for Pierce to look at,' said Nel. 'That would work for me.'

'I don't think your priorities are quite the same as Pierce's. You realise if they're going to reveal their real intentions, the Hunstantons will probably be there, and invite Jake too. How will you feel about that?'

'OK! Now the scales have fallen from my eyes, I'll know him for the snake he is.'

'You may have got your metaphors a bit mixed there.'

Nel shrugged. 'We'll divide the committee members into two lists and take half each. I'll get as many promises to buy bits of land as I can . . . There's one person you have to do, though, Viv.'

'Who?'

'Pierce Hunstanton. You need to convince him that he really doesn't want a whole huge housing estate on his doorstep, however rich it would make him. It's perfectly possible he doesn't know everything that Gideon Freebody has in mind.'

'Let's face it, Nel, we don't know anything that he has in mind. It's all speculation.'

'But it might be true. And you need to convince Pierce—'

The phone rang again. 'Blast it! Who is it this time?' Viv snatched the receiver from the wall. 'Hello!' she said crossly. Then her expression changed. She didn't speak,

242

she just made little whimpers. Then she said, 'Fine. I'll be there in an hour,' and put the phone down. 'It's Mum! That was her neighbour. She's fallen over and is in hospital.'

'Oh Viv! Poor Florence! How is she?'

'The neighbour's not sure. I'm going there now to pick up some things and go and visit her.'

'I'll bring up those books I promised her. Where is she?'

'Just the local hospital, thank goodness.'

'Then it can't be too bad. Anything remotely serious and they take them into the Royal.'

'That's true. But I'm afraid it means I won't be able to—'

'Talk to the committee and see Pierce. That's OK. I'll do it.'

'Will you remember everyone's names?' As she talked, Vivian was going through her cupboards, finding packets of biscuits, homoeopathic remedies and various health foods. She filled a plastic carrier with fruit.

'I'll manage. Now will you be all right? Do you need me to come with you?'

'I shouldn't think so. I'll ring you if things are really bad. Poor Mum! It's the first time anything like this has happened. It'll knock her confidence terribly. Now, have I got everything?'

'Shall I take Hazel with me? In case you're late?'

The little whippet, hearing her name, looked up with dark, anxious eyes at her mistress.

'That would be a good idea. I can come and pick her up later, but she'll have company, and you can feed her.'

'Yes, but not on tripe. I can't stand the smell.'

'It's so good for them!'

'I know. But it makes me vomit.'

'Well, you're lucky I haven't got any defrosted then. Come on now. I'll lock the door.'

'Viv, I think you've forgotten something.'

'No, I haven't. I'll get most of the stuff from Mum's house.'

'You've got your appointment book with you then?'

'No! Why should I need that?'

'So you can cancel your afternoon client?'

Vivian banged her forehead. 'Oh God! How could I have forgotten!'

'I can recommend some really good supplements . . .'

Chapter Eighteen

Nel gathered up her little extra passenger, the passenger's coats, her bed and her toys, and took her home. It was only when the other dogs had finished greeting her, and when they were all settled in a heap in front of the Rayburn that she noticed her answerphone flashing.

There was a certain amount of muttering and throat clearing before a voice said, 'Sorry you're not there to talk to lass, and I've got to go out myself, but I thought you'd like to know that the copy of the will's arrived, and the hospice do own that ransom strip! Sir Gerald bequeathed it . . .'

Abraham was cut off before he could finish, but he'd said enough. It was brilliant news! Nel danced round her kitchen shouting 'Yes' a few times before the dogs' silent reproach made her calm down. It was too exciting to keep to herself. Even though Vivian was having a crisis, Nel decided to ring her. It might cheer her up a bit.

She got her on her mobile.

'Viv! Love! Sorry to bother you when I know you're so busy, but I had to tell you! There was a message from Abraham when I got back! The strip is ours! Sir Gerald left it to us in his will!'

'Oh that's fantastic!'

'I can't believe it, it's such good news!' Nel was still jigging up and down as she spoke on the phone.

'But you need to convince Pierce that he should let Abraham be his builder, and not bloody old Gideon Freebody. Or we'll lose access to the river.' Vivian, stuck in traffic, and worried about her mother, was less euphoric.

Hearing this in her voice, Nel said, 'How are things there?'

'Well, obviously I haven't seen Mum yet. I'm just on my way to the hospital, but this is such good news. It'll give me something nice to tell her. Provided we can win over the rest of the committee—'

'We wouldn't have to win them all over, even – I think seventy-five per cent would do—'

'Oh, I must go. The lights have changed. Speak to you later!'

It took Pierce Hunstanton quite a long time to be persuaded to see Nel, partly because he didn't remember who she was, and partly because, when he'd finally placed her, he assumed she would be haranguing him about the buildings.

Nel decided to meet him in the local wine bar. Their appointment was for six. She knew she would have spent all day touring the county signing up not only farmers interested in coming to the market, but people willing to buy unspecified amounts of land for an unspecified price. Alcohol would be necessary, and she could walk home if she had to. She also knew most of the bar staff and felt at home there. Although she was buoyed up by the knowledge that the hospice owned the vital strip of land, she wanted to persuade Pierce to pick the right builder, and his and his wife's greed might encourage him to do otherwise.

She had already finished her first white wine spritzer when her quarry arrived, so she didn't refuse his offer of another one. Of course it was bad to use alcohol as a prop, but she needed props. Having right on your side wasn't always enough.

'Is that with water, or with lemonade?'

'Water, please. I'm trying to reduce the calories, not add to them.'

He gave the kind of smile used by people who didn't have much sense of humour, were aware this was a bad thing, and so smiled whenever there was a pause in the conversation, which was sometimes quite the wrong place. How he'd managed to inherit none of his father's considerable charm was a mystery and a shame. There was a faint family likeness, but as Pierce Hunstanton came back to the table with the drinks, Nel cursed the bit of water on Vivian's mother's kitchen floor. Had she not slipped on it, she wouldn't be in hospital, being tended to by her daughter, and her daughter would be here, flashing her cleavage and making little fluttery gestures with her hands. Vivian was so lovely, and so confident, she could have had Pierce Hunstanton eating out of her hand in moments. Nel had to depend on being kind and friendly and smiling a lot, and while this method had sold a lot of raffle tickets in the past, she wasn't sure if it was quite what was required to persuade Pierce Hunstanton that he only wanted a small fortune, not a huge one.

With a flash of genius brought about by panic, she remembered a Theatre Studies essay she had helped Fleur with. It was about Method Acting, and said you had to live your role. If Nel pretended she was Vivian she might become like Vivian and thus be charming and persuasive and sexy. The sexy part was important, she decided, because everyone knew that sex sold, and Nel wanted to sell her plans to Pierce.

'It's terribly kind of you to see me,' she cooed when she'd taken a sip of her drink. 'Kerry Anne not with you?'

'She's in London. Due back tomorrow. Now what is it you wanted to see me about, Mrs Innes? I'm sure I don't need to tell you I'm a busy man.'

'Nel, please.' She laughed, she hoped warmly. 'I'm only

ever called Mrs Innes at school. I'll think you're referring to my mother-in-law, who's been dead for years. The thing is,' she went on in a more businesslike way, realising the reference to her dead mother-in-law had probably been a mistake, 'I've come to ask you something.'

'Oh, why?'

'What do you mean, why?' Nel forgot to be Viv and frowned. He was supposed to say, 'What?'

'What have you come to ask me? I know you're against the fields being built on, and I fully intend to build on them. What can you possibly have to say?' He cleared his throat. 'If you've come to say you've discovered some wildflower or rare bug or some such on the land, don't tell me about it, tell the relevant authorities.' He laughed again, although why, Nel couldn't imagine.

She stopped trying to be anyone other than herself. 'No, no, it's nothing like that! In fact, I'm not against the building plans any more. At least, not all of them.'

'What? What on earth has happened to make you change your mind! You were rabid!'

'I was not rabid, but I've come to see that building on that land is more or less inevitable.' She shifted her glass around on the beer mat. 'It's just what kind of development might be there that I want to discuss.'

'I fail to see what on earth it has to do with you.'

'I do live very near those fields. The development will affect everyone in the area. Which is why I think it behoves you—'

'What?'

'Obliges you to choose the least invasive option. Don't you think?' she added, to make what she'd said seem less threatening and more appealing.

He frowned and ruffled his hair in a confused way and it occurred to Nel that he looked rather like Hugh Grant, minus a few of his brain cells and all of his sex appeal. 'Well, there's a turn-up for the books. I thought you were dead against any sort of building, going on what Chris Mowbray told me.'

Nel smiled, to stop herself seething audibly. 'Chris Mowbray doesn't know me as well as he thinks he does.'

'Well, that's good. I mean that you're not against the building completely.'

Nel smiled again, aware it was possible that she might have picked up Piece's habit of smiling at inappropriate moments; her own sense of humour seemed to be leaching into the vacuum of his missing one. 'I wonder if you've really thought about what it's going to be like, looking at all those little houses, having them interrupting your view of the river.' She didn't mention the executive housing, because that would still be there with Abraham's plan.

'Oh it won't do that, not from the penthouse.'

Nel tried again. 'But the noise, Pierce, screaming children, chainsaws, lawn mowers, it'll be terrible in summer when you've got the windows open.'

'We don't plan to spend much time down here. Kerry Anne's family live in America.'

'And she sees a lot of her family?' From Nel's point of view, Kerry Anne couldn't see enough of her family unless she actually went to live with them.

'Oh yes. She likes to be up and doing.'

And what she was doing, Pierce would probably rather not know, thought Nel, somewhat bitterly. 'She's very keen on Sacha's cosmetics, isn't she?' This presumably was a safe thing to say. 'It's nice for her to have a project while she's down here in the country. Otherwise she might get bored.'

Pierce's eyes narrowed. 'Bored?' He sounded a little anxious. 'How so? She's a married woman with a husband to look after.'

'She hasn't got children yet. And you're a big strong man. I don't suppose you take a lot of looking after.' She

249

smiled, aware she was being coy, and not sure if this was the right tack to be on.

He laughed, flattered. 'Well, no.'

'And you're away a lot, I gather?' Nel wasn't quite sure about this, but fortunately for her, he confirmed it with a nod.

She took a breath, not quite sure what argument she could put forward to convince him to go with Abraham. She leaned forward as she got into her role. 'Which is why Kerry Anne needs an interest.'

'What are you talking about?'

Nel had very little idea, but she hoped it didn't show. 'I mean Kerry Anne's very interested in Sacha's beauty products. If she wants to be near Sacha, she'll want to live somewhere pleasanter, don't you think?'

She smiled again, imagining herself a pretty, younger woman, who got what she wanted by smiling in the right way at the right time.

'Frankly I don't much care about the estate and I don't think Kerry Anne does either. I'll quite likely sell the house when all the work is done. Move on, somewhere quieter. Kerry Anne can find another hobby.'

Nel almost choked into her spritzer, wishing she'd gone for straight white wine, something to bolster her a little. 'But Pierce,' she said desperately, 'don't you see . . .'

'What?'

What indeed? What on earth could she think of to say that would make him make the right decision? Oh Viv, if only you were here. 'It's not just a hobby she wants. That wouldn't keep her from . . .' She hesitated, mostly to give herself time to think, but she was aware that Pierce was frowning slightly again.

'Pierce, I'm telling you this as a friend, as a woman, older and wiser than Kerry Anne . . .'

'Yes? I wish you'd spit it out.'

Nel wished she would too, but still hadn't quite decided

what to spit. 'If she doesn't have this project, this enthusiasm, as I said, she's liable to get bored. And you do know, don't you, what happens to pretty young wives with a lot of money who are bored, don't you?' He obviously didn't. 'They are preyed on by young, attractive men.'

This sounded a bit desperate and she didn't really believe it. She knew that pretty young women were preyed on by men who would be classed as older. Younger than Nel, of course.

'What on earth are you talking about?'

Nel decided she had nothing left to lose. Jake was not interested in her, never had been. And perhaps she was behaving like a woman scorned, but she felt she might as well tell Pierce about it, if it would keep the desecration of Paradise Fields to an almost acceptable level.

She leaned in and lowered her voice to an extent that Pierce had to lean forward to hear her. 'I really hate to be the one to tell you this, and I'm quite sure that if her time was more occupied, you could nip it in the bud before anything happened, but Jake Demerand—'

'Do I hear my name being taken in vain?' Jake's voice was commanding and Nel looked up, straight into his eyes. For once, they were not laughing and sexy, but cold, critical and dismissive. Nel felt a familiar stab of pain just below her breastbone. And she felt guilty, guilty of telling tales on him, and so miserable she wished she could die of it. Somehow she managed to keep her desperate feelings to herself.

'Yes,' she said smoothly. 'I was just about to tell Pierce that you have been implicated in a very dodgy building deal, and that I thought he ought to know.'

Oh God, that wasn't what she'd meant to say at all. Nel had never intended telling Pierce anything about Jake's possible connection to a dodgy building deal. She had no idea whether the rumours were true or not, and she was not in the habit of slandering people without access to the facts. Warning Pierce to keep Kerry Anne away from Jake would have been one thing – she'd seen them together – but now, with both Jake and Pierce actually sitting there in front of her, she couldn't quite bring herself to accuse him of seducing Pierce's wife. And so she'd landed herself in something even more complicated.

Jake raised a hand to attract the attention of the barman. 'Diet cola, please. So tell me, Nel, what is it I am supposed to have done?'

Nel looked down at the table, her brain working furiously as Jake collected his drink from the bar, came back and pulled out a chair.

'Well,' he demanded when he'd sat on it.

Nel had had precious seconds in which to think up what to say. 'I have heard, on quite good authority, that you might not just be a solicitor assisting the Hunstantons to sell their land.'

'So what have you heard, then?' He sounded more irritated than anything else.

'That you narrowly escaped being prosecuted for a dodgy deal concerning old peoples' homes.'

'Oh, well, that didn't take long. I thought that old chestnut would follow me here eventually, but I didn't realise it would be so soon.'

'So you're not denying it?' asked Nel, astounded by his casual attitude.

'Nope. Now, was that all you wanted to see Pierce about? He told me you'd asked for a meeting. Was it only to tell unsubstantiated tales about me?'

He seemed terribly unconcerned. She was quietly dying. 'I actually came to tell him about a meeting that's been called of the hospice committee, but I hadn't quite got round to it.'

'No, she was telling me a lot of nonsense about my wife! As if I don't know what she's up to!'

'And what nonsense is that?'

Nel looked at Jake straight in the eye. He looked right back. Not for a second did he look away, or show any sign of guilt or discomfort. He was annoyed, angry even, but he was not feeling remotely guilty. Which, considering what she'd seen, was slightly odd. She looked away first. She felt she was the one with the secret romance, not him.

'That's not important,' she declared, as breezily as she possibly could. 'What I really want to do is persuade Pierce and Kerry Anne that they'd be much better off with the plans Abraham has created.'

'Chris Mowbray says that Gideon Freebody's are the ones to go for, and I respect his opinion,' said Pierce. 'He's got a lot of experience of this type of project.'

I bet he has, thought Nel. 'Well anyway, there's going to be a meeting, at the hospice, about the buildings. What isn't quite clear – to me, anyway – is why the hospice is involved.' She looked at her two companions, hoping one of them might give her a clue. Nothing.

'Oh. I don't suppose I need to go to that.' Losing interest, Pierce got up and headed in the direction of the Gents. 'Chris will make all the right decisions.'

'I see,' said Jake when they were alone. 'And you weren't going to tell me about this meeting at the hospice?'

'No! It's not for me to invite you! You're Pierce's solicitor. It's up to him if he wants you there.'

'So you wouldn't have told me as a friend?'

'No! We're not friends!' And she sighed, far too deeply.

He didn't say anything for a few moments and then said, 'Can I get you another drink?' She nodded. She should have refused but she was too desolate to argue. While he was getting it, she slumped back in her chair, fighting despair.

He put a glass of whisky in front of her. 'Now,' he said

firmly. 'Let me tell you what's what. You really shouldn't listen to gossip, you know. People do it all the time, but it leads them quite off track.'

'Does it?' She sipped her drink, aware that if she wasn't careful it would be gone in two goes. I'm turning into an alcoholic, she thought.

'Yes. Now, because I've suffered from gossip myself, I am not going to pass any on, but I do wish you'd keep your eyes open, use your brain and think about just who is the good guy around here.'

Nel regarded him. He was so attractive, so good-looking. It would be so nice just to think of him as a knight in shining armour and believe every word that fell from his sexy mouth in his sexy voice. But she knew she couldn't. Trusting him now would be madness, and while she might be seven-eighths besotted, she wasn't entirely deluded. Pierce was her unlikely saviour. 'Another drink, anyone? No? Barman! Another half, please.'

'So, Pierce,' said Nel, fighting the desire to shrink back into her coat and disappear. 'Will you come to the meeting? I really think you should be there. And Kerry Anne.'

Pierce sighed. 'If you insist. But it'll be a complete waste of time.'

'I'm sure it won't. I'm sure you'll find it very helpful when it comes to making up your mind. I think you should know how awful the Gideon Freebody scheme is likely to look. Goodbye. Thanks for the drinks.'

Then she picked up her coat and walked out of the wine bar, aware that the mutterings she left behind her from the bar staff and the regulars who knew her would go on a long time. She could feel Jake's eyes burning accusingly into her back.

As she marched up the hill as fast as she could, to assuage the pain and feeling of utter despair the meeting had left her with, something Vivian said came into her head. 'The nice bastards are harder to get over than the nasty ones.' Jake was, could be, had been, a nice bastard, but a bastard right enough.

Fleur was whisking about the house looking for something. 'Oh God, Mum, thank goodness you're back. I can't find the parcel tape.'

Sam, Nel's eldest, had christened this item as 'tape that can also be used to pack parcels'. Nel and Fleur used it to get dog hairs off their clothes.

'Just let me get my coat off, I'll have a think.'

'Hurry, Mum! I'm meeting Jamie off the bus!'

'But it's not the weekend! Surely his mother wouldn't let him come during the week!'

'He's got study leave or something. Anyway, who cares? I need my black top!'

Refraining from mentioning that she was, personally, a little concerned about her daughter's education, Nel thought hard.

'It's probably in an overnight bag or something,' went on Fleur. 'You know how you never unpack.'

This was true. Nel cast her mind back to when she last spent a night away from home, and left the room quickly. At the top of the stairs she leant her head against the banister and let tears seep through her screwed-up eyelids. Along with the tears were the sort of hard, painful sobs that Nel hadn't experienced since she'd stopped sobbing over Mark. This was what a broken heart felt like. She was over forty and she'd never felt it before. That meant she was lucky. But as she went to the bedroom and retrieved the tape from where it lay among the remnants of her night with Jake, she didn't feel lucky. Anything but.

'So, tell us what happened!'

Vivian was perched on the end of her mother's bed. Nel had the chair. Vivian's mother, Florence, was sitting up in her hospital bed, eager for news.

255

'Tell me how you are, first,' said Nel, encouraged to see her old friend looked so well, in spite of being in hospital.

'There's absolutely nothing wrong with me!' insisted the old lady. 'Just because I slipped on some water and stubbed my toe and fell over, they drag me in here "for tests". Huh! Anyone would think there was no shortage of beds in the National Health. Now, tell all.'

'I've brought you something to read. I thought you might be getting bored.'

'Thank you, dear, that's very kind. But Vivian's told me all about you having to meet that dreadful man.'

'Yes,' said Vivian, 'and I'm gagging to know how you got on.'

Nel laughed. Somehow the prospect of relating her recent humiliations to Florence and Viv, in the bright, clinical atmosphere of the hospital, diminished their awfulness.

'You would have done it much better, Viv. I kept changing horses mid-stream.'

'Don't talk to me about mid-stream,' said Florence with a shudder. 'If I have to pee into—'

'Mother!'

'Oh, don't fuss. I'm sure Nel's heard the word pee before.'

'What do you mean?' asked Viv.

'Well, first of all I thought I should try and be like you and seduce him' – Florence snorted with laughter – 'but that failed miserably. So I thought I'd resort to blackmail.'

'Blackmail! You, Nel!' Vivian was almost impressed.

'Yes, I told him if Kerry Anne couldn't do the cosmetic thing with Sacha, she'd get bored and stray.'

'And how did that go down?'

'It didn't, really. I didn't actually get to go through with it.'

'Why not?' Florence leaned forward to hear better.

'Well, I'd just begun to tell him, more or less in so many words, that Jake and Kerry Anne had something going, but I didn't get a chance to say it.'

'Why not?' asked Viv.

'Oh, do stop interrupting, child! She's just getting to the good bit. All anyone talks about in here is bowel movements. A little scandal is just what I need.'

'Because Jake appeared. Pierce had obviously asked him to come.' Nel paused a moment to compartmentalise what happened from her feelings. 'Anyway, with him looking over my shoulder, I could hardly tell Pierce I thought he had the hots for Kerry Anne. So I said he had been involved in a dodgy building deal instead.'

Vivian laughed far too loudly. 'I don't know about scandal, Mum. Slander seems a bit more in Nel's line. Or is it libel?'

'I know I shouldn't have said it! I would never have said it if I hadn't been put on the spot. I don't know what came over me.'

'That's what they say when they've been caught shoplifting,' said Florence authoritatively.

'Mum! How do you know?' Nel could see the horror on Vivian's face as she imagined her mother having her collar felt by a burly security man.

'The woman in the next bed told me.'

'Oh, that's all right.' Nel glanced across at the now empty bed. 'Did she go home?'

'In a manner of speaking. She died.'

'Oh,' said Vivian, giggling. 'Not of hypothermia, I hope.'

'No,' said Florence. 'I think it was her heart. Why should it be hypothermia?'

'From stuffing frozen turkeys up her vest,' said Vivian.

Nel found herself laughing quite immoderately, and put it down to the relief of tension. All her emotions seemed extreme lately.

'So is Pierce coming to the meeting?' asked Viv, handing Nel a medical wipe.

'I think so. And I think Jake is too. So if he is doing a dodgy deal with Gideon Freebody, we're in trouble. He'll take us apart and convince everyone to vote for pulling down the hospice.'

'We don't know they plan to pull down the hospice, that's just speculation at the moment.'

'But I've got a bad feeling about it. I think Chris Mowbray has done this kind of thing before. It's probably why he went on the committee in the first place.'

'Well, we'll just have to get as many people on our side as possible,' said Vivian firmly, possibly sensing that Nel's recent laughter was a sign of latent hysteria. 'How have you been doing with the list?'

'I went for the soft targets first. The vicar was on our side, and he's going to get as many people as possible to buy chunks of the ransom strip.'

'I could do that too,' said Florence. 'How much are they? And how much land do you get? Enough to plant a row of beans on?'

Nel and Vivian regarded each other. 'The trouble is, we don't know. We haven't had time to work things like that out. We'll have to get it properly measured. Then we'll have to think if it's best to count all the people committed to buying it, and divide it up into that many squares, or the other way round,' said Nel.

'Mmm,' said Florence. 'That does make it a little harder. But there are one or two wealthy widows in the bridge club. I'll try and twist their arms.'

'Now you've got to concentrate on getting better,' said Nel.

'Nonsense! There's nothing wrong with me. I only stubbed my toe, for God's sake!'

'And does that explain all the bruising and the possible hairline fracture of your hip?' said Vivian, rearranging the get-well cards on her mother's locker.

'I shall be out by next week,' went on Florence. 'Can I come to the meeting?'

'No,' said Vivian.

'Not really,' said Nel, more gently. 'You would have to be on the hospice committee, or something.'

'Huh! I've spent my life on committees. You think that would count for something!'

'It does, Mum, and we'll be really grateful when you sell all our plots for us, but you can't come to the meeting.'

Florence sat back on her now replumped pillows. 'Very well, I suppose you're right. Now tell me, girls, what are you going to wear?'

Surprised, Nel considered. She would not have thought that was important, but now Florence had asked the question, she realised that it was.

'Will you be wearing mud again, Nel?' asked Vivian.

'It is vital that you feel right!' said Florence. 'Whenever I had a difficult meeting to go to, I knew I had to be wearing the right thing, from my underwear to my hat.'

'I hadn't thought about wearing a hat,' said Vivian.

'I know no one wears hats nowadays, more's the pity,' went on Florence. 'But the right clothes will give you confidence.'

'We might have to do a trawl of the charity and second-hand shops,' said Viv. 'Are you up for that, Nel?'

Nel sighed, infinitely tired. 'I would really love that, but I just don't have time. I do promise you, though,' she added reassuringly to the two women who were looking at her with critical consideration, 'that I will get the dog hairs off everything I do wear, and that I won't fall over in the mud first.'

'Ah ha!' declared Florence, triumphantly. 'You fall over too! And no one put you in hospital for it!'

'I didn't fall over, quite. I just got a nasty attack of muddy football in my cake . . . Oh, never mind. You had to be there.'

Vivian was laughing. 'I was!'

Chapter Nineteen

❧

When Fleur heard about the meeting, she insisted on taking her mother shopping.

'I know you're really busy, I know you're getting people signed up for the market, and to buy these plots of land, blah, blah, blah, but if you're going to wow them at the meeting you can't turn up in that navy blue number which makes you look like Mary Poppins without the good bits.'

'You only want me to go shopping so I'll bring my credit card and you're at a loose end because Jamie's gone back.' Normally, Nel loved buying size ten clothes and shopping with Fleur was always fun, but she wasn't in the mood for girly trips to town at the moment. 'He is a nice boy, isn't he?'

'Careful, Mum, you'll make me go off him.'

'Well, not that nice, obviously,' said Nel hurriedly. 'He has dreadful taste in music.'

'You don't care what sort of music he listens to, but I'm glad you're not freaking about him coming from London any more. So, shopping?'

'I told Florence and Viv I didn't have time to go shopping. And I haven't. You'll have to buy whatever it is you're after with your own money.'

'Well, I do need a pair of jeans rather badly, but honestly, Mum, this is for you. If Jake is going to be there you have to look gorgeous.'

'I am not interested in Jake. Any slight interest I may have had in him has long gone.' This wasn't remotely true, but she felt if she said it enough times it might one day become so. Besides, she was getting used to lying; she could even do it without blushing.

'Derr! That is so not the point! You want to make him sorry he did whatever he did to make you stop liking him!'

'But he did that before he met me, sweetheart. I told you. Simon brought round that bit of paper, and when I spoke to him about it at the wine bar, he didn't deny anything. He's a no-good rotten scoundrel.'

'Well, I like him. He's not patronising or bossy.' She mouthed, 'Like Simon.' She added aloud, 'And Viv agrees with me.'

'Not now, she doesn't. Not now she knows what a black-hearted devil he is.'

'You do have some quaint expressions, Ma, but trust me on this one. Even if you genuinely don't like him any more' – Fleur's raised eyebrows indicated her how much she believed in that particular myth – 'you want to make him sorry.'

'Darling, I don't play those sort of games.'

'Bollocks,' Fleur said bluntly. 'I'm far more experienced with all this than you are. Now, pick me up after school and we'll hit the shops. I finish at two.'

Realising she was vanquished, not so much by her daughter's bullying but by her own need to spend a little time being frivolous, Nel muttered for a few minutes about how in her day she had to stay at school all day, whether she had lessons or not, and Fleur muttered back that it was not her day now.

Nel rang Viv to confess that she would be taking an afternoon off from her labours, having told herself that if Viv sounded remotely disapproving, she wouldn't go.

'Good idea! You can't work every minute God sends, and Mum is right. You will feel much more confident about the meeting if you're looking fab.'

'I do feel a bit guilty. A whole afternoon. I could visit two point four potential farmers' market stallholders in that time. The rent from them is going to be much more important to the hospice when we lose our fields.'

'You can still have some time off. Besides, I'm going to be ringing a few of Mum's old friends, tell them she's been in hospital etc., and I shall just throw into the conversation about the hospice. Several of them are on the crochet squares team. What would they do with their time if there was no hospice to support?'

'Support an animal charity, I expect, or something that won't ask them to buy bits of old field they can't even use.' Nel paused, and Viv knew what she was thinking.

'Look, I know you think that Jake slept with you for all the wrong reasons.'

'There are no right reasons, Viv. Whatever his motives were they were bad.'

'Rubbish! What about desire! That's perfectly acceptable.'

'Desire is too nice a word for it. It was lust.'

'Even so, there's nothing wrong with honest lust—'

'Except there was nothing honest about it!'

'You don't know that. And one day you'll be able to think of the experience as lovely, just for itself, with no pain or bitterness.'

Nel considered this for a few seconds. 'I might think that if it was lust, or desire or whatever, but I won't think that if I believe what happened happened because he wanted to subdue me. God! I'd rather be seduced for my money! At least that's a positive thing.'

'Except you haven't got any money.'

'That's not the point.'

'Well, I think you're wrong. I think he wanted you as much as you wanted him.'

Nel thought for a heart-churning second. 'Possibly.'

'And you had a really good time, didn't you? It was fantastic?'

'Yes. But what about that whole morning-after pill fiasco? That was pretty dreadful.'

'Not really. It worked, didn't it? The pill? You're not pregnant. I'm not saying you're going to feel fine about it immediately. But, one day, you'll look at that time you spent together as something really nice that happened to you.' Viv paused. 'After all, if Simon is all you've got in mind, you may never have sex again.'

'Viv!' wailed Nel. 'I'm going now.'

'Good. Don't forget your credit card, and don't worry about how much you spend. That's what credit cards are for. Oh, and can we have something a little more exciting than our normal black or navy blue? I know you think you're the size of a house, but no one else agrees with you.'

Fleur's first requirement on hitting Cheltenham was to eat. 'You need energy for shopping, Ma. If you're hungry you just grab anything. I know a little place.'

It was a good choice. Owner-run, it did home-made soup, wonderful salads, and, Fleur pointed out, it had a licence. 'Have a glass of wine, Mum. Go on.'

'But I haven't eaten all day! It'll go straight to my head. I am driving.'

'A spritzer then, and we'll share it. You need a bit of alcohol to make you try new colours and things. Viv gave me strict orders that you're not to come back with black or navy.'

'That leaves me with bottle green or brown, then,' said Nel. 'Or possibly dark grey.'

Fleur grimaced hideously and then smiled at the waitress. 'Two soups and a Caeser salad to share, please.'

While they were eating soup and bread and butter, picking at the salad, Fleur regarded her mother with her head on one side. It made Nel nervous.

'I'm not having a makeover. Don't even suggest it! We

haven't time for one thing. And if you bully me too much I won't buy you anything.'

'I was just thinking a slightly brighter lipstick. That brown colour you wear is OK, but it doesn't exactly make a statement.'

'It's not brown! It's soft rose! And it's only on my lips! It's my mouth that makes the statements!'

Fleur made a face and tore off another hunk of bread.

'The trouble is,' said Nel as they contemplated the racks of clothes, 'I can't tell what I like when there are so many of them. In a charity shop, you usually only like one thing, and it either fits or it doesn't. I get confused when faced with rows and rows of jackets all the same. Like a fox in a hen house, I don't know which one to kill.'

Fleur gave her mother a frown and a shake of her head, in acknowledgement of her insanity. 'There aren't rows and rows! Just a couple in each size!'

'And there's another thing! Fancy spending' – she looked at a label in horror – 'all that money, only to find someone else wearing the same thing. In a size eight.'

'You won't, Mum,' said Fleur with confidence. 'No one who's a size eight would wear anything like that. Unless they're really old and sad.'

Nel looked anxiously round to make sure no one really old and sad was within earshot. 'Honestly, Fleur!'

'And I don't think you should wear it either. Come with me, over here.'

'Darling!' Nel braked hard. 'This label charges nearly a hundred pounds for a T-shirt!'

'They have a sale! Like always! Now stop being difficult.'

'You're so bossy.'

'Well, one of us has to be. Now, what about that?'

Forced by Fleur to go through the torture of trying it on, Nel emerged onto the shop floor uncertain of how she felt.

It was a sort of long cardigan coat made of merino wool and hung beautifully. It was designed to go over a skirt, but Fleur pushed that aside with disdain. 'I know we're trying to get you out of black trousers, but they do look good with that.'

'But is it smart enough for a meeting?'

By now the shop assistant was on the case, and, to Nel's slight annoyance, firmly on Fleur's side. 'Absolutely! It will take you anywhere, that coat. You'll live in it once you get used to it. It's elegant, practical, smart, warm and slimming.'

'And does it also provide tasty snacks and dog-sitting services?' asked Nel sarcastically, aware she was beginning to feel wonderful in it.

'If you let the dogs near that, I'll kill you!' said Fleur. 'It's gorgeous. But do you love it?'

Fleur, who had enough clothes to supply a whole town's worth of charity shops, had a strict rule. If she didn't love it, she didn't buy it. Nel tended to buy things if they vaguely fitted and she could afford them, not caring to fly in the face of coincidence. Viv was constantly threatening to go through her wardrobe and throw half of it out.

Nel sighed. 'Yes, I do, actually. I don't want to take it off.'

'Excellent! Now, what to go with it?'

'I thought you said black trousers looked OK!'

Fleur sighed. 'Not those black trousers! You need better ones!'

Reluctantly Nel agreed with her. Besides, the trousers she was now wearing, and wore almost like a uniform, were inextricably connected with Jake. She remembered him taking them off with hideous regularity. If the memories weren't triggered every time she went to the loo, it would definitely make the getting-over process a whole lot easier.

Fleur convinced Nel to go to the cosmetics department.

'Look, there's a really good free gift if you buy two products.'

'Darling, I don't need two products! I've already spent a small fortune on clothes I can't strictly justify. I don't need make-up as well.'

'You do, you know. That eye-shadow is a bit blah. Makes you look old. I don't think you should wear it.'

'But you're always stealing it!'

'You've always taught us to share, Mum, and I just think you need another one, to go on top. Give you a bit of shape. Now let's see what we've got.'

Nel, who liked bargains as much as anyone, did concede that there were quite a lot of useful little bottles and tubes in the make-up bag they gave you if you spent a week's housekeeping on an eye-shadow and some tinted moisturiser.

'You have got lovely skin,' said the saleswoman, who was reassuringly old, but, more disconcertingly, wearing white lipstick. 'This is just what you need to even out the skin tones and give you a lovely natural look. See how easily it blends in. Now, what you need with that . . .'

Ten minutes later, Fleur and Nel left the counter, bearing two very attractive carrier bags, and no end of cures for fine lines (the word 'wrinkle' being totally non p.c in the beauty world), enlarged pores and broken veins.

'I can't believe I have just spent so much money. Nor that I've just taken beauty advice from someone who wears white lipstick. I must be even more mad than I realised. Just because she said I had nice skin!'

'She was really generous with the free gifts, though, and that's a lovely shade . . .'

'I don't mind sharing, but it lives in my house, OK?'

'OK. Now, cup of tea? Or shall we go home?'

'Home. I have tea at home, and a sample of lemon cake someone gave me.'

'Oh, excellent.'

When Simon rang to ask her out for a drink she didn't like to admit she was too tired, having spent the afternoon shopping, so she said yes. She would have much preferred to watch back numbers of *Sex and the City* with Fleur, who had them all on video. As she put on the new eye-shadow, and evened out her skin tones, she wondered if this was a sign she should definitely tell Simon she couldn't see him any more. Except she might need Simon. Did she want to end up a lonely old lady? It was one thing preferring to spend an evening with Fleur when Fleur was there. Would old episodes of *Sex and the City* seem so appealing when she was watching them on her own and had no one to comment on the clothes with?

Also, could she cope with any more upset just now? Simon might well be devastated, especially when he'd done so much work for her. Did she want to put him through what Jake had put her through? Certainly not! Simon was a kind and honest man. When she'd got over this emotional blip with Jake, she'd recognise him for what he was, and possibly agree to marry him.

While she was tweaking her fringe and borrowing Fleur's hair wax for blondes, she remembered what Viv had said about men, when Fleur had asked her why she had never married. 'Men are like elephants, practically my favourite thing. But you wouldn't want to own one.'

'Do I want to own one?' she asked, peering into the mirror, trying to see if her pores really did look refined with their new make-up, or if they were as coarse as ever, swearing and drinking tea out of the saucer.

'You're looking tired, Nel,' Simon said when they were seated at too small a table on rather uncomfortable chairs.

Nel's hackles rose, possibly visibly. 'Well, I shouldn't!

I've got new make-up on which is supposed to bring out my sparkle.'

'New make-up doesn't do anything for lack of sleep, or stress, pickle.' He took hold of her hand and squeezed it gently.

Nel regarded him. It was nice of him to be concerned. She was tired and stressed, and, no, different make-up couldn't really be expected to change anything. She should value his caring nature. Instead she felt slightly suffocated by it.

'I think you need to do less. Why don't you concentrate on the farmers' market, and give up with this hospice nonsense . . . I don't mean nonsense!' he added quickly. 'I mean, the hospice is terribly important. But you can't really do much about the building scheme. And if the hospice land gets sold, well, think of the lovely new building you could get with the money.'

Nel couldn't remember telling Simon all this. She supposed she must have at some time, or how would he know? But there was no harm in him knowing. None of the information was confidential, was it?

'I see what you mean. We are facing huge opposition. But I have a feeling that the new hospice wouldn't get built. That the money would just disappear into people's pockets.' She didn't say Jake Demerand's, or Chris Mowbray's pocket, but she thought it.

'I don't think you should worry about that. After all, you're not responsible for the hospice. You're only one committee member. I really think you should cut down on your good works, Nel. I know they were what got you through when Mark died, but you're over him now. You don't have to cut your heart out for every good cause now.'

For a brief, wild moment, it was as if Simon had an hidden agenda. Nel dismissed this as early-onset paranoia and wished she could tell Simon that he was a good cause in a way, that he took up her time too, time when she could be relaxing with her daughter. She smiled. The grip on her hand became tighter.

'Darling, I wish you'd let me look after you more.'

'Simon! You look after me brilliantly! You're always fixing things for me, sorting out the car, stuff like that.'

'But I'd like to do it on a more full-time basis. I want to marry you, Nel. I think you know that.' He released her hand and raised his own. 'No, I know what you're going to say! You're going to say, "Wait until the children have left home," but they have, nearly. I don't want to wait any longer, I want to marry you now, while we've still got time ahead of us.'

Rather desperately, Nel tried to lighten the mood. 'We're not that old! We've got a few more years before we're likely to shuffle off this mortal coil! Or at least, I have.'

'Trust you to make a joke of it, but I'm serious. I love you and I want to marry you. Now. Soon.' Then, to Nel's growing horror, he put his hand in his pocket and produced a box. 'I know all girls appreciate a romantic gesture. This is a little something I picked up in Cirencester the other day. Try it on.'

It not only fitted, it looked fabulous. It was a huge oval aquamarine, surrounded by tiny diamonds. Nel starred down at it, momentarily hypnotised by the sight of it on her wedding finger. Mark hadn't been able to afford diamonds, and her engagement ring had been lovely, but semi-precious, and she had stopped wearing it years ago, when she realised it couldn't take the battering being a wife and mother gave it. Suddenly her hand looked complete, the narrow gold band enhanced by the larger ring. So why did she think back to the moment when Mark had pulled a screwed-up paper bag from his pocket and given her a ring that was initially so big she had to pack her finger with sticking plaster and cotton wool to keep it on? It had cost more to make smaller than it did to buy.

Would Mark feel she was being disloyal if she married again?

Dismissing this fleeting nonsense, she said, 'Simon, I couldn't possibly get engaged to you without talking to the children.'

'Would they talk to you if they were getting engaged?'

'Probably not, but it's not the same. I'm their mother—'

'Which means you don't have to answer to them.'

'Yes, I do! They're still young! They still live at home! I can't just get married, change their lives completely, without consulting them!'

'Obviously, you'd have to tell them, but not ask their permission. They're young adults, they've got their own lives to lead. They can't dictate what you do.'

'No! Of course not. And they wouldn't dream of doing that, or trying to do that. But I would have to give them plenty of warning. I couldn't just go home with a dirty great rock on my hand.' She looked at it. 'Although it is glorious.'

'Don't wear it immediately then. Give them a chance to get used to the idea, and then wear your ring.' He smiled, and when he did, the corners of his eyes crinkled attractively. His smile was one of the things that made Nel say yes when he first asked her out. She'd rejected many other invitations prior to his. At the time she'd seen it as a sign that she was ready for another relationship.

'After all,' he said now. 'It's not going to affect your children all that much. We don't need to move house, or anything. I could move in with you. There'd be plenty of room for us both, especially when the children do leave home.'

A terrifying sense of suffocation flashed through Nel. She tried hard to dismiss it. She was only being neurotic because she was so stressed. Simon would keep her safe. Simon wouldn't sleep with her because he wanted her influence. He wouldn't take advantage of her age or desperation, or the fact she was a sensual woman who had suppressed her sensuality for years. He probably didn't know that; she'd only just discovered it herself. She was so confused. Would she be mad to turn down Simon and all he represented because she'd been mad enough to fall in love with Jake?

'Don't answer now. Think about it. Talk it over with the boys – not Fleur straightaway. She's so indulged she's bound to be against it.'

As always, Nel prickled at the merest hint of criticism of her children. She made herself calm down. Fleur *was* indulged. Only that afternoon she had bought her some very expensive jeans for no reason other than she loved her, and had appreciated her help buying clothes. The trouble was, Fleur was easy to indulge. She was always so delighted, so grateful and so loving. Which was how she knew she wasn't spoilt, Nel always thought. Spoilt children were never pleased, never happy with anything they were given. It was, she convinced herself, the vital difference.

'I don't think Fleur would be against anything which would make me happy,' she said.

'Not consciously, but she wouldn't like sharing you with me. She wouldn't get the amount of attention you give her now. Viv too. She'd feel she would lose you as a friend if you married me – or anyone. So just think about it, don't talk about it. But keep the ring, and look at it from time to time. It's a symbol of all the good things I can give you.'

Nel looked down at the ring, part entranced by its sparkliness, part horrified at what it implied. Horrified that she was seriously considering accepting Simon's offer. She didn't love him, there was no doubt about that – at least she didn't feel about him the way she felt about Jake. He didn't preoccupy her, and make her lose track of herself; being with him didn't make her feel all overexcited. But neither did he make her doubt herself, and her judgement. He might not set her on fire, but she knew where she was with him – something that certainly couldn't be said for Jake.

Before Jake had come along and confused everything, she'd been perfectly happy with Simon, hadn't she? What if Jake had just temporarily muddled things? What if, by turning down Simon, she'd actually be turning down a very comfortable, companionable future? It wasn't as if Jake was likely to offer the same commitment. She took a deep breath.

'All right. I'll think about it. But I'm not saying yes, Simon, not until I've thought things through. And, as you say, I've got a lot on my plate at the moment. I'll need to wait until I've got a time slot for thinking.' She smiled, to point up her little joke, which sounded extremely pathetic.

'You don't need to think too hard. After all, if you married me, you wouldn't have so much on your plate, would you?'

'Well, no.'

Rather frantically she tried to think of what Simon would remove from her area of responsibility. Car servicing, possibly paperwork, tax forms, DIY and house maintenance. It seemed a lot, and she smiled, suppressing thoughts of what work he would create: proper cooking all the time, washing, ironing, extra house cleaning, tidiness. Would they even each other out? And would watching war documentaries rather than makeover programmes be a sacrifice she could willingly make?

It would be a familiar sacrifice. Mark had been addicted to any programme involving war, war machines, or re-enactments of battles fought long ago. And she could always get another television and watch it in another room.

'Promise me you'll think about it, and not spend so much time thinking about things you can't change?'

'OK, Simon, I will,' she said softly, knowing that a large proportion of her warm feelings for him came from gratitude that he wasn't pressing her for an answer.

Chapter Twenty

❧

Nel decided not to think about Simon's offer of marriage until after the meeting. She knew he'd understand; she could hardly think about turning her life upside down when she didn't know how much it was going to be turned upside down anyway. If they lost the hospice land, it might be nice to start a new life with Simon. He'd help her get over Jake. They could perhaps sell both their houses, buy something bigger, start afresh. It would be fun, decorating somewhere different. After all, would she want to go on living in this house if there was a vast housing estate at the bottom of her garden? Simon's vague suggestion made when she and Jake met him at the Black Hart, and he was with that woman, that she might sell off the end bit was a silly idea. He'd see that when she'd had a chance to talk to him about it.

As she applied her new make-up and put on her new clothes, Nel realised she was a classic Nimby: Not In My Back Yard. 'So,' she asked herself out loud, 'if the hospice survived, with a new roof, but you still had the housing estate, would you still want to move?'

No, the garden was huge. She wouldn't need to look at the housing estate if she didn't want to. She could grow more trees, put up a screen. She'd only really hate the housing estate if it took the place of the hospice.

Relieved to discover she wasn't a wholly despicable person, she took one last look at herself in the mirror, took her long coat out of its plastic bag, put it on.

She was just about to leave the house when Fleur leapt out of the sitting room.

'Let me look at you.'

'It's only a meeting!'

'An important meeting and Jake will be there. Hang on.' Fleur withdrew a piece of crumpled tissue from up her sleeve. 'You've got a bit of mascara on your cheekbone. There.'

'I suppose I should be grateful you didn't spit on the tissue!' said Nel and then left the house before too many dog hairs could leap off the furniture and stick to her, like iron filings to a magnet.

'Wow, you look wonderful!' said Vivian as they met up in the Ladies of the hospice. 'Fleur did really well! Designer?'

Nel nodded. 'Don't ask how much it cost. I don't know. I've blotted it out of my consciousness. It was extremely well reduced, but it was still a fortune.'

'Worth every penny. You'll wear it for years. I can't help noticing it is predominantly black, though.'

'Well, yes. You can't have stylish, almost affordable and wear-it-for-years and not have black. Have you noticed my new make-up, though? Apparently it's what I need, because I have beautiful skin. They must sell an enormous about of make-up by telling people they have beautiful skin and then making them buy something to cover it up.'

'You do have beautiful skin, though. You're looking really good, girl.'

'Don't be silly.'

'And you've got a game plan?'

'Sort of.' Nel's instinct was to fly off the seat of her pants (new, plain but elegant), but she knew that Vivian would not approve. She and Abraham had decided to keep their information to themselves, until they discovered how much Chris Mowbray knew, or was willing to reveal. Then, when they thought the moment was right, they would tell the committee about the ransom strip, and their plan to divide it into plots. 'It's a shame we didn't get a chance to discuss it, really. How's Florence? Home?'

Vivian dried her hands on a paper towel, peering into the mirror as she did so. 'Home, but still a bit restricted as to what she can do. However, she's been busy on the telephone. She's getting all her groups to buy chunks of land, and the richer members to buy them individually. How many committee members know about the ransom strip?'

'Apart from those we've told? I haven't a clue. I think we have to assume everyone knows everything. Especially people we don't want to know.'

'Do you think Jake will come? Oh, hi, Kerry Anne. Nice to see you.'

'Kerry Anne!' Nel was far more enthusiastic. 'Excellent! I hope you're going to encourage Pierce to go for the smaller building plan? After all,' she leaned in, 'you wouldn't want cheap housing in front of your health spa, would you? Tasteful executive housing would fit the image much better.'

'Not really, Nel,' said Kerry Anne. 'We're going to need every penny we can get to set it up. I'm going to be investing in Sacha's cosmetics, too.' She curled back her lips in a sinister gesture, checking for lipstick on her teeth, no doubt. 'There would be a wall between the spa and the houses, anyway.'

'Oh.' Nel's brief flash of optimism evaporated.

Kerry Anne looked into the mirror more closely, opened her eyes very wide and examined herself. She didn't make the slightest adjustment. 'No, I think the plan Chris Mowbray is suggesting will be fine. Either way I guess I'll have to go along with Pierce. It's his money, after all.'

'If you're married to him, it's half yours,' said Viv. 'Where did you get married? If it was in California, you're entitled to half everything he's got if you get divorced.'

'It was in England. And I'm not planning on getting divorced,' said Kerry Anne.

'Oh. Good,' said Nel, sounding disturbingly like Joyce Grenfell, trying not to demand what she was doing messing round with another man then. 'Shall we go in, now?'

Nel walked in with her shoulders back, determined she would act with perfect confidence and thus acquire it. She had used all the beauty tips given to her by the woman with white lipstick, and while this could have been a mistake, first Fleur and then Viv had approved of her new look.

Several of the committee were already seated, but there were lots of empty seats. The secretary was obviously expecting several extra people. Nel realised that if Jake wasn't one of them she would be very disappointed. Then she realised this was the emotional equivalent of pressing her nose up against a shop window, yearning for things she couldn't have.

Pierce and Kerry Anne came in together. Nel smiled at Abraham who came in with another, younger man, also wearing a suit, and appearing uncomfortable in it.

Christopher Mowbray, as chairman, came in wearing not only a suit but an air of self-importance that made Nel want to hit him. He nodded to Nel and Viv and smiled in a way that made Nel yearn to see him in the tabloids, involved in a sordid sex scandal. After all, if he did do anything to jeopardise the hospice, he would be a kind of child molester.

The vicar, who Nel always thought of as Father Ted, smiled at everyone and Muriel, Nel's friend, gave Nel and Viv an approving look, obviously on side and fit for battle, two plastic hips notwithstanding.

A man who was greeted warily by Pierce and more enthusiastically by Chris Mowbray, Nel took to be Gideon

Freebody. Abraham nodded towards him; he appeared ambivalent but not aggressive. He had an air of self-assurance Nel hadn't seen in meetings before. It was as if by going back into the building business he was wearing the status and confidence his standing in that world gave him.

Jake was the last to arrive. Nel allowed herself a tiny glimpse of him as he sat down, so he wouldn't see her looking. He was wearing the most heavenly suit. Her heart, or her desire, whichever it was, lurched at the sight of him. She lowered her eyes quickly, and started doodling frantically on the pad in front of her. How was she going to cope? Would she ever get over him if the sight of him made her practically melt? But you won't have to see him after today, she told herself. When you leave the meeting today your paths may never cross again, especially if you leave the county. Instead of relief, she felt total devastation.

'Well, ladies and gentleman,' said the chairman briskly, 'I know we've all felt a bit like a ship without a rudder, without a director in post, but I think between us we can make these important decisions regarding the future of what is close to all our hearts,' – Nel's own heart contracted at the thought of being close to Chris's – 'the hospice.'

He paused, looking round for possible applause. There was none forthcoming.

'You may all be wondering why I've called this meeting to discuss the building on Paradise Fields when really –' he looked round the room and smiled, 'we can have no say on the matter. We don't own the fields –' he glared at Nel, Viv and Muriel, who were all sitting together, 'and so we just have to accept that our jamborees and boat trips are a thing of the past.'

Abraham and Nel exchanged glances and silently agreed not to say anything just then.

'Well,' he continued. 'The reason I've called this meeting

278

is to tell you all about a very exciting proposal planned that would spread further than the fields and would affect us.'

Next to Nel, Muriel squirmed indignantly. Nel put a soothing hand on her arm, to silence her.

'We've got a lot of ground to cover, a lot of decisions to make, so I suggest that I ask Mr Freebody to give his presentation. I think when you've heard it, you'll agree that his plans are the way forward for the hospice.' He gave Abraham an irritated glare over the top of his reading glasses. 'Mr Abraham will give a presentation too, naturally, and then it's up to us, as the committee of the hospice, currently responsible for fiscal matters, to decide our best course. Mr Freebody.'

Mr Freebody wore a navy blue suit, white shirt and scarlet tie. He bulged over his trousers and his hair was black and greasy. He reminded Nel of some comedian or other who, according to the tabloids, had significant success with women. Nel could never understand why. Mr Freebody also had a sort of buoyancy, possibly brought about by his self-inflated image. He was used to winning, and assumed he would this time.

'My plan is an all-win offer which would not only make Mr Hunstanton here a substantial amount of money, but would also create enough wealth for the hospice for a brand-new, purpose-built hospital which will give youngsters with fatal illnesses every facility. It does entail pulling down the present building, but, I can assure you, it'll be cheaper in the end.'

'Nonsense!' said Muriel.

'I doubt that very much,' said Vivian.

'Don't you want the best for the kiddies? They are dying, you know!'

Everyone who actually worked with the children winced. No one ever referred to the children as having fatal illnesses, they had 'life-threatening conditions'. And the word 'hospital' was not popular, either. Muriel drew breath to protest but was silenced by a hand from Father Ted. 'Let the man speak, Muriel. We might as well know what his plans are.'

'At the moment,' Gideon Freebody went on, unaware how many people he was offending, 'the hospice has a constant battle to keep the building in good repair, raising funds, time after time, to replace windows, gutters and now a roof, when these items will have to be replaced again within a short time.'

'Not as quickly as they would if you'd built it,' said Muriel. 'I've been doing some research *on the Net*!' she confided to Nel, quite loudly.

'Here, here,' said Abraham.

'Please!' said Chris Mowbray. 'Let Mr Freebody finish! He has a very generous offer to make. Let him make it in peace!'

'I'm sure it must be wrong that the chairman has already decided in favour, before we've even heard the proposition,' muttered Vivian to Nel. 'Isn't it against the constitution?'

'I don't know,' Nel whispered. 'I haven't ever read the constitution.'

Viv sighed. 'Nor me.'

They sat back to listen to Gideon Freebody talk about drainage. It was when he got onto access that Nel really concentrated. But try as she might, she couldn't understand him. Then she realised he was deliberately obfuscating; the committee weren't meant to understand.

Nel never had what anyone would call a career. She had had jobs appropriate for an eighteen-year-old, but then she had got married. Since being married for years and becoming a widow she was given more responsibility in the part-time jobs she had had, but setting up the farmers' market was the only remotely businesslike thing she had ever attempted. She was aware she was inexperienced and untrained. She was accustomed to speaking at committee meetings when only the committee members were present, but arguing against hostile witnesses was completely new to her. Yet she couldn't afford to get it wrong. She took notes. She listened intently, she read the notes of her fellow committee members where she could. It was while she was trying to grasp what Gideon Freebody was saying about profit margins, explaining how the hospice would somehow get far more than the property and the land were worth, that she brought into play her ability to read upside down.

She'd developed this skill when going to parents' evenings. She didn't even know she could do it until she found herself reading what the teacher had really said about her child while listening to how they had translated that for parental consumption. Now, although she was too far away to see everything, she could read where Gideon Freebody had made notes. She hadn't even done it on purpose. She was just looking in his direction, frantically trying to decipher his double-speak, when she noticed his papers in front of him. She was sure she could see figures crossed out and replaced by other figures.

It was so frustrating, not being able to read clearly, and she wondered if they could be what she thought they were. After all, if she could nearly read them from where she was sitting, what was to stop the people sitting nearer reading them? Then she realised; the people sitting nearer probably didn't need to read the figures covertly. They probably knew if they'd been adjusted for the purposes of the meeting, because on one side of Gideon Freebody sat his side-kick, and Chris Mowbray, chairman of the committee, sat on the other.

Judging by the stack of notes in his hand, Gideon Freebody was not going to finish his spiel anytime soon. Nel wrote a quick note to Viv. *I'm going to the loo for tactical reasons. Make sure you write down anything that's important.*

Viv nodded, and Nel got up. As she reached the top of the table, she dropped her handbag. As she scooped up the contents, which were fairly embarrassing, she made sure she had a good look at Gideon Freebody's notes. No one noticed, she was sure. They were all just dismissing her as a daffy female who carried far too much clutter around with her. The chairman was particularly patronising as he handed her a very grubby hairbrush with a dog-chewed handle. Nel smiled sweetly and moved on, but she was pleased to note, as she did so, that Gideon Freebody had responded to her smile. Perhaps the white-lipsticked saleswoman had known her stuff after all.

Nel stayed out of the room for as brief a time as she reasonably could. When she came back in, Gideon Freebody was still intoning about giving the sick kiddies the best chance possible of a bit of decent medical care before they snuffed it. Nel could tell by the expressions on the faces of the really committed hospice people how well this had gone down. They all looked as if they were sucking on lemons.

At last Gideon Freebody drew to a close. Viv wrote a note. *I think he's trying to bore us into submission.*

Nel scribbled: *Did I miss anything vital?*

Viv replied: *Don't think so. I was struggling to keep awake.*

'Well, now, I think that was very interesting,' said the chairman. 'And obviously it will be easier for the committee to find a new director of the hospice if we have a nice new building. Shall we take a vote?'

Abraham got to his feet. 'I think maybe our chairman has forgotten something.' He looked sternly at Chris Mowbray. 'Gideon Freebody isn't the only builder present. While it might be questioned that this committee has anything to do with what Mr Hunstanton decides to do with his land, the building will affect the hospice and I think the committee have a right to know the full implications of the plans that have already been presented to them.'

Gideon Freebody muttered something to Chris Mowbray and then stood up. 'Hang on! You can't present your plans to the committee if you're on the committee! It would be an unfair advantage.'

'I think Mr Mowbray has unintentionally misinformed you, Mr Freebody,' said Abraham calmly, although Nel had suddenly found herself panicking. 'I resigned from the committee the instant the building issue came up. I did it in writing and by telephone.'

Chris Mowbray looked down at the papers in front of him, coughed and said, 'Do carry on Mr Abraham.'

'Well,' Abraham cleared his throat. 'I'll not be as long in the process of telling you all about my plans as my friend here. I might add that he builds houses quicker than he talks about them, but I won't—'

He held up his hand to stem the murmur of protest which arose from the Gideon Freebody camp. 'I've a bit to say about the plans I have devised with the help of an architect, who sadly, couldn't be here today.'

The chairman looked at his watch. Abraham began. 'The plans don't affect the hospice much—'

'Apart from taking away our playing fields and preventing us getting access to the river!' said Muriel indignantly, forgetting that Abraham was now a good guy.

'Very well, I'll rephrase that. Our plans don't affect the hospice as much as Mr Freebody's do. The hospice building is *not* affected, but, as I said at the outset, I'll put a new roof on the building for the cost of the materials. I was also persuaded by Nel . . .' Here he paused. 'She is a very persuasive young lady.' Nel blushed and looked down, aware that Jake's eyes were on her. 'Persuaded to rejig the plans somewhat, so there is still access to the river. With no reduction in the amount of houses which can be built.'

'Are you running a business or a charitable institution?' asked Gideon Freebody. 'Mr Hunstanton stands to make

283

much more money with my scheme. And there's more affordable housing in my plan than there is in yours!'

The vicar, sensing there was something more between the two builders than straight competition, stood up, giving them both disapproving looks. 'Gentleman! I'm sure you don't want this to become personal. It is for us as a committee to decide if we want to sell our building and build another one in its place. Not to hear about the money-making potential of the two schemes.'

'Except that if the hospice gets pulled down, it won't be in its place,' said Viv. 'It may not be anywhere near here. And I think we all agree that one of the reasons the hospice has been such a success is because so many local people support it. It's part of our community.'

'We do have to be businesslike,' said the man whose name Nel never knew, until she saw Viv scrawl it down for her. Fred Axminster. 'I'm a businessman myself.'

'Except we *are* a charitable institution, not a business,' said Nel.

'Do you think these comments could go through the chair?' demanded Chris Mowbray, who, as chairman, felt his authority was being challenged.

'Not unless we want to be here all night,' said Muriel briskly.

'What choice do we have, anyway?' said Fred Axminster, self-declared businessman. 'We can't afford to keep up the hospice building, we might as well sell it and build a new one.'

'Perfectly possible with the amount I'm offering for it,' said Gideon Freebody. 'As you know,' he looked at his audience in a rather patronising way, 'Mr Hunstanton owns Paradise Fields already. If I buy the hospice building, and then develop his site as well, we'll be quids – in a profitable position. And so will the hospice,' he added as an afterthought.

'Exactly,' said the chairman. 'Shall we vote?'

'No!' said Nel. 'I would like to speak, if the committee don't object.'

'We haven't got time for a lot of hearts-on-sleeves nonsense,' said Gideon Freebody's side-kick, who only needed a badge saying 'Security' to turn him into a nightclub bouncer.

Nel got to her feet. 'Everyone knows that I have an axe to grind. I have supported this hospice for ten years. I have been party to raising thousands and thousands of pounds. I am reluctant to see the hospice disappear.'

'It's not going to disappear!' Gideon Freebody was losing patience. 'I've explained! You can have a new hospice.'

'Not with the money you're offering us,' said Nel. 'The figures don't add up. Have you any idea how much a new building would cost, from scratch?' It was a rhetorical question, but she was very glad when Abraham answered it.

'A sight more than he's offering you, that's for sure.'

'If we allowed the hospice building to be sold, we'd lose it for ever. Even if there was enough money to build a new one, and I don't believe there is—'

'My figures show that you can,' said Gideon Freebody.

'Not the figures you're keeping to yourself,' said Nel. 'Those figures leave us with about enough for a one-up one down, if we're lucky with the price of the land.'

'That's slanderous!' said the chairman. 'Mrs Innes, I insist you withdraw that statement.'

'It's not slanderous if it's true,' said Nel, 'but I will withdraw it, because there are other arguments I'd like to put forward.'

'Oh, get out the violins,' said Gideon Freebody's side-kick.

'Please allow others to speak!' said Jake, who had been silent up until then.

Nel looked down at her notes. 'The plans and figures

you've put before us, Mr Freebody, overlook a couple of important facts.'

'And what might those be?' he demanded.

'The fact that your plans are completely useless if you don't have access. So while it might be perfectly possible for you to persuade the committee to sell the hospice, it isn't of any use if you can't get to the houses.'

'What do you mean?' asked the chairman.

'There's a ransom strip,' said Nel. 'Some committee members already know about it. But you seem to have overlooked it, Mr Chairman.'

He blushed. 'I don't know what you're talking about. All the hospice land is of a piece. There is no ransom strip. Hospice land is hospice land.'

'Yes, but I don't think everyone knows about this ransom strip,' said Nel, aware that she hadn't managed to contact everybody, and determined that it should be talked about, in the open.

'It would be nice to have it clarified,' said Chris Mowbray. 'If it exists.'

'It does exist,' said Jake. 'The late Sir Gerald Hunstanton left a small strip to the hospice in his will.'

'Thank you,' said Nel, still keeping her eyes firmly averted. 'And I think we should vote, as a committee, on what we want to do with this strip, as well as the rest of the hospice property.'

Chris Mowbray sighed with exaggerated patience. 'Well, you can vote if you want, but I do advise the committee, that for the sake of the hospice, Gideon Freebody's plans are the ones to go for.'

'For the sake of the hospice chairman, more like,' muttered Vivian to Muriel.

'I think the committee would, if presented with all the arguments, vote against selling the building.'

'The figures are there,' said Gideon Freebody.

'Yes, both sets,' said Nel, risking slander again. 'But

without the ransom strip, neither of your plans – either with or without the hospice land – can go forward, because you'd have no proper access. Which means the ransom strip is far more valuable than the sum you've put on it, just lumping it in with the hospice. Unless you're prepared to offer us at least four times what you have already, it would not be in the hospice's interest to accept your offer.'

'Can you afford to ignore it?' said Mr Freebody. 'You know yourselves how much the roof is going to cost to repair.'

'Well, we know how much it would cost if you repaired it,' said Nel. 'But Mr Abraham has offered to do it for nothing.'

'But the roof is only a tiny part of the upkeep!' said the chairman.

'And may I point out that the woman putting up all the objections—' Gideon Freebody began, before he was interrupted.

'The woman's name is Mrs Innes,' said Jake. 'I think you know that. Would you be kind enough to use it?' Nel blushed and all the women in the room sighed a little.

'I'll use the name I think fit!' Gideon Freebody set spittle arcing out of his mouth onto his notes. 'And that's Nimby! Not In My Back Yard! She doesn't want houses at the bottom of her garden! It's all very well to be sentimental about sick kids, but put a few cheap houses on her back lawn and she's up in arms!'

Jake half got to his feet, but was pulled down again by Father Ed.

'Except,' said the chairman, leaping up. 'She's not just a Nimby! She's been doing a bit of investigation as to how much her garden would be worth as building land! She wants to have her cake and eat it too!'

'I never did understand that expression,' said Viv.

Nel felt dizzy. She had never been attacked personally

like this before and it was strange, and yet oddly exhilarating. 'I beg your pardon, Mr Chairman. What did you say I'd done?'

'I said you'd been making enquiries as to how much your garden would be worth as building land. All this talk about ransom strips and saving the bloody hospice! You're just waiting for us to get planning permission for a big scheme so you can cash in yourself. You could get a three-bed executive home, on that bit of land. Garage with up and over doors.'

Nel wondered if she was going to faint. It was quite interesting, waiting to see if the room really would go black and fill with silver stars. 'I'm sorry, Chris,' she said quietly. 'I must be being particularly dense, but what the hell are you talking about?'

Muriel liberated a glass of water from the chairman's end of the table and handed it to her.

'Oh, you haven't done it yourself! You're far too clever for that! You got your boyfriend to do it for you!'

Before she could think what she was doing she looked at Jake. He shook his head so slightly she could hardly see the movement, and then she realised. It was Simon.

'Oh yes,' Chris Mowbray went on. 'Your boyfriend Simon Butcher – the estate agent. He made some very interesting enquiries on your behalf.'

Nel got to her feet. 'Really, I have no responsibility for what Mr Butcher does. But I can assure you that he did not act on my behalf. I would not dream of selling my garden in order to put houses on it!'

'See, I told you she was a Nimby,' said Gideon Freebody.

'This is a side issue,' said Jake. 'Now, everyone knows, I think, that I act for Mr Hunstanton, and therefore cannot be considered unbiased. But for common courtesy's sake, I would ask you all to listen to what Mrs Innes has to say without interruption.'

Chris Mowbray sighed. 'Carry on, Mrs Innes.'

'I propose,' said Nel, feeling both shocked and bolstered up by Jake's support, 'that the committee votes on whether or not we want our hospice building pulled down.'

'Can't afford to keep it up, if you'll pardon the pun,' said Chris Mowbray.

'And that to raise money for the upkeep of the building,' persisted Nel, 'we divide the ransom strip into plots, to be sold to individuals.' She sent a quick glare in the direction of Chris Mowbray. 'Which would have the effect of making it difficult for future committees to threaten to sell the building.'

'Well, I think that's a ridiculous idea,' said Chris Mowbray. 'But I'm keen to have a vote on whether we should maximise our opportunities, sell the hospice land and rebuild somewhere else. All those in favour of selling the hospice building and land to Mr Freebody and partners—'

Chris Mowbray looked round the table, his own hand up.

'May I point out that,' said Jake, 'as chairman, you don't have a vote unless it is a draw, and you need a casting vote.'

'Oh yes. Let's see?'

Not many hands were up, although Gideon Freebody and his sidekick both tried to vote, seemingly unaware they were not entitled to.

'Very well,' said the chairman. 'Now, who's against?'

'Would that be voting in favour of Nel's idea?' asked Muriel.

'Yes.'

Most of the people Nel had lobbied put their hands up. Nel counted, and it seemed to be evenly split. She curled her fingers so that her nails bit into her palms. If only she'd tried harder, said more, done more! The fate of the hospice now hung in the balance.

'I reckon that's an even split, so with my vote—' Chris Mowbray began.

'Excuse me,' said Jake, 'I know it's not strictly my business, but I do feel it would look very bad if a vote of such importance was taken while not all the committee members are present. I gather your legal advisor is in the Maldives?'

How did he know that? Nel scrawled to Viv.

'I told him ages ago. He must have stored up the information,' whispered Viv.

'So?' demanded Chris Mowbray.

'I don't know if he'd be pleased to discover that the committee had been talked into making a decision like this when he might say they didn't have an opportunity to discuss the matter completely fully,' went on Jake steadily.

'How would he know?' demanded Chris Mowbray.

'He would read the minutes,' said Jake.

Chris Mowbray exhaled loudly, exasperated.

'Can I suggest a compromise?' said Jake. 'That you bring the matter up again at the next meeting?'

There was a hurried consultation between Chris Mowbray and Gideon Freebody. Nel might have been mistaken, but she thought she heard something about 'planning permission' and it expiring.

'No, we can't do that,' said Chris. 'We have to decide now.'

Nel got to her feet. 'There's got to be a way round this! Can I suggest a compromise?'

'What?' demanded Chris Mowbray.

'That we give my idea of selling the plots a chance. If we can sell them, raise a certain amount of money, by a certain time, it would give the community a chance to say how they felt about their hospice being pulled down. And if we fail, well then, we'll accept the inevitable.'

'I won't,' said Muriel.

She was ignored. Chris Mowbray was looking at Nel with narrowed eyes as if plotting how to bring about her downfall. 'Very well,' he said. 'I'll give you a chance. If Mrs Innes raises say, ten thousand pounds,' he seemed to Nel to have thought of a figure he knew would be downright impossible to raise 'by –' he consulted Gideon Freebody 'the end of March, we'll discuss this again. If not, we sell. Agreed?'

Gideon Freebody sneered. 'Why not make it the first of April, make an April Fool of the whole stupid scheme.'

'Good idea!' said Nel rashly, refusing to be daunted by two such disgusting characters. 'And April the first happens to be the date we've decided on to have our next fundraising event. It's to include a farmers' market, as well. All those in favour?'

Most people raised their hands, but Nel's fellow members of the fundraising committee did look at her with some bemusement.

'You know I'm always prepared to back you up,' said Muriel. 'But I was going on a cruise on the first of April. Now I'll have to reschedule it.'

Chapter Twenty-one

❧

Nel felt as if she either had a very bad hangover, or was about to go down with flu. She realised it was shock. She must have looked odd too, as Viv offered to go home with her.

'No, you go and tell Florence all about the meeting. She'll be desperate to know what I wore. I need to go home and sort my head out.'

'OK. I'll come round later.'

'I'll ring if I need you. I've got to see Simon.'

'Ohmygod, I'd forgotten for a moment. Yes, of course.'

Although she was aware of his presence at every second, and thought she could avoid catching his eye, Nel found herself looking at Jake just as he was looking at her. He was putting his keys in his car just as she was doing the same. She wanted to cry, to laugh with embarrassment, to be sick, but she did nothing. She felt she should thank him for his support, but she couldn't shout her thanks across the hospice car park. She just stood there.

He saw her, and shrugged very slightly, and made the tiniest gesture towards a smile. Then he opened his car door, got in and started the engine.

Nel's own car was going by the time he drove away.

She went to see Simon at his office. She couldn't wait until six o'clock, and besides, she didn't want the visit to be remotely social.

'I'm afraid Simon's not back from lunch yet,' said a girl

Nel did know, but now couldn't remember the name of.

'I'll wait. He hasn't got an appointment immediately after lunch, has he?'

The girl checked. 'No.'

'Is it all right if I wait in his office, then? I've got some papers to look at.'

'No, I'm sure that will be fine.'

Simon was surprised to see her, and, as far as Nel could tell, not wholly pleased.

'Nel, what brings you into the office? You're not putting your house on the market, are you?'

'No. And I'm not interested in selling the garden for building land, either.'

'Oh.'

'There was a hospice committee meeting today. You knew that. You probably also knew the subject of my garden would come up.'

'I had no idea—'

'You had absolutely no right to enquire about my house, my land, on my behalf, without my permission.'

'Now calm down. I know I should have told you what I was doing, but you'd have had a fit!'

'Yes!'

'And I thought you ought to have the facts. We are practically engaged. It's my job to do these things for you.'

'No, it's not! And we're not practically engaged! It's not your job to do anything to do with me, unless I specifically ask you to, and then it's a favour, not a job!'

'Nelly, there's no need to get so worked up—'

'This is not worked up! This is calm and reflective! I've had time to think things over while I was waiting for you!'

'For God's sake—'

'And one of the things I thought was, there is no earthly point in you finding things out for me if you don't pass on the information! I had to put up with being called a

Nimby by a crooked builder before I knew what was going on. You made such a fool of me, Simon.'

'Sweetheart! Nel! Darling, it's not like that! Really, it's not. I made enquiries because I'm in a position to. Information is power! The more you know, the better you can make decisions!' He manoeuvred her onto a chair and handed her a glass of water. 'Just think about it; when the building has gone ahead, are you sure you'll still want to live where you do now?'

As she'd already asked herself this question, Nel didn't hesitate. 'Yes. There'd be no reason to move. I'll just plant trees down the end and screen off the houses.'

'And lose all your winter sunshine?'

'Would I? Oh well, I'd cross that bridge when I came to it. I'm not selling, Simon.'

'Fine. It's your decision. But if you did decide to sell, wouldn't it be better if you could put it on the market at a price which reflected that valuable bit of land you've got?'

'In theory. I suppose.'

'So I've done nothing wrong, then. I've only made some enquiries and found out some facts for you. As I did when I went through the *Yellow Pages* looking up farmers.'

Nel sipped the water. It was tepid, and now, so was her argument. 'You have been really helpful about that, Simon. I do appreciate it.'

'So you're not annoyed with me for making enquiries, then?'

'I do wish you hadn't. It was embarrassing for me at that meeting, being called a Nimby and not really knowing why.'

'You'd have got upset if I'd told you about it beforehand.'

'Well, yes, I would have, but only with you there. I wouldn't have got upset in front of a whole lot of strangers.'

'How did the meeting go?'

'It was hell! I feel as if I've been on the rack.'

Simon ignored her anguish. 'So, what was decided?'

Nel sighed. 'Well, it went to a casting vote. Obviously Chris wanted Gideon Freebody's plans, but Jake Demerand said that we couldn't take a vote on such an important issue without all the committee being there.'

'For God's sake! What is it to him!'

This seemed a bit of an overreaction, but as her own reactions to Jake were distinctly irrational, she didn't comment. 'He was just advising. Anyway, we reached a compromise.'

'What compromise? Did you agree to sell the building or not?'

'No! We're going to sell the chunks of land.'

'What chunks of land?'

'The ransom strip. You did know about the ransom strip? Simon, I thought you knew everything!' The sarcasm in her voice was so slight he didn't notice.

'Tell me!'

'There's a bit of land that Sir Gerald bequeathed to the hospice. It's vital access for Gideon Freebody's plan. Without it, he can't build. We're going to divide it into plots so it would be difficult to sell. There'd be so many legal costs, buying each one individually, it wouldn't be worth it. And then, most people would refuse to sell. It's why they've bought them, after all, to save the hospice.'

'Oh.' Simon seemed genuinely shocked. Nel couldn't help wondering why. Part of her realised he probably had some financial link with Gideon Freebody. She put it out of her mind; time enough later to chew on that.

She went on. 'The only trouble is, we have to sell all the plots by the first of April. I think that's a significant date for the planning permission or something, although no one said anything about it out loud. I don't think Chris Mowbray thinks we can do it.'

'Frankly, nor do I!'

'We're determined to. We're having a big fundraising event on the first anyway. We're doing a farmers' market, too. Give everyone new to it a dry run, sort of.'

'Nel, is this sensible?'

'Well, obviously the weather might be terrible, but we haven't got time to wait until summer.'

'No! I mean trying to hang onto the ransom strip! You'll never do it!'

Why was Simon so definite about this?

'Wouldn't it be better to sell it, and buy land and build a new hospice? Think how long it's taken you to find a new director. It would be much easier if you had a shiny new building to offer him.'

Nel was getting tired of this argument. 'Not necessarily! It's just possible that a new director might like lots of lovely high-ceilinged rooms with period detail! I know the offices are a bit cramped, but if the hospice had a bit of money to play with, it could convert the stables or something.'

'I don't know why you're so set on keeping that old building.'

'Well, you should do by now, Simon! We've known each other long enough! I have a fondness for elegant old houses. Besides,' she paused, not quite sure how to put her next point, 'I feel a bit worried about what would happen to the money if we did sell.'

'What could possibly happen to it?'

'Without a director, and a chairman of the committee who's definitely dodgy—'

'Chris Mowbray's all right! I play golf with him.'

'He's not all right. He's slimy. And I'm worried that if there's a large chunk of money, lying around in some account or other, waiting for us to find another plot and get a building plan organised, it just might leach away into people's pockets. And you can never build a new house for the money you could get an old house for. I've seen enough programmes on television about it.'

'The hospice could buy another old house, then.'

'But why should it? Why should it lose all its connections with the area, when it's ideally sited where it is now? It wouldn't make sense.'

Simon hesitated, as if Nel was slightly better informed than he'd thought she'd be – depended on her being, even. 'Well, say what you like, Chris Mowbray's an honest bloke! And Gideon Freebody's got a good reputation . . .'

'Has he, Simon? I thought you looked up that item in the newspaper on the net, and showed it to me, to tell me that Gideon Freebody didn't have a good reputation.' She paused. Simon had gone rather red in the face. 'Or did you show me that to tell me that Jake Demerand was crooked?'

'I meant it all for the best!'

'I'm sure you did, Simon. Just whose best, is what we need to consider!'

She left his office, leaving him trying to explain, but unable to find the words.

She drove home, tired and disheartened. She should have felt victorious; the hospice was safe for the time being. All she had to do now was get her son down from university and divide the land into plots for her. She also needed to find a solicitor to make it all legal.

Even if there was nothing personal between them, Jake was out of the question. He was working for the opposition. Pierce Hunstanton must be furious that his option of selling to Gideon Freebody had been taken away, by her, in particular. Both Gideon Freebody and Chris Mowbray must be pretty fed up with her as well. Not usually given to such thoughts, Nel suddenly wondered if they might take it out on her in some way. Kidnap Fleur, send in the heavies, fire-bomb her house? Or, at least, put a brick through her windows? She wished that things between her and Simon were OK. If they were friends, she could just ask him to come and stay for a few days until her irrational fears subsided. As things were, if she even mentioned that she was worried about having upset Gideon Freebody, he'd just lecture her about keeping her nose out of things she didn't understand and make her talk the committee back round into selling the building.

When she finally parked the car and came into the house she saw that someone had put a note through her door. She picked it and put it in her pocket while she greeted the dogs. When at last they'd agreed that it really was her, and they hadn't been abandoned for ever, she retrieved it.

It said: *If you need a good solicitor . . .* There followed a name and number. *Best, Jake.*

She carried the note through to the kitchen, holding it to her. She was grateful for the name, and would use it without hesitation, but at that moment, she felt more grateful for a few words on a scrap of paper – from Jake.

Even his handwriting was somehow sexy. Slightly old-fashioned, very black, angled. She read the note again. What did 'Best' mean? Could she possibly divine from those four letters that he had not slept with her for devious reasons? That he didn't just think of her as over forty, a widow and grateful?

She put the note on the dresser, tucked between a couple of her favourite antique jugs, and then filled the kettle.

Jake had gone a little way towards proving he was one of the good guys. He'd given her the tip about looking at the will, stuck up for her at the meeting. And giving her the name of a solicitor meant he was good, too. He knew she'd need one, and to save her time, he'd provided the name of one. That was at least three big ticks for Jake.

She put a Women's Tea bag in a mug. And what of

Simon? Could she tolerate such behaviour? Should she regard his enquiring about the value of her garden as helpful, or horribly intrusive?

It was hard not to think of it as intrusive. He may have been a friend for a good while, and helped her out many times, but ever since Mark died she'd been an independent woman, and she'd made her own decisions. Could she tolerate a man in her life making them for her?

She thought about the wonderful aquamarine ring that was hidden upstairs. She hadn't put it in her jewel case in case Fleur found it. Was losing her independence worth a gorgeous ring? No. Hell, she could save up her money and buy her own rings. She'd finish with Simon, in fact, probably all men, and carry on life as before, independent and happy, with her children about her.

She sipped the tea. It was very hot and peppery and it gave her courage. It was, she and Viv had decided, the tea-equivalent of neat whisky. What about when her children weren't about her? In about five minutes, the way the time went. Would she be happy to be on her own then?

Another sip, another answer: better to be on her own, and lonely, than to sacrifice her independence for one who might not be worth it. It was sad about Simon. She'd known him a long time, had trusted him and even depended on him in small ways. But recently he'd revealed himself as someone she didn't quite recognise, who played golf with influential people; who did things behind her back; took, she realised now, too much interest in her house. Was his plan to marry her for her property? Would he have been so fond, so attentive if she'd lived in a modern semi, with a garden there was no possible opportunity to build on?

It was a very lowering thought. No one wanted her unless there was something else with the package: influence on an important committee, a house with a valuable garden.

No. The last gulp of Women's Tea held the solution. Lonely widowhood was the answer. It was a pity this conclusion didn't make her dance with joy.

Villette put her paws up, and Nel heaved her onto her lap. There were lots of compensations to being alone. It wasn't only sexual love that made one happy. Apart from her children, there were gardens, decorating, her animals. There would be grandchildren one day, not too soon, she hoped, but all these things would bring contentment, and the sort of everyday happiness which made the world function. One day she would become the sort of woman whose most pressing problem would be deciding whether to decorate her hall in Farrow and Ball or Colefax and Fowler. Thousands of happy, contented women lived without sex. She had done so herself for years. She could do it again.

'Maybe I'll turn into an eccentric dog-breeder,' she said to Villette, who sighed, sounding tired. 'And just turn the dog hairs into a decorative effect.'

'So, Mum, this plot is approximately a hundred metres long and ten metres wide?' Sam, down from university, wanted to go and find some old friends, but he was having to give his mother a course in basic maths first.

'I think so.' When maths was concerned, Nel's brain went fuzzy, and she found it terribly hard to concentrate. She could do sums perfectly well when she needed to, if she didn't know she was doing them, like adjusting a recipe or deciding how much paint to buy. But now, because it was important (and because, she was forced to admit, her brain was addled by unrequited love), she felt tired and out of her depth.

'So, you could do it the easy way, and have a thousand plots of a square metre each. Charge, say, a hundred pounds each, and you've got a hundred grand, just like that.'

'No! Not just like that! For a start, I couldn't find a

thousand people to sell plots too, not if I had from now until the next Millennium, let alone by April the first, and for a second, I couldn't charge a hundred pounds for each plot! I was thinking more like twenty quid.'

Sam did some more dabbing onto his calculator. 'OK, five hundred people—'

'No, Sam. Think fifty people, possibly a hundred, two hundred at most. How much would I have to charge?'

A few seconds later, he said, 'Well, to get ten thousand pounds – that was the amount? You need to find two hundred people and charge them fifty quid a throw. Can't say fairer than that.'

Nel rested her face in her hands. 'Two hundred people! That's an awful lot.'

'Well, don't worry. Some people will buy more than one plot.'

'They're not allowed to!'

'Why not?'

'Because I deliberately made it be like that so Chris Mowbray couldn't buy up all the plots himself.'

'Oh. Chris Mowbray is a bad thing, is he?'

'Definitely.'

'And talking of bad things, who's this Jake guy Fleur keeps going on about?'

'He's definitely a bad thing.'

'Fleur didn't seem to think so. Says he's much nicer than Simon.'

'In some ways, I suppose . . .'

'Personally, I don't think Simon's a bad bloke, I just don't fancy him as a stepfather.'

'I would never inflict anyone on you whom you didn't like, but he wouldn't be a stepfather, really, not now you're this age.'

'Mum, Simon's been a stepfather every time he's come into this house and I've been here. I know he means well, I know he does it to support you, but he does it. Asks about uni, whether I'm going to lectures, have I got a job, that sort of thing.'

'Oh God, I'm sorry.'

'The sort of stuff you don't ask me.'

'But the sort of stuff I would quite like to know.'

Sam grinned. 'Mum, you know I'm a good boy, really.'

His mother smiled back, feeling she should make the most of this quality time with her eldest child. 'Cup of tea, darling?'

Sam glanced at the clock. 'OK, quick one. Shall I make it?'

'That would be lovely! You're so sweet to me!'

'It's easy to be the good son when I'm not here much. Especially as you might give me some money, Mummy.'

Nel sighed and reached for her handbag. 'Sometimes I think you children think those words are interchangeable.'

'There you are, *Mummy*.' Sam put down the tea, and Nel handed over a ten-pound note.

'Very expensive café, this.'

'Yes, but you get therapy thrown in. What gives, Ma?'

'Simon has asked me to marry him.' Nel could see her son controlling his reaction. 'I'm not going to, I don't think.'

'Why not? Don't worry about us kids. We'll cope. But what's wrong with him?'

It was a relief to talk about it. 'Well, apart from the fact that he's always known that I don't want to have a permanent relationship while you kids are still at home . . .' She frowned, suddenly. 'And yet he asked me anyway, and came up with a ring.'

'A ring, eh? What does my sister have to say about that?'

'She doesn't know. Simon asked me not to tell her.'

'Why not? Does he think she'll talk you out of it?'

'I think so.'

'And will she?'

'She doesn't have to. I think Simon only wants me for my house.'

302

'That's a bit unfair, isn't it?'

'I wish it was, but we were bumbling along, nothing much happening, and then, when this whole building fiasco erupts, he's asking me to marry him. Well, I told him the very first time we went for a drink that I wouldn't be interested. The two things can't be unconnected.'

Sam shrugged and looked at the clock again. 'So tell me about this Jake bloke, then? Fleur likes him.'

'He's not "in the frame", as they say, Sam.'

Sam chuckled. 'You do have some quaint expressions, Ma. So?'

'So, what? I said, he's not an issue.'

'Tell me anyway. So I know what Fleur's talking about. Apparently he's the one who kissed you under the mistletoe?'

And the rest, she thought. 'Sam, if I have to give you a rundown on everyone who kissed me under the mistletoe, which would be rather a strain on my ageing memory—'

'Don't give me that baloney. Fleur said he came here and helped you make a cake.'

'Oh yes. Well, he did. But he ruined the first one, it was only fair.'

'She said he was really fun.'

'Yes, he is, but he's younger than me, and he's not really interested, and I'm never going to see him again, so he's not relevant.'

'To what?'

'To my life. Now, don't you think you ought to be going? Your friends will be waiting.'

Sam got up and took his jacket from the back of the chair. 'Not like you to urge me out drinking.'

'Anything to stop the third degree, Sam. Don't forget to drink plenty of water.'

'Cheers, Mum.'

*

The solicitor recommended by Jake was fatherly and kind. His offices were also a lot more elegant than Jake's were when Nel last saw them.

'Mr Demerand told me you might get in touch. It's about dividing a ransom strip currently owned by the local hospice so it can't be bought by developers?'

'That's right. We also need to make it so people can only buy one bit each. Otherwise the developers would just buy them all themselves. And we also have to be sure that the land is safe from future hospice committees who may want to sell it.'

Mr Tunnard put his pen down and regarded Nel over the top of his spectacles. 'Mrs Innes, there's something I feel I should tell you.'

'What?' Nel had had so many shocks lately that her heart jerked every time anyone said anything to her in that confidential, almost doom-laden, voice.

'The legal expenses of such a thing would be high. There's a lot of paperwork involved.'

'You mean I'd have to factor that in to the price of each plot?'

'No, you couldn't do that.'

'So you're asking me how I'll pay?' For a moment, she allowed herself to speculate on the value of a certain aquamarine ring hidden in her knicker drawer.

'No. I'm telling you that Jake Demerand has asked me to act for you *pro bono*, for nothing.'

'Oh – he shouldn't have done that! It's not fair! Unless you're devoted to the cause, why should you?'

'Because Jake agreed to give me his time in lieu.'

'Sorry, I don't understand.'

'I'll make a note of the hours I do, and then he'll do those hours for me, when I need him to.'

'So . . .'

'So it's Jake who's working for nothing, not me.'

'Oh.'

'I'm telling you because I got the impression from Jake that you didn't have a very high opinion of him. Now, I don't know Jake well personally, but professionally I know him well enough to be certain that he's a thoroughly good man.'

Feeling this was an opportunity, Nel asked him, 'I thought he'd been involved in some scandal about selling off old peoples' homes or something.'

'I know the case to which you're referring. But he was on the losing side. One of the good guys.'

'I see,' she said, to stop herself saying 'oh' again. But she didn't see, really.

'In this case, he could hardly offer to do the work himself, when he's involved with one of the developers.'

'No, but why did he want to? Why get involved with this bit at all?'

Mr Tunnard raised a bushy eyebrow. 'I really couldn't say, Mrs Innes.'

Chapter Twenty-two

❧

'It'll be easy, don't worry about it,' said Fleur, who was painting her toenails in the sitting room, her nail varnish balanced perilously on the arm of the sofa.

Nel was watching the bottle, ready to catch it if it wobbled, having abandoned the notion of asking her daughter to beautify herself in her bedroom, the bathroom, or indeed, anywhere except the drawing room.

'Darling, I'm not selling pints on a Friday night! I'm asking people to donate fifty pounds to charity. That's quite a lot. When those lovely young men stop you in the street, they never ask you to sign up for more than a couple of quid a month.'

'And you've already asked lots of people already.'

'I know, but I didn't say how much they'd have to fork out, and most of those people were farmers' market bods. A lot of them are very hard up as it is. Why should they pay to stop a building they're never likely to see from being pulled down?'

'You have to tell them about the children. Lay it on thick.'

'You know I'm hopeless doing things like that.'

'You mean you cry.'

'Well! Even you, Hard-Hearted Hannah, must feel just a little bit sad.'

'Of course I do. But I don't actually have to cry about it in public.'

'No, well, nor would I if I could help it.'

'Is it because Dad died, do you think?'

Nel shook her head. 'No. My hormones were shot to

pieces when I was first pregnant, and they never recovered. It was years before I could watch the news without weeping.'

'*Really?* I hope that doesn't happen to me when I get pregnant.'

'You're not planning on getting pregnant, are you?' This was all she needed, suffering acutely from a broken heart, having to find two hundred people with fifty pounds to spare, organise a jamboree for the hospice combined with a farmers' market, plus a teenage daughter expecting a baby. Just at that moment, she didn't feel she could offer appropriate support.

'Derr! Of course not! I haven't even left school yet! Let alone gone travelling and gone to uni.'

'That's all right then.' Now the toenails were a suitably vivid pink, Nel took away the bottle and screwed on the lid.

'Did you thank Jake, by the way?' Fleur was now doing damaging things to her hair.

'I told you. I tried to. I went to his office, the moment after I left the other one, but he wasn't there. What else can I do? I haven't got his telephone number.'

'You could try and find his telephone number. Someone must know it. Did you ask at his office?'

'Darling, you don't ask for people's home telephone numbers at their offices! It would look desperately needy for a start, and they wouldn't give it to you anyway.'

'I bet they would if you explained.'

Nel shook her head. 'I wrote a letter and sent it. That will be fine.'

Fleur shook her head, her mouth full of hairgrips. 'It's not the same as saying it face to face, or on the phone.'

'No, it's better. More polite.'

'You're just being cowardly. Do you think I should have my eyelashes tinted?'

'What's wrong with mascara? No, I'm not.'

'What?'

'Being cowardly. I just don't want to see him. There's no point.'

'You really like him, don't you?'

Nel knew this question had a lot more weight that it might have sounded. She sighed. Was there any point in trying to protect her daughter from how she felt? No, she decided. If Fleur was old enough to have sex (which, as her mother, she doubted), she was old enough to know about men who used you and then left you. Except had Jake used her? If so, for what?

'Mum? Do you really like Jake?'

'Yes, I do. He's – well – lovely. And we did flirt, I admit that. But there's nothing more to it than that. On his part, anyway.'

'How do you know that?'

'Oh, honey! It's not rocket science! He's younger than me! He's extremely attractive, he's single, why would he want me?'

'Mum! It's not rocket science! You're very attractive, you're a widow, why wouldn't he?'

'Darling, it's so sweet of you to say that I'm attractive. But it's only because I'm your mother, and you love me, that you think so. To the rest of the world I'm just frumpy, overweight Nel.'

'If Viv could hear you she'd go mad! You're not frumpy – at least, not when I'm around to check you're not, and you're not overweight! Lots of people fancy you!'

'Lots of people are very kind to me. And why shouldn't they be? I'm kind to lots of people, and what goes around, comes around. But I'm not a sex symbol.'

Fleur opened her mouth to disagree but then shut it again. It was hard to think of your mother as a sexual being – harder, possibly, than thinking of your daughter as one. 'You probably are to the right person,' she said after some thought.

'Yes, I probably am. But probably not to someone like Jake, who could have anyone.' And has had me, she added privately, to torture herself.

'Well, I'm off out now. Why don't you give Viv a ring and get her to come round, share a bottle of wine?'

In spite of her despair, Nel laughed. 'Why do I let you get away with telling me how to run my life?'

Fleur scooped up the accoutrements of her beauty regime into a bag. 'Because I've got one, that's why.'

'Are you telling me to get a life?' Nel was indignant.

'Not a life. You have a life. But you need a love life. Look at Viv. She really knows how to enjoy herself.'

'Which probably means she doesn't want to come round here and share a bottle of wine with me.'

'No, but if you rang her, she'd tell you what a twit you're being. She'd see it as an emergency.' Fleur kissed Nel's cheek. 'Bye. Have fun. Don't do anything I wouldn't do.'

'As if,' said Nel, and went to hang socks on the airer over the Rayburn. There seemed to be hundreds of them. They were all much the same colour, but there didn't seem to be any pairs. As always, she thought about the puzzle which asked: if a drawer is full of black socks and white socks, how many would you have to pull out before you got a pair? The answer was three, but Nel knew it wouldn't work in her case.

Harry, the owner of approximately half the socks, came into the kitchen.

'I do wash them myself,' he said. 'But it seemed pointless to do it when I was coming home for the weekend.'

'Obviously. It's so sensible to carry a bag of dirty washing with you when you're on the coach from Newcastle.'

'It's just a few socks, Ma, the rest of them are Sam's.'

Nel sighed. 'You know I don't really mind. It's nice that you're both home together.'

'There's this party we want to go to in Bristol.'

309

'Oh? And I thought you'd come to see your darling mother.'

'That too, of course. And check out this new bloke. Sam told me about him.'

'Sam did? Well, he's made a mistake. There is no new bloke.'

'I don't mind Simon, myself. I mean, he's never going to set the world on fire, but he's OK.'

'Exciting enough for your old mother, obviously.'

'I didn't mean that!' Harry put his arm round Nel's shoulders and squeezed. She'd forgotten how strong and muscly he was nowadays. 'I meant that if you want to marry Simon, you should just go ahead. We can look after ourselves now.'

Nel put the kettle on. 'Well, for a start, I don't want to marry Simon, and for a second, Fleur is still at school. She couldn't look after herself.' Nel was not entirely sure this was true, but as she had no intention of letting Fleur loose on the world just yet, it might as well have been.

'So what about this new bloke, then?'

'There is no new bloke! He's a figment of Fleur's imagination, probably because she doesn't like Simon.'

'Doesn't like Simon? What's not to like? Just get him a tweed jacket with leather patches on the elbows, and he'd be perfect! Fleur's a fashion-fascist, that's all.'

'Yes, probably. But I told you, I'm not going to marry Simon – and there is no new bloke,' she repeated hurriedly.

'But Fleur said he came here and helped you make a cake.'

'Yes, he did, but it was just a cake. Do you remember that ski slope cake I made you? I got Viv to make a figure out of silver foil?'

'You're changing the subject, Ma.'

'No, I'm not. I'm segueing from a subject that has lost interest into another, more interesting one.'

'If you think that cakes are more interesting than blokes, Fleur must have been adopted.'

'I think I would have remembered doing that, but it is possible she was swapped in the hospital. She's the only organised member of the family. Oh, that reminds me.' She went to the dresser. 'I took this stuff out of your jeans pocket. I wish you'd empty your pockets yourself. I don't want to be the sort of person who goes into other people's pockets, but nor do I want tissues in the tumble drier, covering Fleur's little black tops with fluff. She makes enough fuss about the dog hair as it is.'

Harry rolled his eyes, then dashed past her to the Rayburn. 'Did you want tea, Mum, or did you just boil the kettle over for fun?'

'So, how are you?' asked Viv, on her mobile, from a hotel where they had fluffy white robes on the backs of the doors, and very expensive freebies in the bathroom, all of which Viv had just described.

'Fine, the boys are here. How about you?'

'Oh, the boys are here, too. Different boys, of course.'

'So I should hope. I don't think I could cope with my best friend showing my sons the way. So, is there an ironing board in the room, or did you have to ring for one?'

'No, it was here. And there were herb tea bags. It really is an awfully good hotel.'

Nel sighed. 'You're a lucky girl. There is nothing I would like more than spending the weekend in a really nice hotel.'

'With the right man, of course.'

Nel considered. 'Well, for preference, but even on my own would be quite good.'

'And the right man would be?'

'My fantasies are my own. How are you doing with your list?'

'Well, I've sold a plot to most of the people I'm with, which, before you ask, is why I go out with rich people.' Vivian managed to say this without sounding in the least smug. 'What about you?'

Nel yawned. 'Lots of them would give a tenner to a good cause. They're not mean. But fifty quid is a lot when you're on a low income.'

'You could club them together, make little syndicates.'

'Well, yes, I could. If I had till next Christmas to do it in, instead of only until April Fools' day.'

'April the first sounds much better,' Viv said reprovingly.

'I know what I mean. And I just don't have time to go around matching up people. When people know each other, I have suggested it, but they all have their own lives, their own agendas.'

'Hey, I've got an idea,' Viv exclaimed. 'I think we should advertise in the paper. Or get them to write an editorial, giving a contact name for people who are interested.'

'That's a good idea. And the contact name would be yours, I presume?' Nel asked hopefully.

'Fine, if you don't want to do it. I am a bit rushed at the moment—'

'No, no, that's all right. I just sit and twiddle my thumbs all day. I'll be the contact name. But you have to ask your friend who works on the paper to do the article.'

'I'll get to it the minute I'm home. Is my little dog all right?'

'She's fine. Curled up on the sofa with the rest of them.'

'Good. Now, I must dash. The bubbles are threatening to topple over onto the bathroom floor.'

Nel put the phone down with a sigh. It would be nice to be taken somewhere really lovely, to be spoilt, pampered and looked after, just once. And then, inevitably, her mind on its single track, she thought of what she and her fantasy spoiler might do in the king-sized bed with the very fine cotton sheets. The trouble was, it was a very precise fantasy. She knew exactly who she wanted to be in that hotel bedroom with.

It was getting frighteningly near the end of March and it was snowing, when Abraham telephoned Nel.

'All right, lass?' he asked her.

She felt instantly comforted. 'OK, sort of. I haven't sold nearly enough plots, though.'

'I was just ringing to ask if you'd like a bit of steam at the hospice jamboree.'

'What do you mean?'

'I've got some friends who own steam engines, organs, rollers, all that sort of stuff, and after I'd told them the story, they volunteered to come along. They'd collect money and buy a plot with it. It would belong to the Old Steamers' Association.'

'That sounds wonderful! We've always had steam boats before, but not land-based things. Do they take up a lot of space?'

'A fair bit.'

Nel mentally rearranged the farmers' market, which was also going to buy a plot. 'That will be lovely! Do say "yes please" to them.'

'But there will need to be a beer tent. Think you can arrange that?'

Nel wrote down 'beer tent' on her list, her heart sinking as she thought of licences and all the red tape that accompanied public drinking.

'Real ale for preference.'

'Real ale.'

'We'll have a right good time.'

'Yes. If the weather clears up.'

'In like a lion, out like a lamb. That's March for you.'

'I don't remember the weather starting to get bad until about the fifteenth. I think it might be in like a lamb,

313

out like a lion, this time. Oh Abraham, if the weather's foul no one will come! I still have twenty-five plots to sell!'

She wanted him to say, 'Dinna fash yissen, lass,' but he didn't. He just said, 'That many? Oh dear.'

'Pinch and a punch for the first of the month,' said Sam as Nel came into the kitchen.

'It doesn't count, I've been up for hours.' She smiled and hugged him. She and Mark had always pinched and punched each other, and now Sam had stepped into his father's shoes. 'I do appreciate you coming down for this Jamboree. It'll probably be a complete fiasco.'

Sam shrugged. 'Jamboree, fiasco, they both sound pleasantly foreign. And the sun is shining, look!'

'Yes, but it was fine before seven, that means it'll rain before eleven.' Much as Nel had been looking forward to it, the fact that April the first had arrived without all the plots being sold couldn't help but depress her. But she decided to put it out of her mind – her only way to help the hospice now was to make a success of the jamboree.

Sam seemed unfazed by her pessimism about the weather. 'Rubbish. You shouldn't listen to all those old wives' tales. Now, what do you want me to do? I've come down from London, I've got up early—'

'It's half past ten. It's hardly early.'

'I'm a student. That's early. So use me.'

'I want you to bike down to Paradise Fields and see if everyone's all right. The Old Steamers all arrived yesterday, but the beer tent couldn't come until today. It's going to make us awfully late.'

'Bike down! Can't I take the car?'

'No! I need it. I've got to collect the banner from Muriel and put it up. It's beautiful, a real work of art. It's going in the local museum when we've finished with it.'

'Why can't Muriel put it up?'

314

'Because she's nearly eighty, has two plastic hips and hasn't got a long ladder.'

'Nor have you.'

'I'm going to borrow Simon's.'

'He'll never let you have it. He'll make a fuss and say you'll fall off—'

'I'm not going to tell him, I'm not speaking to him. I'm just going to take it. It's in his garage. Now, I haven't got time to stand here arguing the toss. On yer bike!'

As she stood on the top rung of the ladder with one arm out at right angles, holding a banner which seemed to be getting heavier by the second, Nel conceded that Simon might have had a point about the ladder. Wearing wellingtons might have been a mistake, too, but as Paradise Fields were extremely muddy, she hadn't had a choice.

'Can you let me have a bit more rope?' asked Ben, the chef, who fortunately had arrived early and, being extremely good-natured, was fixing the other side.

'If I give you enough, you'll hang yourself,' said Nel, who was getting skittish, but decided it was better than becoming tearful, which, considering the state of the fields, the unreliability of the weather, and the fact that the beer tent had still not arrived, was not an unreasonable alternative.

'Thanks. That OK?'

'I'll have to come down the ladder to look,' said Nel, suddenly finding coming down the ladder a bit of a problem. Every time she tried to move, the instep of her boot got stuck on the rung and made it wobble. She couldn't possibly spare the time to go to A. and E. with a broken leg.

Ben jumped off his ladder from about six feet. 'Hang on. I'll give you a hand.'

He put his big hands on her waist and held her while

she disengaged her feet and then swept her down off the ladder and into the mud. 'Thank you,' she said. 'My boots are a bit big. They're my son's.'

'No problem.'

He was extremely attractive, Nel decided as she watched him brush his hands together and stride off towards some women who were putting up a coconut shy. Perhaps she should consider a toy boy, a proper boy, not just a man who was only a couple of years younger than she was. They would be a lot of fun and wouldn't expect major life changes.

She allowed herself a glance at the man who was always in her thoughts, who was right over the other end of the field, marking out the field for the five-a-side football competition, which he was organising. She hadn't thanked him personally for doing this, but Viv had, so she didn't feel obliged. She had felt such a lowering pang of jealousy when she realised he and Viv must have spent several minutes in conversation together that she had even considered some sort of therapy.

She took a moment to scan the field and check her list, which was getting increasingly muddy. If she were a proper organising woman, she'd have a clip-board and a list of people delegated to help. She just smiled and cajoled and got people to help anyway.

The steam people had their machines – wonderful beasts, seemingly alive – ranged down the far end. They had fallen on the *Lady Elizabeth*, the hospice steam yacht, with glee and had spent a happy time arguing amiably with Jack, who usually ran it, about the finer points of steam power.

The boat looked like a royal barge, all decked out with bunting, courtesy of Muriel, and was going to give trips up and down the river. There was still argument going on about how much to charge. Viv felt the trips should be fairly expensive, so they would make a lot of money, and Muriel thought they should be cheap, so people would take more than one trip. Nel, who had enough to think about, was keeping out of it.

The spot for the beer tent – close enough to the steam crowd to satisfy them, not too near the farmers' market which was selling apple juice and soft drinks as well as their usual fare – was still looking frighteningly empty. Frantically, Nel tried to think of a plan B, in case it didn't arrive on time, or at all. Unfortunately, nothing occurred to her beyond asking the local pub to drag a few kegs of beer into the field and she didn't think they'd fancy it.

She could have asked Sam, of course; he often organised parties, which involved invading a distant field, or railway arches, hiring a generator for the sound equipment, and buying a sufficient number of cans of beer to require several trips to the recycling centre. But somehow Nel didn't think the Old Steamers would be happy with budget lager. They wanted beer with unspeakable names and unmentionable ingredients.

It was nearly twelve. The grand opening was scheduled for two o'clock. The fields were a mass of scurrying people, floundering in mud, laughing, cursing, battling with ropes, sheets of canvas, corrugated plastic, and bits of board which moved in the wind. There were people struggling to put up awnings, ramming posts into the ground, tying bits of rope together and stretching them at neck height across the pathways. It was chaos. There was no other word for it.

Sam appeared. 'Hi, Mum, how you doing? It's just like Glastonbury, isn't it?'

Nel had never been to Glastonbury, which, to the amusement of her children, she pronounced with a long A, but she knew it was inclined to be muddy.

'Do you want me to nip into town and stock up on black plastic bags?' he went on.

'Why? What for?'

'To stop everyone getting trench foot.'

'Oh, go away, Sam!'

'Only joking, Mother.'

Nel went to find Viv, for some moral support. She had a honey stall in the market, but it was being minded by Lavender, with her lavender-scented candles, wheat compresses, soap and linen bags.

'How's it going, kid?' asked Viv, who was managing to look attractively wind-blown. 'Look, that must be the beer tent arriving. Has Chris arrived yet?'

'Oh God no! He wouldn't be seen before the moment he opens it! He wants all the bells and whistles. The band are all set to play "Anchors Aweigh" because he was once in the Sea Scouts.'

'I'm still not sure we should have asked him to do it. We could have got a local actor to do it so easily.'

'I know, but he was so flattered he bought a plot of land himself. And not even he could do a dodgy deal with a plot that size.'

'You don't think we've panicked over it all, do you?' Viv brushed a strand of hair out of her eyes streaking her face with mud as she did so.

'Definitely not. He's a crook and a toad.' She paused. 'Do you want me to spit on my hanky and get the mud off, or will you brave the Ladies?'

Viv rubbed at her face. 'I'll brave the loos. They're OK if you go early. Were they terribly expensive, by the way?'

'Yes. That's why there are only two. I did get a special deal, though. The man was so nice.'

'I don't know why you don't realise how attractive to men you are, Nel.'

'Don't start, Viv! There're a thousand things I have to do before lift-off. Do you think the pig will be roasted in time for people to actually eat it today?'

'Don't ask me, I'm a vegetarian.'

'No need to be smug about it.'

'Nel! Lighten up! We're supposed to be having fun here!'

'You may be, but I'm not. I'm supposed to be making sure that all the stallholders are happy with their site and that the steam people like the real ale, which is called Pig's Bottom, or something equally gross. The band only drink Streaked Lightning, by the way.'

'What's that when it's at home?'

'Some sort of cider from the Forest, I think. It's probably illegal, but would clean your drains, no problem. I haven't actually tasted it myself.'

'Well, perhaps you should. It might cheer you up.'

'The only thing that would cheer me up is being cloned enough times so I can be everywhere I need to be at the same time.'

'Make-up tips I can do. Cloning is beyond me. I'm going to talk to Jake.'

Nel watched her beautiful best friend stalk off in the direction of the love of her life and forced herself to smile. Not as genuine a reaction as bursting into tears, but less messy.

Chapter Twenty-three

❦

'So, how many plots have you sold, then?' Chris Mowbray oiled up to Nel through the mud. He was dressed in a blue blazer with shiny buttons, a very regimental-looking tie, white drill trousers and new-looking wellington boots, possibly bought that morning.

Before she replied, Nel was pleased to observe that flecks of mud sullied the creases of his slacks. She was sure he'd refer to them as slacks. He looked, she thought, like a 1950s advertisement for cigarettes. Then she beamed. 'Hello, Chris. How thoughtful of you to be on time. We're all ready. And aren't we lucky with the weather? It's cleared up beautifully. Bright sunshine, after all the showers. Perfect.'

'You know they've all got to be sold today. In fact, if you haven't sold them already, I reckon it's too late.'

Nel went on beaming. Her smile muscles were in danger of going into spasm. She had not sold all the plots, but she was determined not to spoil the jamboree because of it. She would sort something out tomorrow, now she had to put on a happy face.

'I don't think so,' she said through her teeth. 'I don't think April the first ends until midnight. I might be wrong, of course, but I think that's generally accepted to be the end of the day.'

Chris Mowbray snorted and marched off. Nel offered a silent prayer that he might trip over something and fall into the mud, but sadly, at ten minutes to two, the site was remarkably organised.

Even in her depressed and panicky state, Nel could not avoid noticing that everything looked lovely, a modern Brueghel scene, full of life, colour and activity.

A row of white awnings (bought by Nel out of her new farmers' market overdraft) denoted the market end of the proceedings. As if to co-ordinate with the awnings, but in fact to comply with Health and Safety standards, the food producers were wearing smart white overalls and white hats. They looked hygienic, professional and efficient.

Sacha's stall, like a sapphire among diamonds, had pyramids of blue bottles and jars. Acetate boxes of her special bath chocolates decorated with rosebuds caught the light, and behind the stall, with Sacha, in a short, tight, white nylon uniform, sat Kerry Anne. She looked a confusing mixture of squeaky-clean nurse and sexual fantasy involving tight belts and nappies. Sacha had explained to Nel on the phone that although Kerry Anne was a money-grabbing madam, she had her uses.

Next to them was Lavender, adding amethyst to the sapphire. Bunches of lavender hung all around the top and down the sides of her stall. Within the frame were scented candles, bright cotton lavender bags, white linen lavender-filled pillows and bottles of lavender water. Like Viv's honey stall next to it, it was a foretaste of summer: optimistic, sensual, positive.

Next to them was a more eccentric entry to the farmers' market world, one which Nel feared she would not get past the council. It was hard enough to persuade them that good quality crafts were eligible, but this woman made hats. In her favour was that they were made on a farm: her husband was a farmer, and she had some token eggs displayed in an up-turned straw boater, but what she produced was designed for Ascot, rather than a small local fair.

They were sensational: elegant and pretty and

unashamedly frivolous. Some were huge, flower-covered cartwheels, some were little tight-fitting caps with a swirl of black feathers, others were coy bunches of net, designed to flirt through, and the rest were the sort of straw hat you could wear all summer. Viv had already bought one and was wearing it, displaying both her purchase and herself to maximum advantage. When Nel had visited the stall earlier and seen the price of the produce, she had sold a plot to the creator. 'Just one hat sold, and you're in profit – buy a square, there's a dear!'

The milliner, who had moved down from London to marry her farmer boyfriend, had laughed and produced her cheque book.

'I'll buy more than one if you like.'

'Not allowed, I'm afraid,' Nel had explained. 'Although now,' she added, 'I wish we'd put a maximum number of purchases on it, making it possible for people to buy up to five plots, say. I'm finding it awfully hard to find enough people.'

At the more conventional end of the market, Catherine was already doing a brisk trade in organic burgers, as was Geoff, the ice-cream maker, whom Nel had never got round to meeting, but had said 'yes' to on the phone, thinking the event would need ice cream and it might as well be his. She had sampled it that morning, and decided as soon as his equipment was up to standard, he must become a market regular.

Ewan, the hurdle maker, had set up a whole cluster of wicker wigwams. His wife had made long, silky pennants which now fluttered from their tops, giving the impression of a miniature medieval jousting ground. Apparently they were either for children to play in or for adults to grow beans up, whichever seemed more appropriate.

At the river end of the ground was the steam fair. A steam organ, complete with lovingly restored automata, banging drums and clapping cymbals, added colour and life to the more workaday steamrollers and traction engines. All the machines hissed and steamed gently, like benign dinosaurs in a primeval swamp.

Behind the steam engines, the pièce de résistance was the *Lady Elizabeth*, bedecked with bunting and flowers, as magnificent and stately as any royal barge. The sun shone on the water, all the brighter for the rain which had gone before. A small queue was already forming by the notice advertising boat-trips. Nel still didn't know who'd won the battle regarding prices, but she didn't care. It all looked beautiful.

One of the local primary schools had produced a maypole, and its top class was scheduled to dance round it, weaving in and out, plaiting and unplaiting, just after Chris Mowbray had pronounced the fête open. Nel promised herself a ringside position. The potential for disaster was enormous, but attractive in a bizarre way.

The band, up near the wooden box which was acting as a podium (Nel hadn't thought that she might need a podium until ten minutes earlier, and had frantically begged from stall to stall for something that would do), all looked magnificent in their braided uniforms and peaked caps. The sun sent sunbeams bouncing off their instruments which were polished like mirrors.

Just as she was taking a last look at the river, before finding the megaphone so Chris Mowbray could make his speech, Nel saw a flash of iridescent blue skim the willows. A kingfisher! It had to be a good omen, whatever happened today; a kingfisher had to mean good things.

In a moment of sentimentality, brought on no doubt by love-sickness and the fact she had had no breakfast, it occurred to Nel that events like this, in one form or another, had been going on for centuries: people gathering together, buying, selling, meeting old friends and making new ones. And even when Paradise Fields disappeared under new houses, fairs would still continue, if not here, then somewhere. What was still uncertain was what and how many houses would cover it. In her pocket, Nel had the forms for thirteen unsold plots.

She handed Chris the megaphone. The band were silenced; the steam organ wheezed to a stop.

'You would think,' Chris Mowbray muttered, all pretence of being friendly long gone, 'that you'd have been able to set up a decent public-address system, instead of this bloody thing.'

'And you would think,' said Nel, not bothering to pretend any more either, 'that you might be bit more graceful about doing this. We could have had the actor from that new police series, you know. He'd have done it without making all this fuss! Everyone said we should have a celebrity, but I held out for asking you. For all you've done for the hospice.'

Watching him then, she tried to think of what he'd done for the hospice since he'd been chairman of the board. Apart from encouraging a very good director to leave and trying to close the whole thing down, she couldn't think of a thing.

Chris Mowbray gave her a withering look. 'Fat slag,' he muttered, then brought the megaphone to his lips.

'Ladies and gentlemen . . .' he began.

'And fat slags,' muttered Nel, who, instead of being enraged by it, found his insult had released some of her tension and was making her laugh. She caught sight of Viv and signalled for her to come over. She wanted to share the joke. After he had opened the fête, and the festivities could officially begin, she planned to push him into the mud, preferably when the photographer from the local paper was handy. She'd make a point to warn him, so the moment could be captured for posterity.

'It gives me great pleasure—'

Nel and Viv exchanged bored glances and put their hands over their mouths to hide their yawns. Any minute now they would start getting giggly.

'—to announce the festivities open. But before I do—'

Sadly for Chris Mowbray the band, thinking this was their cue, had started playing again and had to be hushed by Muriel. Someone from the back – Nel had a horrible feeling it was one of her own children – shouted, 'Get on with it!'

'I would just like to say how proud I am to be able to announce that this will be the last such occasion on Paradise Fields.'

There were loud boos, and this time Nel could see it was indeed Sam, Fleur, and several of their friends doing it. She frowned as loudly as she could and shook her head at them.

'In the place of this – er – charming, but let's face it, extremely muddy area of unused land, there will soon be houses, many houses. Homes for men, women and their children – that old building will be gone . . .'

'Just a minute!' From nowhere appeared Jake, muddy but still gorgeous in old jeans and a rugby shirt. 'Just what are you saying?' he demanded.

The audience was completely silent, desperate to hear the altercation that was obviously going on. Nel observed the local photographer, poised to snap the moment when one angry man punched another on the nose.

'Gideon Freebody's plan will go ahead,' said Chris Mowbray, trying to look down his nose at someone who was several inches taller than he was. 'That other plan is just so much waste paper.'

'What makes you say that?' Because she was near, Nel could just about hear what was going on, but Jake was speaking very quietly. Quiet but deadly, she thought, remembering her terrifying headmistress.

'Because they haven't sold all the ransom strip plots.'

He indicated Nel and Viv, who were beginning to bristle like terriers. Viv pushed her hat back a bit, so she wouldn't miss anything.

'Oh really?' Jake was practically whispering now. 'And how up to date is your information?'

Nel felt sick. Jake must think all the plots were sold and was making a grand gesture, but in fact Chris Mowbray was right. The thirteen forms were still in her pocket. She opened her mouth to say something, but all the moisture had dried up and her tongue wouldn't work. She nudged Viv, hoping she would do something useful, but she was just watching Jake, admiration rendering her useless.

'Oh, for Christ's sake!' said Chris Mowbray. 'Ask these madwomen how many plots they've managed to sell! I did, earlier, and didn't get an answer, and I can assure you that if she had sold them, she would have told me.'

'And who is "she"?' demanded Jake, louder now.

Nel was shocked into action. An awful lot of people were watching a public exhibition of what should be done in private, and while they were probably fascinated, it wasn't what they'd come here for.

She grabbed the megaphone, snatching it out of Chris Mowbray's hand before he dropped it in the mud. 'It's open, folks!' she bellowed through it. 'Spend loads of money, and have a good time!'

A few camera flashes flashed, although what they were snapping Nel could only guess. She wished she'd bought one of 'Benita's Bonnets' so she could have pulled it down over her eyes and become unrecognisable.

For a second she wondered if she should stay and sort out the muddle between Chris Mowbray and Jake, but then she realised she couldn't possibly achieve anything. Chris was right and Jake was wrong; that's all there was to it. She headed to where a group of shivering children were waiting at the base of the maypole for the music to begin.

They were extremely good at it. The teacher, young and enthusiastic, gave instructions, and the ribbons at the top formed a smooth plait for quite a long way down. There was a pause, the children all changed direction, then skipped and wove and passed under each other's arms, and the plait came undone again.

'That is so clever!' said Nel enthusiastically to the teacher and her panting charges. 'How did you work out how to do it? It was brilliant!'

The teacher laughed. 'Well, we have been practising a lot, haven't we? We do it round the basketball hoop at school.'

'Well, I think you're wonderful. There are cartons of juice for you all, and mini chocolate bars.' She produced the chocolate from her bag and handed it to the teacher. 'The juice is over there, in that box. It won't be cold, but I don't suppose that matters.'

'Oh! How kind. Children, shall we give Mrs Innes a big cheer?'

'Oh, please don't.'

But it was too late. The children were obviously as well trained in cheering as they were in maypole dancing, and Nel had to stand there blushing while they delivered their three cheers.

'It is kind of you to think of giving them drinks and sweets,' said the teacher. 'Most people wouldn't have.'

'Most people would have arranged a podium and a public-address system,' said Nel. 'I only seem to be able to remember the nice things, not the important ones. Now I'd better see how my farmers are doing.'

'The five-a-side is starting now. Aren't you going to watch them?'

'No. They'll be fine. I've given their goodies to one of the mums to hand out.' Nel had no intention of going anywhere near Jake. She had almost absolved him of sleeping with her for political reasons, but she couldn't forget seeing Kerry Anne with her arms round him and she was so bruised and thrown off course by the whole thing, she couldn't rely on herself to behave properly.

Abraham caught her on her way to Sacha's stall, where Nel planned to buy something for stress.

'Hey, lass, it's a grand do, isn't it?'

His wife was with him, wearing a fetching straw bonnet decorated with poppies. 'He bought it for me. I never wear hats as a rule.'

'I've always liked you in hats, you know that. She gets embarrassed wearing them,' he explained.

'So do I,' said Nel, 'though I wished I'd bought one earlier, so no one would recognise me.'

'And why don't you want people to recognise you?'

Nel flapped her hands and shrugged, ending with a nervous laugh. 'It's all gone so horribly wrong. Not the fair, that seems to be fine, the building thing.'

'It's not over till it's over,' said Abraham sagely.

Nel exchanged glances with his wife. Men were so good at pointing out the obvious.

'Go and have something to eat, lass,' Abraham ordered. 'That young lad is making some smashing pancake jobs. You go and get some of them inside you, and things won't seem so black.'

'He's right, you know,' said his wife. 'You probably need food. When my children got scratchy with each other I gave them a snack.'

'I haven't been scratchy with anyone!' said Nel. 'Yet!'

'No, but you're nervy,' went on Mrs Abraham from beneath her poppies. 'I can tell. Eat something, you'll feel better.'

It was quite nice to be parented, thought Nel. She'd been without her own parents for so long, and she spent most of her life mothering people. It was pleasant to be on the receiving end for once.

'OK, I'll go and see what Ben has to offer.'

'And the ice cream's very good too,' said Mrs Abraham. 'More like it was in the old days.'

Aware that Chris Mowbray had not done the decent thing and gone from stall to stall, buying something from each, but had got into his previously-mud-free four-wheel drive and gone off, she felt obliged to take on the task herself. Most of the people were known to her, and now they had finally fought for their territory (the organisation of which had given Nel sleepless nights), they were all ready to congratulate her.

'I like the hats myself,' said Catherine, loading a burger with home-made mayonnaise and chopped onion. 'They're not what people traditionally made on farms, I dare say, but why not have a bit of variety? And she's such fun. I went on a computer course she ran a couple of years ago.'

'I should go on a computer course,' said Nel. 'I should know how to do spreadsheets and things. It would be really useful for the market.'

'Have you seen Sacha's new stuff? That new girl seems to have given her some really good ideas. She's got loads more products.'

Nel needed no more encouragement to visit Sacha. Sacha produced an oil which was almost guaranteed to rub away the cares of the day. It would take several oil wells full of oil to do this, Nel felt, but you had to start somewhere.

'Hi, you guys!' she said. She kissed Sacha, and then – slightly reluctantly – kissed Kerry Anne, so she didn't feel left out. 'How are you doing? The stall looks amazing! Catherine tells me you've got some wonderful new products. But before you tell me about them, give me a bottle of that anti-road-rage oil, will you? I've got stress to beat the band.'

'And they're doing pretty well,' said Sacha, opening a

bottle and handing it to Nel. 'Why are they playing all those sea shanties, do you think?'

Nel dabbed oil on her finger and started rubbing her temples. 'Because I told them Sir had been a Sea Scout and fancied himself as naval. It's a compliment to him and he's buggered off already.'

'Why did you have him to open it?' asked Kerry Anne. 'He's so . . .' She hesitated, searching for the word. 'Yeuch! He may know how to make money, but otherwise . . .'

'But I thought you liked him!' said Nel. 'When I was last in his house you were ringing him up, asking him to dinner!'

Kerry Anne shuddered. 'That was Pierce's idea, to get to know him better. But after I told Pierce Chris had put his hand on my butt, he didn't press it.'

Confused as to whether it was Kerry Anne's butt or their connection with Chris Mowbray that wasn't pressed, Nel changed the subject.

'So, what's the new product, then?'

'Body polish,' said Kerry Anne, producing a sachet.

'Brown sugar and almond oil,' said Sacha. 'Much less harsh than salt. It'll rub away all the dead skin cells and leave you soft and shining.'

'Sounds lovely. Can I buy some?'

'Have a free sample. It's the least I can do,' said Sacha. 'Finding me Kerry Anne has made such a difference to my business.'

'We sell to California, now,' said Kerry Anne. 'Only through personal recommendation, until we get into the new premises.'

'Which are where?'

'Oh, a little way away,' said Sacha. 'We've gone for somewhere quite big.'

'Well, that is nice,' said Nel, feeling a little abandoned. 'Will you still have time to come to the markets?'

'Oh yes,' said Sacha.

Kerry Anne looked at her. 'If we can get someone to do them. But really, they don't contribute much to our sales figures. Once the spa is up and running, we'll use almost all we can make just through that.'

'The market represents my first loyal customers,' said Sacha firmly. 'I won't abandon it.'

Kerry Anne shrugged. 'Well, maybe until the stuff's available locally elsewhere.'

Nel moved on. She had enough conflict in her own life without engaging in other people's. But she was pleased things were going so well for Sacha.

'Hi, Mum!' It was Fleur.

'Hello, darling. Do you want more money?'

'No! I was coming to ask you if you had any make-up in your handbag.'

'Well, only the usual stuff. There's a few centimetres of kohl pencil, a sample tube of foundation, a dried-up mascara. Oh, and a lipstick. You can borrow it if you want. Are you planning to abandon Jamie for Ben?'

Fleur rolled her eyes. 'He is rather gorgeous. I've been helping him on his stall.'

'He's nice, isn't he? Very laid back.'

'Laid back? Prop him up a bit and he'd be horizontal! But then I thought I ought to see how you were getting on.'

'By checking what make-up I had with me? You can have the mascara, but don't spit on it.'

'As if I would! I'm just going to pop and get something from Sacha. See you in a mo.'

Nel moved on. She tasted and bought rather more cheese than her household was likely to eat. Stocked up on chutney, which her family hardly ate at all, and then found some lemon curd, which she loved. By this time her carrier bag was getting quite heavy. She took it to Viv's stall.

'You wouldn't mind me leaving this here for now,

would you? The circulation is going in my fingers, my bag's so full.'

'You should buy a basket from Ewan,' said Viv. 'They're gorgeous. I'm planning to fill one of those shallow square ones with pebbles, and put it by the fire.'

'Sounds very tasteful and artistic,' said Nel, knowing from experience that Viv's taste was always good, but wondering why anyone would want to keep pebbles by a fireplace. 'So can I leave this here?'

Nel and Viv were speculating how the conversation between Jake and Chris Mowbray had ended when Fleur came up. She thrust a square, paper-wrapped package into her hand.

'It's a present. It's a little travel pack of moisturiser, cleanser and body lotion. From Sacha. It's a new line. She gave it to me to give to you.'

'Oh. That's very kind. I wonder why she didn't give it to me when I was over there. I'll stick it with my other stuff, behind Viv's stall.'

'Oh no! Put it in your handbag. It's specially designed to go in your handbag, so you'd better put it there. Don't you think, Viv?'

Viv nodded. 'Otherwise you'll freeze it by mistake.'

Nel was just about to protest when she heard the mega-phone.

'Will Mrs Nel Innes please come to the five-a-side com-petition.' It was Jake behind the megaphone. She could see him.

'No, I won't. I'm not a first-aider, so if someone's hurt themselves they'd be better off with Viv. She's a trained physiotherapist.'

'They may want you to present the prize,' said Fleur after a moment.

'Well, I won't. I'm not dressed for the public. You go, Viv. You're looking gorgeous as usual, and you're wearing a hat.'

Viv regarded Fleur and Nel briefly. 'OK. You mind my stall for me.'

'Of course. And if it's a medical emergency, ask for a doctor. I've seen at least two members of our local practice wandering round.'

The next thing Nel heard was, 'Could Mrs Nel Innes please come to the five-a-side section of the field.'

'No,' said Nel quietly. 'I can't. I'm minding Viv's stall.'

'I can mind Viv's stall,' said Fleur. 'No one's here anyway.'

'That's not the point.'

'If Nel doesn't come to the five-a-side section, I will say what I want to say over this megaphone,' Jake boomed and crackled from across the field.

'He's not going to blackmail me into it,' said Nel, who was now blushing ferociously.

'Nel, if you don't come now, I'll tell the whole world what happened on a certain night in London.'

'Oh shit!'

As she began racing across the field, she heard her daughter's shocked exclamation behind her. 'Language!'

Chapter Twenty-four

Nel ran as fast as she could through mud wearing welling-tons. She was aware that people were watching her, smiling, but she didn't raise her eyes from the ground. When she got to Jake she was out of breath and hot. Clothes suitable for ambling slowly about are not the same as those you'd choose for sprinting the hundred metres.

'What the hell are you doing?' she demanded when she was within earshot. 'If you want to talk to me so badly, you could have come across and found me!'

'What I have to say needs to be said in private.' Jake was unmoved and seemingly unsurprised by her anger.

'Well then, you could have phoned me, sent me an email, written me a letter, even.'

Now she was no longer running, and was actually looking at him, she became aware of a trickle of sweat running down her spine, of how red her face must be, and how little of the make-up she had applied that morning would be left on. She was also aware that she hadn't had time to think carefully enough about what to wear that day. She was wearing her inevitable black trousers, a warm but old cashmere sweater and a waxed jacket that used to belong to Mark. She had intended to go back home and change before the festivities, but what with one thing and another, hadn't had time. Jake was muddy too, but it somehow suited him.

'Would you have taken my call?'

Nel shrugged. She didn't want to lie and say yes, and she didn't want to go on with an argument which might easily deteriorate into 'would, wouldn't, would, wouldn't'.

'Besides,' Jake went on. 'I couldn't say what I wanted to say until today.'

'Oh?'

'It concerns today.'

Nel sighed. 'Listen, I'm very tired and very busy, not to mention very depressed. Could you please spit out whatever it was you wanted to say to me.'

He reached down and put an arm round her shoulders. 'Come with me.'

She began to protest, but found the weight of his arm and the pressure of his hand on the top of her shoulder quite difficult to argue with. It seemed easier just to allow herself to be steered in whatever direction he chose.

He held her very tightly against him, as if he didn't want her to escape.

'What are you doing?' she demanded, feeling she should make some objection, even if she couldn't physically run away.

'Kidnapping you.'

'Don't be ridiculous. I'm not a kid and you're a solicitor. You don't do things like that.' Then she paused, aware that they were walking away from the field, which was full of friends who would come to her rescue in a second, up towards where the four-wheel drives were parked, where it was extra muddy. 'Oh my God! You *are* kidnapping me! Help!'

He laughed. 'If you're going to call for help, you'll have to do it a bit louder than that.'

'I was just having a practice run. Help!' she called again, louder this time. Either no one heard, or no one had any intention of helping her. 'Are you planning to keep me for long? Or just until the ransom shows up?'

'Just until Tuesday, and there will be no ransom demand.'

335

'Just as well. We haven't got a bean. You may as well take me home. It will save you money in the long run.'

'I told you, I don't want money for your return. I just want you, for a long weekend, or what's left of this one.'

A large bubble began to form in Nel's stomach and rise. When it reached her throat she felt as if she needed to either cough, burst into tears, or vomit. She coughed, hard, to make the bubble go away.

'Well, you can't have me, as you know perfectly well. I have children, dogs, a house. They all need me.'

'No, they don't.'

'Yes, they do! How dare you say that!'

'Viv's going to walk the dogs and Fleur and Sam are going to look after the house, although that may include having a party.'

'But who's going to look after them?'

'They don't need looking after. Fleur looks after you, anyway.'

'You mean she bosses me. It's not the same thing.'

'Yes, it is. Now get in.'

They had reached a large dark purple Jeep. 'No! Not until I get some explanation! Have you been conspiring with my friends and family to kidnap me? It's outrageous.' Nel was finding it quite hard to keep up the indignation. Being with Jake was so lovely, she probably would have gone with him if he'd said they were going to visit a sewage plant.

'Look, just get in and we can talk as we drive.'

'I'm not getting in until you tell me where we're going.' She only noticed that she'd said 'we're going' instead of 'you're taking me' when it was too late. And Jake definitely noticed too.

'Cornwall.'

'Cornwall! That's miles away!'

'About three hours.'

He had opened the door and was waiting for her to get

in. She closed her eyes. 'Really, I can't do this. It sounds lovely, but I'm a grown-up woman with responsibilities. I can't just take off.'

Before she knew what he was planning, he had caught her behind the knees and heaved her up onto the seat and closed the door, catching a bit of waxed jacket as he did so. He was sitting next to her before she had worked out why the door wouldn't open, and then he locked them in.

'Listen, Nel, I know this all seems a bit extreme, but I wanted to take you somewhere where we wouldn't be interrupted and you could relax, we could get to know each other, and . . .' He hesitated, his breathing suddenly a bit ragged, then he swallowed. '. . . things,' he finished finally.

Nel's heart was thumping so hard she thought it was quite likely visible through the waxed jacket. 'I can't, Jake, you don't understand.'

'Tell me then. But let's get out of here first, before someone comes up and asks you something.'

She sat in silence while Jake manoeuvred the Jeep out of the parking area and was back on the road. Then she said, 'This isn't the car you had before. Is it yours?'

'Yup. I thought this was a bit more suitable for the country.'

'But you know what they call them in town: Chelsea tractors.'

'I'm not planning to be in town much. Although I will keep my flat on.'

Mention of his flat made Nel catch her breath. She must get a grip. She burrowed in her handbag and found Sacha's calming oil.

'What's that?' he asked.

'It's very soothing. Guaranteed to prevent road rage and exam nerves.'

'And which are you suffering from?'

'Both.'

He laughed. He wasn't meant to. Nel was being perfectly serious.

'Honestly, Jake. A joke's a joke, but please take me home now. I've got all sorts of stuff to sort out from the fête. I'm going to have to give back all the money to the people who bought plots of land.'

'No, you won't.'

'Of course I will! I can't just keep it! They're not going to get their squares and they've paid for them. They must have their money back. Some people had to struggle to find fifty quid, you know, although I don't suppose you can imagine that.'

'You're making several vast assumptions there. Which one shall I disabuse you of first?'

Nel put a hand on the dashboard. 'Seriously, Jake, unless you turn off here you'll be on the motorway before you know it. Take me home!'

'No! I want to be on the motorway, and I'm not taking you home. Not yet, anyway.'

Helpless, Nel watched as they reached the point of no return and were firmly pointed in the direction of Cornwall. 'Please, Jake! I haven't got anything with me!'

'Look in the back.'

Nel looked and saw a familiar bag which was still thickly layered in Glastonbury mud. 'Oh my God.'

'Fleur packed it, and Viv told her what to pack.'

Nel closed her eyes and winced. Fleur might not be aware that there were clothes in Nel's wardrobe that she couldn't get into, but that she kept there for inspiration. 'If Fleur packed my bag, why did she want to know if I had any make-up with me?'

'She forgot your sponge bag. She told me at the five-a-side. She said she could sort it out.'

That explained the travel pack from Sacha. 'Well, for your information, I have very little make-up with me. And presumably not a toothbrush either.'

'We're going to a very good hotel. They will provide anything we need.'

'Did Viv have anything to do with this?' Nel was getting angry. All her family and friends, the very people who should rally round and protect her, seemed to be in cahoots with the man she'd sworn off for ever.

'She just confirmed that you'd like to be taken to a good hotel and pampered for a couple of days.'

'Well, she's wrong! I won't like it at all!'

'She told me you'd told her you would.'

'That's just silly! Of course I'd like it if I had time to think about it, pack properly, make sure I had something half decent to wear, but not if I'm going to turn up in Mark's old jacket and my wellington boots!'

Jake looked at her for a moment and laughed. 'I do realise that a bit of notice would have been useful, but I promise you it will be all right. Fleur's definitely packed shoes.'

Nel sighed and looked at the road ahead. There was a good view from the Jeep and if everything in the world had been different, she would have enjoyed thundering along, on the way to a weekend in a good hotel in Cornwall.

'It's not just my own feelings,' she explained. 'I can't run out on the hospice, and the plan to save it. It would be OK if we'd stopped bloody Gideon Freebody, and sold all the plots. But we haven't. As I said earlier, there's money to be returned, explanations, all that stuff. If I leave now, they might think I've absconded with the cash.' She shot him a quick glance, hoping this reference to a possible crime might gain attention from the legal part of his mind and stop him.

'But you have stopped Gideon Freebody.'

'No, I haven't! I've still got the certificates for thirteen unsold plots.' She put her hand in her pocket and withdrew them. 'They're about the only things I have got with me.'

'And I've got the money for the plots. So that's all right.'

'But, Jake, you know perfectly well we made it so each plot had to be sold individually, so that no one could buy more than one! I really regretted we did it like that, we could have had a limit of five, or something. But we didn't. You can't buy the plots yourself. God! If I could have, I would have! Even if I'd had to sell something.'

'I haven't bought the plots myself. I've sold the plots and issued promissory notes.'

'Which are?'

'Bits of paper saying that the documentation will be along soon.'

'Oh. Well, who have you sold them to?'

'My colleagues in the office. You've met some of them.'

'You haven't got thirteen colleagues. You've got about six colleagues.'

'Yes, and they all have mothers and fathers. It was easy to sell them.'

'But why should they give a damn about what sort of buildings go up? They don't live down here.'

'No, but they are quite fond of me, and were probably hoping for invitations to my rural retreat.'

'So you're buying a house?'

'Yup. You must come and see it sometime.'

A little of Nel's tension eased away. 'Jake, have you really sold all the plots?'

'Yes. And had great pleasure in telling Chris Mowbray so.'

'He must have been livid.'

'He was. Not a pretty sight. Except to me, of course. He's such an ar— horrible man. I also managed to convince Pierce that Abraham's plan would be for the best, too. In spite of Kerry Anne's urgings to go for the big bucks.'

Nel sighed. 'Kerry Anne. I saw you kissing her, you know.'

Jake frowned. 'Did you? I don't think I've ever kissed her, but I suppose it could have slipped my mind.'

'Jake! It was outside the Black Hart, a few weeks ago! I was caught up in those road works. I saw you!'

'I expect she was kissing me goodbye. It couldn't have been much else, because Pierce was with us. Honestly, she's just a child. I couldn't ever fancy her.'

'Are you sure?'

'Quite sure. She's too thin.'

'I thought thin was good. God, I've spent enough of my own life trying to become thin.'

'Most men prefer flesh, though I do realise you might not know that, having lead a very sheltered life.'

'With three children, two of them at university, it's not as sheltered as it was!' Feeling she need no longer worry about Kerry Anne, she went back to what they'd first been arguing about. 'But if you'd sold the plots, why didn't you tell me?'

'Because I couldn't have got you alone, and I had the five-a-side to organise.' He looked at her again. 'I wanted you to present the cup.'

'Viv was a much better choice. She's young and lovely and was wearing a hat.'

'I don't fancy Viv, though.'

Nel found herself blushing. 'So? What's that got to do with it?'

'If I spend hours and hours on a muddy football ground with a lot of little boys, I want a reward.'

A little sigh escaped Nel as she tried to stop a feeling which could have been smugness. 'You had the pleasure of knowing you were working for a good cause.'

'Good causes are all very well, but there are other things in life.'

'What's that supposed to mean?'

'I mean that you seem to devote your life to good causes and don't pay enough attention to your personal life.'

'Oh, that's not true! You just happened to meet me when we were having this building on Paradise Fields to deal with. Normally I am entirely selfish and sybaritic, whatever that means.'

He chuckled and glanced at her before indicating and roaring past a row of cars in the middle lane. 'I'm glad to hear about the sybaritic bit – there's no point in taking you where I'm taking you if you don't appreciate luxury.'

'There's a "but" there, somewhere.'

'Yes, there is.'

'So? Tell me!'

Jake didn't tell her immediately. He fiddled with the radio, found a channel he liked, turned down the volume, passed a caravan and muttered about the driving of someone on the inside lane.

'Yes? I'm dying of suspense here.'

'It's about Simon,' said Jake eventually.

'Oh? I have no intention of marrying him, you know, or indeed anyone.'

'That's a relief.'

A tiny part of Nel had wanted Jake to protest at this determined statement. 'Oh?'

'Not the getting married at all part, but that you're not going to marry Simon.'

'Oh? Are you going to tell me why?' She bit back the rider, 'If you don't want to marry me yourself.' She didn't want to marry him, she was almost sure, but she didn't want him to have made that decision before she had.

'I did a bit of research on him.'

'I know he was in cahoots with Gideon Freebody and that lot. That's not news.'

'But did you know he's been married twice before, and the women in question had to sell their houses in order to get rid of him?'

Nel went cold. 'No, I didn't. How did you find out?'

'Friends in the trade.'

'But that's horrendous!'

'Yes, it is. And one of the women lost the house she'd lived in with her late husband, and brought all her children up in.'

'How on earth did he do that?'

'He was clever and the judges were stupid. I'm quite sure it was what he planned for you.'

'Huh! As if he could have got away with it! Besides, he bossed the children. I could never have married him. And he didn't like the dogs on the furniture. It's why I won't marry again.' Then she frowned. 'So why did you bother to find out about Simon's past life?'

Jake shrugged. 'I had my own reasons.'

'Which were?' She wasn't going to let him get away without telling her.

'When you're thinking about moving into an area and you meet a woman you really fancy, it's only natural to check out the opposition.'

An involuntary sound emerged from Nel, but she suppressed it. She couldn't quite decide if Jake 'checking out the opposition' was intensely flattering, or a bit stalkerish.

'But having found out all that stuff, I didn't want to tell you, in case it looked like I was claiming an unfair advantage.'

'What, by not being a man who marries women for their property?'

'There is something else, Nel . . .'

The bubbles of excitement and happiness which had been beginning to form suddenly went flat. This was when he told her he was still married, that they were only separated or worse, giving themselves a break. 'What?' she demanded crisply.

'I've applied for a job.'

'Well, that's not usually a reason to behave as if you have a secret life. What sort of job? Besides, I thought you'd got one.'

343

'You are a bit involved.'

'Am I? How can I be? You're not planning to take my job setting up the farmers' market out of my hands, are you?'

'No, you idiot! At the hospice!'

'The hospice?'

'Yes! The one you've just spent the best years of your life trying to save! I've got the job as the director!'

'But why didn't I know about it! I'm always involved in interviewing.'

Jake was getting more and more uncomfortable. 'I had to declare an interest.'

'What?'

'I had to explain that I – entertained certain feelings for you.'

'Jake, when did you apply for the job? We've been looking for someone for ages—'

'It was before we'd slept together.'

Nel was suddenly far too hot. She fought her way out of her waxed jacket and pushed it out of the way. 'I can't believe that no one told me.'

'Very few people knew. Chris Mowbray didn't, but although he's the chairman, he's not the real power on the committee. It's Father Ed. He's been looking for ages, which you know. It was when I went for the interview I had to tell him about you.'

Nel now wanted to take off her jumper, but didn't think she should, given she wasn't wearing much underneath. 'What did you tell him about me?'

'That I found you very attractive, but I couldn't pursue a relationship with you if you knew I was applying for the job. You would have thought I was doing it for the wrong reasons.'

Aware that this was exactly what she'd have thought didn't help her internal thermostat. 'It's not very well paid, you know.'

'I can do a bit of consultancy on the side. They've agreed to let me do that. And living in the country will be so much cheaper than in town.'

'Oh. Good.' Nel had a sudden desire for deodorant. She didn't know if anxiety and heat had given her an unpleasant 'glow' but she couldn't take the chance. 'I don't suppose you might be stopping for fuel anytime soon?'

'I've got enough to take us all the way' – Nel winced – 'but if you want to stop, there's a services coming up soon.'

'Oh good. I could do a little essential shopping.'

'As long as you promise not to escape.'

Nel gave him a withering look. It was nice to be able to do so. 'Oh yes, I'm very likely to run away in a service station and hitch a lift back home. Obviously, I'd get dozens of offers.'

'You'd get a lot more offers than I care to think of. You're a very lovely woman. The fact that you're unaware of it does not make you any less attractive.'

Chapter Twenty-five

❧

Nel wondered if there was something inherently sluttish about trying to re-do your make-up in a motorway service station when all you have is a stump of pencil, a dried-up mascara and one lipstick, or was it just her own anxiety that made it seem so? Her feelings weren't helped by the fact she was still wearing her wellington boots.

She had heaved her bag over to the front of the Jeep and found that the shoes Fleur had put in were what were known as her 'Killer Heels'. Nel called them that because she did find it hard to walk in anything too high, and these had heels of nearly two inches. Fleur and Viv called them that because they thought it was killingly funny that she could refer to such mild shoes as 'Killer'. Call them what you like, she thought now, they would not look right with thick, albeit laddered, black tights and her old black trousers. Smart trousers possibly, but not mud-splattered ones.

What was it about Jake and her and mud? There seemed to be a symbiotic relationship she couldn't avoid.

But she was edgy, and she knew it wasn't really her make-up, or lack or it, or the fact her hair needed washing that was making her so. And she should have been blissfully happy.

She had so much to be happy about. The least awful scheme for Paradise Fields had triumphed over the expensive, badly built rabbit hutches which would have covered every inch of land if their plan had failed. She was on her way to a good hotel in Cornwall with the man who had taken up every waking thought and many of her sleeping ones for months, who was not only too gorgeous to live but had turned out to be a thoroughly nice man. They'd even slept together and knew it was fantastic. There was absolutely no reason for Nel to be anything but ecstatic.

As she rinsed her hands she noticed the women on either side of her looking at her oddly. She hoped they didn't think she was on the game. After all, why else was a middle-aged woman desperately trying to glam herself up at six o'clock at night? No, if she was on the game, she'd have her kit with her. She probably looked like she'd run away from home and was desperately trying to look respectable enough to be taken in somewhere for the night. Which was actually the case.

As she wet her fingers and started pulling at her hair she concluded her edginess was because what was about to follow was a foregone conclusion. Jake would expect her to sleep with him. God! If she'd gone to all that trouble, she'd expect it too – it was not remotely unreasonable. She hadn't exactly been unwilling to be seduced before, in fact she had been embarrassingly eager.

But it had been entirely spontaneous. So spontaneous it had required a humiliating trip to the chemist the following day. Now she looked at the condom machine with trepidation. Should she take responsibility for her fertility and buy some? Or should she assume that he would have thought about this unromantic aspect of weekends away and dealt with the matter himself?

A glance at the women (why were they spending so long in here?) and Nel's overstretched brazenness quota expired; she couldn't buy condoms – at least, not from a machine while she was being watched. After all, if the hotel was really all that good, they could probably supply them. Jake could just pick up the phone and say, 'Send up some double-ribbed, extra fine' or something that

347

sounded equally like knitwear. A slightly hysterical giggle erupted from somewhere and she had to disguise it as a cough. Why didn't the women leave? Were they the service station equivalent of store detectives? Would they check to see she hadn't vandalised her cubicle with her lipstick?

She dragged her mind back to condoms. One thing was certain, she couldn't have unprotected sex again. She had just about forgiven herself for the first time, but to have it again would be completely unforgivable. How cross she would be with her children if she thought they weren't taking proper precautions.

She could buy some in the shop. She'd already been in there to buy a toothbrush, toothpaste and a better hair-brush than the hairy, broken-handled thing she had in her bag. She'd seen them by the counter. She would just go up, select some chewing gum and then pick up a packet of condoms and say, 'Oh, I'd better have these.' How hard could that be?

Not hard at all if she were in her twenties or thirties. The fact that she had definitely hit forty did make it a tad worse. Indeed, it made it nearly impossible.

She peered into the mirror and took a brief count of the wrinkles round her eyes. There was, she concluded, not just the feet but the nest of the crow on either side – laughter lines be damned. She was too old for this, that was the problem.

Her mind went back to one of those conversations she had had with Fleur and Viv, one about taking your clothes off in front of a man you didn't know. It would be all right if one's body was smooth and tanned and slim, but Nel had stretch marks, cellulite, and, not having been given any warning of this weekend, hairy legs. Not very hairy, admittedly, as she'd been waxing them for years and a lot of hairs had given up the struggle, but her legs weren't shining and sleek. Half of her cursed Fleur and Viv for colluding with Jake. Didn't they realise she wouldn't want to do this sort of thing without having had a facial, a thorough exfoliation and possibly a fake tan as well?

She almost groaned aloud. Vivian and Fleur wouldn't understand her anxieties. They had womanly confidence. They were gorgeous and they knew it. And while Nel knew she had quite a lot of followers, as her mother would have called them, for the most part they weren't men who did her ego any good. Only Jake did that, but even now he didn't do it quite well enough for her to believe she was an attractive, sexy woman who was entitled to an attractive, sexy man.

She gave her hair a last despairing tweak and forced herself out of the brightly lit safety of the Ladies. Jake wanted her, fancied her, and had gone to a lot of trouble to kidnap her: she must have something about her. She put her shoulders back and went to find him in the shop.

'You were a long time. I thought you'd skipped off back home.' He kissed her cheek. Someone kissed her cheek almost every day, but now, it seemed the tenderest gesture anyone had ever made to her.

'Well, I did try my luck with the lorry drivers but it was no good. They said the black heels with the trousers and tights made me look like an Essex Girl in mourning. And the wellington boots are the wrong sort of kinky.'

He grinned. 'Shall we go?' He took her hand and led her back to the Jeep. We must look like lovers, she thought. I wonder if we are?

'You're very quiet. You haven't said a word for hours.' They had turned off the motorway, which they had thundered down at a speed which should have been terrifying, but somehow wasn't, and were now on narrow, high-sided roads which all looked the same and were all sprinkled with primroses, just visible in the evening light.

'Oh well, I'm tired, you know, and enjoying the scenery.

It's so lovely here. I love the moment when you see that the soil has turned that deep red colour and you know it's growing grass that's feeding cows who are making all that clotted cream—'

'And now you're gabbling. Are you nervous?'

She gave a long, shuddering sigh. There seemed no point in denying it. 'The thing is, Jake, although this is a really lovely idea – really, really, lovely – I am a bit – well . . .'

'Nervous?'

'Yes.'

'Why?'

'To be brutally frank' – after all, that 'why' had been quite brutal. He should have just said, 'Don't worry, I won't make you do anything you feel uncomfortable with.' – 'it's the whole taking my clothes off thing.'

'Oh?' He was polite but disbelieving, as if she'd admitted to an inability to handle zips.

'Yes! Jake, I have a body that is less than perfect. I am overweight. I have stretch marks and cellulite. In fact, I could be in a painting by Lucian Freud!'

'Could you?' He seemed much more interested now. 'Which one? I'll buy it immediately.'

Nel giggled. 'You are a twit! You won't be able to afford paintings by anyone if you become the director of the hospice, let alone by Lucian Freud. We pay peanuts.'

'I know you do and I told you, I'm going to do a bit of agency work on the side. My present firm are happy to keep me on to do bits and pieces they haven't time for.'

'But going back to my body—'

He put his hand on hers and squeezed it. 'If you don't mind, I'd rather not talk about your body while I'm driving. These lanes are quite confusing and it's getting dark. We'll get to the hotel, and then we'll go for a walk along the beach. Then we can talk about whatever you like.'

*

Wellingtons and a waxed jacket were the perfect clothes for walking on the beach in April. The sky was a strange mixture of mauve and pink, brighter than the night surrounding it, and the sea beneath reflected all the lights of Padstow, which twinkled like Christmas decorations. They'd checked in to the hotel and left their bags, but Jake had insisted on going for a walk before they went upstairs.

'I'm stiff. I need some exercise.'

Nel was glad to go along with his plan. It was easy, just walking, side by side, admiring the curve of the harbour, the boats, the little lanes, the houses. They peered into the window of a bookshop which seemed tiny, yet was obviously crammed with books.

'In summer it's open all evening,' said Jake.

'Have you been here before, then?' Nel asked, her head on one side, trying to see if the book she was looking at really was one she'd wanted for ages.

'Oh yes. We used to come here as kids. It's great. There's a cycle path now. We can hire bikes tomorrow, if you'd like.'

Although Nel was relaxing more and more by the minute, mention of tomorrow did remind her of what might happen before tomorrow.

'I haven't ridden a bike for years,' she said.

'No, I rather thought you hadn't.'

'Now why – oh.' Blushing desperately, she realised he was referring to a conversation they had had shortly after that fatal night in London.

'But don't worry,' he went on. 'You'll soon pick it up, it's just like—'

'Riding a bike?'

'Exactly. Shall we go back? I've booked a table for eight-thirty. Presumably you'll want to change, although it is very informal.'

Without waiting for her comments, he took her hand and led her towards the good hotel.

*

It occurred to Nel that it was probably totally obvious that she was not in the habit of having dirty weekends. It had been a joke between her and Mark that they had never had one, having neither the time nor the money to fit one in before they got married. And after they were married there were other things to spend money on. So following a sweet young thing in a white blouse and black skirt upstairs and along corridors was embarrassing. She tried to convince herself that the sweet young thing had probably shown so many guests to bedrooms, she didn't give a thought to what they might get up to in them. Also, no one ever believed that anyone outside their own generation had sex. At least, young people certainly didn't think that grown-ups did.

This girl, who was about the same age as Fleur, probably thought that Jake would put on his stripy pyjamas, and she her rollers and her winceyette nightie and cold cream, and then they'd get into bed on their respective sides (the same sides as at home, naturally) and stay there for the entire night, having shared nothing more passionate than a peck on the cheek and a late-night sachet of hot chocolate.

Having created this little scenario, Nel felt less like a scarlet woman, and therefore became a little less scarlet. For all she knew, she and Jake looked like an old married couple.

'Here we are,' said the sweet young thing, unlocking the door. 'You were lucky to get the suite. We'd had a cancellation.'

Jake put the bags down and thanked her. Nel took off her wellingtons and then went to inspect the bathroom. It was beautiful. Well lit, it had huge bales of fluffy white towels, large bottles of Molton Brown shower gel, body lotion and shampoo. White woodwork and artistically placed shells made the room seemed homely, in spite of the extravagant luxury of it all.

352

'I'm afraid there's only one bathroom,' said Jake, coming in behind her and making her jump. 'But there's a bed in the sitting room. I just thought I'd tell you that. In case you wanted to know.'

'Thank you.' It came out rather huskily.

'Why don't you explore the suite, or unpack or something, while I have a quick shower? Then you can be as long as you like getting ready.'

'Good idea.' It would also mean she wouldn't have to worry about leaving the bathroom spotless.

Nel took her bag into the sitting room and tipped out its contents. There was a nightie, and she was pleased to see it was a less ragged one than some. No dressing gown, but that was no problem, there were robes in the bathroom. There was a bundle of knickers and tights all tangled together, which was how they came out of the washing machine, and how they were dried over the Rayburn. She took a moment to reflect that Viv probably separated her silk French knickers and her thongs, put them into special net bags and washed them on 'delicates'. She just bunged everything in on 'easy care' and hoped for the best. It made the process quicker at the time, but now, when she realised that all her pants were a pale mud colour, she wished she'd kept a few pairs for best.

Apart from the underwear, Fleur had also packed Nel's little black top, a long velvet skirt with a slit up it, which definitely came from the thin end of her wardrobe, and a sort of gypsy top, which Nel couldn't remember buying. In theory the top and the skirt would look fine together, but until she tried them on, Nel had no idea whether she'd be able to fit into the skirt, and the gypsy top might look like a dog's breakfast. She wished Fleur had put in the long coat she had bought for the meeting, but she hadn't. She felt safe in that. Perhaps that was why Fleur had decided against it.

Did she have time to try on her outfit while Jake was

in the shower? She risked him coming in while she was struggling with a zip, trying to squash a segment of fat in between two edges which were destined never to meet. Or at least, not until a good half-stone had been disposed of. No, he seemed to have been in there quite a long time, better not chance it.

What was her fallback position? There was a white silk shirt, which needed an iron, but would look sort of OK if she wore it open over the little black top. Fleur hadn't done a bad job, Nel decided, and there were a couple of jumpers and her new pair of black trousers in the bag as well. She'd manage, especially if there was an iron somewhere about. There was.

The skirt fitted beautifully, and with the silk blouse and black top, looked quite sophisticated, Nel decided, emerging from the bathroom.

'You look – and smell – delicious,' said Jake, who was wearing a charcoal grey suit, but with the top two buttons of his shirt undone. 'I can't decide whether to wear a tie or not. What do you think?'

Nel couldn't think. He looked so completely sexy and gorgeous, she couldn't possibly comment on whether the tie was necessary or not. 'You said it was informal here. Would you feel happier in a tie?'

Jake looked at her, then at her mouth and then, she couldn't help noticing, at her cleavage. He bit his lip and swallowed. 'I'll just put it in my pocket and then I can put it on if necessary. Shall we go down? If we don't, we might stay here, and miss our table.'

Nel was still trying to work this out when they reached the restaurant.

They shared a lobster to start with. It was delicious, messy and a wonderful way to forget about nerves, thought Nel, wondering vaguely if she'd ever get the butter out of her shirt. But by the time she had drunk at least half a bottle of very delicious white wine, and had cracked and pulled, sucked and chewed and generally wallowed in shell and flesh and sundry bits and pieces, she felt much more relaxed.

She took her hands out of the bowl of hot water and lemon and dried them. 'That was such fun, and really delicious.' She was about to add, 'Terribly extravagant too,' but realised that neither Viv nor Fleur would say that. They would assume they deserved extravagance. 'Thank you, Jake.'

He pulled his napkin out from where he'd tucked it in his shirt. 'My pleasure entirely, Nel. I've fantasised about taking you somewhere like this for ages.'

'Oh?' Was this piece of information unnerving, or romantic?

'Yes. I've thought a lot about how to proceed with you, and I've come to the conclusion that slowly is the answer.'

Nel put her elbows on the table and looked up at him. 'Would you care to elaborate?'

'Mm. I thought at first, while we're still getting to know each other, we'd go away for weekends to nice places, where we can talk.'

'Without my family constantly making demands, you mean?'

'Don't get me wrong, I adore your family – the one I've met, anyway – but I don't want to have to fight for your attention, not straight away. Later, when we know each other better, and they've had time to get used to the idea, I thought you could spend the odd night at my house.'

'Your house?'

'Yes. My new house. Did I tell you I've bought one? As soon as I heard the job was mine. It's going to be very nice when I've finished it. It's still a building site at the moment, but the builders say it should be habitable by

Christmas.' He gave a slight, crooked smile which sent Nel's insides into spasm. 'They didn't say which Christmas, of course.'

'Well, it is only April. There must be a good chance it's this one.' Suddenly the thought of being curled up with Jake in front of a roaring fire made Christmas into something to look forward to. Then she frowned. 'If you hadn't bought a house last Christmas, what were you doing buying mistletoe?'

'I was taking the opportunity to get close to the most attractive woman I'd seen in ages.'

Nel looked down at her plate, just as it was whisked away.

'But going back to our courtship,' said Jake.

'That's a lovely, old-fashioned word.'

'When you've stayed with me a few times—'

'It's not easy for me to get away, you know, what with the dogs and everything.'

'I thought perhaps the dogs could stay too, or wouldn't they like that?'

Nel began to giggle. 'You'd have my dogs to stay in your new house? And cover it with hair?'

'Well, yes. It's not that bad, is it?'

'It's worse, but it's such a kind thought.'

'Anyway,' Jake went on, when your family are used to you having me in your life, I thought I could stay with you from time to time.' His voice faltered and he stopped. He took hold of her wrist. 'Nel, do you want me in your life?'

She knew her pulse was racing, knew he would feel it under his thumb. 'I think so,' she breathed.

'Because I want you in mine. I'm not asking you to marry me, or anything like that, because I was told in no uncertain terms by Viv how you felt about that while your children are still at home. But we can be lovers, can't we?'

Nel sighed. 'I do hope so.'

Jake swallowed. 'I wish they'd hurry up with our fish.'

It arrived at that moment, covered in the crispest batter in the world, accompanied by the best chips, served with malt vinegar and the most tender vegetables. Nel was aware of the most delicious food passing through her lips and into her mouth, but she could hardly enjoy it. She was longing for him, longing for the moment when they could go upstairs and be alone.

'I'll tell you what,' said Jake, crunching a chip with very white teeth, 'shall we ask for a bottle of champagne and our pudding to be sent upstairs?'

'What will they think?'

'I don't care what they think, what do you think?'

'I think that's a very good idea.'

Nel noticed that it was the sweet young thing who came to take their order, and realised that now she'd know that Nel and Jake weren't planning to stay on their own sides of the bed all night. In fact, while they were discussing what to have for pudding, it seemed that Jake had some interesting ideas for that, too.

She decided on fresh peaches in champagne with raspberry coulis. Jake went for chocolate mousse. It was because, she decided, he'd never had to consider how hard it would be to get chocolate out of the sheets. She noted that now she had completely stopped worrying about taking her clothes off, and was only concerned about how soon she could do it.

'Come on,' said Jake. 'Let's go.'

They left the restaurant hand in hand.